D1368293

1356

Bernard Cornwell

W F HOWES LTD

This large print edition published in 2016 by
W F Howes Ltd
Unit 5, St George's House, Rearsby Business Park,
Gaddesby Lane, Rearsby, Leicester LE7 4YH

1 3 5 7 9 10 8 6 4 2

First published in the United Kingdom in 2012
by HarperCollins*Publishers*

Copyright © Bernard Cornwell, 2012

The right of Bernard Cornwell to be identified as
the author of this work has been asserted by him
in accordance with the Copyright, Designs and
Patents Act, 1988.

All rights reserved

A CIP catalogue record for this book is available
from the British Library

ISBN 978 1 51001 813 6

Typeset by Palimpsest Book Production Limited,
Falkirk, Stirlingshire

Printed and bound in Great Britain
by TJ International Ltd, Padstow, Cornwall

FSC
www.fsc.org

MIX
Paper from
responsible sources
FSC® C013056

1356

is for my grandson,
Oscar Cornwell,
with love.

CONTENTS

'The English are riding, no-one knows where.'

Warning sent in fourteenth-century France,
quoted in *A Fool and His Money*
by Ann Wroe

PROLOGUE

CARCASSONNE

He was late.

Now it was dark and he had no lantern, but the city's flames gave a lurid glow that reached deep into the church and gave just enough light to show the stone slabs in the deep crypt where the man struck at the floor with an iron crow.

He was attacking a stone incised with a crest that showed a goblet wreathed by a buckled belt on which was written *Calix Meus Inebrians*. Sun rays carved into the granite gave the impression of light radiating from the cup. The carving and inscription were worn smooth by time, and the man had taken little notice of them, though he did notice the cries from the alleyways around the small church. It was a night of fire and suffering, so much screaming that it smothered the noise as he struck the stone flags at the edge of the slab to chip a small space into which he could thrust the long crow. He rammed the iron bar down, then froze as he heard laughter and footsteps in the church above. He shrank behind an archway just before two men came down into the crypt. They carried a flaming torch that lit the long, arched space and showed that there was no easy plunder in sight. The crypt's altar was plain stone with nothing but a wooden cross for decoration, not even a candlestick, and one of the men said something in a strange language, the other laughed, and both climbed back to the nave where the flames from the streets lit the painted walls and the desecrated altars.

The man with the iron crow was cloaked and hooded in black. Beneath the heavy cloak he wore a white robe that was smeared with dirt, and the robe was girdled with a three-knotted cord. He was a Black Friar, a Dominican, though on this night that promised no protection from the army that ravaged Carcassonne. He was tall and strong, and before he had taken his vows he had been a man-at-arms. He had known how to thrust a lance, cut with a sword, or kill with an axe. He had been called Sire Ferdinand de Rodez, but now he was simply Fra Ferdinand. Once he had worn mail and plate, he had ridden in tournaments and slaughtered in battle, but for fifteen years he had been a friar and had prayed each day for his sins to be forgiven. He was old now, almost sixty, though still broad in the shoulders. He had walked to reach this city, but the rains had slowed his journey by flooding the rivers and making fords impassable and that was why he was late. Late and tired. He rammed the crow beneath the carved slab and heaved again, fearing that the iron would bend before the stone yielded, then suddenly there was a coarse grating sound and the granite lifted and then slid sideways to offer a small gap into the space beneath.

The space was dark because the devil's flame-light from the burning city could not reach into the grave, and so the friar knelt by the dark hole and groped. He discovered wood and so he thrust the crow down again. One blow, two blows, and the wood splintered, and he prayed there was no lead coffin inside the timber casket. He thrust the crow a last time, then reached down and pulled pieces of splintered wood out of the hole.

There was no lead coffin. His fingers, reaching far down into the tomb, found cloth that crumbled when he touched it. Then he felt bones. His fingers explored a dry eye-hole, loose teeth, and discovered the curve of a rib. He lay down so he could stretch his arm deeper and he groped in the grave's blackness and found something solid that was not bone. But it was not what he sought; it was the wrong shape. It was a crucifix. Voices were suddenly loud in the church above. A man laughed and a woman sobbed. The friar lay motionless, listening and praying. For a moment he despaired, thinking that the object he sought was not in the tomb, but then he reached as far as he could and his fingers touched something wrapped in a fine cloth that did not crumble. He fumbled in the dark, caught hold of the cloth, and tugged. Some object was wrapped inside the fine cloth, something heavy,

5

and he inched it towards him, then caught proper hold of it and drew the object free of the bone hands that had been clutching it. He pulled the thing from the tomb and stood. He did not need to unwrap it. He knew he had found *la Malice*, and in thanks he turned to the simple altar at the crypt's eastern end and made the sign of the cross. 'Thank you, Lord,' he said in a murmur, 'and thank you, Saint Peter, and thank you Saint Junien. Now keep me safe.'

The friar would need heavenly help to be safe. For a moment he considered hiding in the crypt till the invading army left Carcassonne, but that might take days and, besides, once the soldiers had plundered everything easy they would open the crypt's tombs to search for rings, crucifixes, or anything else that might fetch a coin. The crypt had sheltered *la Malice* for a century and a half, but the friar knew it would offer him no safety beyond a few hours.

Fra Ferdinand abandoned the crow and climbed the stairs. *La Malice* was as long as his arm and surprisingly heavy. She had been equipped with a handle once, but only the thin metal tang remained and he held her by that crude grip. She was still wrapped in what he thought was silk.

The church nave was lit by the houses that burned in the small square outside. There were three men inside the church, and one called a challenge to the dark-cloaked figure who appeared from the crypt steps. The three were archers, their long bow staves were propped against the altar, but despite the challenge they were not really interested in the stranger, only in the woman they had spreadeagled on the altar steps. For a heartbeat Fra Ferdinand was tempted to rescue the woman, but then four or five new men came through a side door and whooped when they saw the naked body stretched on the steps. They had brought another girl with them, a girl who screamed and struggled, and the friar shuddered at the sound of her distress. He heard her clothes tearing, heard her wail, and he remembered all his own sins. He made the sign of the cross, 'Forgive me, Christ Jesus,' he whispered and, unable to help the girls, he stepped through the church door and into the small square outside. Flames were consuming thatched roofs that flared bright, spewing wild sparks into the night wind. Smoke writhed above the city. A soldier wearing the red cross of Saint George was being sick on the church steps and a dog ran to lap up the vomit. The friar turned towards the river, hoping to cross the bridge and climb to the Cité. He thought that Carcassonne's double walls, towers and crenellations would protect him because he doubted that this rampaging army would have the patience to conduct a siege. They had captured the *bourg*, the commercial district that lay west of the river, but that had never been defensible. Most of the town's businesses were in the *bourg*, the leather shops and silversmiths and armourers and poulterers and cloth merchants, yet only an earth wall had surrounded those riches, and the army had swarmed over that puny barrier like a flood. Carcassonne's Cité, though, was a fortress, one of the greatest in France, a bastion ringed by vast stone turrets and towering walls. He would be safe there. He would find a place to hide *la Malice* and wait until he could return it to its owner.

He edged into a street that had not been fired. Men were breaking into houses, using hammers or axes to splinter doors. Most of the citizens had fled to the Cité, but a few foolish souls had remained, perhaps hoping to protect their properties. The army had arrived so swiftly that there had been no time to take every valuable across the bridge and up to the monstrous gates that protected the hilltop citadel. Two bodies lay in the central gutter. They wore the four lions of Armagnac, crossbowmen killed in the hopeless defence of the *bourg*.

Fra Ferdinand did not know the city. Now he tried to find a hidden way to the river, using shadowed alleys and narrow passages. God, he thought, was with him, for he met no enemies as he hurried eastwards, but then he came to a wider street, lit bright by flames, and he saw the long bridge, and beyond it, high on the hill, the fire-reflecting walls of the Cité. The stones of the wall were reddened by the fires blazing in the *bourg*. The walls of hell, the friar thought, and then a gust of the night wind swirled a great mask of smoke down to

8

shroud his view of the walls, but not the bridge, and on the bridge, guarding its western end, were archers. English archers with their red-crossed tunics and their long deadly bows. Two horsemen, mailed and helmeted, were with the archers.

No way to cross, he thought. No way to reach the safety of the Cité. He crouched, thinking, then headed back into the alleys. He would go north.

He had to cross a major street lit by newly set fires. A chain, one of the many that had been strung across the roadway to hold up the invaders, lay in the gutter where a cat lapped at blood. Fra Ferdinand ran through the firelight, dodged into another alley, and kept running. God was still with him. The stars were obscured by smoke in which sparks flew. He crossed a square, was baulked by a dead-end alley, retraced his steps, and headed north again. A cow bellowed in a burning building, a dog ran across his path with something black and dripping in its teeth. He passed a tanner's shop, jumping over the hides that were strewn on the cobbles, and there ahead was the risible earth bank that was the *bourg*'s only defence, and he climbed it, then heard a shout and glanced behind to see three men pursuing him.

'Who are you?' one shouted.

'Stop!' another bellowed.

The friar ignored them. He ran down the slope, heading towards the dark countryside that lay beyond the huddle of cottages built outside the earthen bank, as an arrow hissed past him, missing him by the grace of God and the width of a finger, and he twisted aside into a passage between two of the small houses. A steaming manure heap stank there. He ran past the dung and saw the passage ended in a wall, and turned back to see the three men barring his path. They were grinning.

'What have you got?' one of them asked.

'*Je suis Gascon*,' Fra Ferdinand said. He knew the city's invaders were both Gascons and English, and he spoke no English. '*Je suis Gascon!*' he said again, walking towards them.

'He's a Black Friar,' one of the men said.

'But why did the goddamned bastard run?' another of the Englishmen asked. 'Got something to hide, have you?'

'Give it here,' the third man said, holding out his hand. He was the only one with a strung bow; the other two had their bows slung on their backs and were holding swords. 'Come on, arseface, give it me.' The man reached for *la Malice*.

The three men were half the friar's age, and, because they were archers, probably twice as strong, but Fra Ferdinand had been a great man-at-arms and the skills of the sword had never deserted him. And he was angry. Angry because of the suffering he had seen and the cruelties he had heard, and that anger made him savage. 'In the name of God,' he said, and whipped *la Malice* upwards. She was still wrapped in silk, but her blade cut hard into the archer's outstretched wrist, severing the tendons and breaking

10

bone. Fra Ferdinand was holding her by the tang, which offered a perilous grip, but she seemed alive to him. The wounded man recoiled, bleeding, as his companions roared with anger and stabbed their blades forward, and the friar parried both with one cut and lunged forward, and *la Malice*, though she had been in a tomb for over a hundred and fifty years, proved as sharp as a newly honed blade and her fore-edge skewered through the padded haubergeon of the nearest man and opened his ribs and ripped into a lung, and before the man even knew he had been wounded Fra Ferdinand had swept the blade sideways to take the third man's eyes and blood brightened the alleyway and all three men were retreating now, but the Black Friar gave them no chance to escape. The blinded man tripped backwards onto the manure pile, his companion hacked his blade in desperation, and *la Malice* met it and the English sword broke in two and the friar flicked the silk-wrapped blade to cut that man's gullet and felt the blood splash on his face. So warm, he thought, and God forgive me. A bird shrieked in the darkness, and the flames roared up from the *bourg*.

He killed all three archers, then used the silk wrapping to clean *la Malice*'s blade. He thought of saying a brief prayer for the men he had just killed, then decided he did not want to share heaven with such brutes. Instead he kissed *la Malice*, then searched the three bodies and found some coins, a lump of cheese, four bowstrings, and a knife.

The city of Carcassonne burned and filled the winter night with smoke.

And the Black Friar walked north. He was going home, home to the tower.

He carried *la Malice* and the fate of Christendom.

And he vanished into darkness.

The men came to the tower four days after Carcassonne had been sacked.

There were sixteen of them, all cloaked in fine, thick wool and all mounted on good horses. Fifteen of the men wore mail and had swords at their waists, while the remaining rider was a priest who carried a hooded hawk on his wrist.

The wind came harsh down the mountain pass, ruffling the hawk's feathers, rattling the pines and whipping the smoke from the small cottages of the village that lay beneath the tower. It was cold. This part of France rarely saw snow, but the priest, glancing from beneath the black hood of his cloak, thought there might be flakes in the wind.

There were ruined walls about the tower, evidence that this had once been a stronghold, but all that was left of the old castle was the tower itself and a low thatched building where perhaps servants lived. Chickens scratched in the dust, a tethered goat stared at the horses, while a cat ignored the newcomers. What had once been a fine small fortress, guarding the road into the mountains, was now a farmstead, though the priest noticed that the tower was still in good repair, and the small village in the hollow beneath the old fortress looked prosperous enough.

A man scurried from the thatched hut and bowed low to the horsemen. He did not bow because he recognised them, but because men with swords command respect. 'Lords?' the man asked anxiously.

'Shelter the horses,' the priest demanded.

'Walk them first,' one of the mailed men added, 'walk them, rub them down, don't let them eat too much.'

'Lord,' the man said, bowing again.

'This is Mouthoumet?' the priest asked as he dismounted.

'Yes, father.'

'And you serve the Sire of Mouthoumet?' the priest asked.

'The Count of Mouthoumet, yes, lord.'

'He lives?'

'Praise be to God, father, he lives.'

'Praise be to God indeed,' the priest said carelessly, then strode to the tower door, which stood at the top of a brief flight of stone steps. He called for two of the mailed men to accompany him and ordered the rest to wait in the yard, then he pushed open the door to find himself in a wide, round room used to store firewood. Hams and bunches of herbs hung from the beams. A stair led around one half of the wall, and the priest, not bothering to announce himself or wait for an attendant to greet him, took the stairs to the upper floor where a hearth was built into the wall. A fire burned there, though much of its smoke swirled about the circular room, driven back through the vent by the cold wind. The ancient wooden floor-boards were covered in threadbare rugs; there were two wooden chests on which candles burned because, though it was daylight outside, the room's two windows had been hung with blankets to block the draughts. There was a table on which lay two books, some parchments, an ink bottle, a sheaf of quills, a knife, and an old rusted breastplate that served as a bowl for three wrinkled apples. A chair stood by the table while the Count of Mouthoumet, lord of this lonely tower, lay in a bed close to the smouldering fire. A grey-haired priest sat beside him, and two elderly women knelt at the bed's foot. 'Leave,' the newly arrived priest ordered the three. The two mailed men came up the stairs behind him and seemed to fill the room with their baleful presence.

'Who are you?' the grey-haired priest asked nervously.

'I said leave, so leave.'

'He's dying!'

'Go!'

The old priest, a scapular about his neck, abandoned the sacraments and followed the two women down the stairs. The dying man watched the newcomers, but said nothing. His hair was long and white, his beard untrimmed, and his eyes sunken. He saw the priest place the hawk on the

14

table, where the bird's talons made scratching noises. 'She is *une calade,*' the priest explained.

'*Une calade?*' the count asked, his voice very low. He stared at the bird's slate-grey feathers and pale streaked breast. 'It is too late for a *calade.*'

'You must have faith,' the priest said.

'I have lived over eighty years,' the count said, 'and I have more faith than I have time.'

'You have enough time for this,' the priest said grimly. The two mailed men stood at the stairhead and said nothing. The *calade* made a mewing noise, but when the priest snapped his fingers the hooded bird went still and quiet. 'You were given the sacrament?' the priest asked.

'Father Jacques was about to give it to me,' the dying man said.

'I will do it,' the priest said.

'Who are you?'

'I come from Avignon.'

'From the Pope?'

'Who else?' the priest asked. He walked about the room, examining it, and the old man watched him. He saw a tall, hard-faced man, his priest's robes finely tailored. When the visitor lifted a hand to touch the crucifix hanging on the wall his sleeve fell open to reveal a lining of red silk. The old man knew this kind of priest, hard and ambitious, rich and clever, the kind who did not minister to the poor, but climbed the ladder of clerical power into the company of the rich and privileged. The priest turned and gazed at the

15

old man with hard green eyes. 'Tell me,' he said, 'where is *la Malice*?'

The old man hesitated a second too long. '*La Malice*?'

'Tell me where she is,' the priest demanded and, when the old man said nothing, added, 'I come from the Holy Father. I order you to tell me.'

'I don't know the answer,' the old man whispered, 'so how can I tell you?'

A log crackled in the fire, spewing sparks. 'The Black Friars,' the priest said, 'have been spreading heresies.'

'God forbid,' the old man said.

'You have heard them?'

The count shook his head. 'I hear little these days, father.'

The priest reached into a pouch that hung at his waist and brought out a scrap of parchment. 'The Seven Dark Lords possessed it,' he read aloud, 'and they are cursed. He who must rule us will find it, and he shall be blessed.'

'Is that heresy?' the count asked.

'It is a verse the Black Friars are telling all over France. All over Europe! There is only one man to rule us, and that is the Holy Father. If *la Malice* exists then it is your Christian duty to tell me what you know. She must be given to the church! A man who thinks otherwise is a heretic.'

'I am no heretic,' the old man said.

'Your father was a Dark Lord.'

The count shuddered. 'The sins of the father are not mine.'

'And the Dark Lords possessed *la Malice*.'

'They say many things about the Dark Lords,' the count said.

'They protected the treasures of the Cathar heretics,' the priest said, 'and when, by the grace of God, those heretics were burned from the land, the Dark Lords took their treasures and hid them.'

'I have heard that.' The count's voice was scarce above a whisper.

The priest reached out and stroked the hawk's back. '*La Malice*,' he said, 'has been lost these many years, but the Black Friars say she can be found. And she must be found! She is a treasure of the church, a thing of power! A weapon to bring Christ's kingdom to earth, and you conceal it!'

'I do not!' the old man protested.

The priest sat on the bed and leaned close to the count. 'Where is *la Malice*?' he asked.

'I don't know.'

'You are very close to God's judgement, old man,' the priest said, 'so do not lie to me.'

'In the name of God,' the count said, 'I do not know.' And that was true. He had known where *la Malice* was hidden, and, fearing that the English would discover her, he had sent his friend, Fra Ferdinand, to retrieve the relic and the count assumed the friar had done that, and if Fra Ferdinand had succeeded then the count did not know where *la Malice* was. So he had not lied, but

17

nor had he told the priest the whole truth, because some secrets should be carried to the grave.

The priest stared at the count for a long time, then reached out his left hand to take the jesses of the hawk. The bird, still hooded, stepped cautiously onto the priest's wrist. He lifted it down to the bed and coaxed the bird to stand on the dying man's chest, then gently undid the hood's laces and lifted the leather from the bird's head. 'This *calade*,' he said, 'is different. It does not betray whether you will live or die, but whether you will die in a state of grace and go to heaven.'

'I pray I shall,' the dying man said.

'Look at the bird,' the priest commanded.

The Count of Mouthoumet looked up at the hawk. He had heard of such birds, *calades*, which could foretell a man's death or life. If the bird looked directly into a sick person's eyes then that person would recover, but if not, they would die. 'A bird that knows eternity?' the count asked.

'Look at him,' the priest said, 'and tell me, do you know where *la Malice* is hidden?'

'No,' the old man whispered.

The hawk seemed to be gazing at the wall. It shuffled on the old man's breast, its talons gripping the threadbare blanket. No one spoke. The bird was very still, but then, suddenly, it darted its head down and the count screamed.

'Quiet,' the priest snarled.

The hawk had sliced its hooked beak into the dying man's left eye, pulping it, leaving a trail of bloodied jelly on his unshaven cheek. The count was whimpering. The hawk's beak made a clattering noise as the priest moved the bird back down the bed.

'The *calade* tells me you lied,' the priest said, 'and now, if you wish to keep your right eye, you will tell me the truth. Where is *la Malice*?'

'I don't know,' the old man sobbed.

The priest was silent for a while. The fire crackled and the wind blew smoke into the room. 'You lie,' he said. 'The *calade* tells me you lie. You spit in the face of God and of His angels.'

'No!' the old man protested.

'Where is *la Malice*?'

'I don't know!'

'Your family name is Planchard,' the priest said accusingly, 'and the Planchards were ever heretics.'

'No!' the count protested, and then, sounding weaker, 'Who are you?'

'You may call me Father Calade,' the priest said, 'and I am the man who decides whether you go to hell or go to heaven.'

'Then shrive me,' the old man pleaded.

'I would rather suck on the devil's arse,' Father Calade said.

An hour later, when the count was blinded and weeping, the priest was at last convinced that the old man did not know where *la Malice* was hidden. He coaxed the hawk onto his wrist and placed the hood back on its head, then he nodded to one of the mailed men. 'Send this old fool to his master.'

'To his master?' the man-at-arms asked, puzzled.

'To Satan,' the priest said.

'For God's sake,' the Count of Mouthoumet pleaded, then jerked helplessly as the man-at-arms thrust a fleece-stuffed pillow over his face. The old man took a surprisingly long time to die.

'We three go back to Avignon,' the priest told his companions, 'but the rest stay here. Tell them to search this place. Pull it down! Stone by stone.'

The priest rode east towards Avignon. Later that day some snow fell, soft and thin, whitening the pale olive trees in the valley beneath the dead man's tower.

Next morning the snow had gone, and a week later the English came.

PART I

AVIGNON

CHAPTER 1

The message arrived in the town after midnight, carried by a young monk who had travelled all the way from England. He had left Carlisle in August with two other brethren, all three ordered to the great Cistercian house at Montpellier where Brother Michael, the youngest, was to learn medicine and the others were to study at the famous school of theology. The three had walked the length of England, sailed from Southampton to Bordeaux and then walked inland, and, like any travellers committed to a long journey, they had been entrusted with messages. There was one for the abbot at Puys, where Brother Vincent had died of the flux, then Michael and his companion had walked on to Toulouse, where Brother Peter had fallen sick and been committed to the hospital where, as far as Michael knew, he still lay. So the young monk was alone now and he had just one message left, a battered scrap of parchment, and he had been told that he might miss the man to whom it was addressed if he did not travel that same night. '*Le Bâtard*,' the abbot at Paville had told him, 'moves swiftly. He

23

was here two days ago, now he is at Villon, but tomorrow?'

'*Le Bâtard?*'

'That is his name in these parts,' the abbot had said, making the sign of the cross, which somehow suggested that the young English monk would be lucky to survive his encounter with the man named *le Bâtard*.

Now, after a day's walking, Brother Michael stared across the valley at the town of Villon. It had been easy to find because, as night fell, the sky was lit with flames that served as a beacon. Fugitives passing him on the road told him that Villon was burning, and so Brother Michael merely walked towards the bright fire so that he could find *le Bâtard* and thus deliver his message. He crossed the valley nervously, seeing fire twist above the town walls to fill the night with a churning smoke that was touched livid red where it reflected the flames. The young monk thought this was what Satan's sky must look like. Fugitives were still escaping the town and they told Brother Michael to turn around and flee because the devils of hell were loose in Villon, and he was tempted, oh so tempted, but another part of his young soul was curious. He had never seen a battle. He had never seen what men did when they unleashed themselves to violence, and so he walked on, putting his faith in God and in the stout pilgrim's staff he had carried all the way from Carlisle.

The fires were concentrated around the western

gate, and their flames lit the bulk of the castle that crowned the hill to the east. It was the Lord of Villon's castle, that was what the abbot at Paville had told him, and the Lord of Villon was being besieged by an army led by the Bishop of Lavence and by the Count of Labrouillade, who together had hired the band of mercenaries led by *le Bâtard*.

'Their quarrel?' Brother Michael had asked the abbot.

'They have two quarrels,' the abbot had answered, pausing to let a servant pour him wine. 'The Lord of Villon confiscated a wagon of hides belonging to the bishop. Or so the bishop says.' He grimaced, for the wine was new and raw. 'In truth Villon is a godless rogue, and the bishop would like a new neighbour.' He shrugged, as if to admit that the cause of the fighting was trivial.

'And the second quarrel?'

The abbot had paused. 'Villon took the Count of Labrouillade's wife,' he finally admitted.

'Ah.' Brother Michael had not known what else to say.

'Men are quarrelsome,' the abbot had said, 'but women always make them worse. Look at Troy! All those men killed for one pretty face!' He looked sternly at the young English monk. 'Women brought sin into this world, brother, and they have never ceased to bring it. Be grateful that you are a monk and sworn to celibacy.'

'Thanks be to God,' Brother Michael had said, though without much conviction.

25

Now the town of Villon was filled with burning houses and dead people, all because of a woman, her lover, and a cartload of hides. Brother Michael approached the town along the valley road, crossed a stone bridge and so came to Villon's western entrance, where he paused because the gates had been torn from the arch's stonework by a force so massive that he could not imagine what might do such a thing. The hinges were forged from iron, and each had been attached to its gate by brackets longer than a bishop's crozier, broader than a man's hand and thick as a thumb, yet the two leaves of the gate now hung askew, their scorched timbers shattered and their massive hinges wrenched into grotesque curls. It was as though the devil himself had plunged his monstrous fist through the arch to rip a path into the city. Brother Michael made the sign of the cross.

He edged past the fire-blackened gate and stopped again because, just beyond the arch, a house was burning and in the door opposite was the body of a young woman, face down, quite naked, her pale skin laced with rivulets of blood that appeared black in the firelight. The monk gazed at her, frowning slightly, wondering why the shape of a woman's back was so arousing, and then he was ashamed that he had thought such a thing. He crossed himself again. The devil, he thought, was everywhere this night, but especially here in this burning city beneath the fire-touched clouds of hell.

Two men, one in a ragged mail coat and the other in a loose leather jerkin and both holding long knives, stepped over the dead woman. They were alarmed by the sight of the monk and turned fast, eyes wide, ready to strike, but then recognised the grubby white robe and saw the wooden cross about Brother Michael's neck and ran off in search of richer victims. A third soldier vomited into the gutter. A rafter collapsed in the burning house, venting a blast of hot air and whirling sparks.

Brother Michael climbed the street, keeping his distance from the corpses, then saw a man sitting by a rain barrel where he was trying to staunch the bleeding from a wound in his belly. The young monk had been an assistant in his monastery's infirmary, and so he approached the wounded soldier. 'I can bind that up,' he said, kneeling, but the wounded man snarled at him and lashed out with a knife, which Brother Michael only avoided by toppling sideways. He scrambled to his feet and backed away.

'Take off your robe,' the wounded man said, trying to follow the monk, but Brother Michael ran uphill. The man collapsed again, spitting curses. 'Come back,' he shouted, 'come back!' Over his leather jerkin he wore a jupon that showed a golden merlin against a red field and Brother Michael, dazedly trying to make sense of the chaos about him, realised that the golden bird was the symbol of the town's defenders, and that the wounded man had wanted to escape by stealing his monk's robe and using it as a disguise, but instead the man was trapped by two soldiers in green and white colours who cut his throat.

Some men wore a badge showing a yellow bishop's staff surrounded by four black cross-crosslets, and Brother Michael decided they had to be the bishop's soldiers, while the troops who wore the green horse on the white field must serve the Count of Labrouillade. Most of the dead displayed the golden merlin, and the monk noted how many of those corpses were spitted by long English arrows that had blood-speckled white feathers. The fighting had passed through this part of the town, leaving it burning. Fire leaped from thatched roof to thatched roof, while in the places where the fire had not reached a horde of drunken, undisciplined soldiers plundered and raped amidst the smoke. A baby cried, a woman shrieked, then a blinded man, his eyes nothing but blood-weeping pits, staggered from an alley to collide with the monk. The man shrank away, whimpering, holding up his hands to ward off the expected blow.

'I won't hurt you,' Brother Michael said in French, a language he had learned as a novice so he would be fitted to finish his education at Montpellier, but the blinded man ignored him and stumbled down the street. Somewhere, incongruous in the blood and smoke and shouting, a choir sang, and the monk wondered if he was dreaming, yet the voices were real, as real as the screaming women and sobbing children and barking dogs.

He went cautiously now, for the alleys were dark and the soldiers wild. He passed a tanner's shop where a fire burned and he saw a man had been drowned in a vat of the urine used to cure the hides. He came into a small square, decorated with a stone cross, and there he was attacked from behind by a bearded brute wearing the bishop's livery. The monk was pushed to the ground and the man bent to cut away the pouch hanging from his rope belt. 'Get away! Get away!' Brother Michael, panicking, forgot where he was and shouted in English. The man grinned and moved the knife to threaten the monk's eyes, then he opened his own eyes wide, looked horrified and the flame-lit night went dark with a spray of blood as the man slowly toppled over. Brother Michael was spattered with the blood and saw that his assailant had an arrow through his neck. The man was choking, clawing at the arrow, then began to shudder as blood pulsed from his open mouth.

'You're English, brother?' an English voice asked, and Michael looked up to see a man wearing a black livery on which a white badge was slashed with the diagonal bar of bastardy. 'You're English?' the man asked again.

'I'm English,' Brother Michael managed to speak.

'You should have clouted him,' the man said, picking up Brother Michael's staff, then hauling the monk to his feet. 'Clouted him hard and he'd have toppled over. Bastards are all drunk.'

'I'm English,' Brother Michael said again. He was shaking. The fresh blood felt warm on his skin. He shivered.

'And you're a long bloody way from home, brother,' the man said. He had a great war bow strung across his muscled shoulders. He stooped to the monk's assailant, drew a knife and cut the arrow out of the man's throat, killing him in the process. 'Arrows are hard to come by,' he explained, 'so we try to rescue them. If you see any, pick them up.'

Michael brushed down his white robe, then looked at the brutal badge on his rescuer's jupon. It showed a strange animal holding a cup in its claws. 'You serve . . .' he began.

'The Bastard,' the man interrupted. 'We're the Hellequin, brother.'

'The Hellequin?'

'The devil's souls,' the man said with a grin, 'and what the hell are you doing here?'

'I've a message for your master, *le Bâtard*.'

'Then let's find him. My name's Sam.'

The name suited the archer, who had a boyish, cheerful face and a quick grin. He led the monk past a church that he and two other Hellequin had been guarding because it was a refuge for some of the townsfolk. 'The Bastard doesn't approve of rape,' he explained.

'Nor should he,' Michael responded dutifully.

'He might as well disapprove of rain,' Sam said

cheerfully, leading the way into a larger square where a half-dozen horsemen waited with drawn swords. They were in mail and helmets, and all wore the bishop's livery, and behind them was the choir, a score of boys chanting a psalm. '*Domine eduxisti,*' they sang, '*de inferno animam meam vivificasti me ne descenderem in lacum.*'

'He'd know what that meant,' Sam said, tapping his badge and evidently meaning *le Bâtard.*

'It means God has brought our souls out of hell,' Brother Michael said, 'and given us life and will keep us from the pit.'

'That's very nice of God,' Sam said. He gave a perfunctory bow to the horsemen and touched his hand to his helmet. 'That's the bishop,' he explained, and Brother Michael saw a tall man, his dark face framed by a steel helmet, sitting on his horse beneath a banner showing the crozier and the crosses. 'He's waiting,' Sam explained, 'for us to do the fighting. They all do that. Come and fight with us, they say, then they all get pissing drunk while we do all the killing. Still, it's what we're paid for. Careful here, brother, it gets dangerous.' He took the bow from his shoulder, led the monk down an alley, then checked at the corner. He peered around. 'Bloody dangerous,' he added.

Brother Michael, fascinated and repelled by the carnage all about him, leaned past Sam and discovered they had reached the top of the town and were at the edge of a big open space, a marketplace

31

perhaps, and on its far side was a road cut through black rock to the castle gate. The gatehouse, lit by the flames in the lower town, was hung with great banners. Some enjoined the help of the saints, while others showed the badge of the golden merlin. A crossbow bolt struck the wall near the priest then skittered down the cobbled alley. 'If we capture the castle by sundown tomorrow,' Sam said, putting an arrow on his string, 'our money is doubled.'

'Doubled? Why?'

'Because tomorrow is Saint Bertille's day,' Sam said, 'and our employer's wife is called Bertille, so the fall of the castle will prove that God is on our side and not on hers.'

Brother Michael thought that was dubious theology, but he did not argue the point. 'She's the wife who ran away?'

'Can't blame her. He's a pig, the count, a bloody pig, but marriage is marriage, ain't it? And it'll be a chill day in hell that a woman can choose a husband. Still, I do feel sorry for her, married to that pig.' He half drew the bow, stepped around the corner, looked for a target, saw none and stepped back. 'So the poor girl's in there,' he went on, 'and the pig is paying us to fetch her out double fast.'

Brother Michael peered around the corner, then twitched back as a pair of crossbow bolts caught the firelight. The bolts banged into the wall close to him, then ricocheted on down the alley. 'Lucky, aren't you?' Sam said cheerfully. 'Bastards saw me, took aim, then you showed yourself. You could be in heaven by now if the bastards could shoot straight.'

'You'll never get the lady out of that place,' Brother Michael opined.

'We won't?'

'It's too strong!'

'We're the Hellequin,' Sam said, 'which means the poor lass has got about an hour left with her lover boy. I hope he's giving her a good one to remember him by.'

Michael, unseen, blushed. He was troubled by women. For most of his life that temptation had not mattered because, closed away in the Cistercian house, he rarely saw any women, but the journey from Carlisle had strewn a thousand devil's snares across his path. In Toulouse a whore had grabbed him from behind, fondled him, and he had torn himself free, shaking with embarrassment, and fallen to his knees. The memory of her laughter was like a whip on his soul, as were the memories of all the girls he had seen, stared at, and wondered about, and he remembered the white naked skin of the girl at the town gate and he knew the devil was tempting him again, and he was about to say a prayer for strength when he was distracted by a whirring sound and saw a shower of crossbow bolts slashing down to the marketplace. Some, striking the cobbles, gave off bright sparks, and Brother Michael wondered why the defenders

33

were shooting, then became aware that dark-cloaked men were running from every alleyway to line the open space. They were archers, who began loosing arrows at the high battlements. Flights of arrows; not the short, leather-fledged, metal bolts of crossbowmen, but English arrows, white-feathered and long, speeding silently up to the wall's top, propelled by the great yew war bows with their hempen strings that gave a harp's sharp note for every missile shot. The arrows trembled as they left the string, then their feathers caught the air and they streaked up, white flashes in the dark, the firelight glistening from their steel points, and the monk noted how the defenders' bolts, so thick a moment ago, were suddenly sparse. The archers were drenching the castle's defenders with arrows, forcing the cross-bowmen to duck behind the wall's parapet, while other bowmen shot at the slits in the flanking towers. The sound of the steel heads striking the castle walls was like hail on cobbles. One archer fell back, a bolt in his chest, but that was the only casualty the monk saw, and then he heard the wheels.

'Stand back,' Sam warned him, and the priest stepped into the alley as a cart thundered past him. It was a small cart, light enough for six men to push, but it had been made heavier because ten great pavises, man-sized shields designed to protect a crossbowman as he reloaded his clumsy weapon, had been nailed to the front and sides to protect the men who pushed the cart, which was loaded with small wooden barrels.

'Much less than an hour,' Sam said, stepping into the street when the cart had passed. He drew the big bow and sent an arrow towards the castle's gate.

It was all strangely silent. Bother Michael had expected battle to be noise, he had expected to hear men calling to God for the sake of their souls, to hear voices raised in fear or pain, but the only sounds were the shrieks of the women in the lower town, the crackle of the flames, the harp-notes of the bows, the sound of the cart's wheels on the cobbles, and the rattle of bolts and arrows clattering on stone. Michael stared in awe as Sam kept shooting, not seeming to aim, but just whipping shaft after shaft at the castle's battlements.

'Good thing we can see,' Sam said, releasing another arrow.

'The flames, you mean?'

'That's why we set fire to the houses,' Sam said, 'to light up the bastards.' He loosed another shaft, seemingly without effort; when Brother Michael had once tried to draw a yew bow he had not been able to pull the string more than a hand's breadth.

The cart had reached the castle's gate now. It stopped there, a black shadow inside the dark archway, and Brother Michael saw a flicker of light spring up in that darkness, fade, revive, then steady to a dull glow as the six men who had pushed the cart ran back towards the archers. One of them fell, evidently struck by a crossbow bolt. Two of the others snatched his arms and dragged him back, and it was then that the monk caught his first sight of *le Bâtard*.

'That's him,' Sam said fondly, 'our bloody bastard.' Brother Michael saw a tall man dressed in a belted haubergeon of chain mail that had been painted black. He had high boots, a black sword scabbard and his helmet was a simple bascinet that was black like his mail. His sword was drawn and he used it to wave a dozen men-at-arms forward, forming them in a line, shields overlapping, in the open space. He glanced towards Brother Michael, who saw *le Bâtard*'s nose was broken and his cheek scarred, but he also saw a force in the face, a savagery, and he understood why the abbot at Paville had spoken of this man with awe. Brother Michael had expected *le Bâtard* to be an older man, and was surprised that the black-armoured soldier looked so young. Then *le Bâtard* saw Sam. 'I thought you were guarding the church, Sam,' he said.

'Poxface and Johnny are still there,' Sam said, 'but I brought this fellow to see you.' He jerked his head towards Brother Michael.

The monk took a step forward and felt the full force of *le Bâtard*'s gaze. He was suddenly nervous and his mouth went dry with fear. 'I have a message for you,' he stammered, 'it's from . . .'

'Later,' *le Bâtard* interrupted. A servant had

brought him a shield that he looped onto his left arm, then turned to look at the castle.

Which suddenly gouted flame and smoke. The smoke was black and red, shot through with stabbing flames, and filling the night with a bursting thunder that made Brother Michael crouch in fear. Scraps of flaming wreckage seared through the night as the heated air punched past the alley's mouth. Smoke shrouded the open space as the noise of the blast echoed and rolled back from the valley's far side. Birds that had been nesting in crevices of the castle wall flapped into the smoky air, while one of the great banners, calling on the help of Saint Joseph, caught the fire and blazed bright against the battlements. 'Gunpowder,' Sam explained laconically.

'Gunpowder?'

'He's a clever bastard, our bastard,' Sam said. 'Knocks down gates fast, don't it? Mind you, it's expensive. The wifeless pig had to pay double if he wanted us to use powder. He must want the bitch bad to pay that much! I hope she's bloody worth it.'

Brother Michael saw small flames flickering in the archway's thick smoke. He understood now why the town's entrance looked as though it had been torn, blackened and wrenched apart by the devil's fist. *Le Bâtard* had forced his way into the town with gunpowder, and he had repeated the trick to blow down the castle's great wooden gates. Now he led his twenty men-at-arms towards the wreckage.

'Archers!' another man called, and the bowmen, including Sam, followed the men-at-arms towards the gate. They advanced in silence, and that too was terrifying. These men in their black and white livery, Brother Michael thought, had learned to live calmly and fight ruthlessly in the dark valley of death. None of them appeared to be drunk. They were disciplined, efficient and frightening.

Le Bâtard vanished in the smoke. There were shouts from the castle, but the monk could not see what was happening there, though it was plain the attackers were inside, for the archers were now streaming through the smoking gate-arch. More men were following, men wearing the badges of the bishop and the count, going to seek more plunder in the doomed fortress.

'It could be dangerous,' Sam warned the young monk.

'God is with us,' Brother Michael said, and wondered at the fierce excitement he felt, so fierce that he hefted the pilgrim's staff as though it were a weapon.

The castle had looked big from the alleyway, but as he jostled through the scorched gate Brother Michael saw it was much smaller than it had appeared. It had no bailey and no great keep, but merely the gatehouse and one tall tower, which were separated by a small courtyard where a dozen crossbowmen in the red and gold livery lay dying. One man had been eviscerated by the explosion at the gate and, though his intestines had spilt across the yard's stones, he still lived and moaned. The monk paused to offer the man some help, then sprang back as Sam, with an ease that was as casual as it seemed heartless, cut his throat. 'You killed him!' Brother Michael said in horror.

'Of course I bloody killed him,' Sam said cheerfully. 'What did you expect me to do? Kiss him? I hope someone does the same for me if I'm in that state.' He wiped the blood from his short knife. A defender screamed as he fell from the gatehouse parapet, while another man staggered down the tower steps to collapse at the foot.

There was a door at the top of the steps, but it had not been defended, or else the defenders' courage had evaporated when the main gate exploded inwards, and so le Bâtard's men were streaming into the tower. Brother Michael followed, then turned as a trumpet sounded. A cavalcade of horsemen, all in green and white, were forcing their way through the castle gate where they used swords to drive their own men from their path. At the centre of the horsemen, where he was protected by their weapons, was a monstrously fat man clad in mail and plate and mounted on a huge horse. The cavalcade stopped at the foot of the steps and it took four men to ease the fat one out of his saddle and steady him on his feet. 'His piggy lordship,' Sam said sardonically.

'The Count of Labrouillade?'

'One of our employers,' Sam said, 'and here's the other one.' The bishop and his men had followed the count through the gate, and Sam and Michael went onto their knees as the two leaders mounted the steps and went into the tower.

Sam and Brother Michael followed the bishop's men into the entrance chamber, up a flight of shallow stairs and into a great hall that was a high, pillared space lit by a dozen smoking torches and hung with tapestries showing the golden merlin on its red background. There were at least sixty men already in the hall and they now shuffled to the edges, allowing the Count of Labrouillade and the Bishop of Lavence to walk slowly towards the dais where two of *le Bâtard*'s men were holding the defeated lord on his knees. Behind them, tall and black in his armour, was *le Bâtard* himself, his face expressionless, while beside him, unrestrained, was a young woman in a red dress. 'That's Bertille?' Brother Michael asked.

'Must be,' Sam said appreciatively. 'And a nice little mare she is too!'

Brother Michael held his breath, stared, and, for an heretical moment, he regretted ever taking holy orders. Bertille, the faithless Countess of Labrouillade, was more than a nice little mare, she was a beauty. She could not have been a day over twenty and had a sweet face, unmarked by scars or disease, with full lips and dark eyes. Her hair was black and curly, her eyes wide, and despite the obvious terror on her face she was so lovely that Brother Michael, who was only twenty-two himself, trembled. He thought he had never seen a creature so beautiful, and then he breathed again, made the sign of the cross, and uttered a silent prayer that the Virgin and Saint Michael would keep him from temptation. 'She's worth the price of the gunpowder, I'd say,' Sam commented cheerfully.

Brother Michael watched as Bertille's husband, who had taken off his helmet to reveal a head of greasy grey hair and a heavy, porcine face, waddled towards her. The count's breath was short because of the effort of walking in his heavy armour. He stopped a few paces from the dais and stared at the breast of his wife's dress, which was blazoned with the golden merlin, the symbol of her defeated lover. 'It seems to me, madame,' the count said, 'that you show poor taste in clothing.'

The countess dropped to her knees and held her clasped hands towards her husband. She wanted to speak, but the only sound she made was a whimpering sob. Tears on her cheeks reflected the flames of the torches. Brother Michael reminded himself that she was an adulteress, a sinner, a fornicator lost to grace, and Sam glanced at the young monk and thought that one day a woman would cause trouble in his life.

'Take that badge off her,' the count ordered two of his men-at-arms, gesturing at the golden merlin embroidered on his wife's dress, and the two men, their chain mail clinking and plated boots heavy on the flagstones, climbed the dais and seized the countess. She tried to resist them, shrieked once,

41

but then surrendered as one man held her arms behind her back and the other drew a short knife from his belt.

Brother Michael instinctively moved as though to help her, but Sam checked him with his one hand. 'She's the count's wife, brother,' the archer said softly, 'which means she's his property. He can do with her whatever he wants, and if you interfere he'll slit your belly open.'

'I was not . . .' Brother Michael began, then fell silent rather than tell a lie, for he had been moved to intervene, or at least protest, but now he just watched as the man-at-arms slashed at the precious fabric, ripping the golden threads away from the scarlet, tearing the bodice down to the countess's waist and finally pulling the embroidered merlin free and throwing it at the feet of his master. The countess, released from the second man's grip, crouched and clutched the remnants of the dress to her breasts.

'Villon!' the count commanded. 'Look at me!'

The man held by *le Bâtard*'s two soldiers reluctantly looked up at his enemy. He was a young man, handsome as a hawk, and, till an hour before, he had been ruler of this place, lord of its lands and owner of its peasants, but now he was nothing. He was in mail, with a breastplate and leg plates, and a smear of blood in his dark hair showed that he had fought the besiegers, but now he was in their grasp and he was forced to watch as the fat count fumbled to drag up the skirt of his chain

42

mail. No one in the hall moved or spoke, they just watched as the count wrenched leather and steel aside and then, with a smile on his face, pissed on the merlin torn from his wife's dress. He had the bladder of an ox and the urine splashed for a long time. Somewhere in the castle a man screamed and the scream went on and on, until at last, blessedly, it stopped.

The count finished at the same time, then held out a hand to his squire, who gave him a small knife with a wickedly curved blade. 'See this, Villon?' The count held the knife up so its blade caught the light. 'Know what it is?'

Villon, held by the two men-at-arms, said nothing.

'It's for you,' the count said. 'She,' he pointed the knife at his wife, 'will go back to Labrouillade, and so will you, but only after we've cut you.'

The men in green and white livery grinned, anticipating the pain and pleasure to come. The knife, its blade rusted and its handle a worn sliver of wood, was a castrator's knife, used to geld rams or calves or the small boys destined for the choirs of great churches. 'Strip him,' the count ordered his men.

'Oh, God,' Brother Michael murmured.

'No stomach for it, brother?' Sam asked.

'He fought well,' a new voice intervened, and the monk saw that *le Bâtard* had stepped to the edge of the dais. 'He fought bravely and he deserves to die like a man.'

Some of the count's men put their hands on their sword hilts, but the bishop waved them down. 'He has offended the laws of man and God,' the bishop told *le Bâtard*, 'and placed himself beyond the boundaries of chivalry.'

'The quarrel is mine,' the count snarled at *le Bâtard*, 'not yours.'

'He is my prisoner,' *le Bâtard* said.

'When we hired you,' the bishop said, 'it was agreed that all prisoners would belong to the count and myself, regardless of who captured them. Do you deny that?'

Le Bâtard hesitated, but it was clear the bishop had spoken the truth. The tall, black-armoured man glanced about the room, but his men were far outnumbered by the forces of the bishop and count. 'Then I appeal to you,' he said to the bishop, 'to let him go to his God like a man.'

'He is a fornicator and sinner,' the bishop said, 'and so I give him to the count to do with as he wishes. And I would remind you that your fee is contingent on obeying all our reasonable commands.'

'This is not reasonable,' *le Bâtard* insisted.

'The command for you to step aside is reasonable,' the bishop said, 'and I give it to you.'

The count's men-at-arms thumped their shields on the floor to show their agreement, and *le Bâtard*, knowing himself outnumbered and out-argued, shrugged and stepped away. Brother Michael saw a man-at-arms take the castrating knife and, unable to bear what was about to happen, he pushed his way out to the steps of the tower where he breathed the smoky night air. He wanted to get farther away, but some of the count's men had found an ox in the castle's stable and were torturing the beast, prodding it with spears and swords, skipping away when it lumbered around to face them, and he did not dare try to thread his way through the vicious game. Then the screaming began in the hall behind.

A hand touched his shoulder and he turned, raising the heavy staff, only to see it was a priest, an older man, who offered the monk a skin of wine. 'It seems,' the older man said, 'that you do not approve of what the count does?'

'You do?'

The priest shrugged. 'Villon took the count's wife, so what does he expect? And our church gave its blessing to the count's revenge, and with reason. Villon is a despicable man.'

'And the count is not?' Brother Michael decided he hated the fat count, with his greasy hair and heavy jowls.

'I am his chaplain and confessor,' the older priest said, 'so I know what he is.' He sounded bleak. 'And you,' he asked the monk, 'what brings you to this place?'

'I bring a message for *le Bâtard*,' Brother Michael said.

'What message?'

The English monk shook his head. 'I've not read it.'

'You should always read messages,' the older man said with a smile.

'It's sealed.'

'A hot knife will solve that.'

Brother Michael frowned. 'I was told not to read it.'

'By whom?'

'By the Earl of Northampton. He said it was urgent and private.'

'Urgent?'

Brother Michael crossed himself. 'It's said that the Prince of Wales is gathering another army. I think *le Bâtard* is ordered to join it.' He shrugged. 'That would make sense, anyway.'

'It would.'

The conversation had distracted Brother Michael from the terrible screams that sounded inside the hall. Those screams slowly subsided, became a pathetic whimpering, and only then did the count's chaplain lead the monk back to the flamelight in the pillared chamber. Brother Michael did not look at the naked thing on the bloody floor. He stayed at the back of the hall, hidden from the gelded man by the crowd of mailed soldiers.

'We are done,' the Count of Labrouillade said to *le Bâtard*.

'We are done, my lord,' *le Bâtard* agreed, 'except you owe us the money for capturing this place swiftly.'

'I owe you the money,' the count agreed, 'and it waits for you at Paville.'

'Then we shall go to Paville, my lord.' *Le Bâtard* offered the count a bow, then clapped his hands to get his men's attention. 'You know what to do! Do it!'

Le Bâtard's men had to collect their own wounded, pick up their dead, and retrieve the arrows shot in the fight, because English arrows were hard to find in Burgundy, Toulouse and Provence. It was dawn before *le Bâtard*'s men filed out of the city's ravaged gate, crossed the bridge in the valley and turned eastwards. The wounded were carried in carts, but every other man rode, and Brother Michael, who had snatched a few hours' sleep, could at last count *le Bâtard*'s company. He had learned that some of the Hellequin were still guarding the castle at Castillon that was their refuge, but *le Bâtard* still led a formidable force. There were just over sixty archers, all of them English or Welsh, and thirty-two men-at-arms, mostly from Gascony, but some from the Italian states, a handful from Burgundy, a dozen from England, and some from further away, all of them adventurers who sought money and had found it with *le Bâtard*. With their serv-ants and squires, they formed a war band that could be hired by any lord who had the resources to afford the best, though any lord who wished to fight against the English or their Gascon allies had to look elsewhere because *le Bâtard* would not help. He liked to say that he helped England's enemies kill one another, and those enemies paid him for that help. They were mercenaries and they called themselves the Hellequin, the devil's beloved, and they boasted that they could not be defeated because their souls had already been sent to hell.

And Brother Michael, after witnessing his first fight, believed them.

CHAPTER 2

The Count of Labrouillade was eager to leave Villon and gain the safety of his own fortress, which, because it possessed a moat and drawbridge, was safe from *le Bâtard*'s method of opening gates with gunpowder, and the count needed to be safe because *le Bâtard*, he was certain, would soon have a quarrel with him. And so he had left the bishop's men to hold the newly captured castle at Villon while he and his force, sixty men-at-arms and forty-three crossbowmen, hurried home to Labrouillade.

His journey, though, was slowed by his captives. He had contemplated beating Bertille in Villon, and had even ordered one of his servants to bring a whip from the castle stables, but then had delayed the punishment to hasten his return home. Yet he wanted to humiliate her, and to that end he had brought a cart from Labrouillade. The cart had been in the stables for as long as he could remember, and on its bed was a cage big enough to hold a dancing bear or a fighting bull, and that was probably why it had been made. Or perhaps one of his ancestors had used the cart for prisoners, or for transporting the savage mastiffs used to hunt boars, but whatever its original function, the heavy cart was now a cage for his wife. The Count of Villon, bloody and weak, was being transported in another cart. If the man lived the count planned to chain him naked in his courtyard as an object for men's laughter and as a pissing post for dogs, and that prospect cheered the count as he lumbered slowly southwards.

He had sent a dozen lightly armed horsemen eastwards. Their job was to trail *le Bâtard*'s mercenaries and return with a report if the Englishman pursued him. Yet that now seemed unlikely, for the count's chaplain had good news. 'I suspect he has been summoned by his liege, sire,' the chaplain told the count.

'Who is his liege?'

'The Earl of Northampton, sire.'

'In England?'

'The monk had travelled from there, sire,' the chaplain said, 'and reckoned *le Bâtard* is ordered to join the Prince of Wales. He said the message was urgent.'

'I hope you are right.'

'It is the best explanation, sire.'

'And if you are right then *le Bâtard* will be gone to Bordeaux, eh? Gone!'

'Though he might return, sire,' Father Vincent warned the count.

'In time, maybe, in time,' Labrouillade said carelessly. He was unconcerned, for if *le Bâtard* did go to Gascony then the count would have time to raise more men and strengthen his fortress. He slowed his horse, letting the carts catch up so he could stare down at his naked and bloody enemy. The count was pleased. Villon was in agony, and Bertille could expect an adulteress's punishment. Life, he decided, was good.

His wife wept. The sun rose higher, warming the day. Peasants knelt as the count passed. The road climbed into the hills that separated the lands of Villon and Labrouillade, and, though there had been death in the first, there would be rejoicing in the second because the count was revenged.

Paville was only two hours' ride west of the fallen castle. It had once been a prosperous town, famed for its monastery and for the excellence of its wine, but now there were only thirty-two monks left, and fewer than two hundred folk lived in the small town. The pestilence had come, and half the townsfolk were buried in the fields beside the river. The town walls were crumbling, and the monastery's vineyards choked with weeds.

The Hellequin gathered in the marketplace outside the monastery where they carried their wounded into the infirmary. Tired horses were walked and arrows repaired. Brother Michael wanted to find something to eat, but *le Bâtard* approached him. 'Six of my men are dying in there,' he jerked his head at the monastery, 'and another four might not live. Sam tells me you worked in an infirmary?'

'I did,' the monk said, 'but I also have a written message for you.'

'From whom?'

'The Earl of Northampton, lord.'

'Don't call me that. What does Billy want?' *Le Bâtard* waited for an answer, then scowled when none came. 'Don't tell me you didn't read the letter! What does he want?'

'I didn't read it!' Brother Michael protested.

'An honest monk? The world sees a miracle.' *Le Bâtard* ignored the proffered message. 'Go and tend to my wounded men. I'll read the letter later.'

Brother Michael worked for an hour, helping two other monks wash and bind wounds, and when he had finished he went back to the sunlight to see two men counting a vast pile of shoddy-looking coins. 'The agreement,' *le Bâtard* was saying to the abbot, 'was that the payment should be in genoins.'

The abbot looked worried. 'The count insisted on replacing the coins,' he said.

'And you permitted that?' *le Bâtard* asked. The abbot shrugged. 'He cheated us,' *le Bâtard* said, 'and you allowed it to happen!'

'He sent men-at-arms, lord,' the abbot said unhappily. Labrouillade had agreed to pay *le Bâtard*'s fee in genoins, which were good golden coins, trusted everywhere, but since *le Bâtard*'s men had first checked the payment the count had sent men to take away the genoins and replace them with a mixture of obols, écus, agnos, florins, deniers and sacks of pence, none of them gold and most of them debased or clipped, and, though the face value of the coins was for the agreed amount, their worth was less than half. 'His men assured me the value is the same, lord,' the abbot added.

'And you believed them?' *le Bâtard* asked sourly.

'I protested,' the abbot declared, concerned that he would not receive the customary fee for holding the cash.

'I'm sure you did,' *le Bâtard* said in a tone suggesting the opposite. He was still in his black armour, but had taken off his bascinet to reveal black hair cut short. 'Labrouillade's a fool, isn't he?'

'A greedy fool,' the abbot agreed eagerly. 'His father was worse. The fief of Labrouillade once encompassed all the land from here to the sea, but his father gambled away most of the southern part. The son is more careful with his money. He's rich, of course, very rich, but not a generous man.' The abbot's voice trailed away as he gazed at the piles of shoddy, misshapen and bent coins. 'What will you do?' he asked nervously.

'Do?' *Le Bâtard* seemed to think about it, then shrugged. 'I have the money,' he finally said, 'such as it is.' He paused. 'It is a matter for lawyers,' he finally decided.

'For lawyers, yes.' The abbot, worried that he

would be blamed for the substitution of the coins, could not hide his relief.

'But not in the count's own courts,' *le Bâtard* said.

'It might be argued in the bishop's court?' the abbot suggested.

Le Bâtard nodded, then scowled at the abbot. 'I shall depend on your testimony.'

'Of course, lord.'

'And pay well for it,' *le Bâtard* added.

'You may depend on my support,' the abbot said.

Le Bâtard tossed one of the coins up and down in a hand that was misshapen, as though the fingers had been mangled by a great weight. 'So we shall leave it to the lawyers,' he announced, then ordered his men to pay the abbot with whatever good coin they could find among the dross. 'I have no quarrel with you,' he added to the relieved churchman, and turned to Brother Michael, who had taken the parchment from his pouch and was trying to deliver it. 'In a moment, brother,' *le Bâtard* said.

A woman and child were approaching. Brother Michael had not noticed them till this moment, for they had been travelling with the other women who followed the Hellequin and who had waited outside Villon as the castle was assaulted. But the young monk noticed her now, noticed her and trembled. He had been haunted all day by the memory of Bertille, but this woman was just as beautiful, though it was a very different kind of beauty. Bertille had been dark, soft and gentle, while this woman was fair, hard and striking. She was tall, almost as tall as *le Bâtard*, and her pale gold hair seemed to shine in the early winter sun. She had clever eyes, a wide mouth and a long nose, while her slim body was dressed in a coat of mail that had been scrubbed with wire, sand and vinegar so that it appeared to be made of silver. Dear God, the monk thought, but flowers should blossom in her footsteps. The child, a boy who looked to be about seven or eight years old, had her face but hair as black as *le Bâtard*'s.

'My wife Genevieve,' *le Bâtard* introduced the woman, 'and my son, Hugh. This is Brother . . .' He paused, not knowing the monk's name.

'Brother Michael,' the monk said, unable to take his eyes from Genevieve.

'He brought me a message,' *le Bâtard* said to his wife, and gestured that the monk should give Genevieve the battered fold of parchment on which the earl's seal was now dried, cracked and chipped.

'Sir Thomas Hookton,' Genevieve read the name written across the folded parchment.

'I'm *le Bâtard*,' Thomas said. He had been christened Thomas and for most of his life had called himself Thomas of Hookton, though he could call himself more if he wished, for the Earl of Northampton had knighted him seven years before and, though bastard born, Thomas had a claim to a county in eastern Gascony. But he preferred to be known as *le Bâtard*. It put the fear of the devil into enemies, and a frightened enemy was already half beaten. He took the missive from his wife, put a fingernail under the seal, then decided he would wait before reading the letter and so, instead, he tucked it under his sword belt and clapped his hands to get the attention of his men. 'We're riding west in a few minutes! Get ready!' He turned and offered a bow to the abbot. 'My thanks,' he said courteously, 'and the lawyers will doubtless come to talk with you.'

'They shall receive heaven's assistance,' the abbot said eagerly.

'And this,' Thomas added more money, 'is for my wounded men. You will tend them and, for those who die, bury them and have masses said.'

'Of course, lord.'

'And I shall return to see they were properly treated.'

'I shall anticipate your return with joy, sire,' the abbot lied.

The Hellequin mounted and the bad coins were scooped into leather bags that were loaded onto packhorses as Thomas said his farewells to the men in the infirmary. Then, when the sun was still low in the east, they rode west. Brother Michael rode a borrowed horse alongside Sam who, despite his young face, was evidently one of the archers' leaders. 'Does *le Bâtard* often use lawyers?' the monk asked.

'He hates lawyers,' Sam said. 'If he had his way he'd bury every last bloody lawyer in the deepest pit of hell and let the devil shit on them.'

'Yet he uses them?'

'Uses them?' Sam laughed. 'He told that to the abbot, didn't he?' He jerked his head eastwards. 'Back there, brother, there's a half-dozen men following us. They ain't very clever, 'cos we spotted them, and by now they'll be talking to the abbot. Then they'll go back to their master and say they saw us go west and that his fat lordship is to expect a visit from a man of law. Only he won't get that. He's going to get these instead.' He patted the goose feathers of the arrows in his bag. Some of those feathers were speckled with dried blood from the fight at Villon.

'You mean we're going to fight him?' Brother Michael said, and did not notice that he had used the word 'we', any more than he had thought about why he was still with the Hellequin instead of walking on towards Montpellier.

'Of course we're bloody going to fight him,' Sam said scornfully. 'The bloody count cheated us, didn't he? So we'll cut south and east as soon as those dozy bastards have finished chatting with the abbot. 'Cos they won't follow us to make sure we've gone west. They're the sort of dozy bastards who don't think beyond their next pot of ale, but Thomas does, Thomas is a two-pot thinker, he is.'

Thomas heard the compliment and twisted in his saddle. 'Only two pots, Sam?'

'As many pots as you like,' Sam said.

'It all depends,' Thomas let Brother Michael catch up with him, 'on whether the Count of Labrouillade stays in that castle we gave him. I suspect he won't. He doesn't feel safe there, and he's a man who likes his comfort, so I reckon he'll head south.'

'And you'll ride to meet him?'

'Ride to ambush him,' Thomas said. He glanced back at the sun to judge the time. 'With God's help, brother, we'll bar his road this afternoon.' He took the parchment from under his belt. 'You didn't read this?'

'No!' Brother Michael insisted, and spoke truly. He watched as *le Bâtard* cracked the seal apart and unfolded the stiff parchment, then he gazed at Genevieve who rode a grey horse on *le Bâtard*'s far side. Thomas saw the monk's yearning gaze and was amused. 'Didn't you see last night, brother, what happens to a man who takes another man's wife?'

Michael blushed. 'I . . .' he began, but found he had nothing to say.

'And besides,' Thomas went on, 'my wife is a heretic. She was excommunicated from the church and consigned to hell. As was I. Doesn't that worry you?'

Brother Michael still had nothing to say.

'And why are you still here?' Thomas asked.

'Here?' The young monk was confused.

'Aren't you under orders?'

'I am supposed to go to Montpellier,' Brother Michael confessed.

'It's that way, brother,' Thomas said, pointing south.

'We're going south,' Genevieve said drily, 'and I think Brother Michael would like our company.'

'You would?' Thomas asked.

'I would be glad of it,' Brother Michael said, and wondered why he had spoken so eagerly.

'Then welcome,' Thomas said, 'to the devil's lost souls.'

Who now turned south and east to teach a fat and greedy count a lesson.

The Count of Labrouillade made slow progress. The horses were tired, the day grew warmer, most of his men were suffering from the wine they had drunk in the captured city, and the carts lumbered awkwardly on the rough road. Yet it did not matter, for shortly after midday the men he had sent to spy on *le Bâtard* returned with the news Labrouillade wanted.

The Englishman had ridden west. 'You're sure?' the count snapped.

'We watched him, my lord.'

'You watched him do what?' the count asked suspiciously.

'He counted the money, lord, his men stripped off their armour, then they rode westwards. All of them. And he told the abbot he would send lawyers to demand payment.'

'Lawyers!' The count laughed.

'The abbot said so, and he promised your lordship that he would speak for you in any proceedings.'

'Lawyers!' The count laughed again. 'Then the quarrel won't be settled in our lifetime!' He was safe now and the slowness of his journey did not matter. He stopped in a miserable village and demanded wine, bread and cheese, none of which he paid for, but the peasants' reward was to be in his presence and that, he sincerely believed, was recompense enough. After the meal he rattled the gelding knife on the bars of his wife's cage. 'You want it as a keepsake, Bertille?' he asked.

Bertille said nothing. Her throat was raw from sobbing; her eyes were red and fixed on the rusted blade.

'I shall shave your hair off, madame,' the count promised her, 'and make you go on your knees to the altar to beg for forgiveness. And God may forgive you, madame, but I shall not, and you'll go to a convent when I've done with you. You will scrub their floors, madame, and wash their habits until your sins have been cleansed, and then you can live in regret for the rest of your miserable days.'

She still said nothing, and the count, bored that he could not provoke her to protest, called for his men to heave him into the saddle. He had discarded his armour now and was wearing a light surcoat blazoned with his badge, while his men's armour was piled on packhorses along with their shields and lances. They rode carelessly, unthreatened, and the crossbowmen walked behind packhorses that were laden with sacks of plunder.

They followed a road that wound into the hills between chestnut trees. Pigs rooted between the trunks, and the count ordered a couple of them killed because he liked pork. The carcasses were thrown on top of the countess's cage so that the blood dripped down onto her tattered dress.

By mid afternoon they were approaching the pass that would lead them into the count's own land. It was a high place of scrawny pines and massive rocks, and legend said a force of Saracens had fought and died in the pass many years before. The country people went there to cast curses, a practice officially disapproved of by both the count and by the church, though when Bertille had first run off with her lover the count had gone to the Saracen's Pass and buried a coin, struck the high rock at the top of the hill three times, and so put a curse on Villon. It had worked, he thought, and Villon was now a gelded lump of bleeding misery chained to the bed of a dung-cart.

The light was fading. The sun was low over the western hills, but there was an hour of daylight left and that should be sufficient to see the tired soldiers over the pass, and from there the road ran straight downhill to Labrouillade. The bells of the castle would ring for the count's victory, filling the new darkness with jubilation.

And just then the first arrow flew.

★　　★　　★

Le Bâtard had led thirty archers and twenty-two men-at-arms southwards while the rest of his force was continuing westwards with those wounded who could still ride. *Le Bâtard*'s horses were tired, but they kept a steady pace, following paths they had reconnoitred in the long days as they waited for the attack on Villon.

Thomas read the Earl of Northampton's message as he rode. He read it once, then again, and his face betrayed nothing. His men watched him, suspecting the message might affect their future, but Thomas just folded the parchment and pushed it into a pouch hanging from his sword belt. 'Has he summoned us?' Sam finally asked.

'No,' Thomas said. 'And why would he summon us? What use are you to the earl, Sam?'

'None at all!' Sam said cheerfully. He was pleased that the Earl had not called Thomas back to England or, more likely, to Gascony. The Earl of Northampton was Thomas's liege lord, his master, but the earl was happy to let Thomas and his men serve as mercenaries. He shared the profits, and those profits were lavish.

'He says we must be ready to join the prince's army in the summer,' Thomas said.

'Prince Edward won't need us,' Sam replied.

'He might if the King of France decides to play games,' Thomas said. He knew the Prince of Wales was ravaging southern France and that King Jean was doing nothing to stop him, but he would surely march if the prince conducted another

62

chevauchée. And that must be tempting, Thomas thought, because France was weak. The King of Scotland, France's ally, was a prisoner in the Tower of London, and there were Englishmen in Normandy, Brittany and Aquitaine. France was like a great stag being mauled by hounds.

'And that's all the message says?' Sam asked.

'No,' Thomas said, 'but the rest of it is none of your business, Sam.' Thomas spurred his horse ahead and beckoned Genevieve to follow him. They went into the trees, seeking privacy. Hugh, their son who was mounted on a small gelding, had followed his mother, and Thomas nodded to show the boy he was allowed closer. 'You remember that Black Friar who came to Castillon?' Thomas asked Genevieve.

'The one you threw out of the town?'

'He was preaching nonsense,' Thomas said sourly.

'What was his nonsense called?'

'*La Malice*,' Thomas said, 'a magic sword, another Excalibur.' He spat.

'Why do you remember him now?'

Thomas sighed. 'Because Billy has heard of the goddamned thing.' 'Billy' was Thomas's lord, William Bohun, Earl of Northampton. Thomas handed Genevieve the letter. 'It seems another Black Friar preached in Carlisle and spouted the same nonsense. A treasure of the Seven Lords.'

'And the earl knows . . .' Genevieve began uncertainly, then checked.

'That I'm one of the Seven Lords.' Some people had called them the Seven Dark Lords of hell, and all were dead, but their descendants lived. Thomas was one. 'So Billy wants us to find the treasure.' He sneered as he said the last three words. 'And when we find it we're to deliver it to the Prince of Wales.'

Genevieve frowned over the letter. It was, of course, written in French, the language of England's aristocracy. 'The Seven Dark Lords possessed it,' she read aloud, 'and they are cursed. He who must rule us will find it, and he shall be blessed.'

'The same nonsense,' Thomas said. 'It seems the Black Friars have got excited. They're spreading the tale everywhere.'

'So where do you look?'

Thomas wanted to say nowhere, that the nonsense was not worth a moment of their time, but the Abbé Planchard, the best man he had ever known, a Christian who was truly Christ-like and also a descendant of one of the Dark Lords, had an elder brother. 'There's a place called Mouthoumet,' Thomas said, 'in Armagnac. I can think of nowhere else to look.'

'"Do not fail us in this",' Genevieve read the letter's last line aloud.

'Billy's caught the madness,' Thomas said, amused.

'But we go to Armagnac?'

'Once we're finished here,' Thomas said.

Because before the treasure could be sought the

Count of Labrouillade must be taught that greed has a price.

So *le Bâtard* set up the ambush.

It was raining in Paris. A steady rain that diluted the filth in the gutters and spread its stink through the narrow streets. Beggars crouched under the overhanging houses, holding out skinny hands to the horsemen who threaded through the city gate. There were two hundred men-at-arms, all big men on big horses, and the riders were shrouded in woollen cloaks with their heads protected from the rain by steel helmets. They looked about them as they rode through the rain, plainly astonished by such a great city, and the Parisians sheltering beneath the jutting storeys noted that these men looked wild and strange, like warriors from a nightmare. Many were bearded and all had faces roughened by weather and scarred by war. Real soldiers, these, not the followers of a great lord who spent half their time quarrelling in castle precincts, but men who carried their weapons through snow and wind and sun, and men who rode battle-scarred horses and carried battered shields. Men who would kill for the price of a button. A standard bearer rode with the men-at-arms and his rain-soaked flag showed a great red heart.

Behind the two hundred men-at-arms came packhorses, over three hundred of them, loaded with bags, lances and armour. The squires and servants who led the packhorses wore blankets, or so it seemed to the onlookers. The garments, little more than matted and grubby rags, were thrown over a shoulder then wrapped and belted at the waist, and the servants wore no breeches, though no one laughed at them because their belts carried weapons, either crude long swords with plain hilts, or chipped axes, or skinning knives. They were country weapons, but weapons that looked as though they had received much use. There were women with the servants and they were dressed in the same barbaric manner, with their bare legs muddied and red. They wore their hair loose, but no Parisian would dare mock them, for these ragged women were armed like their men and looked just as dangerous.

The horsemen and their servants stopped beside the river at the city's centre and there they divided into small groups, each going to find their own lodgings, but one group of half a dozen men, attended by servants better dressed than the others, crossed the bridge to an island in the Seine. They twisted down narrow alleys until they came to a gilded gatehouse where liveried spearmen stood guard. Inside was a courtyard, stables, a chapel and stairways leading into the royal palace, and the half-dozen horsemen were greeted with bows, their horses were taken away and they were led up stairs and down corridors to their quarters.

William, Lord of Douglas and leader of the two hundred men-at-arms, was given a chamber facing the river. Sheets of horn covered the windows, but he knocked them out to let the damp air into the room, where a great fire burned in a hearth carved with the French royal coat of arms. The Lord of Douglas stood by the fire as servants brought in bedding, wine, food and three women. 'You may take your choice, my lord,' the steward said.

'I'll take all three,' Douglas said.

'A wise choice, my lord,' the steward replied, bowing, 'and is there anything else your lordship desires?'

'Is my nephew here?'

'He is, my lord.'

'Then I want him.'

'He shall be sent,' the steward said, 'and His Majesty will receive you for supper.'

'Tell him I am filled with happiness at the prospect,' Douglas said flatly. William, Lord of Douglas, was twenty-eight years old and looked forty. He had a clipped brown beard, a face scarred from a dozen skirmishes, and eyes as cold as the winter sky. He spoke perfect French because he had spent much of his boyhood in France, learning the ways of French knights and perfecting his skills with sword and lance, but for ten years now he had been home in Scotland where he had become the leader of the Douglas clan and a magnate in the Scottish council. He had opposed the truce with England, but the rest of the council had insisted, and so the Lord of Douglas had brought his fiercest warriors to France. If they could not fight the English at home then he would unleash them on the old enemy in France.

'Take off your clothes,' he told the three girls. For a heartbeat they looked astonished, but the expression on Douglas's grim face persuaded them to obey. A good-looking man, all three thought, tall and well muscled, but he had a warrior's face, hard as a blade and with no pity. It promised to be a long night. The three were naked by the time Douglas's nephew arrived. He was not much younger than his uncle, had a broad, cheerful face, and was wearing a velvet jerkin trimmed with gold embroidery above sky-blue skin-tight leggings that were tucked into soft leather boots tasselled with gold thread. 'What the hell are you wearing?' Douglas asked.

The young man plucked the embroidered hem of the jerkin. 'It's what everyone wears in Paris.'

'Good Christ, Robbie, you look like an Edinburgh whore. What do you think of those three?'

Sir Robert Douglas turned and inspected the three girls. 'I like the one in the middle,' he said.

'Jesus Christ, she's so skinny you could use her as a needle. I like girls with meat on the bone. So what has the king decided?'

'To wait on events.'

'Jesus Christ,' Douglas said again, and went to the window where he stared at the river, which was being dappled by rain. The stench of sewage seeped from the slow swirling water. 'Does he know what's looming?'

'I have told him,' Robbie said. He had been sent to Paris to negotiate terms with King Jean, and he had arranged for his uncle's men to be paid and armoured by the French king, and now the men had come and the Lord of Douglas was eager for them to be unleashed. There were English forces in Flanders, in Brittany and in Gascony, and the Prince of Wales was raping southern France, and Douglas wanted a chance to kill some of the bastards. He hated the English.

'He knows the boy Edward will likely strike north next year?' Douglas asked. The boy Edward was the Prince of Wales.

'I have told him.'

'And he's havering?'

'He's havering,' Robbie confirmed. 'He likes feasts and music and entertainment. He's not fond of soldiering.'

'Then we'll have to put some backbone into the bloody man, won't we?'

Scotland had known little but disaster in the last few years. The pestilence had come and emptied the valleys of souls, but almost ten years before, at Durham, a Scottish army had been defeated and the King of Scotland had been taken prisoner by the hated English. King David was now a prisoner in London's Tower, and the Scots, to get him back, were expected to pay a ransom so vast that it would impoverish the kingdom for years.

But the Lord of Douglas reckoned the king could be restored in a different way, a soldier's way, and that was the main reason he had brought his men to France. In the spring the Prince of Wales would probably lead another army out of Gascony, and that army would do what English armies always did, rape and burn and pillage and destroy, and the purpose of that *chevauchée* was to force the French to bring an army against them, and then the dreaded English archers would go to work and France would suffer another defeat. Its great men would be taken prisoner and England would get even wealthier on their ransoms.

But the Lord of Douglas knew how to defeat archers, and that was the gift he brought to France, and if he could persuade the French king to oppose the boy Edward then he saw the chance of a great victory, and in that victory he planned to capture the prince. He would hold the prince to ransom, a ransom equal to that of the King of Scotland. It could be done, he thought, if only the King of France would fight.

'And you, Robbie? You'll fight?'

Robbie coloured. 'I took an oath.'

'Damn your bloody oath!'

'I took an oath,' Robbie persisted. He had been a prisoner of the English, but he had been released and his ransom paid on a promise not to fight the English ever again. The promise had been extracted and the ransom had been paid by his friend, Thomas of Hookton, and for eight years Robbie had kept the promise, but now his uncle was pushing him to break the oath.

'What money do you have, boy?'

'Your money, uncle.'

'And do you have any left?' Douglas waited, saw his nephew's sheepishness. 'So you've gambled it away?'

'Yes.'

'In debt?'

Robbie nodded.

'If you want more, boy, you fight. You strip off that whore's jacket and put on mail. For Christ's sake, Robbie, you're a good fighter! I want you! Have you no pride?'

'I took an oath,' Robbie repeated stubbornly.

'Then you can untake the bloody thing. Or become a pauper. See if I care. Now take that skinny bitch and prove you're a man, and I'll see you at supper.'

When the Lord of Douglas would try to make the King of France into a man.

The archers lined the woods. Their horses were picketed a hundred yards away, guarded by two men, but the bowmen hurried to the edge of the trees and, when the leading horsemen of the Count of Labrouillade's straggling column were less than one hundred yards away, they loosed their arrows.

The Hellequin had become rich on two things. The first was their leader, Thomas of Hookton, who was a good soldier, a supple thinker, and clever in battle, but there were plenty of men in southern France who could match *le Bâtard*'s cleverness. What they could not do was deploy the Hellequin's second advantage, the English war bow, and it was that which had made Thomas and his men wealthy.

It was a simple thing. A stave of yew, a little longer than the height of a man and preferably cut from one of the lands close to the Mediterranean. The bowyer would take the stave and shape it, keeping the dense heartwood on one side and the springy sapwood on the other, and he would paint it to keep the moisture trapped in the stave, then nock it with two tips of horn that held the cord, which was woven from fibres of hemp. Some archers liked to add strands of their woman's hair to the cord, claiming that it stopped the strings from breaking, but Thomas, in twelve years of fighting, had found no difference. The cord was whipped where the arrow rested on the string, and that was the war bow. A peasant's weapon of yew, hemp and horn, shooting an arrow made from ash, hornbeam or birch, tipped with a steel point and fledged with feathers taken from the wing of a goose, and always taken from the same wing so that the feathers curved in the same direction.

The war bow was cheap and it was lethal. Brother Michael was not a weak man, but he could not draw a bow's cord more than a hand's breadth, but Thomas's archers hauled the string back to their ears and did it sixteen or seventeen times a minute. They had muscles like steel, humps of muscle on their backs, broad chests, thick arms, and the bow was useless without the muscles. Any man could shoot a crossbow, and a good crossbow outranged the yew bow, but it cost a hundred times as much to manufacture and it took five times longer to reload, and, while the crossbowman was winding the ratchet to haul back his cord, the English archer would close the range and shoot a half-dozen points. It was the English and the Welsh archers who had the muscle, and they began training as children, just as Hugh, Thomas's son, was training now. He had a small bow and his father expected him to shoot three hundred arrows a day. He must shoot and shoot and shoot until he no longer had to think about where the arrow would go, but would simply loose in the knowledge that the arrow would speed where he intended, and every day the muscle grew until, in ten years' time, Hugh would be ready to stand in the archers' line and loose goose-feathered death from a great war bow.

Thomas had thirty archers at the edge of the wood and in the first half-minute they launched more than one hundred and fifty arrows, and it was not war, but massacre. An arrow could pierce chain mail at two hundred paces, but none of the Count of Labrouillade's men were wearing armour or carrying shields, all of which they had loaded onto packhorses. Some of the men had leather coats, but all had taken off their heavy plate or mail, and so the arrows slashed into them, wounding men and horses, driving them to instant chaos. The crossbowmen were on foot and a long way behind the count's horsemen, and anyway they were cumbered with their sacks of plunder. It would take minutes for them to ready for battle, and Thomas did not give them the minutes. Instead, as the arrows plunged into the screaming horses and fallen riders, Thomas led his twenty-two men-at-arms out of the woods onto the count's flank.

Thomas's men were mounted on destriers, the great stallions that could carry the weight of man, armour and weapons. They had not brought lances, for those weapons were heavy and would have slowed their march; instead they drew their swords or wielded axes and maces. Many carried a shield on which the black-barred badge of *le Bâtard* was painted, and Thomas, once they were out of the trees, turned the line to face the enemy and swung his sword blade down as a signal to advance.

They trotted forward, knee to knee. Rocks studded the high grassland and the line would divide around them, then rejoin. The men were in mail. Some had added pieces of plate armour, a breastplate or perhaps an espalier to protect the shoulders, and all wore bascinets, the simple open-faced helmet that let a man see in battle. The arrows continued to fall. Some of the count's horsemen were trying to escape, wrenching their reins to ride back northwards, but the thrashing of the wounded horses obstructed them and they could see the black line of Hellequin men-at-arms coming from the side, and some, in desperation, hauled out their swords. A handful broke clear and raced back towards the northern woods where the crossbowmen might be found, while another handful gathered around their lord, the count, who had one arrow in his thigh despite Thomas's orders that the count was not to be killed. 'A dead man can't pay his debts,' Thomas had said, 'so shoot anyone else, but make certain Labrouillade lives.' Now the count was trying to turn his horse, but his weight was too great and the horse was wounded, and he could not turn, and then the Hellequin spurred into the canter, the swords were lowered to the lunge position, and the arrows stopped.

The archers stopped for fear of hitting their own horsemen, then discarded their bows and pulled out swords and ran to join the killing as the men-at-arms struck.

The sound of the charge striking home was like butchers' cleavers hitting carcasses. Men screamed. Some threw down swords and held their hands out in mute surrender. Thomas, not as comfortable on horseback as he was with a bow, had his lunge deflected by a sword. He crashed past the man, backswung his blade that hammered harmlessly against leather, then swept it forward into a man's red hair. That man went down, spilling from his saddle, and the Hellequin were turning, coming

75

back to finish the enemy. A rider wearing a black hat plumed with long white feathers lunged a sword at Thomas's belly. The blade slid off his mail, and Thomas brought his sword back in a wild swing that sliced into the man's face just as Arnaldus, one of the Gascons in the Hellequin, speared the man's spine with another sword. The count's rider was making a high-pitched keening sound, shaking uncontrollably, blood pouring from his shattered face. He let his sword drop, and Arnaldus speared him again. He fell slowly sideways. An archer seized the reins of the man's horse. The dying man was the last to offer any resistance. The count's men had been taken by surprise, they had fought an unequal skirmish against men in armour whose lives were spent fighting, and the struggle was over in seconds. A dozen of the count's men escaped, the rest were dead or prisoners, and the count himself was captured. 'Archers!' Thomas shouted. 'Bows!' Their job would be to watch the northern woods in case the crossbowmen had fight in them, though Thomas doubted any would want to fight after their lord was captured. A dozen archers collected arrows, cutting them out of dead and wounded horses, picking them from the ground and filling their arrow bags. The prisoners were herded to one side and made to yield their weapons as Thomas walked his horse to where the wounded count lay on the turf. 'My lord,' he greeted him, 'you owe me money.'

'You were paid!' the count blustered.

'Sam,' Thomas called to the archer, 'if his lord-ship argues with me you can fill him with arrows.' He spoke in French, which Sam understood, and the bowman put an arrow on his string and offered the count a happy grin.

'My lord,' Thomas said again, 'you owe me money.'

'You could have pleaded your case,' Labrouillade said.

'Pleaded? Argued? Wrangled? Delayed? Why should I let your lawyers weave spells?' Thomas shook his head. 'Where are the genoins you took from Paville?'

The count thought of claiming that the coins were still at Villon's castle, but the archer had his string half drawn and *le Bâtard*'s face was implac-able, and so the count reluctantly told the truth. 'They are in Labrouillade.'

'Then you will send one of your men-at-arms to Labrouillade,' Thomas said courteously, 'with orders that the money is to be brought here. And when it is, my lord, we shall let you go.'

'Let me go?' The count was surprised.

'What use are you to me?' Thomas asked. 'It would take months to raise your ransom, my lord, and in those years you'd consume a greater value than the ransom in food. No, I shall let you go. And now, my lord, when you have sent for the coins you might permit my men to take that arrow from your thigh?'

A man-at-arms was summoned from the prisoners, given a captured horse and sent south with his message. Thomas then called Brother Michael. 'You know how to take arrows out of flesh?'

The young monk looked alarmed. 'No, sir.'

'Then watch as Sam does it. You can learn.'

'I don't want to learn,' Brother Michael blurted out, then looked abashed.

'You don't want to learn?'

'I don't like medicine,' the monk confessed, 'but my abbot insisted.'

'What do you want?' Thomas asked.

Michael looked confused. 'To serve God?' he suggested.

'Then serve him by learning how to extract arrows,' Thomas said.

'You'd better hope it's a bodkin,' Sam told the count cheerfully. 'It's going to hurt either way, but I can get a bodkin out in an eyeblink. If it's a flesh arrow I'll have to cut the bastard out. Are you ready?'

'Bodkin?' the count asked faintly. Sam had spoken in English, but the count had half understood.

Sam produced two arrows from his bag. One had a long slender head without barbs. 'A bodkin, my lord, made for slipping through armour.' He tapped it with the second arrow that had a barbed triangular head. 'A flesh arrow,' he said. He drew a short knife from his belt. 'Won't take a moment. Are you ready?'

'My own physician will treat me!' the count shouted at Thomas.

'If you wish, my lord,' Thomas said. 'Sam? Cut the shaft off, bind him up.'

The count yelped as the arrow was cut. Thomas rode away, going to where the Lord of Villon lay in his cart. The man was curled up, naked and bloody. Thomas dismounted, tied his horse to the shafts and called Villon's name. The count did not move and Thomas clambered into the wagon, turned the man over, and saw he had died. There was enough congealed blood in the cart to fill a pair of buckets, and Thomas grimaced as he jumped down, then wiped his boots on the pale grass before going to the caged cart where the Countess Bertille watched him with wide eyes. 'The Lord of Villon is dead,' Thomas said.

'Why didn't you kill the Lord of Labrouillade?' she asked, jerking her head towards her husband.

'I don't kill a man for owing me money,' Thomas said, 'but only for refusing to pay it.' He drew his sword and used it to snap the feeble lock of the cage door, then held out his hand to help the countess down to the grass. 'Your husband,' he said, 'will be free to go soon. You also, my lady.'

'I'm not going with him!' she said defiantly. She stalked to where the count lay on the grass. 'He can sleep with the pigs,' she said, pointing to the two carcasses on top of the cage, 'he won't know the difference.'

The count tried to get to his feet to slap his wife, but Sam was binding his wound with a strip of linen torn from a corpse's shirt and he yanked the linen tightly so that the count yelped with pain again. 'Sorry, my lord,' Sam said. 'Just stay still, sire, won't be but a moment.'

The countess spat at him and walked away.

'Bring the bitch here!' the count shouted.

The countess kept walking, clutching her torn dress to her breasts. Genevieve touched her shoulder, said something, then approached Thomas. 'What will you do with her?'

'She's not mine to do anything with,' Thomas said, 'but she can't come with us.'

'Why not?' Genevieve asked.

'When we leave here,' Thomas said, 'we have to go to Mouthoumet. We might have to fight our way there. We can't take useless mouths that will slow us down.'

Genevieve smiled briefly, then gazed at the crossbowmen who were sitting at the edge of the northern woods. None of them had a weapon, instead they just watched their lord's humiliation. 'Your soul has hardened, Thomas,' she said softly.

'I'm a soldier.'

'You were a soldier when I met you,' Genevieve said, 'and I was a prisoner, accused of heresy, excommunicated, condemned to death, but you took me away. What was I but a useless mouth?'

'She's trouble,' Thomas said irritably.

'And I wasn't?'

'But what will we do with her?' he asked.

'Take her away.'

'From what?'

'From that hog of a husband,' Genevieve said, 'from a future in a convent? From being clawed by dried-up nuns who hate her beauty? She must do what I did. Find her future.'

'Her future,' Thomas said, 'is to cause dissension among the men.'

'Good,' Genevieve said, 'because men cause enough trouble for women. I'll protect her.'

'Dear God,' Thomas said in exasperation, then turned to look at Bertille. She was, he thought, a rare beauty. His men were staring at her with undisguised longing, and he could not blame them. Men would die for a woman who looked like Bertille. Brother Michael had found a cloak rolled up behind the cantle of the count's saddle and he shook it out, carried it to her and offered it as a covering for her torn dress. She said something to him and the young monk blushed as scarlet as the western clouds. 'It looks,' Thomas said, 'as though she already has a protector.'

'I will do a better job,' Genevieve said, and she walked to the count's horse and reached for the blood-stained gelding knife that hung by a loop from the saddle's pommel. She crossed to the count, who flinched at the sight of the blade. He glowered at the silver-mailed woman who looked down at him with disdain. 'Your wife will ride with us,' Genevieve told him, 'and if you make any attempt to take her back then I will cut you myself. I will cut you slowly and make you squeal like the pig you are.' She spat at him and walked away.

Another enemy, Thomas thought.

The genoins came as dusk shaded into night. The coins were loaded on two packhorses and, once Thomas was satisfied that all the coins were there, he went back to the count. 'I shall keep all the coins, my lord, the bad and the good. You've paid me twice, the second payment for the trouble you caused me today.'

'I'll kill you,' the count said.

'It was our pleasure to serve you, my lord,' Thomas said. He mounted, then led his men and all the captured horses westwards. The first stars pricked the darkening sky. It was cold suddenly because a northern wind had blown up, bringing a hint of winter.

And in the spring that followed, Thomas thought, there would be another war. But first he must go to Armagnac.

And so the Hellequin rode north.

CHAPTER 3

It would have been easy enough for Fra Ferdinand to steal a horse. The Prince of Wales's army had left their horses outside Carcassonne, and the few men guarding the animals were bored and tired. The destriers, those big horses that the men-of-arms rode, were better guarded, but the mounts of the archers were in a paddock and the Black Friar could have taken a dozen, but a lone man on a horse is noticeable, a target for bandits, and Fra Ferdinand dared not risk the loss of *la Malice*, and so he preferred to walk.

It took him ten days to reach home. For a time he travelled with some merchants who had hired a dozen men-at-arms to guard their goods, but after four days they took the road south to Montpellier, and Fra Ferdinand continued northwards. One of the merchants had asked him why he carried *la Malice*, and the friar had shrugged the question away. 'It's just an old blade,' he had said, 'it might make a good hay knife?'

'Doesn't look like it could cut butter,' the merchant had said, 'you'd do better to melt it down.'

'And maybe I will.'

He had heard news on the journey, though such travellers' tales were always unreliable. It was said that the rampaging English army had burned Narbonne and Villefranche, others said Toulouse itself had fallen. The merchants had grumbled. The English *chevauchée* was a tactic to destroy a country's power, to starve the lords of taxes, to burn their mills, uproot their vines, to demolish whole towns, and the only way such a destructive force could be stopped was by another army, yet the King of France was still in the north, far away, and the Prince of Wales was running riot in the south. 'King Jean should come here,' one of the merchants had said, 'and kill the English princeling, or else there'll be no France to rule.'

Fra Ferdinand had kept silent. The other travellers were nervous of him. He was gaunt, stern and mysterious, though his companions were grateful that he did not preach. The Black Friars were a preaching order, destined to wander the world in poverty and encourage it to godliness, and when the merchants turned southwards they gave him money, which Fra Ferdinand suspected was in gratitude for his silence. He accepted the charity, offered the donors a blessing, and walked north alone.

He kept to the wooded parts of the country to avoid strangers. He knew there were *coredors*, bandits, and routiers who would think nothing of robbing a friar. The world, he thought, had become evil, and he prayed for God's protection and his prayers were answered because he saw no bandits and found no enemies, and late on a Tuesday evening he came to Agout, the village just south of the hills where the tower stood, and he went to the inn and there heard the news.

The Lord of Mouthoumet was dead. He had been visited by a priest accompanied by men-at-arms, and when the priest left the Sire of Mouthoumet was dead. He was buried now, and the men-at-arms had stayed at the tower until some Englishmen had come and there had been a fight and the Englishmen had killed three of the priest's men and the rest had run away.

'Are the English still there?'

'They went away too.'

Fra Ferdinand went to the tower the next day where he found the Sire of Mouthoumet's housekeeper, a garrulous woman who knelt for the friar's blessing, but hardly ceased her chatter even as he gave it. She told how a priest had come, 'He was rude!', and then the priest had left and the men who remained behind had searched the tower and the village. 'They were beasts,' she said, 'Frenchmen! But beasts! Then the English came.' The English, she said, had worn a badge showing a strange animal holding a cup.

'The Hellequin,' Fra Ferdinand said.

'Hellequin?'

'It is a name they take pride in. Men should suffer for such pride.'

'Amen.'

'But the Hellequin did not kill the Sire of Mouthoumet?' the friar asked.

'He was buried by the time they arrived.' She made the sign of the cross. 'No, the Frenchmen killed him. They came from Avignon.'

'Avignon!'

'The priest came from there. He was called Father Calade.' She made the sign of the cross. 'He had green eyes and I did not like him. The sire was blinded! The priest gouged his eyes out!'

'Dear God,' Fra Ferdinand said quietly. 'How do you know they came from Avignon?'

'They said so! The men he left behind told us so! They said if we didn't give them what they wanted then we would all be damned by the Holy Father himself.' She paused just long enough to make the sign of the cross. 'The English asked too. I didn't like their leader. One of his hands was like the devil's paw, like a claw. He was courteous,' she said that grudgingly, 'but he was hard. I could tell from his hand that he was evil!'

Fra Ferdinand knew how superstitious the old woman was. She was a good woman, but saw omens in clouds, in flowers, in dogs, in smoke, in anything. 'Did they ask about me?'

'No.'

'Good.' The friar had found a refuge in Mouthoumet. He was becoming too old to walk the roads of France and rely on the kindness of strangers to provide a bed and food, and a year earlier he had come to the tower and the old man had invited him to stay. They had talked together, eaten together, played chess together, and the count had told Fra Ferdinand all the ancient stories of the Dark Lords. 'The English will come back, I think,' the friar said now, 'and perhaps the French too.'

'Why?'

'They search for something,' he said.

'They searched! They dug up the new graves even, but they found nothing. The English went to Avignon.'

'You know that?'

'That's what they said. That they would follow Father Calade to Avignon.' She crossed herself again. 'What would a priest from Avignon want here? Why would the English come to Mouthoumet?'

'Because of this,' Fra Ferdinand said, showing her the old blade.

'If that's all they want,' she said scornfully, 'then give it to them!'

The Count of Mouthoumet, fearing that the rampaging English would plunder the graves of Carcassonne, had begged the friar to rescue *la Malice*. Fra Ferdinand suspected that the old man really wanted to touch the blade himself, to see this miraculous thing that his ancestors had protected, a relic of such power that possession of it might take a man's soul directly to heaven, and such was the old man's desperate pleading that

Fra Ferdinand had agreed. He had rescued *la Malice*, but his fellow friars were preaching that the sword was the key to paradise, and all across Christendom men were lusting after the blade. Why would they preach that? He suspected that he was to blame himself. After the count had told him the legend of *la Malice*, the friar had dutifully walked to Avignon and recounted the story to the master general of his order and the master general, a good man, had smiled, then said that a thousand such tales were told each year and that none had ever held the truth. 'Do you remember ten years ago?' the master general had asked, 'when the pestilence came? And how all Christendom believed the Grail had been seen? And before that, what was it? Ah, the lance of Saint George! And that was a nonsense too, but I thank you, brother, for telling me.' He had sent Fra Ferdinand away with a blessing, but maybe the master general had told others of the relic? And now, thanks to the Black Friars, the rumour had infested all Europe. '"He who must rule us will find it, and he shall be blessed",' the friar said.

'What does that mean?' the old woman asked.

'It means that some men go mad in search of God,' Fra Ferdinand explained, 'it means that every man who wants power seeks a sign from God.'

The old woman frowned, not understanding, but she believed Fra Ferdinand was strange anyway. 'The world is mad,' she said, picking on that one word. 'They say the English devils have burned half of France! Where is the king?'

'When the English come,' Fra Ferdinand said, 'or anyone else, tell them I have gone to the south.'

'You're leaving?'

'It's not safe for me here. Perhaps I will return when the madness is over, but for now I am going to the high hills by Spain. I shall hide there.'

'To Spain! They have devils there!'

'I shall go to the hills,' Fra Ferdinand reassured her, 'close to the angels,' and next morning he walked southwards and only when he was well out of sight of the village and sure that no one watched him did he turn north. He had a long journey to make and a treasure to protect.

He would return *la Malice* to her rightful owner. He would go to Poitou.

A small man, dark-faced and scowling, with a paint-spattered shock of black hair, was perched on a high trestle and using a brush to touch brown pigment onto an arched ceiling. He said something in a language Thomas did not understand.

'You speak French?' Thomas asked.

'We all have to speak French here,' the painter said, changing to that language, which he spoke with an execrable accent, 'of course we damned well speak French. Have you come to give me advice?'

'On what?'

89

'On the fresco, of course, you damned fool. You don't like the colour of the clouds? The Virgin's thighs are too big? The angels' heads are too small? That's what they told me yesterday,' he pointed his paintbrush across the ceiling to where flying angels played trumpets in the Virgin's honour, 'their heads are too small, they said, but where were they looking from? From up one of my ladders! From the floor they look perfect. Of course they're perfect. I painted them. I painted the Virgin's toes too,' he dabbed the brush angrily at the ceiling, 'and the goddamned Dominicans told me that was heresy. Heresy! To show the Virgin's toes? Sweet holy Christ, I painted her with naked tits in Siena, but no one threatened to burn me there.' He dabbed with the brush, then leaned back. 'I'm sorry, *ma chérie*,' he spoke to the image of Mary that he was painting onto the ceiling, 'you're not allowed to have tits and now you've lost your toes, but they'll come back.'

'They will?' Thomas asked.

'The plaster's dry,' the painter snarled as though the answer was obvious, 'and if you paint over a fresco when it's dry then that paint will peel off like a whore's scabs. It will take a few years, but her heretical toes will reappear, but the Dominicans don't know that because they are damned fools.' He switched into his native Italian and screamed insults at his two assistants, who were using a giant pestle to mix fresh plaster in a barrel. 'They are also fools,' he added to Thomas.

'You have to paint on wet plaster?' Thomas asked.

'You came here to have a lesson in how to paint? You damned well pay me. Who are you?'

'My name is d'Evecque,' Thomas said. He had no wish to be known by his real name in Avignon. He had enemies enough in the church, and Avignon was the home of the Pope, which meant the town was packed with priests, monks and friars. He had come here because the disagreeable woman in Mouthoumet had assured him that the mysterious Father Calade had come to Avignon, but Thomas now had a sinking feeling that his time was being wasted. He had enquired of a dozen priests if they knew of a Father Calade, and none had recognised the name, but equally no one had recognised Thomas either or knew he had been excommunicated. He was a heretic now, outside the church's grace, a man to be hunted and burned, yet he could not resist visiting the great fortress-palace of the Papacy. There was a Pope in Rome too, because of the schism in the church, but Avignon held the power, and Thomas was astonished by the riches displayed in the vast building.

'From your voice,' the painter said, 'I'd guess you're a Norman? Or perhaps an Englishman, eh?'

'A Norman,' Thomas said.

'So what is a Norman doing so far from home?'

'I wish to see the Holy Father.'

'Of course you damned well do. But what are you doing here? In the Salle des Herses?'

91

The Salle des Herses was a room that opened from the great audience chamber of the Papal palace, and it had once contained the mechanism that lowered the portcullis in the palace gate, though that winch and pulley system had long been taken out so that, evidently, the room could become another chapel. Thomas hesitated before answering, then told the truth. 'I wanted somewhere to piss.'

'That corner,' the painter gestured with his brush, 'in that hole beneath the picture of Saint Joseph. It's where the rats get in, so do me a favour and drown some of the bastards. So what do you want of the Holy Father? Sins remitted? A free pass to heaven? One of the choirboys?'

'Just a blessing,' Thomas said.

'You ask for so little, Norman. Ask for much, then you might get a little. Or you might get nothing. This Holy Father is not susceptible to bribes.' The painter scrambled down from the scaffold, grimaced at his new work, then went to a table covered with small pots of precious pigments. 'It's a good thing you're not English! The Holy Father doesn't like the English.'

Thomas buttoned up his breeches. 'He doesn't?'

'He does not,' the painter said, 'and how do I know? Because I know everything. I paint and they ignore me because they can't see me! I am Giacomo on the scaffold and they are talking beneath me. Not in here,' he spat, as if the chamber he decorated was not worth the effort, 'but I am also painting over the angels' naked tits in the Conclave Chamber, and that's where they talk. Chatter, chatter, chatter! They're like birds, their heads together, twittering, and Giacomo is busy hiding tits on the scaffold above and so they forget I am up there.'

'So what does the Holy Father say about the English?'

'You want my knowledge? You pay.'

'You want me to throw paint on your ceiling?'

Giacomo laughed. 'I hear, Norman, that the Holy Father wants the French to defeat the English. There are three French cardinals here now, all yammering in his ear, but he doesn't need their encouragement. He's told Burgundy to fight alongside France. He has sent messages to Toulouse, to Provence, to the Dauphiné, even to Gascony, telling men it is their duty to resist England. The Holy Father is a Frenchman, remember. He wants France strong again, strong enough to pay the church its proper taxes. The English are not popular here,' he paused to give Thomas a sly look, 'so it is good you're not an Englishman, eh?'

'It is good,' Thomas said.

'The Holy Father might curse an Englishman,' Giacomo chuckled. He climbed the scaffolding again, talking as he went. 'The Scots have sent men to fight for France and the Holy Father is pleased! He says the Scots are faithful sons of the church, but he wants the English,' he paused to make a brush-stroke, 'punished. So you came all this way just for a blessing?'

Thomas had walked to the chamber's end where an old painting faded on the wall. 'For a blessing,' he said, 'and to look for a man.'

'Ah! Who?'

'Father Calade?'

'Calade!' Giacomo shook his head. 'I know of a Father Callait, but not Calade.'

'You're from Italy?' Thomas asked.

'By the Grace of God I come from Corbola, which is a Venetian city,' Giacomo said, then nimbly descended the scaffolding and went to the table where he wiped his hands on a rag. 'Of course I come from Italy! If you want something painted, you ask an Italian. If you want something daubed, smeared or splattered, you ask a Frenchman. Or you ask those two fools,' he gestured at his assistants, 'idiots! Keep stirring the plaster! They might be Italians, but they have the brains of Frenchmen. Nothing but spinach between their ears!' He picked up a leather quirt as if to strike one of his assistants, then abruptly fell to one knee. The two assistants also knelt, and then Thomas saw who had entered the room and he also snatched off his hat and knelt.

The Holy Father had come into the chamber, accompanied by four cardinals and a dozen other priests. Pope Innocent smiled absently at the painter, then stared up at the newly painted frescoes.

Thomas raised his head to look at the Pope. Innocent VI, Pope now for three years, was an old man with wispy hair, a drawn face, and hands that shook. He wore a red cloak, edged with white fur, and he was slightly bent as if his spine was crippled. He dragged his left foot as he walked, but his voice was strong enough. 'You're doing good work, my son,' he said to the Italian, 'most excellent work! Why, those clouds look more real than real clouds!'

'All for the glory of God,' Giacomo muttered, 'and your own renown, Holy Father.'

'And for your own glory, my son,' the Pope said, and sketched a vague blessing towards the two assistants. 'And are you a painter too, my son?' he asked Thomas.

'I am a soldier, Holy Father,' Thomas said.

'From where?'

'From Normandy, Holy Father.'

'Ah!' Innocent seemed delighted. 'You have a name, my son?'

'Guillaume d'Evecque, Holy Father.'

One of the cardinals, his red robe belted tightly about a glutton's belly, turned fast from examining the ceiling and looked as if he was about to protest. Then he shut his mouth, but went on glaring at Thomas. 'And tell me, my son,' Innocent was oblivious of the cardinal's reaction, 'whether you have sworn fealty to the English?'

'No, Holy Father.'

'So many Normans have! But I don't need to tell you that. I weep for France! Too many have died and it is time there was peace in Christendom.

My blessing, Guillaume.' He held out his hand and Thomas stood, walked to him, knelt again and kissed the fisherman's ring that the Pope wore above his embroidered glove. 'You have my blessing,' Innocent said, laying a hand on Thomas's bare head, 'and my prayers.'

'As I shall pray for you, Holy Father,' Thomas said, wondering if he was the first excommunicate ever to be blessed by a pope. 'I shall pray for your long life,' he added the polite phrase.

The hand on his head quivered. 'I am an old man, my son,' the Pope said, 'and my physician tells me I have many years left! But physicians lie, don't they?' He chuckled. 'Father Marchant says his *calade* would tell me I have a long life yet, but I would rather trust my lying physicians.'

Thomas held his breath, conscious suddenly of his heartbeat. There seemed a chill in the room, then a quiver of the Pope's hand made Thomas breathe again. '*Calade*, Holy Father?' he asked.

'A bird that tells the future,' the Pope said, taking his hand from Thomas's. 'We do indeed live in an age of miracles when birds deliver prophecies! Isn't that so, Father Marchant?'

A tall priest bowed to the Pope. 'Your Holiness is miracle enough.'

'Ah no! The miracle is in here! In the painting! It is superb. I congratulate you, my son,' the Pope spoke to Giacomo.

Thomas stole a glance at Father Marchant, seeing a slim, dark-faced man with eyes that seemed to glitter; green eyes, forceful eyes, frightening eyes that suddenly looked straight at Thomas, who dropped his gaze to stare at the Pope's slippers, which were embroidered with Saint Peter's keys.

The Pope blessed Giacomo and then, pleased with the progress of the new frescoes, limped from the room. His entourage followed him, all but for the fat cardinal and the green-eyed priest, who stayed. Thomas was about to rise, but the cardinal placed a heavy hand on Thomas's bare head and pressed him back down. 'Say your name again,' the cardinal demanded.

'Guillaume d'Evecque, Your Eminence.'

'And I am Cardinal Bessières,' the red-robed man said, keeping his hand on Thomas's head, 'Cardinal Bessières, Cardinal Archbishop of Livorno, Papal Legate to King Jean of France, whom God blesses above all earthly monarchs.' He paused, plainly wanting Thomas to echo his last words.

'May God bless His Majesty,' Thomas said dutifully.

'I heard Guillaume d'Evecque died,' the cardinal said in a dangerous tone.

'My cousin, Your Eminence.'

'How did he die?'

'The plague,' Thomas said vaguely. Sire Guillaume d'Evecque had been Thomas's enemy, then his friend, and he had died of the plague, but not before he had fought on Thomas's side.

'He fought for the English,' the cardinal said.

'I have heard as much, Your Eminence, and it

is to our family's shame. But I hardly knew my cousin.'

The cardinal withdrew his hand and Thomas stood. The priest with the green eyes was staring at the faded painting on the end wall. 'Did you paint this?' he demanded of Giacomo.

'No, father,' Giacomo answered, 'it is a very old painting and very badly done, so it was probably daubed there by a Frenchman or perhaps a Burgundian? The Holy Father wants me to replace it.'

'Make sure you do.'

The priest's tone drew the attention of the cardinal who now stared at the old painting. He had been looking at Thomas, frowning as if he doubted the truth of what Thomas had said, but the sight of the painting distracted him. The faded picture showed Saint Peter, identifiable because in one hand he held two golden keys, offering a sword towards a kneeling monk. The two men were in a snow-covered field, though the patch of ground about the kneeling man had been cleared of snow. The monk was reaching for the sword, watched by a second monk who peered apprehensively through the half-opened shutter of a small snow-covered house. The cardinal gazed at it for a long time and looked surprised at first, but then shuddered in anger. 'Who is the monk?' he demanded of Giacomo.

'I don't know, Your Eminence,' the Italian answered.

The cardinal glanced quizzically at the green-eyed priest, who merely answered with a shrug. The cardinal glowered. 'Why haven't you covered it over already?' he demanded of the painter.

'Because the Holy Father ordered the ceiling painted before the walls, Your Eminence.'

'Then cover it now!' the cardinal snarled. 'Cover it before you finish the ceiling.' He snatched a glance at Thomas. 'Why are you here?' he demanded.

'To receive the Holy Father's blessing, Your Eminence.'

Cardinal Bessières frowned. He was plainly suspicious of the name Thomas had given, but the existence of the old painting seemed to trouble him even more. 'Just cover it!' he ordered Giacomo again, then looked back to Thomas. 'Where do you lodge?' he asked.

'By Saint Bénézet's church, Your Eminence,' Thomas lied. In truth he had left Genevieve, Hugh and a score of his men in a tavern beyond the great bridge, far from Saint Bénézet's church. He lied because the last thing he wanted was Cardinal Bessières to take a sudden interest in Guillaume d'Evecque. Thomas had killed the cardinal's brother, and if Bessières knew who Thomas really was then the fires of heresy would be lit in the great square beneath the Papal palace.

'I am curious,' the cardinal said, 'about the state of affairs in Normandy. I shall send for you after the None prayers. Father Marchant will fetch you.'

99

'I shall indeed,' the priest said, and made the words sound like a threat.

'I shall be most honoured to assist Your Eminence,' Thomas said, keeping his head bowed.

'Get rid of that painting,' the cardinal said to Giacomo and then led his green-eyed companion from the room.

The Italian, still on his knees, let out a long breath. 'He didn't like you.'

'Does he like anyone?' Thomas asked.

Giacomo stood and screamed at his assistants. 'The plaster will set hard if they don't stir it!' he explained his anger to Thomas. 'They have porridge for brains. They are Milanese, yes? So they are fools. But Cardinal Bessières is no fool, he would be a dangerous enemy, my friend.' Giacomo did not know it, but the cardinal was already Thomas's enemy, though fortunately Bessières had never met Thomas and had no idea that the Englishman was even in Avignon. Giacomo went to the table where his pigments were in small clay pots. 'And Cardinal Bessières,' he went on, 'has hopes of being the next Pope. Innocent is frail, Bessières is not. We may have another Holy Father soon.'

'Why doesn't he like this painting?' Thomas asked, pointing to the end wall.

'Perhaps he has good taste? Or perhaps because it looks as if it was painted by a dog holding a brush stuck up its arsehole?'

Thomas stared at the old picture. The cardinal

had wanted to know what story it told, and neither Giacomo nor the green-eyed priest could answer him, but plainly he wanted the painting destroyed so no one else could find the answer. And the picture did tell a story. Saint Peter was handing his sword to a monk in the snow, and the monk must have a name, but who was he? 'You really don't know what the picture means?' Thomas asked Giacomo.

'A legend?' the Italian guessed carelessly.

'But what legend?'

'Saint Peter had a sword,' Giacomo said, 'and I suppose he's handing it to the church? He should have used it to cut off the painter's hand and saved us from having to look at his horrible daubs.'

'But usually the sword is painted in Gethsemane,' Thomas said. He had seen many church walls painted with the scene before Christ's arrest when Peter had drawn a sword and cut off the ear of the high priest's servant, but he had never seen Peter placed in a snowstorm.

'So the fool who painted this didn't know his stories,' Giacomo said.

Yet everything in pictures had a meaning. If a man held a saw then he was Saint Simon, because Simon had been sawn to pieces at his martyrdom. A bunch of grapes reminded folk of the eucharist, King David carried a harp, Saint Thaddeus a club or a carpenter's rule, Saint George faced a dragon, Saint Denis was always painted holding his own severed head: everything had a meaning, yet

Thomas had no idea what this old picture meant. 'Aren't you painters supposed to know all these symbols?'

'What symbols?'

'The sword, the keys, the snow, the man in the window!'

'The sword is Peter's sword, the keys are the keys of heaven! You need teaching how to suck at your mother's tit?'

'And the snow?'

Giacomo scowled, plainly uncomfortable with the question. 'The idiot couldn't paint grass,' he finally decided, 'so he slapped on some cheap limewash! It has no meaning! Tomorrow we chip it off and put something pretty there.'

Yet whoever had painted the scene had taken the trouble to clear that patch of snow from around the kneeling man, and he had painted the grass cleverly enough, scattering it with small yellow and blue flowers. So the cleared snow had a meaning, as did the presence of the second monk looking fearfully from the cottage window. 'Do you have charcoal?' Thomas asked.

'Of course I have charcoal!' Giacomo gestured to the table where his pigments stood.

Thomas went to the door and looked out into the great audience chamber. There was no sign of Cardinal Bessières or of the green-eyed priest, and so he picked up a lump of charcoal and went to the strange painting. He wrote on it.

'What are you doing?' Giacomo asked.

'I want the cardinal to see that,' Thomas said.

He had scrawled *Calix Meus Inebrians* in great black letters across the snow. 'My cup makes me drunk?' Giacomo asked, puzzled.

'It's from a psalm of David,' Thomas said.

'But what does it mean?'

'The cardinal will know,' Thomas said.

Giacomo frowned. 'Sweet Christ,' he said, 'but you play dangerously.'

'Thanks for letting me piss here,' Thomas said. The painter was right, this was dangerous, but if he could not track down Father Calade in this city of his enemies, then he would invite Father Calade to follow him, and Thomas suspected that Father Calade would turn out to be the priest with very green eyes.

And the priest with the green eyes was interested in an old, badly painted picture of two monks and Saint Peter, but the centre of the painting had not been the kneeling monk, nor even the gowned figure of Saint Peter himself, but the sword.

And Thomas, though he could not be certain, was suddenly convinced that the sword had a name: *la Malice*.

And that day, long before the None prayers, and before anyone could find him and put him to the church's torture, Thomas and his company left Avignon.

The warm weather came. It was campaigning weather, and all across France men sharpened weapons, exercised horses and waited for the summons to serve the king. The English were sending reinforcements to Brittany and to Gascony and men thought that surely King Jean would raise a great army to crush them, but instead he took a smaller army to the edges of Navarre, to the castle of Breteuil, and there, facing the stronghold's gaunt walls, his men constructed a siege tower.

It was a monstrous thing, taller than a church's spire, a scaffold of three floors perched on two iron axles joined to four massive wheels of solid elm. The front and sides of the tower were sheathed in oak planks to prevent the castle's garrison from riddling the platforms with crossbow bolts, and now, in a cold dawn, men were nailing stiff leather hides to that wooden armour. They worked a mere four hundred paces from the castle and once in a while a defender would shoot a crossbow bolt, but the range was too long and the bolts always fell short. Four flags flew from the tower's summit, two with the French fleur-de-lys and two showing an axe, the symbol of France's patron saint, the martyred Saint Denis. The flags stretched and twisted in the wind. There had been a gale in the night and the wind still blew strong from the west.

'One shower of rain,' the Lord of Douglas said, 'and this damn thing will be useless. They'll never move it! It'll bog down in mud.'

'God is on our side,' his young companion said placidly.

'God,' the Lord of Douglas said disgustedly.

'Watches over us,' the young man said. He was tall and slender, scarce more than twenty or twenty-one years old, with a strikingly handsome face. He had fair hair that was brushed back from a high forehead, blue eyes that were calm, and a mouth that seemed constantly hovering on the edge of a smile. He was from Gascony, where he owned a fief that had been sequestered by the English, leaving him without the income of his lands, which loss should have rendered him poor, but the Sire Roland de Verrec was renowned as the greatest of France's tournament fighters. Some had claimed that Joscelyn of Berat was the better man, but at Auxerre, Roland had defeated Joscelyn three times, then tormented the brutal champion, Walther of Siegenthaler, with quicksilver sword-play. At Limoges he had been the only man standing at the end of a vicious melee, while in Paris the women had sighed as he destroyed two hardened knights who had twice his years and many times his experience. Roland de Verrec earned the fees of a champion because he was lethal.

And a virgin.

His black shield bore the symbol of the white rose, the rose without thorns, the flower of the Virgin Mary and a proud display of his own purity. The men he so constantly defeated in the lists thought he was mad, the women who watched him thought he was wasted, but Roland de Verrec had devoted his life to chivalry, to sanctity and to goodness. He was famous for his virginity; he was also mocked for it, though never to his face and never within reach of his quick sword. He was also admired for his purity, even envied, because it was said that he had been commanded to a life of sanctity by a vision of the Virgin Mary herself. She had appeared to him when he was just fourteen, she had touched him and she had told him he would be blessed above all men if he kept himself chaste as she was chaste. 'You will marry,' she had told him, 'but till then you are mine.' And so he was.

Men might mock Roland, but women sighed over him. One woman had been driven to tell Roland de Verrec that he was beautiful. She had reached out and touched his cheek, 'All that fighting and not one scar!' she had said, and he had drawn back from her as if her finger burned, then said that all beauty was but a reflection of God's grace. 'If I believed otherwise,' he had told her, 'I would be tempted to vanity,' and perhaps he did suffer from that temptation because he dressed with inordinate care and always wore his armour blanched: scrubbed with sand, vinegar and wire until it reflected the sun with dazzling brilliance. Though not on this day because the sky above Breteuil was low, grey and dark.

'It's going to rain,' the Lord of Douglas growled, 'and this damned tower will go nowhere.'

'It will bring us victory,' Roland de Verrec said,

sounding quietly confident. 'The Bishop of Châlons blessed it last night; it will not fail.'

'It shouldn't even be here,' Douglas snarled. The Scottish knights had been summoned by King Jean to join this attack on Breteuil, but the defenders were not Englishmen, they were other Frenchmen. 'I didn't come here to kill Frenchmen,' Douglas said, 'I came here to kill the English.'

'They're Navarrese,' Roland de Verrec said, 'the enemies of France, and our king wants them defeated.'

'Breteuil is a goddamned pimple!' the Lord of Douglas protested. 'For Christ's sake, what importance does it have? There are no bloody Englishmen inside!'

Roland smiled. 'Whoever is inside, my lord,' he said quietly, 'I do my king's bidding.'

The King of France, ignoring the Englishmen in Calais, in Gascony and in Brittany, had instead chosen to march against the Kingdom of Navarre on the edge of Normandy. The quarrel was obscure and the campaign a waste of scarce resources, for Navarre could not threaten France, yet King Jean had chosen to fight. It was evidently a family quarrel, one the Lord of Douglas did not comprehend. 'Let them rot here,' he said, 'while we march against England. We should be chasing the boy Edward and instead we're pissing on a spark at the edge of Normandy.'

'The king wants Breteuil,' Roland said.

'He doesn't want to face Englishmen,' the Lord

of Douglas said, and he knew he was right. Ever since the Scottish knights had come to France, the king had hesitated. Jean had chosen to go south one day, west the next, and to stay put on the third. Now, finally, he had marched against Navarre. Navarre! And the English had erupted from their strongholds in Gascony and were ravaging inland again. Another army was gathered on England's south coast, doubtless to be landed in Normandy or Brittany, and King Jean was at Breteuil! The Lord of Douglas could weep at the thought. Go south, he had urged the French king, go south and crush the puppy Edward, capture the bastard, trample his men's guts into the mud, and then imprison the prince as a bargaining piece for Scotland's captured king. Instead they were besieging Breteuil.

The two men were standing on the topmost platform of the tower. Roland de Verrec had volunteered to lead the attack. The siege tower would be trundled forward, pushed by dozens of men, some of whom must fall to crossbow bolts, but others would replace them, and eventually the whole tower would crash against the castle wall and Roland's men would slash through the ropes holding the drawbridge that protected the front of the upper platform. The drawbridge would fall, making a wide bridge to Breteuil's battlements, and then the attackers would stream across, screaming their war cry, and those first men, the men most likely to die, must hold the captured

108

battlement long enough to let hundreds of the King of France's troops climb the tower's ladders. They had to climb those ladders while cumbered by mail, by plate armour, by shields, and by weapons. It would take time, and the first men across the drawbridge had to buy that time with their lives. There was great honour in being among those first attackers, honour earned by the risk of death, and Roland de Verrec had gone on his knees to the King of France and begged to be granted that privilege.

'Why?' the king had asked Roland, and Roland had explained that he loved France and would serve his king, and that he had never been in battle, he had only fought in tournaments, and that it was time his talents as a fighter were put to a noble cause, and all that had been true. Yet the real reason Roland de Verrec wished to lead the assault was because he yearned for a great deed, for a quest, for some challenge that would be worthy of his purity. The king had graciously given Roland permission to lead the attack, and then granted the same honour to a second man, the Lord of Douglas's nephew, Robbie.

'You want to die,' the Lord of Douglas had grumbled at Robbie the night before.

'I want to feast in that castle's hall tomorrow night,' Robbie had answered.

'For what?' the Lord of Douglas demanded. 'For what goddamned purpose?'

'Talk to him,' the Lord of Douglas now appealed

to Roland de Verrec. That was why Douglas had come to the tower, to persuade Roland de Verrec, reputed to be the greatest fool and most chivalrous knight in all France, to urge Robbie to his duty. 'Robbie respects you,' he told Roland, 'he admires you, he wants to be like you, so tell him it's his Christian obligation to fight the English and not die in this miserable place.'

'He took an oath,' Roland de Verrec said, 'an oath not to fight against the English, and that oath was taken freely and piously. I cannot advise him to break it, my lord.'

'Damn his oath! Talk to him!'

'A man cannot break an oath and keep his soul,' Roland said calmly, 'and your nephew will win great renown by fighting here.'

'Bugger renown,' the Lord of Douglas said.

'My lord,' Roland turned to the Scotsman, 'if I could persuade your nephew to fight the English, I would. I am flattered you think he would listen to me, but in all Christian conscience I cannot advise him to break a solemn oath. It would be unchivalrous.'

'And bugger chivalry too,' the Lord of Douglas said, 'and bugger Breteuil and bugger the bloody lot of you.' He went down the ladders and scowled at Robbie, who waited with the forty other men-at-arms who would lead the assault across the tower's drawbridge. 'You're a damned fool!' he shouted angrily.

It was an hour before the hides were finally nailed

into place and had been soaked with water, and by then a small cold rain had begun to spit from the west. The men-at-arms filed into the tower, the bravest climbing the ladders to the topmost platform so they would be first across the drawbridge. Robbie Douglas was one. He had armoured himself in leather and mail, but had decided against wearing any plate except for greaves to cover his shins and a vambrace on his right forearm. His left arm was protected by his shield, which bore the red heart of Douglas.

His sword was an old one, old but good, with a plain wooden hilt in which was concealed a fingernail of Saint Andrew, Scotland's patron. The sword had belonged to another uncle, Sir William Douglas, Knight of Liddesdale, but he had been murdered by the Lord of Douglas in a family quarrel. Robbie, afterwards, had been forced to kneel to the Lord of Douglas and swear allegiance. 'You're mine now,' the Lord of Douglas had said, knowing Robbie had been fond of Sir William, 'and if you're not mine you're no man's, and if you're no man's then you're an outlaw, and if you're an outlaw I can kill you. So what are you?'

'Yours,' Robbie had said meekly, and knelt. Now, as he joined Roland de Verrec at the top of the tower, he wondered if he had chosen right. He could have ridden back to Thomas of Hookton's friendship, but he had made his choice, sworn allegiance to his uncle, and now he would charge across a drawbridge to probable death on the wall of a fortress that meant nothing to him, nothing to Scotland, and little to anyone else. So why join the attack? Because, he thought, it was his gift to his family. A gesture to show the French the quality of Scottish fighting men. This was a battle he could fight with a clean conscience even if it meant his death.

It was an hour after dawn that the King of France ordered his crossbows forward. There were eight hundred of them, mostly from Genoa, but a few from Germany, and each crossbowman had an attendant carrying a great shield, a pavise, behind which the archer could shelter as he rewound the bow. The crossbowmen and their shield carriers made phalanxes at either side of the tower, which now had long poles thrust through its base so that men could push the vast contraption forward.

Behind the tower were two lines of men-at-arms, the men who would follow the first attackers up the ladders to flood Breteuil's ramparts, and they gathered beneath the banners of their lords. The wind was still strong enough to spread the colourful flags; a flaunting of lions and crosses, harts and stars, stripes and gryphons, the barony of France gathered for the attack. Priests walked in front of the men, offering blessings, assuring them that God favoured France, that the Navarrese scum were doomed to hell, and that Christ would aid the assault. Then a new banner appeared, a blue banner blazoned with golden fleurs-de-lys, and the men-at-arms cheered as their king rode between their lines. He wore plate armour that had been polished to brilliance, and around his neck was a cloak of red velvet that lifted in the wind. His helmet glittered, and about it was a gold crown set with diamonds. His horse, a white destrier, lifted its feet high as Jean of France rode between his soldiers, looking neither right nor left, and then he reached the long poles waiting for the peasants who would thrust the tower forward, and there he turned. He curbed the horse and men thought he was about to say something and silence spread across the field, but the king merely raised his left hand as if offering a blessing, and the cheers began again. Some men knelt, others looked in awe at the king's long, pale face, which was framed by his polished helmet. Jean the Good, he was called, not because he was good, but because he enjoyed the worldly pleasures that were a king's prerogative. He was not a great warrior, and he had a famous temper, and he was reputed to be indecisive, yet at this moment the chivalry of France was ready to die for him.

'Not much point in the man riding a bloody horse,' the Lord of Douglas grumbled. He was waiting with a half-dozen of his Scotsmen behind the tower. He was dressed in a simple leather haubergeon, for he had no intention of joining the attack. He had brought his company to kill

Englishmen, not swat a few Navarrese. 'You can't ride a bloody horse up stone walls.'

His men growled agreement, then stiffened as the king, followed by his courtiers, rode towards them. 'Kneel, you bastards,' Douglas ordered them.

King Jean curbed his horse close to Douglas. 'Your nephew fights today?' he asked.

'He does, Your Majesty,' Douglas said.

'We are grateful to him,' King Jean said.

'You'd be more grateful if you led us south, sire,' Douglas said, 'south to kill that puppy Edward of Wales.'

The king blinked. Douglas, who alone among the Scotsmen had not gone down on one knee, was publicly reprimanding him, but the king smiled to show no offence had been taken. 'We shall go south when this business is settled,' the king said. He had a thin voice with a tone of petulance.

'I'm glad of it, sire,' the Lord of Douglas said fiercely.

'Unless other business intrudes,' the king qualified his first remark. He raised a hand in a gesture of vague benediction and rode on. The rain became more insistent.

'Unless other business intrudes,' the Lord of Douglas said savagely. 'He's got Englishmen harrowing his lands, and he thinks other business might intrude?' He spat, then turned as a cheer from the waiting men-at-arms announced that the tower was at last being pushed towards the high walls. Trumpets blared. A great banner showing

Saint Denis had been unfurled from the tower's top. The flag displayed the martyred Denis holding his own severed head.

The great siege tower lurched as it was shoved forward, and Robbie needed to hold on to one of the stanchions that held the drawbridge in place. The long poles had been pushed clean through the tower's base so they protruded on either side and scores of men were thrusting on them, encouraged by men with whips and by drummers who beat a steady rhythm on nakers, great goat-skin tubs that boomed like cannon.

'We should have had cannon,' the Lord of Douglas grumbled.

'Too expensive.' Geoffrey de Charny, one of King Jean's greatest warlords, had come to stand beside the Scottish lord. 'Cannons cost money, my friend, and gunpowder costs money, and France has no money.'

'It's richer than Scotland.'

'The taxes are not collected,' Geoffrey said bleakly. 'Who will pay these men?' He gestured at the waiting soldiers.

'Send them to collect the taxes.'

'They would keep the taxes.' Geoffrey made the sign of the cross. 'Pray there is a pot of gold inside Breteuil.'

'There's nothing but a pack of bloody Navarrese inside Breteuil. We should be marching south!'

'I agree.'

'Then why don't we?'

'Because the king has not ordered it.' Geoffrey watched the tower. 'But he will,' he added softly.

'He will?'

'I think he will,' Geoffrey said. 'The Pope is pushing him to war, and he knows he can't let the damned English run riot over half France again. So yes, he will.'

Douglas wished de Charny sounded more certain, but he said nothing more and followed the Frenchman to watch the tower sway and lurch across the turf. The crossbowmen advanced, keeping pace with the tower, and after fifty yards the first bolts came from the castle walls and the crossbowmen ran forward and shot back. Their job was simple: to keep the defenders crouched behind their battlements as the gaunt tower trundled on. The bolts hissed up, clattered on stone and shook the great banners hanging from the crenellations; bolt after bolt flew as the crossbowmen shot, then they ducked behind their pavises and turned the big handles that winched back the strings. The defenders shot back, their bolts thumping into the turf or banging into the pavises, and soon the first bolts hammered into the tower itself.

Robbie heard them. He saw the drawbridge shudder with the strikes, but the bridge, which was now hinged upright to form a wall at the front of the top platform, was made of thick oak covered with hides, and none of the Navarrese bolts penetrated the leather and timber. They just struck home, a constant banging, and beneath him the tower swayed and creaked and juddered forward. It was just possible to peer past the right-hand edge of the drawbridge, and he saw the castle was two hundred paces away. Great banners hung down the wall's front, many of them pierced by crossbow bolts. The defenders' bolts slammed into the tower, making its leading wall a pincushion of leather-fledged missiles. The drums were banging, and trumpets were calling and the tower rolled another few yards, sometimes dipping as the turf dropped, and a few crossbow bolts, shot from the walls to either side, slashed into the labouring peasants. More were brought up to replace the wounded or dead, and the men-at-arms shouted at them, whipped them, and they heaved on the poles and the great tower trundled on, going faster now, so fast that Robbie drew his sword and looked up at one of the twisted ropes that held the drawbridge in place. There were two hemp ropes, one on either side, and when the tower was close enough they had to be cut to send the great bridge crashing down onto the battlements. Not long now, he thought, and he kissed the hilt of his sword where the relic of Saint Andrew was hidden.

'Your uncle,' Roland de Verrec said, 'is angry with you.' The Frenchman looked absolutely calm as the tower thundered slowly forward and as the defenders' bolts thumped harder into the drawbridge.

'He's always angry,' Robbie said. He was nervous

of Roland de Verrec. The young Frenchman was too composed, too certain of his own certainty and Robbie felt inadequate. He was certain of nothing.

'I told him you could not break your oath,' Roland said. 'It was not forced on you?'

'No.'

'What was in your heart as you made it?' the Frenchman asked.

Robbie thought. 'Gratitude,' he said after a while.

'Gratitude?'

'A friend tended me through the pestilence. I should have died, but didn't. He saved my life.'

'God saved your life,' Roland corrected him, 'and he saved it for a special purpose. I envy you. You have been chosen.'

'Chosen?' Robbie asked, clinging to the stanchion as the tower rocked.

'You were sick with the pestilence, yet you survived. God needs you for a reason. I salute you.' Roland de Verrec lifted his drawn sword in salute. 'I envy you,' he said again.

'Envy me?' Robbie asked, surprised.

'I search for a cause,' Roland said.

And then the tower stopped.

It stopped dead with such a lurch that the men on board were thrown to one side. One wheel had dropped into a hole, a hole big enough to trap the vehicle, and no amount of shoving would drive the wheel up and out, instead the heaves only skewed the tower further to the left. 'Stop,' a man shouted, 'stop!'

The defenders jeered. Crossbow bolts drove through the thin rain to slash into the peasants who had been pushing the tower. Blood coloured the turf and men screamed as the thick quarrels bored into flesh and shattered bones.

Geoffrey de Charny ran forward. He wore a mail coat and helmet, but carried no shield. 'The levers,' he shouted, 'the levers!' He had hoped this would not happen, but the French were ready for it, and a group of men equipped with stout oak poles ran to the trapped side of the tower where they placed anvil-like blocks of timber that would be used as fulcrums so that the levers could lift the left-hand side of the tower and allow it to be shoved on. Other men brought buckets of stones to fill the hole so that the rearward wheel could roll over it.

The crossbow bolts poured down from the walls. Two, three men were down, then Geoffrey bellowed at the nearest pavise holders to bring their shields to protect the men hauling on the levers, and it all took time, and the defenders, emboldened by the stalled tower, rained down more bolts. Some Navarrese defenders were hit by the French crossbow bolts, but only a few, as the garrison ducked behind their stone merlons to rewind their bows. Geoffrey de Charny seemed to have a charmed life because he was not protected by any shield and though the bolts seared close to him none struck as he organised the men who would thrust down on the great oak levers to free the tower. 'Now!' he called, and men tried to lift the monstrous tower with the long oak poles.

And the first fire arrow streaked from the castle.

It was a crossbow bolt, wrapped with kindling that was protected by a leather skirt, and the kindling was soaked in pitch that left a black wavering trail of smoke as the bolt streaked from the rampart and thumped into the lower part of the tower. The flame flickered briefly, then went out, but a dozen more fire arrows followed.

'Water! Water!' Roland de Verrec called. There were already some leather pails of water on the top platform, and the lurching tower had spilt much of it, but Roland's men tipped what was left over the top of the drawbridge so that it cascaded down the tower's front face to soak the already wet hides. More and more fire arrows were thumping home so that the front of the tower smoked in a score of places, but the smoke came only from burning arrows. So far the dampened hides were protecting the tower.

'Heave!' Geoffrey de Charny shouted, and the men on the levers hauled down, and the levers bent, and the tower creaked, then one of the levers snapped, sending a half-dozen men sprawling. 'Bring another pole!'

It took five minutes for another pole to be fetched, then the men hauled down again and the peasants were told to shove forward at the same time, and some men-at-arms ran to help the peasants. Crossbow bolts came thick. More fire arrows were shot, this time at the right-hand side of the tower, and one struck under the edge of a hide and lodged in the oak sheathing. No one saw it. It burned there, the flames creeping up into the space between the hides and the planks, hidden by the leather, and though smoke seeped from beneath the stiff leather sheets, there was so much other smoke that it went undetected.

Then the Navarrese crossbowmen changed their tactics. Some kept shooting the fire arrows, and some, from the slits in the walls, aimed at the men clustered by the left side of the tower, while the rest aimed their crossbows high in the air so that the bolts screamed into the sky, hung there an instant, then plummeted down onto the tower's open platform. Most of the bolts missed. Some struck the men waiting to heave on the poles, but a few crashed down onto the platform, and Roland, fearing that his men would be killed, ordered them to hold up their shields, but then they could not pour the water that had started to arrive in leather pails. The tower was jerking now as some men levered at the side and others shoved at the back. There was a smell of burning.

'Pull it back!' the Lord of Douglas advised Geoffrey de Charny. A crossbow bolt slammed down to bury itself in the turf at the Scotsman's feet and he kicked it irritably. The drums were beating still, the trumpets were tangling their notes, the defenders were shouting at the French, who heaved again at the levers and shoved again at the tower that would not move, and it was now that the Navarrese defenders unveiled their last weapon.

It was a springald, an oversized crossbow, which had been mounted on the wall and was drawn back by four men cranking on metal handles. It shot a quarrel fully three feet long and as thick about as a man's wrist, and the garrison had chosen to keep it hidden until the tower was just a hundred paces away, but the French disarray persuaded them to use it now. They pulled away the great timber screen that had sheltered the weapon and released its metal arrow.

The quarrel hammered into the face of the tower, rocking it back, and such was the force in the steel-reinforced bow yard, which was fully ten feet across, that the great iron head pierced leather and wood to stick halfway through the tower's front. It sprayed sparks and buckled one of the hides, revealing the planks beneath, and three fire arrows thumped home into the bare wood as the springald was laboriously rewound.

'Pull the damn thing back!' the Lord of Douglas snarled. Maybe the tower could be backed out of the hole instead of being pushed through it, then the dip could be filled and the great contraption started forward again.

'Ropes!' Geoffrey de Charny shouted. 'Fetch ropes!'

The watching men-at-arms were silent now. The tower was slightly canted and wreathed in gentle smoke, but it was not obvious what was wrong except to the men close by the stalled tower. The king, still mounted on his white horse, rode a few yards forward, then checked. 'God is on our side?' he enquired of a chaplain.

'He can be on no other, sire.'

'Then why . . .' the king began the question and decided it was better not answered. Smoke was thickening on the right-hand side of the tower now, which shuddered as a second springald bolt crashed home. A man-at-arms limped away from the levers with a bolt through his thigh as squires ran with armfuls of rope, but it was too late.

Fire suddenly showed in the centre floor. For a moment there was just a great billow of smoke, then flames shot through the grey. The planks on the right side were alight and there was not enough water to douse the blaze. 'God can be very fickle,' the king said bitterly, and turned away. A man was waving a flag to and fro on the ramparts, revelling in the French defeat. The drums and the trumpets fell silent. Men were screaming in the tower; others were jumping to escape the inferno.

Roland was unaware of the fire until the smoke began churning up through the ladder's hole. 'Down!' he shouted. 'Down!' The first men scrambled down the ladder, but one of their scabbards became entangled in the rungs, and then flame burst through the hole as the trapped man screamed. He was being roasted in his mail. Another man jumped past him and broke a leg when he fell. The burning man was sobbing now, and Roland ran to help him, beating out the flames with his bare hands. Robbie did nothing. He was cursed, he thought. Whatever he touched turned to ash. He had failed Thomas once, he failed his uncle now, he had married, but his wife had died in her first child-birth, and the child with her. Cursed, Robbie thought, and he still did not move as the smoke thickened and the flames licked at the platform beneath him, and then the whole tower lurched as a third springald bolt crashed home. There were three men left on the top platform with him and they urged him to try to escape, but he could not move. Roland was carrying a wounded man down the ladders, and God must have loved the virgin knight because a fierce swirl of wind blew the flames and smoke away from him as he descended the rungs. 'Go!' a man shouted at Robbie, but he was too dispirited to move.

'You go,' he told the men with him, 'just go.' He drew his sword, thinking at least he could die with a blade in his hand, and he watched as the three men tried to climb down the scaffold of timbers at the tower's open back, but all were scorched by the fierceness of the flames and they jumped to save their lives. One was unharmed, his fall cush-ioned by men beneath, but the other two broke bones. One of the four flags topping the tower was burning now, the fleurs-de-lys turning into glowing cinders, and the whole tower collapsed. It fell slowly at first, creaking, throwing sparks, then the fall became faster as the great contraption keeled over like a proud ship foundering. Men scattered from its base, and still Robbie did not move. Roland had reached the ground, and Robbie was now alone and rode the burning tower down, clinging to the great stanchion, and the tower fell with a thump and an explosion of sparks and Robbie was thrown clear, rolling amidst small flames and thick smoke, and two Frenchmen saw him and ran into the smoke to pull him out. He had been knocked unconscious by the impact, but when men splashed his face with water and pulled off his mail coat they found him miraculously uninjured.

'God saved you,' one of the men said. The Navarrese on Breteuil's wall were jeering. A crossbow bolt slapped into a timber of the fallen tower, which was now an inferno of blazing wood. 'We must get away from here,' Robbie's rescuer said.

The second man brought Robbie his sword while the first helped him to his feet and guided him towards the French tents. 'Roland,' Robbie asked, 'where's Roland?' A last crossbow quarrel pursued him, skidding uselessly in the mud. Robbie clutched his sword. He was alive, but why? He wanted to weep, but dared not because he was a soldier, but a soldier for whom? He was a Scot, but if he could not fight against the English then what use was he?

'God saved you, my friend.' Roland de Verrec,

quite unharmed by the tower's destruction, spoke to Robbie. The Frenchman held out his hand to help steady Robbie. 'You have a holy destiny,' he said.

'Tournament!' a second voice snarled.

Robbie, still dazed, saw his uncle, the Lord of Douglas, standing in the smoke of the burning tower. 'Tournament?' Robbie asked.

'The king is going back to Paris and he wants a tournament! A tournament! The English are pissing all over his land and he wants to play games!'

'I don't understand,' Robbie muttered.

'Wasn't there someone who played the lute while his city burned?'

'Nero,' Robbie said, 'I think.'

'We're to play at tournaments while the English piss all over France. No, not piss, while they drop great stinking turds all over King Jean's precious land, and does he give a rat's fart for that? He wants a tournament! So get your horse, pack up, be ready to leave. Tournament! I should have stayed in Scotland!'

Robbie looked around for Roland. He was not sure why, except that he admired the young Frenchman and if anyone could explain God's reason for inflicting this defeat then surely it was Roland, but Roland was deep in conversation with a man who wore a livery unfamiliar to Robbie. The man's jupon displayed a rearing green horse on a white field, and Robbie had seen no other men in King Jean's army wearing that badge. The man spoke softly and earnestly to Roland, who appeared to ask a few questions before shaking the stranger's hand, and when Roland turned towards Robbie his face was suffused with happiness. The rest of the king's army might be dejected because the hopes of France were now a burning mass of timber in a wet field, but Roland de Verrec fairly glowed with joy. 'I have been given a quest,' he told Robbie, 'a quest!'

'There's going to be a tournament in Paris,' Robbie said, 'I'm sure you'll be needed there.'

'No,' Roland said. 'A maiden is in trouble! She has been snatched from her lawful husband, carried off by a villain, and I am charged with her rescue.'

Robbie just gaped at the virgin knight. Roland had said those words with utmost seriousness, as if he believed he truly was a knight in one of the romances that the troubadours sang.

'You will be paid generously, sire,' the knight in the green and white jupon said.

'The honour of the quest is payment enough,' Roland de Verrec said, but added hastily, 'though if your master the count should offer some small token of thanks then I will, of course, be grateful.' He bowed to Robbie. 'We shall meet again,' he said, 'and do not forget what I said. You have been saved for a great purpose. You are blessed. And so am I! A quest!'

The Lord of Douglas watched Roland de Verrec

walk away. 'Is he really a virgin?' he asked in disbelief.

'He swears so,' Robbie said.

'No wonder his right arm is so bloody strong,' the Lord of Douglas said, 'but he must be mad as a sack of bloody stoats.' He spat.

Roland de Verrec had a quest, and Robbie was jealous.

PART II

MONTPELLIER

CHAPTER 4

'Forgive me,' Thomas said. He had not meant to speak aloud. He spoke to the crucifix above the main altar in the little church of Saint Sardos that stood beneath Castillon d'Arbizon's castle. Thomas was kneeling. He had lit six candles, which burned on the side altar of Saint Agnes where a young, pale-faced priest counted bright new genoins.

'Forgive you for what, Thomas?' the priest asked.

'He knows.'

'And you don't?'

'Just say the masses for me, father,' Thomas said.

'For you? Or for the men you killed?'

'For the men I killed,' Thomas said. 'I gave you enough money?'

'You gave me enough to build another church,' the priest said. 'Remorse is an expensive thing, Thomas.'

Thomas half smiled. 'They were soldiers, father,' he said, 'and they died in obedience to their lord. I owe them peace in their afterlife, don't I?'

'Their liege lord was an adulterer,' Father Levonne said sternly. Father Medous, his predecessor, had

131

died a year before and the Bishop of Berat had sent Father Levonne as his replacement. Thomas had suspected the newcomer was a spy, because the bishop was a supporter of the Count of Berat, who had once possessed Castillon d'Arbizon and wanted the town back, but it seemed the bishop had sent the priest in order to rid himself of a nuisance. 'I pricked the bishop's conscience,' Levonne had explained to Thomas.

'Pricked it?'

'I preached against sin, sire,' Levonne had said, 'and the bishop did not like my sermons.'

Since that conversation, Father Levonne had learned to call Thomas by his name, and Thomas had come to depend on the young, earnest priest for advice, and whenever he returned from a foray into enemy territory he would come to the church of Saint Sardos, say confession and pay for masses to be said for the men he had killed. 'So if the Count of Villon was an adulterer,' Thomas now asked, 'he deserved to be castrated and killed? Father, you'd have to put half this town to death if that was true.'

'Only a half?' Father Levonne asked, amused. 'Speaking for myself,' he went on, 'I would have preferred God to determine Villon's punishment, but perhaps God chose you as his instrument?'

'Did I do wrong?'

'You tell me.'

'Just say the masses, father,' Thomas said.

'And the Countess of Labrouillade,' Father

Levonne went on, 'a brazen adulteress, is here in the castle.'

'You want me to kill her?'

'God will choose her fate,' the priest said gently, 'but the Count of Labrouillade may not wait for that. He will try to reclaim her. The town prospers, Thomas. I don't want it invaded by Labrouillade or by anyone else. Send her away, far away.'

'Labrouillade won't come here,' Thomas said vengefully, 'he's nothing but a fat fool and he fears me.'

'The Count of Berat is also a fool,' the priest said, 'and a rich one, and a brave one, and he's looking for allies to fight against you.'

'Only because he's lost every time he's tried before,' Thomas said. Thomas had captured the town and castle from the count, who had twice tried to reclaim the property, and twice had been defeated. The town lay on the southern edge of the County of Berat and was protected by high stone walls and by the river that flowed around three sides of the crag on which the town was sited. Above the town was the castle on the crag's high rocky summit. The castle was not large, but it was high and strong, and protected by a new gatehouse, turreted and massive, which replaced the old entrance that had been battered down by a cannon. The Earl of Northampton's banner, the lion and stars, flew from the gatehouse and from the keep, but everyone knew that it was Thomas of Hookton, *le Bâtard*, who had taken the castle. It was the base from which his Hellequin could ride east and north into enemy country.

'The count will try again,' Levonne warned Thomas, 'and Labrouillade might help him next time.'

'And not just Labrouillade,' Thomas said grimly.

'You've made new enemies?' Father Levonne asked with mock scorn. 'I am astonished.'

Thomas gazed up at the crucifix. The church of Saint Sardos had been poor when he first captured the town, but now it glittered with wealth. The saints' statues were newly painted and hung with semi-precious beads. The Virgin wore a crown of silver. The candlesticks and vessels on the altar were silver and gilt; the walls glowed with pictures of Saint Sardos, Saint Agnes, and the final judgement. Thomas had paid for it all, just as he had paid to decorate the other two churches in the town. 'I've made new enemies,' he said, still gazing at the blood-spattered Christ on his gilt-bronze cross, 'but first, father, tell me what saint kneels in a cleared patch of snow?'

'In a cleared patch of snow?' Father Levonne asked, amused, then saw that Thomas was serious. 'Saint Eulalia, perhaps?'

'Eulalia?' Thomas asked.

'She was persecuted,' Father Levonne said, 'and her tormentors threw her naked into the street to shame her, but the Blessed Lord sent a snowstorm to cover her nakedness.'

'No,' Thomas said, 'this was a man, and the snow seemed to avoid him.'

'Saint Wenceslaus then? The king? We're told the snow melted where he walked.'

'This was a monk,' Thomas said, 'and in the picture I saw he's kneeling on the grass and there's snow all around him, but none on him.'

'Where was this picture?'

Thomas told him of meeting the Pope in Avignon's Salle des Herses, and of the old painting on the wall there. 'The man wasn't alone,' he said, 'there's another monk watching from a cottage, and Saint Peter is handing him a sword.'

'Ah,' Father Levonne said in an oddly regretful tone, 'Peter's sword.'

Thomas frowned at the priest's tone. 'You make it sound evil. Is the sword bad?'

Father Levonne ignored the question. 'You say you met the Holy Father? How was he?'

'Frail,' Thomas said, 'and very gracious.'

'We're asked to pray for his health,' the priest said, 'which I do. He's a good man.'

'He hates us,' Thomas said, 'the English.'

Father Levonne smiled. 'As I said, he's a good man.' He laughed, then looked serious again. 'It isn't surprising,' he said carefully, 'that a painting of Peter's sword should be in the Holy Father's palace. Perhaps it just means that the papacy has abandoned the use of the sword? A picture to demonstrate that we must give up our weapons if we are to be holy?'

Thomas shook his head. 'It's a story, father. Why else would another monk be watching from a cottage? Why the cleared snow? Pictures tell stories!' He pointed at the church walls. 'Why do we put these paintings here? To tell the unlettered the stories we want them to know.'

'Then I don't know that story,' Father Levonne said, 'though I have heard of Peter's sword.' He made the sign of the cross.

'In the picture,' Thomas said, 'the sword had a thick upper blade. More like a falchion.'

'*La Malice*,' Father Levonne said very quietly.

Thomas was silent for a few heartbeats. 'The Seven Dark Lords possessed it,' he quoted the verse that the Black Friars had been spreading through Christendom, 'and they are cursed. He who must rule us will find it, and he shall be blessed.'

'The sword of the fisherman,' Father Levonne said. 'It isn't a sword, Thomas, but the sword. The sword that Saint Peter used to Christ's displeasure, and because of that disapproval they say the blade is cursed.'

'Tell me.'

'I've told you all I know!' Father Levonne said. 'It's only an old story, but the story says *la Malice* carries Christ's curse in her blade and if that's true then *la Malice* must be horribly powerful. Why else would the sword bear that name?'

'And Cardinal Bessières searches for her,' Thomas said.

Levonne looked sharply at Thomas. 'Bessières?'

'And he knows I look for her too.'

'Oh dear God, but you choose powerful enemies, Thomas.'

Thomas climbed from his knees. 'Bessières,' he said, 'is a devil's turd.'

'He's a prince of the church,' Levonne said in mild admonishment.

'He's a prince of turds,' Thomas said, 'and I killed his brother not a quarter-mile from here.'

'And Bessières wants revenge?'

'He doesn't know who killed his brother. He knows me, though, and he'll pursue me now because he thinks I know where *la Malice* is.'

'Do you?'

'No, but I let him think I knew.' Thomas genuflected to the altar. 'I dangled a bait in front of him, father. I invited him to pursue me.'

'Why?'

Thomas sighed. 'My liege lord,' he said, meaning the Earl of Northampton, 'wants me to find *la Malice*. And Bessières, I think, is looking for the same thing. The trouble is I don't know how to find it, father, but I want to be close to Bessières in case he finds it before I do. Keep your enemies close, isn't that good advice?'

'*La Malice* is an idea, Thomas,' Father Levonne said, 'an idea to inspire the faithful. I doubt she exists at all.'

'But she must have existed once,' Thomas said, 'and why is there a picture of Saint Peter giving the sword to a monk? That monk must have possessed it!

So I need to know which saint is painted kneeling in a cleared patch of snow.'

'God alone knows,' Levonne said, 'but I don't. Maybe it's a local saint? Like Sardos here.' He waved at a wall painting of Saint Sardos, a goat-herd, who was driving wolves away from the lamb of God. 'I'd never heard of Sardos before I came here,' the priest went on, 'and I doubt anyone ten miles from here has ever heard of him! The world is full of saints, there are thousands! Every village has a saint no one else knows.'

'Someone must know.'

'A learned man, yes.'

'I thought you were learned, father.'

Father Levonne smiled sadly. 'I don't know who your saint is, Thomas, but I do know that if your enemies come here then this town and its good people will be destroyed. Your enemies may not capture the castle, but the town can't be defended for long.'

Thomas smiled. 'I have forty-two men-at-arms, father, and seventy-three archers.'

'Not enough to hold the town walls.'

'And Sir Henri Courtois commands the castle garrison. He won't be beaten easily. And why would my enemies come here? *La Malice* isn't here!'

'The cardinal doesn't know that. You risk the safety of all these good people,' Father Levonne said, meaning the townsfolk.

'Protecting these good people is my task and Sir

138

Henri's responsibility.' Thomas spoke more harshly than he had intended. 'You pray and I'll fight, father. And I'll search for *la Malice*. I'll go south first.'

'South? Why?'

'To find a learned man, of course,' Thomas said, 'a man who knows all the stories.'

'I have a feeling, Thomas,' the priest said, 'that *la Malice* is an evil thing. Remember what Christ said when Peter drew the sword.'

'"Put up your sword",' Thomas quoted.

'That is a command from our Redeemer! To abandon our weapons. *La Malice* earned his displeasure, Thomas, so it should not be found, it should be destroyed.'

'Destroyed?' Thomas asked, then turned because hooves and the squeal of ungreased axles sounded loud in the street. 'We can argue about this later, father,' he said, and strode down the nave and pulled open the door to be dazzled by the spring sunshine. Pear blossom was white on the trees around the well where a dozen women watched a cumbersome four-wheeled wagon being dragged by six horses. A score of horsemen accompanied the wagon, all of them Thomas's men except for two strangers. One of those strangers was wearing expensive plate armour beneath a short black jupon on which a white rose had been embroidered. His face was hidden by a tournament helmet that was crested with a black-dyed plume, and his horse, a war-destrier, was swathed in a striped cloth of black and white. He was accompanied by a servant who carried a banner with the same symbol of the white rose.

'These buggers were waiting down the road.' A mounted archer jerked a thumb at the strangers in their white rose livery. The archer, like the rest of the men who guarded the wagon, wore the Hellequin's badge of the yale holding a cup. 'There are eight of the bastards, but we said only two could come into the town.'

'Thomas of Hookton,' the rider wearing plate armour demanded, his voice muffled by the big helmet.

Thomas ignored the man. 'How many barrels?' he asked the archer, nodding at the wagon.

'Thirty-four.'

'Good Christ,' Thomas said in disgust, 'only thirty-four? We need a hundred and thirty-four!'

The archer shrugged. 'Seems the bloody Scots have broken the truce. The king needs every arrow in England.'

'He'll lose Gascony if he doesn't send arrows,' Thomas said.

'Thomas of Hookton!' The rider kicked his horse closer to Thomas.

Thomas still ignored him. 'Did you have any problems on the road, Simon?' he asked the archer.

'None at all.'

Thomas walked past the rider to the big wagon and hauled himself up onto the bed where he used the hilt of his knife to knock off a barrel lid. Inside were arrows. They were stacked fairly loosely to make sure the feathers of the fledging did not become distorted or else the arrows would not fly true. Thomas pulled a couple free and sighted down their ash shafts. 'They look well enough made,' he said grudgingly.

'We loosed a couple of dozen,' Simon said, 'and they flew straight.'

'Are you Thomas of Hookton?' The knight of the white rose had pushed his destrier close to the wagon.

'I'll talk to you when I'm ready,' Thomas said in French, then spoke in English again. 'Cords, Simon?'

'Whole sack of them.'

'Good,' Thomas said, 'but only thirty-four barrels?' One of his constant worries was the supply of arrows for his feared longbowmen. He could provide new bows in Castillon d'Arbizon because the local yew trees were good enough to be fashioned into the long war staves, and Thomas, like a half-dozen of his men, was a proficient enough bowyer, but no one knew how to make English arrows. They looked simple enough: an ashwood shaft tipped by a steel head and flighted by the feathers of a goose; but there were no pollarded ash trees near the town, and the smiths could not fashion the needle-sharp bodkin heads that could pierce armour, and no one knew how to bind and glue the feathers. A good archer could shoot fifteen shafts in a minute, and in any skir-

141

mish Thomas's men could loose ten thousand in ten minutes, and though some arrows could be reused, many were destroyed by fighting, and so Thomas was forced to buy replacements from the hundreds of thousands that were shipped from Southampton to Bordeaux and then distributed to the English garrisons that protected King Edward's lands in Gascony. Thomas put the lid back on the barrel. 'This lot should last us a couple of months,' he said, 'but God knows we'll need more.' He looked at the rider. 'Who are you?'

'My name is Roland de Verrec,' the man said. He spoke French with a Gascon accent.

'I've heard of you,' Thomas said, which was hardly surprising because Roland de Verrec's name was spoken with awe throughout Europe. There was no finer tournament fighter. And, of course, there was the legend of his virginity, imposed by a vision of the Virgin Mary. 'You want to join the Hellequin?' Thomas asked.

'I have been given a mission by the Count of Labrouillade . . .' Roland began.

'The fat bastard will very probably cheat you,' Thomas interrupted, 'and if you want to talk to me, Verrec, take that goddamned pot off your head.'

'My lord the count orders me . . .' Roland began.

'I said take the goddamned pot off your head,' Thomas interrupted again. He had climbed on the wagon bed to inspect the arrows, but also because the bed's height meant he could look down on the mounted man. It was always uncomfortable to confront a horseman on foot, but the discomfort now belonged to Roland. A score of Thomas's men, made curious by the presence of the strangers, had come from the open castle gate. Genevieve was among them, holding Hugh's hand.

'You will see my face,' Roland said, 'when you accept my challenge.'

'Sam?' Thomas shouted up to the gatehouse rampart. 'See this idiot?' He pointed at Roland. 'Be ready to put an arrow through his head.'

Sam grinned, put an arrow on his cord and half drew the bow. Roland, not understanding what had been said, looked up to where Thomas had shouted. He had to crane his head to see the threat through his helmet's eye-slits.

'That's an arrow of English ash,' Thomas said, 'with a scarfed oak tip at the head and a steel bodkin sharp as a needle. It will slice through that helmet of yours, make a neat hole in your skull and come to rest in the open space where your brain ought to be. So either give Sam some target practice or else take the damned helmet off.'

The helmet came off. Thomas's first impression was of an angelic face, calm and blue-eyed, framed by fair hair that had been compressed and shaped by the helmet's liner so that the crown was tight against his skull like a cap, while the fringes jutted out in stubborn curls. It looked so strange that Thomas could not resist laughing. His men were laughing too. 'He looks like a juggler I saw at Towcester Fair,' one said.

Roland, not understanding why men laughed, frowned. 'Why do they mock me?' he asked indignantly.

'They think you're a juggler,' Thomas said.

'You know who I am,' Roland said grandly, 'and I am here to challenge you.'

Thomas shook his head. 'We don't hold tournaments here,' he said. 'When we fight, we fight for real.'

'Trust me,' Roland said, 'so do I.' He kicked his horse closer to the wagon, perhaps hoping he might intimidate Thomas. 'My lord of Labrouillade demands that you return his wife,' he said.

'The scriptures teach us that the dog goes back to its vomit,' Thomas said, 'so your master's bitch is free to return to him whenever she wants. She doesn't need your help.'

'She is a woman,' Roland said harshly, 'and has no freedom outside her master's will.'

Thomas nodded towards the castle. 'Who owns that? Me or your master?'

'You, for the moment.'

'Then for the moment, Roland of wherever it is you're from, the Countess of Labrouillade is free to do what she wishes because she's inside my castle, not yours.'

'We can decide that,' Roland said, 'by fighting. I challenge you!' He tugged off his gauntlet and threw it onto the wagon.

Thomas smiled. 'And what does the fight decide?'

'When I kill you, Thomas of Hookton, I shall take the woman.'

'And if I kill you?'

Roland smiled. 'With God's help I shall kill you.'

Thomas ignored the gauntlet that had come to rest between two of the barrels. 'You can tell your fat master, Roland, that if he wants his woman back then he'd better come and fetch her himself, not send his juggler.'

'This juggler,' Roland retorted, 'has been charged to perform two deeds. To reclaim my lord's lawful wife and to punish you for insolence. So, will you fight?'

'Dressed like this?' Thomas asked. He was in hose and shirt with loose-fitting shoes.

'I will give you time to put on armour,' Roland said.

'Jeanette!' Thomas called to one of the girls at the well. 'Drop your bucket down the well, *chérie*, fill it, then haul it up!'

'Now?' she asked.

'Right now,' Thomas said, then stooped to pick up the gauntlet, which was made of fine leather and plated with scales of steel. He handed it to Roland. 'If you're not out of this town by the time Jeanette hauls that bucket out of the well, I'll let my archers hunt you down. Now go and tell your fat master to come and take his woman for himself.'

Roland looked at Jeanette, who was hauling her bucket's rope with two hands. 'You have no honour, Englishman,' he said proudly, 'and I will kill you for that.'

'Go and dunk your head in a latrine pit,' Thomas said.

'I shall . . .' Roland began.

'Sam!' Thomas interrupted him. 'Don't kill his horse. I'll keep that!'

He had shouted in French and Roland at last seemed to take the threat seriously because he turned his destrier and, followed by his standard bearer, spurred downhill towards the town's southern gate.

Thomas tossed a coin to Jeanette, then walked up to the castle. 'What did he want?' Genevieve asked.

'To fight me. He's Labrouillade's new champion.'

'He would fight to get Bertille back?'

'That's why he was sent, yes.'

Brother Michael came running across the courtyard. 'Did he come for the countess?' he asked Thomas.

'What's it to you, brother?'

The young monk looked confused. 'I was worried,' he said limply.

'Well, you can stop worrying,' Thomas said, 'because tomorrow I'm taking you away.'

'Away?'

'You're meant to go to Montpellier, aren't you? So at dawn tomorrow we leave. Pack your things, if you have any.'

'But . . .'

'Tomorrow,' Thomas said, 'at dawn.'

Because Montpellier had a university, and Thomas needed a learned man.

The Lord of Douglas was angry. He had brought two hundred of Scotland's best warriors to France, and instead of launching them against the English, the King of France was holding a tournament.

A bloody tournament! The English were burning towns beyond the frontiers of Gascony and besieging castles in Normandy, yet Jean of France wanted to play at soldiers. So the Lord of Douglas would play as well, and when the French suggested a melee, fifteen of King Jean's finest knights against fifteen Scotsmen, Douglas took one of his warriors aside. 'Put them down fast,' Douglas growled.

The man, gaunt and hollow-cheeked, just nodded. His name was Sculley. He alone among the Lord of Douglas's men-at-arms was not wearing a helmet, and his dark hair, streaked with grey, was worn long and twisted into pigtails into which he had inserted numerous small bones, and it was rumoured that each bone came from the finger of an Englishman he had killed, though no one ever dared ask Sculley the truth of that statement. The bones could just as easily have come from fellow Scotsmen.

'Put them down and keep them down,' Douglas said.

Sculley smiled, all teeth, no humour. 'Kill them?'

'Christ, no, you bloody fool! It's a goddamned

tournament! Just put them down hard, man, hard and fast.'

Money was changing hands as bets were made, and most of the cash was placed on the French, for they were superbly mounted, beautifully armoured, and each of the fifteen was a renowned tournament fighter. They paraded themselves, trotting their destriers up and down in front of the tiered seats where the king and his court watched, and they glanced patronisingly at the Scots, whose horses were smaller and whose armour was old-fashioned. The French had great helms, padded and plumed, while the Scots wore bascinets, mere skull caps with a tail to protect the neck, and Sculley wore no helmet at all. He kept his great falchion sheathed, preferring a mace.

'Any knight who cries for quarter will be given it,' a herald was reading the rules, which every man knew so no one listened. 'Lances will be blunted. Sword points may not be used. Horses are not to be maimed.' He droned on as the king offered a purse to a servant who hurried off to place the money on the superb French contingent. The Lord of Douglas put all he had on his own men. He had decided against fighting, not because he feared the melee, but because he had nothing to prove, and now he watched his nephew, Sir Robbie, and wondered if the youngster had been softened by his time at the French court. But at least Robbie Douglas could fight, and he was one of the fifteen, his shield, like all the Scotsmen's shields, showing the red heart of Douglas. One of the French knights evidently knew Robbie, for he had ridden to where the Scotsmen readied themselves and the two were deep in conversation.

A fat cardinal, who had been paying court to the king all day, sidled between the padded seats to take the empty space beside Douglas. Most men avoided the hard-faced, dark-faced, grim-faced Scot, but the cardinal smiled a welcome. 'We have not met,' he introduced himself genially. 'My name is Bessières, Cardinal Archbishop of Livorno, Papal Legate to King Jean of France, whom God preserves. Do you like almonds?'

'I've a taste for them,' the Lord of Douglas said grudgingly.

The cardinal held out a plump hand to offer the bowl of almonds. 'Take as many as you wish, my lord. They come from my own estates. I am told you have placed money on your own side?'

'What else would I do?'

'You might have a care of your money,' the cardinal said happily, 'and I suspect you do. So tell me, my lord, what you know and I do not.'

'I know fighting,' Douglas said.

'Then let me try another question,' the cardinal said. 'If I were to offer you one-third of my winnings, and I was to place a large sum of money on the fight, would you advise me to back the Scots?'

'You'd be a fool not to.'

'No one, I think, has ever accused me of foolishness,' Bessières said. The cardinal summoned a

149

servant and gave the man a heavy bag of coin. 'Upon the Scots,' he instructed, then waited for the servant to go. 'You are not content, my lord,' he said to Douglas, 'and today is supposed to be a day of rejoicing.'

Douglas scowled at the cardinal. 'Rejoicing for what?'

'The sunshine, God's blessings, good wine.'

'With the English running loose in Normandy and Gascony?'

'Ah, the English.' Bessières leaned back in the chair, resting the dish of almonds on his protruding stomach. 'The Holy Father urges us to make a peace. An everlasting peace.' He spoke sarcastically. There had been a time, and not so long ago, when Louis Bessières had thought himself certain to become Pope. All it would have needed was for him to produce the Holy Grail, the most desired relic of Christendom, and to ensure that he could produce it he had gone to immense and expensive pains to have the false Grail made, but the cup had been dashed from his hands, and, on the old Pope's death, the crown had gone to another man. Yet Bessières had not given up hope. By the grace of God the Pope was sick and could die any time.

Douglas caught the cardinal's tone and was surprised. 'You do not want peace?'

'Of course I want peace,' the cardinal said, 'indeed I am charged by the Holy Father to negotiate that peace with the English. Would you like another handful of almonds?'

'I thought the Pope wanted the English defeated,' Douglas said.

'He does.'

'But he urges peace?'

'The Pope cannot encourage war,' Bessières said, 'so he preaches peace and sends me to negotiate.'

'And you?' Douglas asked, letting the question hang.

'I negotiate,' Bessières said airily, 'and I shall give France the peace that the Holy Father wants, but even he knows that the only way to give France peace is by defeating the English. So yes, my lord, the road to peace lies through war. More almonds?'

A trumpet sounded, calling the two groups of knights to go to the ends of the tilting ground. Marshals were inspecting lances, making certain they were tipped with wooden blocks so they could not pierce shields or armour.

'There will be war,' Douglas said, 'yet here we are playing games.'

'His Majesty is nervous of England,' Bessières said frankly. 'He fears their archers.'

'Archers can be beaten,' Douglas said vehemently.

'They can?'

'They can. There is a way.'

'No one has found it,' the cardinal observed.

'Because they're fools. Because they think that playing on horseback is the only way to make war. My father was at the Bannock burn; you know of that battle?'

'Alas, no,' the cardinal said.

'We crushed the English bastards, tore them to pieces, archers and all. It can be done. It has been done. It must be done.'

The cardinal watched the French knights form a line of ten men. The remaining five would charge a few paces behind to take advantage of the chaos created by the impact of the ten. 'The one to fear,' Bessières said, gesturing with an almond, 'is the brute with the gaudy shield.' He pointed to a big man on a big horse, a man arrayed in shining plate armour and holding a shield that displayed a clenched red fist against a field of orange and white stripes. 'His name is Joscelyn of Berat,' the cardinal said, 'and he is a fool, but a great fighter. He is undefeated these last five years except, of course, by Roland de Verrec, and he, alas, is not here.'

Joscelyn of Berat was the man Robbie Douglas had been talking with before the knights withdrew to the ends of the field. 'Where's Berat?' Douglas asked.

'South,' Bessières said vaguely.

'How would my nephew know him?'

Bessières shrugged. 'I cannot tell you, my lord.'

'My nephew was in the south,' Douglas said, 'before the pestilence arrived. He travelled with an Englishman.' He spat. 'Some damn archer,' he added.

The cardinal shuddered. He knew the tale, knew it only too well. The damn archer was Thomas of Hookton whom Bessières blamed for the loss of both the Grail and of Saint Peter's throne. The cardinal also knew of Robbie Douglas, indeed that was why he had come to the tourney. 'Your nephew is here?' he asked.

'Piebald horse,' Douglas said, nodding towards the Scots who looked so ill armed compared to their rivals.

'I would like to talk with him,' the cardinal said. 'Would you be so kind as to send him to me?' But before the Lord of Douglas could answer, the king waved, a herald lowered his banner, and the horsemen dug in their spurs.

Bessières immediately regretted his wager. The Scots' horses looked so scrawny compared to the magnificent destriers that the French rode, and the French rode tight, knee to knee, as knights should, while the Scotsmen, slower off the mark, spread out instantly to leave gaps through which their opponents could ride. They had chosen to ride in a single wide line, all fifteen abreast, but they also rode faster, increasing their disarray, while the French came slowly, keeping station, only spurring into the canter when the two groups were about fifty paces apart. The cardinal glanced at the Lord of Douglas to see if the Scotsman shared his apprehensions, but Douglas was smiling sardonically as though he knew what was coming.

The hoofbeats were loud, but drowned by the shouts of the crowd. The king, who was exceptionally fond of jousting, leaned forward expectantly in his chair, and the cardinal looked back to see the leading Frenchmen raise their shields and couch their lances, bracing for the impact, and the crowd went suddenly quiet, as if it held its breath, waiting for the crash of armoured men and horses.

The cardinal never quite understood what happened next, or rather he did not understand until it was explained to him at the feast where cruets were used to represent the horsemen, but when he was watching, when the crash came, he did not understand it at all.

The Scots had seemed so ragged, yet at the last second they suddenly swerved inwards to make a column of horsemen, three riders in the front rank, and that column hammered through the French line like a nail driven through a sheet of vellum. Scottish lances crashed into shields, Frenchmen were thrown back onto their saddles' high cantles, and the column sliced through the line to strike hard against the second smaller group of French riders, who, not expecting to be involved in the fight's opening, were not ready for the impact. A lance caught a Frenchman at the base of his helmet and, though blunted, it cracked the helmet and threw the man back over his cantle. A horse screamed. The Scots in the following ranks had discarded their lances and drawn swords or else carried brutal lead-weighted maces, and they now moved outwards. Most were now behind their opponents who were blind to their attacks. Another Frenchman went down, dragged by his stirrup-trapped boot out of the melee.

154

So far as the cardinal could see it was sheer chaos, but it was clear the Scots were winning. Two more Frenchmen fell, and Sculley, conspicuous because he wore no helmet, was hammering his mace down on a magnificently plumed helm, hammering again and again, grimacing as he stood in his stirrups, and the horseman, plainly stunned, slid down to the turf as Sculley turned on another man, this time swinging the mace so that it slammed straight into the helmet's eye-slits. That man went, felled in an instant, and the Scotsmen were now seeking new enemies, getting in each other's way in their eagerness to finish off the French knights. Joscelyn of Berat was backing his horse, fighting off Robbie Douglas and another man. Joscelyn's swordplay was fast and dangerous, but Sculley came behind him and slammed the mace into the small of his back, and Joscelyn, knowing he could not fight off three men, shouted that he yielded, and Robbie Douglas had to drive his horse between Joscelyn and Sculley to stop the mace coming again in a blow that threatened to snap the Frenchman's spine.

Sculley wheeled away, saw a Frenchman staggering to his feet with a drawn sword, so kicked him in the face and raised the mace to finish the man off, but the heralds were running to intervene and the trumpets were shrilling and another Scotsman stilled Sculley's blow. The crowd was utterly silent. Sculley was growling, twitching, flicking his head from side to side in search of another man to hit, but of the Frenchmen only Joscelyn of Berat was still in his saddle, and he had yielded. The fight had been fast, brutal and one-sided, and the cardinal discovered he had been holding his breath. 'A demonstration of Scottish prowess, my lord?' he enquired of the Lord of Douglas.

'Just imagine they had been fighting the English,' Douglas growled.

'That is a cheering thought, my lord,' the cardinal said, watching as servants ran to rescue the fallen French knights, one of whom was not moving at all. His helm was battered and there was blood seeping from the visor's eye-slits. 'The sooner we release you against the English,' Bessières went on, 'the better.'

Douglas turned to look at the cardinal. 'The king listens to you?' he asked.

'I give him advice,' Bessières said airily.

'Then tell him to send us south.'

'Not to Normandy?'

'Edward's pup is in the south,' Douglas said.

'The Prince of Wales?'

'Edward's pup,' Douglas said, 'and I want him. I want him yielding to me. I want him on his damned knees whimpering for mercy.'

'And will you grant it?' Bessières asked, amused at the passion in the Scotsman's voice.

'You know our king is prisoner in England?'

'Of course.'

'And the ransom will break our backs. I want Edward's pup.'

'Ah!' Bessières understood. 'So your king's ransom will be the Prince of Wales?'

'Exactly.'

Bessières reached out and touched a gloved finger to the Scotsman's hand. 'I shall do as you ask,' he promised warmly, 'but first I want you to introduce me to your nephew.'

'To Robbie?'

'To Robbie,' the cardinal said.

Bessières and Robbie met that evening as the survivors of the tourney feasted with the French court. They ate eels seethed in wine, mutton dressed with figs, roasted songbirds, venison, and a score of other dishes brought into a hall where minstrels played behind a screen. The Scottish warriors ate together, clustered at a table as if protecting themselves from the vengeful French, who had suggested that some strange pagan magic, born of the wild northern hills, had been used against their champions, so that when Robbie was summoned, and ordered by his uncle to obey the summons, he crossed the hall nervously. He bowed to the king, then followed the servant to the table where the cardinal had four trenchers in front of him. 'You will sit beside me, young man,' the cardinal ordered. 'Do you like roasted larks?'

'No, Your Eminence.'

'Suck the flesh from the bones and you will find

the taste delectable.' The cardinal placed a tiny bird in front of Robbie. 'You fought well,' he said.

'We fought as we always fight,' Robbie said.

'I watched you. In another moment you would have beaten the Count of Berat.'

'I doubt it,' Robbie said ungraciously.

'But then your master's beast intervened,' the cardinal said, watching Sculley, who was hunched over his food as though he feared men might take it from him. 'Why does he wear bones in his hair?'

'To remind himself of the men he's killed.'

'Some think it is sorcery,' the cardinal said.

'Not sorcery, Your Eminence, just deadly skill.'

The cardinal sucked at a lark. 'I am told, Sir Robert, that you refuse to fight against the English?'

'I made an oath,' Robbie said.

'To a man who was excommunicated from the church. To a man who married a heretic. To a man who has proven to be an enemy of Mother Church, to Thomas of Hookton.'

'To a man who saved my life when I caught the plague,' Robbie said, 'and to a man who paid my ransom so I could go free.'

The cardinal pulled a sliver of bone from his teeth. 'I see a man who wears bones in his hair, and you tell me you caught the plague and lived with a heretic's help. And this afternoon I watched you defeat fifteen good men, men who are not easily beaten. It seems to me, Sir Robert, that you have unnatural help. Perhaps the devil aids you? You deny using sorcery, but the evidence suggests otherwise, wouldn't you agree?' He asked the questions silkily, then paused to sip wine. 'I might have to talk to my Dominicans, Sir Robert, and tell them that there is the stench of wickedness in your soul. I might be forced to encourage them to heat their fires and wind the ropes of their machines that stretch men till they break.' He was smiling, and his plump right hand was massaging Robbie's left knee. 'One word from me, Sir Robert, and your soul will be in my care.'

'I'm a good Christian,' Robbie said defiantly.

'Then you must prove that to me.'

'Prove it?'

'By realising that an oath made to a heretic is not binding in heaven nor upon earth. Only in hell, Sir Robert, does that oath have power. And I want you to do me a service. If you refuse me then I shall tell King Jean that evil has entered his kingdom and I shall ask the Dominicans to explore your soul and burn that evil from your body. The choice is yours. Are you going to eat that lark?'

Robbie shook his head and watched as the cardinal sucked the meat from the fragile bones. 'What service?' he asked nervously.

'A service for His Holiness the Pope,' Bessières said, carefully not saying which Pope he meant. The service was for himself, who prayed nightly that he would be the next man to wear the fisherman's ring. 'Have you heard of the Order of the Garter?'

'I have,' Robbie said.

'Or the Order of the Virgin and Saint George?' Bessières continued, 'or the Order of the Sash in Spain? Or, indeed, King Jean's Order of the Star? Bands of great knights, Sir Robert, sworn to each other, to their king, and to the noblest aims of chivalry. I have been charged with creating a similar order, a band of knights sworn to the church and to the glory of Christ.' He had made it sound as if the Pope had commanded the creation of the order, but it was all Bessières's idea. 'A man who serves in the church's order,' he went on, 'would never know the torments of hell, nor the agonies of purgatory. A man who serves our new order would be welcomed into heaven and sung into the company of saints by choirs of shining angels! I want you, Sir Robert, to serve in the Order of the Fisherman.'

Robbie was silent. He watched the cardinal. Men were cheering a performer who was juggling half a dozen flaming brands while balancing on stilts, but Robbie did not notice. He was thinking that his soul would be freed of its perplexities if he were to be a knight in the service of the Pope.

'I want the greatest knights of Christendom to fight for the glory of our Saviour,' the cardinal went on, 'and each man, while he fights, will receive a small subvention from the church, enough to feed himself and to keep his attendants and horses.' The cardinal placed three gold coins on the table. He knew Robbie's propensity to gamble, and to lose. 'All your sins will be forgiven,' he said, 'if you become a Knight of the Fisherman and wear this sash.'

He took from a pouch a scapular made of the finest white silk, edged and fringed with cloth of gold, and embroidered with scarlet keys. The Pope received gifts daily that were heaped in the sacristy at Avignon, and Bessières, before he left that town, had hunted through the bundles and discovered a trove of scapulars woven by nuns in Burgundy and sent to the Pope, each of them lovingly embroidered with the keys of Saint Peter. 'The man who wears this sash in battle,' the cardinal continued, 'will have God at his side, the angels will draw their flaming swords to protect him, and the saints will beseech our blessed Saviour to give him victory. A man who wears this sash cannot lose a fight, but neither can a man who wears this sash cleave to an oath made to a godless heretic.'

Robbie stared hungrily at the gorgeous scapular, imagining it around his waist as he rode to battle. 'The Pope has enemies?' he asked, wondering whom he would need to fight.

'The church has enemies,' Bessières said harshly, 'because the devil never ceases his fight. And the Order of the Fisherman,' he went on, 'has a task already, a noble task, perhaps none nobler in all Christendom.'

'What task?' Robbie asked, his voice low.

For answer the cardinal beckoned a priest to his

side. To Robbie the newly invited priest, who had startling green eyes, appeared to be the cardinal's opposite in almost every way. Bessières had charm, but the priest looked stern and unbending; the cardinal was plump, the priest was lean as a blade; the cardinal was swathed in red silk trimmed with ermine, while the lesser cleric was in black, though Robbie caught a glimpse of scarlet lining in one of the hanging sleeves. 'This is Father Marchant,' the cardinal said, 'and he will be the chaplain to our order.'

'By God's grace,' Marchant said. His strange green eyes rested on Robbie and his mouth twitched as if he disapproved of what he saw.

'Tell my young Scottish friend, father, the holy task of the Order of the Fisherman.'

Father Marchant touched the crucifix hanging about his neck. 'Saint Peter,' he said, 'was a fisherman, but he was so much more. He was the first Pope, and God gave him the keys of heaven and earth. Yet he also possessed a sword, Sir Robert. Perhaps you remember the story?'

'Not really,' Robbie said.

'When the evil men came to arrest our Lord in the Garden of Gethsemane it was Saint Peter who drew a sword to protect him. Think of that!' Marchant's voice was suddenly passionate. 'The blessed Saint Peter drew a sword to protect our Redeemer, our precious Christ, our Son of God! The sword of Saint Peter is God's weapon to protect his church, and we must find it! The

162

church is imperilled, and we need God's weapon. It is God's will!'

'Indeed it is,' the cardinal said, 'and if we find the sword, Sir Robert, then the worthiest of the knights in the Order of the Fisherman will be permitted to guard the sword, and to wear it, and to use it in battle, so that God himself will be on his side in every fight. That man will be the greatest knight in all Christendom. So,' he pushed the coins and the scapular a little closer to Robbie, 'as it says in the scripture, Sir Robert, *choisissez aujourd'hui qui vous voulez servir.*' He quoted the French for he was certain Robbie would not understand the Latin. 'Today, Sir Robert, you must choose between good and evil, between an oath made to a heretic or the blessing of the Holy Father himself.' The cardinal crossed himself. 'Choose today whom you wish to serve, Sir Robert Douglas.'

And really there was no choice. Robbie reached for the sash and felt tears in his eyes. He had found his cause and he would fight for God.

'Bless you, my son,' the cardinal said. 'Now go and pray. Thank God that you have chosen rightly.'

He watched Robbie walk away. 'So,' he said to Father Marchant, 'that's the first of your knights. Tomorrow you will endeavour to find Roland de Verrec. But for the moment,' he pointed to Sculley, 'fetch me that animal.'

And so the Order of the Fisherman was born.

★　　★　　★

163

Brother Michael was miserable. 'I don't want to be a hospitaller,' he told Thomas. 'I get dizzy when I see blood. It makes me feel sick.'

'You have a calling,' Thomas said.

'To be an archer?' Brother Michael suggested.

Thomas laughed. 'Tell me that in ten years, brother. It takes that long to learn the bow.'

It was midday and they were resting the horses. Thomas had taken twenty men, all men-at-arms, their job merely to provide protection from the *coredors* who haunted the roads. He dared not take archers. His longbows rode with the Hellequin, but when he travelled in a small group the sight of the dreaded English bows stirred up enemies, so all the men with him spoke French. Most were Gascons, but there were two Germans, Karyl and Wulf, who had ridden to Castillon d'Arbizon to offer their allegiance. 'Why do you want to serve me?' Thomas had asked them.

'Because you win,' Karyl had answered simply. The German was a thin, quick fighter, whose right cheek was scarred by two parallel furrows. 'The claws of a fighting bear,' he had explained. 'I was trying to save a dog. I liked the dog, but the bear didn't.'

'Did the dog die?' Genevieve had asked.

'It did,' Karyl said, 'but so did the bear.'

Genevieve was with Thomas. She would not leave Thomas's side, fearing that if she was alone the church would find her again and try to burn her, and so she had insisted on accompanying him.

Besides, she had told him, there was no danger. Thomas only planned to spend a day or two in Montpellier in search of a scholar who could explain a monk kneeling amidst snow, then they would all hurry back to Castillon d'Arbizon where the rest of his men waited.

'If I can't be an archer,' Brother Michael said, 'then let me be your physician.'

'You haven't finished your training, brother, that's why we're going to Montpellier. So you can be educated.'

'I don't want to be educated,' Brother Michael grumbled. 'I've had enough education.'

Thomas laughed. He liked the young monk and knew well enough that Michael was desperate to escape the cage of his calling, a despair Thomas knew himself. Thomas was the illegitimate son of a priest, and he had obediently gone to Oxford to learn theology so that he could become a priest himself, but he had already found another love, the yew bow. The great yew bow. And no books, no sacrament, no lecture on the indivisible substance of the triple-natured God could compete with the bow, and so Thomas had become a soldier. Brother Michael, he thought, was following the same course, though in Michael's case it was the Countess Bertille who was the lodestar. She was still at Castillon d'Arbizon where she accepted Brother Michael's worship as her due and was kind to him in return, but seemed oblivious to his yearning. She treated him like an indulged puppy and that made the young monk yearn even more.

Galdric, Thomas's servant, and more than able to look after himself in a fight, brought Thomas's horse back from the stream. 'Those folk stopped,' he said.

'Close?'

'A long way back. But I think they're following us.'

Thomas climbed the bank from the stream to the road. A mile away, perhaps more, a small band of men were watering horses. 'It's a busy road,' Thomas said. The men, he thought they were all men, had been behind them for two days now, but they were making no attempt to catch up.

'They're the Count of Armagnac's troops,' Karyl said confidently.

'Armagnac?'

'This is all the Count's territory,' the German said, waving an arm to encompass the whole landscape. 'His men patrol the roads to keep the bandits away. He can't tax merchants if they've nothing to tax, eh?'

The road became even busier as they neared Montpellier. Thomas had no wish to draw attention to himself by entering the city with a large band of armed men so, next afternoon, he looked for a place where most of his men could wait while he entered the city. They found a burned mill on a hilltop to the west of the road. The nearest village was a mile away and the valley beneath the mill was secluded. 'If we're not back in two days,' he told Karyl, 'send someone to discover what's happened and send to Castillon for help. And keep quiet here. We don't want the city consuls sending men to investigate you.' He could tell the city was close by the smear of smoke in the southern sky.

'If people ask us what we do here?'

'You can't afford city prices so you're waiting here to meet the Count of Armagnac's men.' The count was the greatest lord in all southern France and no one would dare interfere with men who served him.

'There'll be no trouble,' Karyl said grimly. 'I promise.'

Thomas, Genevieve, Hugh and Brother Michael rode on. They were accompanied by just two men-at-arms and by Galdric, and they reached Montpellier that evening. The two hills of the city, the towers of its churches and its tile-roofed bastions cast long shadows. The city was surrounded by a high, pale wall from which hung banners showing the Virgin and her child. Others showed a circle, red as the setting sun, against a white field. Outside the wall was a weed-strewn wasteland, and beneath the weeds were ashes, while in a few places there were stone hearths showing where there had once been houses. A woman, stooped and ancient with a black scarf over her hair, grubbed close to one of the hearths. 'You lived here?' Thomas asked.

She answered in Occitan, a language Thomas

scarcely knew, but Galdric translated. 'She lived here till the English came.'

'The English were here?' Thomas sounded surprised.

It seemed that during the previous year the Prince of Wales had come close to Montpellier, very close, but at the last moment his destroying army had sheered away, but not before the city had burned every building outside the walls to deny the English any hiding places for archers or siege engines. 'Ask what she's searching for,' Thomas ordered.

'Anything,' was the answer, 'because she lost everything.'

Genevieve tossed the woman a coin. A bell was tolling inside the city and Thomas feared it was the signal to close the gates, so he spurred his men forward. A line of wagons laden with timber, fleeces, and barrels waited at the gate, but Thomas passed them. He was in mail, carrying a sword, and that marked him as a man of privilege. Galdric, riding close behind, unfurled a banner showing a hawk carrying a sheaf of rye. The badge was the old banner of Castillon d'Arbizon, and a useful device when Thomas did not want to advertise his loyalty to the Earl of Northampton or his command of the feared Hellequin.

'Your business, sire?' a guard at the gate demanded.

'We are on a pilgrimage,' Thomas said, 'so want to pray.'

'Swords must remain sheathed inside the city, sire,' the guard said respectfully.

'We're not here to fight,' Thomas said, 'just to pray. Where do we find lodgings?'

'There's plenty straight ahead, close to Saint Pierre's church. The one showing the sign of Saint Lucia is the best.'

'Because it belongs to your brother?' Thomas guessed.

'I wish it did, sire, but it's owned by my cousin.'

Thomas laughed, threw the man a coin, and rode under the high arch. The sound of his horse's hooves echoed from the buildings, the bell tolled steadily and Thomas rode towards the church of Saint Peter, besieged suddenly by the fecal stench of a city. A man in a red and blue tunic and carrying a trumpet with the banner of the Virgin dangling from its pipes ran past the horses. 'I'm late!' he called to Thomas.

The men guarding the gates began to swing them shut. 'You'll have to wait till morning!' they called to the carters.

'Wait,' another guard called. He had seen eight riders crossing the cleared ground, their horses' hooves kicking up puffs of ash and dust as they hurried towards the city. 'Some bloody lord or other,' the guard grumbled. One of the riders unfurled a banner to show that they came on noble business. The flag displayed a green horse on a white background, though the leading rider had a black jupon that carried the badge of a white rose. All eight

169

horsemen wore mail and carried weapons. 'Make way for them!' the guard shouted at the carters.

'If you're going to let them in,' a carter who had a load of firewood pleaded, 'then why not us?'

'Because you're scum and they're not,' the guard said, then bowed to the riders, who clattered through the arch. 'I have business here,' the leader of the riders explained to the guards, who demanded no further explanation, but just slammed the big gates closed and dropped the bar into its brackets. 'My thanks,' the leader of the riders said, and rode on into the city.

Roland de Verrec had come to Montpellier.

CHAPTER 5

'The proposition,' Doctor Lucius bellowed loud enough for his words to be heard by the fish in the Mediterranean six miles to the south of Montpellier, 'is that a child who dies unbaptised is thereby condemned to the endless torments of hell, to the eternal fires of perdition, and to separation from God for ever with all the pain, agony, remorse, regret and tribulation that this doom entails. My question: is this proposition true?'

No one answered.

Doctor Lucius, who wore an ink-stained white gown of the Dominican order, glared at his cowed students. Thomas had been told that the Dominican was the cleverest man in all Montpellier's university and so had come with Brother Michael to the doctor's lecture hall, which, to Thomas's eyes, appeared to be a hastily constructed chamber made by roofing over a small cloister of the Monastery of Saint Simeon. The good weather had vanished overnight to be replaced by low angry clouds from which the rain fell to drip through the ill-laid tiles of the lecture hall's roof.

Doctor Lucius was sitting on a platform, behind a dais, while facing him were three rows of benches on which a score of dull-faced students slumped in robes of black or dark blue.

Doctor Lucius stroked his beard. It was a massive beard, falling to the frayed rope belted about his waist. 'Are we dull-witted?' he demanded of his students. 'Are we asleep? Did we drink too much of the grape last night? Some of you, God help His holy church, will become priests. You will have a flock to care for, and among that flock will be women whose infants will die before they receive the sacrament of baptism. The mother, tearful and eager for your comfort, will ask whether her infant has been received into the company of the saints, and what will your answer be?' Doctor Lucius waited for a response, but none came. 'Oh, for God's sake,' the doctor snarled, 'one of you must have an answer.'

'Yes,' a young man with a scruffy black student's cap from which long black hair fell half over his face answered.

'Ah! Master Keane is awake!' Doctor Lucius cried. 'He has not travelled all this way from Ireland to no purpose, God be thanked. Why, Master Keane, will you tell the grieving mother that her dead infant is in paradise?'

'Because if I tell her it's in hell, doctor, she'll go on bawling and crying and there's few things worse than a wailing woman. Best just to get rid of her by telling the poor creature what she wishes to hear.'

Doctor Lucius's mouth twitched, perhaps in amusement. 'So you do not care, Master Keane, about the truth of the proposition, only that you will be spared the sound of a woman weeping? You would not think it a priest's duty to comfort the woman?'

'By telling the poor thing that her wee babe has gone to hell? Jesus, no! And if she was comely I'd certainly be wanting to offer her comfort.'

'Your charity knows no bounds,' Doctor Lucius said sourly, 'but let us return to the proposition. Is it, or is it not, true? Anyone?'

A pale young man whose cap and gown were spotless cleared his throat, and most of the other students groaned. The pale boy, skinny as a starved rat, was plainly the assiduous student whose achievements belittled the efforts of the rest of the class. 'Saint Augustine,' he said, 'teaches us that God will not remit the sins of any but the baptised.'

'*Ergo*?' Doctor Lucius asked.

'Therefore,' the young man said in a precise voice, 'the child is condemned to hell because it was born containing sin.'

'So we have our answer?' Doctor Lucius enquired. 'Upon the authority of Master de Beaufort,' the pale boy smiled and tried to look modest, 'and of the blessed Saint Augustine. Do we all agree? Can we now move on to discuss the cardinal virtues?'

'How can a baby go to hell?' Master Keane asked, disgusted. 'What has it done to deserve that?'

'It was born of a woman,' the student called de Beaufort answered sternly, 'and lacking the sacrament of baptism the child is doomed to suffer for the guilt of the sin it thereby contains.'

'Master de Beaufort cuts to the quick of the argument, does he not?' Doctor Lucius suggested to the Irish student.

'God is not commanded by the sacraments,' Thomas interjected, speaking, like everyone else, in Latin.

There was silence as everyone turned to look at the stranger who leaned, dark and hard-faced, against a pillar at the cloister's edge. 'And who have we here?' Doctor Lucius asked. 'I trust you have paid to attend my teaching?'

'I'm here to say that Master de Beaufort is full of shit,' Thomas said, 'and does not understand or has not read the teachings of Aquinas, who assures us God is not bound by the sacraments. God, not Master de Beaufort, will decide the baby's fate, and Saint Paul tells us in his first letter to the Corinthians that a child born to a couple of whom one parent is a pagan is holy to God. And Saint Augustine, in *The City of God*, declared that the parents of the dead child could find a way to redeem its soul.'

'Could, not would,' yapped de Beaufort.

'You are a priest?' Doctor Lucius ignored de Beaufort and asked the question of Thomas, who was swathed in a black cloak.

'I'm a soldier,' Thomas said. He let the cloak fall slightly open to reveal his mail.

'And you?' Doctor Lucius demanded of Brother Michael, who had backed into one of the old cloister arches in an effort to dissociate himself from Thomas. The young monk was unhappy being anywhere near the university and seemed to be sulking. 'Are you with him?' Doctor Lucius asked Brother Michael, gesturing at Thomas.

Brother Michael looked flustered. 'I'm looking for the School of Medicine,' he stammered.

'The bone-setters and piss-sniffers give their lectures in Saint Stephen's.' Master de Beaufort sniggered as the doctor looked back to Thomas. 'A soldier who speaks Latin!' the Dominican said in mock admiration. 'God be praised, but it seems the age of miracles has returned. Shouldn't you be killing someone?'

'I'll get around to that,' Thomas said, 'after I've asked you a question.'

'And once you have paid for my answer,' Doctor Lucius retorted, 'but for the moment,' he now gestured for the attention of his students, 'though I have no doubt our visitor,' he waved an inky hand towards Thomas, 'wins his arguments on the field of battle by brute force, he is entirely wrong in this matter. An unbaptised baby is doomed to the endless torments of hell, and Master de Beaufort will now demonstrate why. Stand, Master de Beaufort, and enlighten us.'

The pale scholar jumped to his feet. 'Man,' he said confidently, 'is made in the image of God, but woman is not. The laws of the church are clear on that distinction. I cite the *Corpus Iuris Canonici* in support of that contention.' But before he could recite the church law there were heavy footsteps in the open corridor outside, and de Beaufort's voice dribbled to nothing as six armed and armoured men came through the arch into the lecture room. They were dressed in mail haubergeons over which they had jupons with the image of the seated Virgin, and all were carrying spears and wearing helmets. They were followed by two men in the blue and rose robes of Montpellier's consuls, the city's governors, and then by a man wearing the badge of the white rose: Roland de Verrec.

'You interrupt us,' Doctor Lucius said indignantly, but in Latin so that none of the newcomers understood him.

'That is him.' Roland de Verrec ignored the doctor and pointed at Thomas. 'Arrest him now!'

'For what?' Doctor Lucius used French this time. He was hardly defending Thomas by the question, instead he was defending his dignity, which had been affronted by the arrival of the armed men, and he was trying to establish his authority in the lecture room.

'For the abduction of another man's lawful wife,' Roland de Verrec answered, 'and for the worse crime of heresy. He is excommunicate, outlawed from the church and hated by men. His name is Thomas of Hookton and I demand he now be given into my custody.' He gestured for the armed men to capture Thomas.

Who swore under his breath and took two steps backwards. He seized Brother Michael, who was still gawking at the newcomers. Thomas had left his sword with Genevieve, for he would have been forbidden entrance to the monastery if he had arrived armed, but he had a short knife at his belt and he drew it, put his left arm around Brother Michael's neck and the point of the knife against his throat. Brother Michael made a strangulated noise that checked the city guards. 'Go back,' Thomas told them, 'or I kill the monk.'

'If you surrender peaceably,' Roland de Verrec told Thomas, 'I shall plead with the Count of Labrouillade to treat you leniently.' He paused, as if expecting Thomas to lower the blade. 'Take him,' he ordered the guards when the knife stayed at Brother Michael's throat.

'You want him dead?' Thomas shouted. He tightened his grip on the young monk's throat, provoking a terrified whimper.

'A reward to the man who takes him,' Roland de Verrec announced, stepping forward himself. The thought of a reward excited the students, who had been gazing wide-eyed at the sudden drama that had enlivened their theology lecture. They gave a roar like hunters seeing their prey close, and kicked over the benches in their hurry to capture Thomas.

'He's dead!' Thomas bellowed, and the students stopped, fearing that the monk's blood would suddenly spurt. 'Tell Genevieve,' Thomas whispered in Brother Michael's ear, 'to join Karyl.' Genevieve, barred by her gender from entering the monastery, had stayed at the tavern with Hugh, Galdric and the two men-at-arms.

'Jesus God, save me!' Brother Michael gasped, and Thomas let go with his left arm and thrust the monk violently forward into the press of students, then ran left into another open corridor. The pursuers roared again, whooping and bellowing. Doctor Lucius shouted for order, but in vain, and Thomas heard the footsteps, saw a door to his right and slammed it open. A lavatorium! Three monks were at stool, perched on stone benches that ran down the sides of the stinking room, which had an arched door at its far end. The monks gaped at Thomas, but dared not move, and Thomas seized one by the beard and spilled him, naked arse, filth and all, across the floor. He did the same to a second one and ran on to the room's far end. Pursuers crowded into the lavatorium, tripped over the fallen monk, and Thomas was through the door. No bolt to lock it shut. A passageway stretched ahead with doors on either side. Monks' cells? He ran hard, cursing the old wound in his leg that meant he was not as fast as he used to be, but he was managing to stay ahead of his pursuers. He burst through a further door with a bolt on the wrong side. Through that into what seemed to be a laundry room with big stone bowls, jugs and heaps of robes. He spilt robes on the floor, pushed through a further door and was in a small enclosed herb garden. No one there and no way out except the door he had just used, and men were shouting in the passage, they were close, too close. It was raining harder. A high wall barred one side of the garden and Thomas jumped, took hold of the coping and used his huge archer's muscles to haul himself up. He kicked up a leg, straddled the wall, stood and ran along the wide coping to where the wall joined a sloping tiled roof. Men spilt into the herb garden as he climbed the roof. The rain made the tiles slippery and he flailed for a few heartbeats before scrambling up to the ridge. 'He's there!' the Irishman Keane shouted enthusiastically. 'Going towards the kitchens!'

Thomas ripped a tile from the roof and hurled it down at the students, then another. Keane swore vilely, ducked, and then Thomas was on the roof ridge, running, lost to sight, but he could hear the students whooping and shouting, released to the joy of the hunt. Chasing an heretical Englishman was far more enjoyable than discussing the four cardinal virtues or the necessity of infant baptism.

A crossbow bolt whipped past Thomas, and he looked left to see a man in the city's livery reloading a weapon on the scaffolding about a church. Damn. He sat on the ridge, then slid down the roof's greasy slope until his feet crashed hard into a small stone parapet. 'He's on the refectory!' a man shouted. Thomas ripped another tile free and hurled it far and high, through the rain and over the roof to fall wherever it might. He heard it crash home, heard the clatter of shards. 'Other way!' a voice called. 'He's on the chapter house!' A bell started to toll, then another joined in, and Thomas heard feet on the roof beyond the ridge. He looked left and right, saw no easy escape, and so peered cautiously over the low stone parapet. There was another garden beneath him, a small one, thick with fruit trees. 'Go left!' a voice shouted somewhere behind him.

'No, he went this way!' It was the Irish student, Keane, and he sounded very sure of himself. 'This way!' he bellowed, 'I saw the bastard!'

Thomas listened as the noise of the pursuit faded. Keane was taking them in entirely the wrong direction, yet even so Thomas was not out of danger. He had to find a way off the rooftops and so he decided to risk the small garden. He swung his legs over the parapet and sat there, hesitant because it was a long drop, then reckoned he had no choice. He jumped, thrashing through blossom and branches and wet leaves. He landed hard and was thrown forward onto his hands. There was a sharp pain in his right ankle so he stayed on all fours, listening to his pursuers, whose voices became fainter. Stay still, he thought. Stay still and let the hunters draw away. Wait.

'This crossbow,' the voice said very close behind him, 'is aimed at your backside. It's going to hurt you. So very much.'

★　　★　　★

180

It had been a stroke of genius, Father Marchant thought, to choose the Abbey of Saint Denis as the place where the Order of the Fisherman would have their vigil and receive their solemn consecration. There, beneath the roof's soaring stone vaults, under the evening light that glowed dust-rich through the glory of the stained-glass windows and before an altar heaped with golden vessels and lustrous with silver, the Knights of the Fisherman knelt to be blessed. A choir chanted, the melody seemed sad yet inspiring as the male voices rose and fell in the great abbey where the kings of France lay cold in their tombs and the oriflamme waited on the altar. The oriflamme was France's war banner, the great red silken pennant that flew above the king when he went into battle. It was sacred. 'It's new,' Arnoul d'Audrehem, a Marshal of France, growled to his companion, the Lord of Douglas. 'The goddamned English captured the last one at Crécy. They're probably wiping their arses with it now.'

Douglas grunted for answer. He was watching his nephew kneeling at the altar with four other men, where Father Marchant, resplendent in robes of crimson and white, said a mass. 'The Order of the bloody Fisherman,' Douglas said sarcastically.

'Rank nonsense, I agree,' d'Audrehem said, 'but a nonsense that might persuade the king to march south. That's what you want, isn't it?'

'I came here to fight the English. I want to march south and thrash the goddamned bastards.'

'The king is nervous,' d'Audrehem said, 'and he looks for a sign. Perhaps these Knights of the Fisherman will convince him?'

'He's nervous?'

'Of English arrows.'

'I've told you, they can be beaten.'

'By fighting on foot?' D'Audrehem sounded sceptical. He was in his fifties, old in war, a hard man with short grey hair and a jaw misshapen from the blow of a mace. He had known Douglas a long time, ever since, as a young man, d'Audrehem had campaigned in Scotland. He still shuddered at the memory of that cold, far land, at the thought of its food, its raw and comfortless castles, its bogs and crags and mists and moors, yet if he disliked the country he had nothing but admiration for its people. The Scots, he had told King Jean, were the finest fighters in Christendom, 'If indeed they are in Christendom, sire.'

'They're pagan?' the king had asked anxiously.

'No, sire, it is just that they live on the world's edge and they fight like demons to keep from falling off.'

And now two hundred of the demons were here in France, desperate for a chance to fight against their old enemy. 'We should be back in Scotland,' Douglas grumbled to d'Audrehem. 'I hear the truce is broken. We can kill the English there.'

'King Edward,' d'Audrehem said calmly, 'recaptured Berwick, the war is over, the English won. The truce is reinstated.'

182

'God damn Edward,' Douglas said.

'And you think the archers can be beaten by men on foot?' d'Audrehem asked.

'On foot,' the Lord of Douglas said. 'You can throw some mounted men at the bastards, but put good armour on their horses. It isn't the archers, it's the horses! Those damned arrows don't pierce armour, not good armour, but they play hell with horses. They drive the beasts mad. So you have knights being thrown, being trampled, their horses running wild with pain, and all because the archers aim at the horses. Arrows turn a cavalry charge into a charnel house, so don't give them horses to kill.' That had been a long speech from the usually taciturn Lord of Douglas.

'What you say makes sense,' d'Audrehem admitted. 'I was not at Crécy, but I hear the horses suffered.'

'But men on foot can carry shields,' Douglas said, 'or wear heavy armour. They can get close to the bastards and kill them. That's how it's done.'

'Is that how your king fought at, where was it? Durham?'

'He chose the wrong ground to fight on,' Douglas said, 'so now the poor bastard's a prisoner in London, and we can't pay the ransom.'

'Which is why you want the Prince of Wales?'

'I want the damned boy on his knees, pissing himself with fear, licking the horse shit off my boots and begging me to be kind.' Douglas gave a snort of laughter that echoed in the great abbey.

'And when I have him, I'll exchange him for my king.'

'He has a reputation,' d'Audrehem said mildly.

'For what? Gambling? Women? Luxury? For Christ's sake, he's a puppy.'

'Twenty-six? A puppy?'

'A puppy,' Douglas insisted, 'and we can cage him.'

'Or Lancaster.'

'Bugger Lancaster!' Douglas spat. Henry, Duke of Lancaster, had led an English army out of Brittany that was ravaging Maine and Anjou. King Jean had considered leading an army against him, leaving his eldest son to harry the Prince of Wales in the south, and that was what Douglas feared. Lancaster was no fool. Faced with a large army he would likely retreat to the great fortresses of Brittany, but Prince Edward of Wales was young and headstrong. He had survived the previous summer, leading his destructive army all the way to the Mediterranean and back to Gascony without meeting real opposition, and that surely had emboldened him for the campaign that had just begun. The prince, Douglas was sure, would march too far from his secure bases in Gascony, and so could be trapped and thrashed. The English prince was too irresponsible, too fond of his whores and of his gold, too addicted to the luxuries of privilege. And his ransom would be huge. 'We should be going south,' Douglas said, 'not farting about with fishermen nonsense.'

'If you want to go south,' d'Audrehem said, 'then give every help you can to the Order of the Fisherman. The king doesn't listen to us! But he listens to the cardinal. The cardinal can persuade him, and the cardinal wants to go south. So do whatever the cardinal wants.'

'I did! I let him take Sculley. For Christ's sake, Sculley isn't a man, he's an animal. He's got the strength of a bull, the claws of a bear, the teeth of a wolf, and the loins of a goat. He terrifies me, so God knows what he'll do to the English. But what in God's name does Bessières want of him?'

'Some relic, I'm told,' d'Audrehem said, 'and he believes the relic will give him the papacy, and the papacy will give him power. And if he does become Pope, my friend, then better to have him on your side than against you.'

'But making Sculley a knight, good Christ Almighty!' Douglas laughed.

Yet Sculley was there, at the steps of the high altar, kneeling between Robbie and a knight called Guiscard de Chauvigny, a man whose lands had been lost to the English in Brittany. De Chauvigny, like the other men, was famous for his exploits in tourneys across Europe. Only Roland de Verrec was missing, and Father Marchant had sent men far across France to find him. These were the best fighters the cardinal could recruit, the greatest warriors, men who struck fear into their opponents. Now they would kill for Christ, or at least for Cardinal Bessières. The last sunlight drained from the sky to leave the stained glass dark. Candles glowed and flickered on the many altars about the abbey where priests muttered prayers for the dead.

'You have been chosen,' Father Marchant said to the men who knelt in their armour before the altar. 'You have been chosen to be Saint Peter's warriors, the Knights of the Fisherman. Your task is great and your reward will be heavenly. Your sins are forgiven, you are freed from all earthly oaths, and you are granted the power of the angels to defeat your enemies. You will go forth from here as new men, bound to each other by loyalty and sealed to God by your sacred oath. You are His chosen and you will do His will and one day be received by Him in paradise.'

Robbie Douglas felt a surge of pure joy. For so long he had looked for a cause. He thought he had found it in the company of women, or in the friendship of other warriors, yet he knew he was a sinner, and that knowledge gave him misery. He gambled; he betrayed his promises. He was a feared fighter in the tournaments of Europe, yet felt himself to be weak. He knew his uncle despised him, but now, before the glittering altar and under the stern voice of Father Marchant, he sensed he had found his salvation. He was a Knight of the Fisherman, given a task by the church and promised a reward in heaven. He felt his soul lift to the moment's solemnity, and he swore to himself that he would serve this company of men with all his heart and strength.

'Stay and pray,' Father Marchant told the men, 'for tomorrow we set forth on our mission.'

'God be thanked,' Robbie said.

And Sculley farted. A noise that echoed off the abbey's walls and seemed to linger.

'Jesus,' Sculley said, 'that was a wet one.'

The Order of the Fisherman was consecrated and would go to war.

'The secret,' Thomas said, 'is to put a bolt in the groove.'

'A bolt?'

'A quarrel. An arrow?'

'Ah!' the woman said. 'I knew I'd forgotten something. That happens when you get ancient. You forget things. My husband did show me how to use one of these things,' she put the crossbow on a small wooden bench that stood between two orange trees, 'but I never did shoot one. I was tempted to shoot him, though. Are you running away?'

'Yes.'

'We're getting wet. Come inside.' The woman was old and bent, a tiny thing, hardly reaching Thomas's waist. Her face was shrewd, wrinkled and dark. She wore a nun's habit, but over it was a rich cloak of crimson wool trimmed with miniver.

'Where am I?' Thomas asked.

'You jumped into a convent. Saint Dorcas's convent. I suppose I should welcome you, so welcome.'

'Saint Dorcas?'

'She was full of good works, they tell me, so I'm sure she was a terrible bore.' The old woman went through a low doorway and Thomas, following her, picked up the crossbow. It was a beautiful weapon with a dark walnut stock inlaid with silver. 'It belonged to my husband,' the woman told him, 'and I have so little of his that I keep it so I can remember him. Not that I really wish to remember him. He was a peculiarly nasty man, rather like his son.'

'His son?' Thomas asked, putting the crossbow on a table.

'My son, too. The Count of Malbuisson. I am the dowager countess of the same county.'

'My lady,' Thomas said, and bowed to her.

'Goodness me! Manners are not dead!' the countess said happily, then sat in a well-cushioned chair and patted her lap. For a heartbeat Thomas thought she wanted him to sit there, but then, to his relief, a grey cat came from behind a chest and leaped onto her knees. She waved as if suggesting Thomas could sit anywhere, though he remained standing. The room was small, just four or five paces in each direction, yet filled with furniture that seemed to belong to a great hall. There was a table draped with a tapestry, two big chests, a bench, and three chairs. Four massive silver candlesticks stood on the table with some bowls, plates, and an ornate chess set, while on the limewashed walls hung a crucifix and three leather panels, one painted with a hunting scene, another with a ploughman, and the third showing a shepherd and his flock. A tapestry depicting two unicorns in a grove of roses hung over a small arch, presumably hiding the countess's bedchamber. 'And you are?' the countess asked.

'My name is Thomas.'

'Thomas! Is that English? Or Norman? You sound English, I think.'

'I'm English, though my father was French.'

'I always liked mongrels,' the countess said. 'Why are you running away?'

'It's a very long story.'

'I like long stories. I have been shut away here, because otherwise I would be spending money that my daughter-in-law would prefer to squander, so here I am with nothing but nuns to keep me company. They're dear women,' she paused, 'on the whole, but quite tedious. You will find some wine on the table. It isn't very good wine, but better than no wine. I like mine mixed with water, which is in the Spanish jug. So who is chasing you?'

'Everyone.'

'You must be a very wicked man! How splendid! What did you do?'

'I'm accused of heresy,' Thomas said, 'and of abducting another man's wife.'

'Oh dear,' the countess said. 'Would you be very charming and give me that blanket? The dark one? It's rarely cold here, but today is distinctly chilly. Are you a heretic?'

'No.'

'Someone must think you are! What did you do? Deny the Trinity?'

'I upset a cardinal.'

'That's not very wise of you. Which one?'

'Bessières.'

'Oh, that man is quite horrid! A pig! But a dangerous pig.' She paused, thinking. There were voices beyond the inner door, women's voices, but faint. 'We hear things in the convent,' the countess went on, 'news from the world. Didn't I hear that Bessières was looking for the Holy Grail?'

'He was. He didn't find it.'

'Oh, my dear, of course he didn't. I doubt it exists!'

'Probably not,' Thomas said, lying. He knew it existed because he had found it, and having found it he had thrown it into the ocean where it could do no harm. And the sword he sought? Was he to hide that too?

'So whose wife did you steal?' the countess asked.

'The Count of Labrouillade's.'

The countess clapped her thin hands. 'Oh, I like you more and more! Well done! Well done! Labrouillade is a vile creature! I always felt sorry for that girl, Bertille. A pretty little thing, too! I can't imagine her marriage bed, or rather I can! How horrible. It would be like being rutted by a grunting sack of rancid lard. Didn't she run off with young Villon?'

'Yes. I got her back, then took her away again.'

'You make it sound very complicated, so you'll have to begin at the beginning.' The countess suddenly paused, bent forward in her chair and hissed between her teeth. The hiss ended in a moan.

'You're unwell,' Thomas said.

'I'm dying,' she said. 'You would think that all the doctors in this city could do something, but they can't. Well, one of them wants to cut me open, but I'm not allowing that! So they smell my water and then say I should pray. Pray! Well, I do.'

'There's no medicine?'

'Not for living eighty-two years, my dear, that is incurable.' She was rocking backwards and forwards in her chair, clutching the blanket to her breasts. She took deep breaths and slowly seemed to feel less pain. 'There's some mandrake wine in a green bottle, there, on the table. The nuns of the infirmary boil it up for me, they're very kind. It does relieve the pain, though it makes my mind very wobbly. Would you pour me a cup? No water with it, my dear, and then you can tell me your tale.'

Thomas gave her the medicine and then told her some of his tale, how he had been hired to defeat Villon and how Labrouillade had tried to cheat him. 'So Bertille is in your fortress?' the countess asked. 'Because your wife likes her?'

'Yes.'

'Does she have children?'

'Bertille? None.'

'That's a blessing. If she had children, that

wretched Labrouillade would use them to lure her back. Instead you can just kill Labrouillade and make her a widow! That's an excellent solution. Widows have so many more choices.'

'Is that why you're here?'

She shrugged. 'It's a refuge, I suppose? My son doesn't like me, his wife hates me, and I was too old to find a new husband. So here I am, just me and Nicholas.' She stroked the cat. 'So Labrouillade wants you dead, but he's not here in Montpellier, is he? So who was chasing you?'

'Labrouillade sent a man to fight me. He started the chase and the students all joined in.'

'Who did Labrouillade send?'

'He's called Roland de Verrec.'

'Oh, my dear!' The countess seemed amused. 'Young Roland? I knew his grandmother very well, poor soul. I hear he's a wonderful fighter, but oh dear, no brain.'

'No brain?'

'It's been rotted by romances, my dear. He reads all those ridiculous stories of knightly valour and, being brainless, believes them. I blame his mother; she's a forceful creature, all prayers and spite, and he, poor thing, believes everything she says. She tells him chivalry exists, which I suppose it does, but never in her husband, who was a goat. Not like his son! The virgin knight!' she chuckled. 'How silly can a young man be? And he's very silly. You heard how the Virgin Mary appeared to him?'

'Everyone's heard that.'

'He was just a silly boy and I suppose his mother made him drunk! I'm sure the Virgin Mary has better things to do than spoil a young man's life. Dear me, poor boy! Now young Roland dreams of being a knight at your King Arthur's round table. I'm afraid you'll have to kill him.'

'I will?'

'You'd better! Or else he'll regard you as a quest and pursue you to the ends of the earth.'

'He pursued me here,' Thomas said ruefully.

'But what on earth are you doing in Montpellier?'

'I wanted to consult a scholar.'

'There are plenty of those here,' she said dismissively, 'and a very motley band they are too. They spend their time fighting each other over the silliest things, but maybe that's what scholars do. Can I ask why you wanted to consult one?'

'I'm looking for a saint.'

'Those are in very short supply! What kind of saint?'

'It was a painting I saw,' Thomas said, and described the monk kneeling in the grass around which the snow had fallen thick. 'It tells a story,' he said, 'but no one seems to know it, and no one can tell me who he is.'

'A frozen saint, by the sound of it, but why do you need to know?'

Thomas hesitated. 'My liege lord,' he finally said, 'has charged me with finding a relic, and I think that saint has something to do with it.'

'You're as bad as Roland! On a quest indeed!'

she chuckled. 'There's a book somewhere on that table, my dear. Bring it to me.'

Before Thomas could find the book there were women's voices sounding close outside, and then a timorous knock on the door. 'Madame? My lady?' someone called.

'What do you want?'

'Are you alone, my lady?'

'I have a man in here,' the countess called, 'a young man, and very virile. You were right, Sister Véronique, God does answer prayers.'

The door was pushed, but the countess had bolted it. 'Madame?' Sister Véronique called again.

'Don't be silly, sister,' the countess said, 'I mumble aloud, nothing more.'

'Very good, madame.'

'Bring me the book,' the countess said, lowering her voice slightly. It was a small volume, hardly bigger than Thomas's hand. The countess untied the laces and unwrapped the soft leather cover. 'It belonged to my mother-in-law,' she said, 'and she was a dear woman! Lord knows how she gave birth to a monster like Henri. I suppose the stars were badly aligned when she conceived him, or else Saturn was in the ascendancy. No child conceived when Saturn is rising will come to any good. Men never care about details like that, but they really should. It's rather pretty, isn't it?' She handed Thomas the book.

It was a psalter. Thomas's father had owned one, though not as richly decorated as this book, which interspersed the words of the seven penitential psalms with beautifully painted illustrations touched with bright gold leaf. The letters were very large so that only a few words could be written on any one page. 'My mother-in-law didn't see well,' the countess explained when Thomas remarked on the size of the words, 'so the monks made the letters big. That was kind of them.'

Most of the pictures, Thomas saw, were of saints. There was Radegonde with her crown, pictured amidst a pile of masonry while, behind her, a great church was being built. He turned the stiff page to see an horrific depiction of Saint Leodeger being blinded, a soldier piercing the bishop's eye with an awl. 'Isn't that horrid?' The countess was leaning forward to see the pictures. 'They tore his tongue out too. Henri always threatened to tear mine out, but he never did. I suppose I should be grateful. That's Clémentin.'

'Being martyred?'

'Oh indeed, disembowelment is a certain path to sainthood, poor man.' Then there was Saint Remigius baptising a naked man in a great cauldron. 'That was Clovis being baptised,' the countess explained, 'and wasn't he the first King of France?'

'I think so,' Thomas said.

'I suppose we should be grateful that he became a Christian then,' the countess said, then leaned forward to turn a page and so reveal Saint Christophe carrying the infant Jesus. The slaughter of the innocents was painted in the background, but the bearded saint had safely taken the baby Christ away from the field littered with dozens of blood-spattered dead and dying children. 'Saint Christophe looks as if he's going to drop the baby, doesn't he? I always think Jesus must have just wet him, or something. Men are quite hopeless with babies. Oh, poor girl.' This last comment was because Saint Apolline was shown being sawn in two by a pair of soldiers. Her belly was ripped open, blood spilling down the page, while she looked prayerfully towards angels peeping from behind a cloud. 'I always wonder why the angels don't come down and save her!' the countess said. 'It must be very unpleasant, being sawn in half, but they just hover in the clouds doing nothing! That's not very angelic. And that man's a fool!' Thomas had turned a page to show a depiction of Saint Maurice kneeling amidst the remnants of his legion. Maurice had encouraged his men to be martyred rather than assault a Christian town, and his fellow Romans had obliged his pious wish, and the painter showed a swathe of broken, bloodied bodies scattered across a field while the killers advanced on the kneeling saint. 'Why didn't he fight?' the countess asked. 'They say he had six thousand soldiers, yet he just encourages them to be slaughtered like lambs. Sometimes I think you must be extremely stupid to become a saint.'

Thomas turned the last page and froze.

Because there he was, the monk in the snow.

The countess smiled. 'You see? You didn't need a scholar, just an old lady.'

This picture differed from the painting in Avignon. The monk in the book was not kneeling in the cleared patch, but lying down, curled up in sleep. There was no Saint Peter, but there was a small house on the right-hand side, and a second monk was peeping through a window. The sleeping monk, who had the halo of a saint, was lying on grass, but the rest of the landscape, like the roof of the cottage, was smothered in deep snow. It was night-time, and the stars were painted against a rich dark-blue sky, and a single angel watched from among those stars, while in the page's flower-painted border was the name of the saint.

'Saint Junien,' Thomas said. 'I've never heard of him.'

'I doubt many people have!'

'Junien,' he said the name again.

'He was a nobleman's son,' the countess said, 'and he must have been very pious because he walked a very long way to study under Saint Amand, but he arrived at night and Amand had locked his door. So Junien knocked on the door. But Saint Amand thought it must be bandits coming to rob him, so he refused to open the door. I can't understand why Junien didn't explain himself! It was winter, it was snowing, and all he had to do was tell Amand who he was! But apparently Junien was as stupid as the rest, and because he couldn't get into Amand's house he lay down to sleep in the garden, and, as you can see, God kindly made sure that the snow didn't fall on him. So he had a good night's sleep and next day the misunderstanding was happily cleared up. It isn't a very exciting story.'

'Saint Junien,' Thomas repeated the name, staring at the sleeping monk. 'But why is he in the book?' he wondered aloud.

'Look in the front,' the countess suggested.

Thomas turned back the stiff pages to see that a coat of arms was painted on the very first page. It showed a red lion rearing against a white background. The lion snarled and had its claws extended. 'I don't know that badge,' he said.

'My mother-in-law came from Poitou,' the countess explained, 'and the red lion is the symbol of Poitou. All the saints in that book, my dear, have connections with Poitou, and I suppose there simply weren't enough of them who were blinded, scalded, beheaded, disembowelled or sawn in half, so they added poor little Junien just to fill a page.'

'But not Saint Peter,' Thomas said.

'I don't think Saint Peter was ever in Poitou, so why would he be in the book?'

'I thought Saint Junien met him.'

'I'm sure all the saints visited each other, my dear, just to chat about happy things like the litany, or which of their friends had recently been burned or skinned alive, but Saint Peter died long before Junien was caught in the snow.'

'Of course he did,' Thomas said, 'but there is a link between Junien and Peter.'

'I wouldn't know,' the countess said.

'But someone will,' Thomas said, 'in Poitou.'

'In Poitou, yes, probably, but first you have to leave Montpellier,' the countess said, amused.

Thomas half smiled. 'Back over the wall to the monastery, I suppose.'

'I'm sure whoever's looking for you will be watching the monastery. But if you can bear to wait till nightfall?'

'If you don't mind,' Thomas said gallantly.

'You can leave after dark. Once Compline is said the nuns do like to sleep. Straight out of my door, down the passage, and there's a way out to the street through the almoner's room which is at the far end. It won't take you more than a minute, but till then we must pass several hours together.' She looked at him dubiously, then suddenly brightened. 'Tell me, do you play chess?'

'A little,' Thomas said.

'I used to be adequate,' the countess said, 'but old age?' She sighed and looked down at the cat. 'My mind is as fluffy as your fur, isn't it?'

'If it would please you to play,' Thomas said.

'I won't play well,' she said sadly, 'but all the same, shall we make it more intriguing by playing for money?'

'If you like,' Thomas said.

'Say a leopard for each game?' she suggested.

Thomas flinched. A leopard was worth almost

five shillings of English money, a week's wages for a highly skilled craftsman. 'A leopard?' he asked, prevaricating.

'Just to make it interesting. But you must pardon my forgetfulness. The mandrake wine makes me dozy, I fear,' she sounded vague, but managed to pull herself together, 'very dozy, and I do make the silliest mistakes.'

'Then perhaps we shouldn't play for money.'

'I can afford a few leopards,' she said tentatively, 'maybe one or two, and it does add spice to the game, doesn't it?'

'A leopard, then,' Thomas agreed.

The countess smiled and gestured that he should bring the chess board and pieces to the small table beside her chair. 'You can play silver, my dear,' she said, and she was still smiling as Thomas advanced his first pawn. 'This is going to hurt you,' she went on, sounding anything but vague, 'so very much!'

CHAPTER 6

It was easier leaving the convent than Thomas had dared to hope. The countess had been right. Down the passage, through a room stacked with vile-smelling cast-off clothes that were to be given to the poor, and out to the street through a door secured by a single bolt. Thomas had been given a lesson in chess and was seven leopards poorer, but he had discovered the name of the saint receiving Peter's sword, though that knowledge was useless unless he managed to escape Montpellier. He had waited till deep in the night before leaving the convent, knowing that the city gates would be locked till dawn. He would have to wait till then, because he doubted he would be able to drop down from the walls. The city's flag-hung ramparts had looked too high and were doubtless well guarded.

He drew his dark cloak around him. It had stopped raining, but the streets were still wet, glistening the shivering reflection of a feeble lantern hanging in the archway of a house across the street. He needed somewhere to hide till sunrise, and then he needed good fortune to escape the men who were doubtless hunting for him.

'A soldier who speaks Latin,' the voice said, 'now isn't that just a miracle?' Thomas turned fast, then stopped. The two tines of a pitchfork were pointing at his belly, and holding the pitchfork was the tall Irish student, Master Keane. He was swathed in his scholar's gown, black in the night. 'I'm supposing you still have the knife,' Keane said, 'but I'm thinking my pitchfork will pierce your guts before you can cut my throat.'

'I don't want to kill you,' Thomas said.

'Now that's a relief to hear, and there was me worrying that I'd be dead before Matins.'

'Just put the pitchfork down,' Thomas said.

'I'm comfortable where it is,' Keane said, 'and feeling sort of pleased with myself.'

'Why?'

'They all chased you half around the town like a bunch of puppies hunting a stag, but I reckoned you could only have dropped into Saint Dorcas's, and right I was. Now isn't that clever of me?'

'Very clever,' Thomas said, 'so why did you send them all away from Saint Dorcas's?'

'Away?'

'I heard you shouting I'd gone in the other direction.'

'Because they're offering money to the man who catches you! To a poor student that's a wonderful enticement! Why share it with others? I keep the pitchfork just where it is and I get a couple of months of free ale, free whores, free wine, and singing.'

'I'll offer you more,' Thomas said.

'Now that's good to hear. The singing's free, of course, but the ale, wine, and the whores? Expensive in this town. Have you ever noticed how the whores' fees go up in towns where there's a lot of churchmen? Strange that, or perhaps not considering how many customers the girls have, and that's a fact. So what will you pay me?'

'I'll spare your life.'

'My God, the mouse offers the pussycat its life!'

'Drop the pitchfork,' Thomas said, 'help me get out of this town and I'll pay you enough to whore for a year.'

'Your woman's been captured,' Keane said.

Thomas felt his body chill. He stared at the young Irishman. 'Is that true?'

'Stopped at the north gate, taken with three men and a bairn. Sire Roland de Verrec has her, so he does.'

'Dear God,' Thomas said. 'Do you know where she is?'

'The rumour says that the virgin knight is taking her west to Toulouse, but that's only what they said in the Stork Tavern, and half the things you hear in there are fables. Last year they said the world would end on Saint Arnulf's Day, but we're still breathing. D'you think he really is a virgin?'

'How would I know?'

'Just seems curious to me. A virgin! And a good-looking fellow he is too.'

Thomas leaned against the convent wall and closed his eyes. Genevieve taken. The church still pursued her because, when Thomas had first met her, she was in a condemned cell, waiting to be burned on the charge of being a *beghard*, a heretic. He swore.

'It's no good quoting the psalmist,' Keane said.

Thomas kept his eyes closed. 'I'm going to take that pitchfork off you,' he said bitterly, 'and ram it through your belly.'

'That's not the best idea you've ever had,' Keane said, 'because I won't be much good to you with a pitchfork through my entrails.'

Thomas opened his eyes. The pitchfork had dropped so that it was pointing at his legs. 'You want to help me?'

'My father's a chief, see? And I'm the third son, and that's a bit like being the fifth hoof on a horse, so he wants me to be a priest, God help me, because it always helps to have a priest in the family. It makes the forgiveness of sins so much more convenient, but it's not to my taste. My elder brothers get to fight and I'm doomed to pray, but I don't do my best work on my knees. So I just need someone to give me a horse, a coat of mail, and a sword and I'll be a great deal happier.'

'Oh God, you and Brother Michael?'

'That monk? I thought he was with you, but no

one would believe me. He didn't look frightened enough when you had that knife at his throat.'

'What's your name?' Thomas asked.

'Éamonn Óg Ó Keane,' Keane said, 'but take no notice of the Óg.'

'Why not?'

'Just don't. It means I'm younger than my father, but we all are, aren't we? It'll be a strange day in paradise when we're older than our fathers.'

'Well, Éamonn Óg Ó Keane,' Thomas said, 'you are now one of my men-at-arms.'

'And thank the good Christ for that,' Keane said, lowering the pitchfork to the cobbles. 'No more of that little turd Roger de Beaufort. How can he believe a wee baby is doomed to hell? But he does! The cretinous little slug will end up as Pope, you mark my words.'

Thomas waved the Irishman to silence. Where was Genevieve? Wherever she was the only thing Thomas could be sure about was that he needed to get out of this city. 'Your first duty,' he told the Irishman, 'is to get us through the gates.'

'That'll be difficult. They're offering a rare reward for your capture.'

'They?'

'The city consuls.'

'So get me out of the city,' Thomas said.

'Shit,' Keane said after a brief pause.

'Shit?'

'Shit-carts, turd-wagons really,' the Irishman said. 'They collect the stuff and cart it out of the city, at least they do from the rich folks' homes. The poor folk just wade in the muck, but there's enough rich people to keep the dung-carts rolling. There's usually a couple of wagons waiting to leave the city when the gates open, and,' he paused to look earnestly at Thomas, 'you can trust my word on this opinion, the city guards don't take a real close look at the carts. They sort of step back, hold their noses, wave them through and wish them God speed.'

'But first,' Thomas said, 'go to the tavern by Saint Pierre's church and . . .'

'The Blind Tits, you mean?'

'The tavern by Saint Pierre's . . .'

'The Blind Tits,' Keane said, 'that's what it's called in town on account that the sign shows Saint Lucia with no eyes and a ripe pair . . .'

'Just go there,' Thomas said, 'and find Brother Michael.' The reluctant monk had been lodging at the tavern, and Thomas hoped he would have reliable news about Genevieve's fate.

'I'll be waking the tavern,' Keane said dubiously.

'Then wake it.' Thomas dared not go himself because he was certain the tavern was being watched. He took a coin from his pouch. 'Buy some wine, loosen their tongues. Look for that monk, Brother Michael. See if he knows what happened to Genevieve.'

'She's your wife, yes?' Keane asked, then frowned. 'Can you believe Saint Lucia dug her own eyes out? Jesus! And all because a man complimented her eyes? Thank Christ he didn't like her tits! Still, she'd have made a good wife.'

Thomas gaped at the young Irishman. 'A good wife?'

'My father always says that the best marriage is between a blind woman and a deaf man. So where will I find you after I've loosened the tongues?'

Thomas pointed at an alleyway beside the convent. 'I'll wait there.'

'And then we become shit-haulers. Jesus, I love being a man-at-arms. Do you want this Brother Michael to join us?'

'Christ, no. Tell him his duty is to learn medicine.'

'Poor fellow. He's going to be a piss-taster?'

'Go,' Thomas said. Keane went.

Thomas hid in the alley, sheltered by shadows black as a monk's cowl. He heard the rats scuttling through the rubbish, a man snoring behind a shuttered window, a baby crying. A pair of watchmen carrying lanterns strolled past the convent, but neither looked down the alley where Thomas closed his eyes and prayed for Genevieve. If Roland de Verrec handed her to the church then she would be condemned again. But surely, he thought, the virgin knight would hold her for ransom, the ransom being Bertille, Countess of Labrouillade, and that meant de Verrec would keep her safe till the exchange was done. The sword of Saint Peter could wait; Thomas would settle with the virgin knight first.

* * *

It was almost dawn when Keane returned. 'Your monk wasn't there,' he said, 'but there was an ostler with a flapping tongue. And you're in trouble because the city guard are told to look for a man with a mangled left hand. Was that a battle?'

'A Dominican torturer.'

Keane flinched as he looked at the hand. 'Jesus. What did he do?'

'A screw-press.'

'Ah, they're not allowed to draw blood, are they, because God doesn't like it, but those fellows can still wake you out of a deep sleep.'

'Brother Michael wasn't at the tavern?'

'He was not, and my fellow hadn't seen him and didn't even seem to know who I was talking about.'

'Good, he's gone to learn medicine.'

'A lifetime of sipping piss,' Keane said, 'but the ostler did tell me your other fellow left the city yesterday.'

'Roland de Verrec?'

'That's the man. He took your wife and bairn westwards.'

'Westwards?' Thomas asked, puzzled.

'He was sure of that.'

So de Verrec was going towards Toulouse? What was at Toulouse? Questions seethed and provoked no answers; all Thomas could be sure of was that Roland had left Montpellier and that suggested the virgin knight was no longer interested in Thomas. He possessed Genevieve and must have known he could exchange her for Bertille, while

Thomas, Roland would assume, would be captured by the city guard of Montpellier. 'Where are these shit-wagons?'

Keane led him westwards. The first house doors were opening. Women carried pails to the city wells, and a stout girl was selling goat's milk beside a stone crucifix. Thomas kept his wounded hand hidden beneath his cloak as Keane led him through alleys and small streets, and past yards where cattle bellowed. The city's church bells were ringing, summoning the faithful to early prayers. Thomas followed the Irishman downhill to where the streets were uncobbled and the mud stained with blood. This was where cattle were butchered, where the city's poor lived, and where the stench of sewage led them to a small square in which three carts were parked. Each cart had a pair of oxen in harness, and their beds were filled with big-bellied barrels. 'Jesus, but rich people's shit stinks,' Keane said.

'Where are the carters?'

'They drink in the Widow,' Keane pointed to a small tavern, 'and the widow is a tough old biddy who also owns the wagons, and the wine is part of their wages. They're supposed to leave when the gates open, but they tend to linger over their wine, which is a surprise.'

'A surprise?'

'The wine is just horrible. Tastes like cow piss.'

'How would you know?'

'That's a question worthy of Doctor Lucius. Are you sure you want to do this?'

'How the hell else do I get out of the city?'

'The trick of it,' Keane said, 'is to wriggle between two of the barrels. Just worm your way in to the centre of the cart and no one will ever know you're there. I'll let you know when it's safe to wriggle out.'

'You're not hiding with me?'

'They're not looking for me!' the Irishman said. 'You're the fellow they want to hang.'

'Hang me?'

'Jesus, you're an Englishman! Thomas of Hookton! Leader of the Hellequin! Sure they want to hang you! There'll be a bigger crowd than Whore Sunday!'

'What's Whore Sunday?'

'Nearest Sunday to the Feast of Saint Nicholas. The girls are supposed to give it away that day, but I've not seen it happen. And you've not a lot of time.' He stopped as an upstairs shutter opened across the small square. A man looked out, yawned, then vanished. Cockerels were crowing all through the town. A pile of rags stirred in a corner of the square and Thomas realised it was a beggar sleeping. 'Not a lot of time at all,' Keane went on. 'The gates are open so the wagons will be rolling soon enough.'

'Sweet Jesus,' Thomas said.

'You'll smell more like Judas Iscariot when you're done. I should jump on now, there's no one watching.'

Thomas ran across the small square and pushed

himself up onto the rearmost wagon. The smell was enough to fell a bear. The barrels were old, they leaked, or rather oozed, and the wagon's bed was inch-deep in slime. He heard Keane chuckle, then took a deep breath and forced his way between two of the vast tubs. There was just space between the rows for a man to be concealed beneath the barrel's bulging bellies. Something dripped on his head. Flies crawled on his face and neck. He tried to breathe shallowly as he wriggled his way to the centre of the cart where he pulled the hood of his cloak over his head. The mail coat with its leather lining offered some protection from the slimy muck, but he could feel the filth seeping beneath the mail to soak his shirt and chill his skin.

He did not need to wait long. He heard voices, felt the wagon lurch as two men climbed up to perch on the foremost barrels, then the crack of a whip. The cart jerked forward, its single axle squealing. Every jolt banged Thomas's head against the seeping side of a barrel. The journey seemed endless, but at least Keane had been right about the guards, who must have simply waved the three carts through the city's gate with no attempt at an inspection because the wagon did not stop as it went from the shadows of the city to the sunlight of the countryside. Keane was walking just beside the oxen, chatting happily to the drivers, and then the cart gave an almighty lurch as it was driven down a bank. Liquid slopped in the barrels and some spilled over onto Thomas's back. He cursed under his breath, then cursed again as the wagon juddered across some ruts. Keane was telling a long story about a dog that had stolen a leg of lamb from Saint Stephen's monastery, but suddenly spoke in English, 'Wriggle out now!' The Irishman went on with his tale as Thomas inched backwards through fresh muck, every jolt of the cart driving the filth deeper into his clothes.

He threw himself off the back, landing on the grassy ridge between the track's wheel ruts. The wagon, oblivious that it had held a passenger, rumbled on. Keane came back, grinning. 'Jesus, you look just terrible.'

'Thank you.'

'I got you out of the city, didn't I?'

'You're a living saint,' Thomas said. 'Now all we have to do is find horses, weapons, and a way to get ahead of Roland.'

He was in a sunken lane between two high banks beyond which were olive groves. The lane dropped to a riverbank where the first cart was tipping its barrels into the water. A brown stain drifted downstream. 'And how do we find horses?' Keane asked wistfully.

'First things first,' Thomas said. He slapped at a fly, then climbed the roadside bank and walked north through the olives.

'So what's first?' Keane asked.

'The river.'

Thomas walked till he was out of sight of the three carts, then stripped off his clothes and

212

plunged into the water. It was cold. 'Jesus, you're scarred,' Keane said.

'If you want to stay beautiful,' Thomas said, 'don't be a soldier. And throw me my clothes.'

Keane kicked the clothes into the river rather than touch them. Thomas kneaded them, trampled them, scrubbed at them with a rock till no more stain coloured the water, then he plunged the mail coat in and out of a pool, trying to rid the links and leather of the stink. He ducked his head a last time, ran fingers through his hair, and climbed onto the bank. He wrung out the clothes as best he could, then put them on still wet. He carried the mail coat. It would be another warm day and his shirt and hose would dry fast enough. 'North,' he said curtly. The first thing was to find the men-at-arms he had left at the ruined mill.

'Horses and weapons, you said?' Keane asked.

'How much are they offering for me?'

'The weight of your right hand in gold coins, I heard.'

'My hand?' Thomas asked, then understood. 'Because I'm an archer.'

'That's just the beginning. The weight of your right hand in gold and the weight of your severed head in silver. They hate English archers.'

'It's a small fortune,' Thomas said, 'so I dare say the horses and weapons will find us.'

'Find us?'

'Soon enough folk will wonder if I escaped the

city, so they'll come looking. Till then we keep going north.'

Thomas thought of Genevieve as he walked. She had been terrified when he first met her, and why not? A pyre had been made outside her prison and she was supposed to have been burned as a heretic, and the prospect of that holy fire was a scar in her memory. It would be torturing her now. He assumed she and Hugh were safe for the moment, at least until Roland could find Bertille, but what then? The virgin knight was mocked for his rectitude, but he was famed for being incorruptible, so would he meekly exchange Genevieve and Hugh for Bertille? Or would he think it his sacred duty to give Genevieve to the church so it could finish the business it had started so long ago? Thomas desperately needed to reach Karyl and his other men-at-arms. He needed men, he needed weapons, he needed a horse.

They were following the river northwards. The sun rose higher and the olive trees gave way to vineyards. He could see five men and three women tilling between the terraces a mile or so away, but otherwise the countryside was empty. He kept to the low ground where he could, but always heading towards the hills. Roland, he thought, would be at least five leagues away from the city by now. 'I should have killed him,' he said.

'Roland?'

'I had an archer aiming at his fat head. I should have let him shoot.'

'A hard man to kill, that one. He looks willowy, doesn't he? But I saw him fight in Toulouse and, by Jesus, he's fast! Quick as a snake.'

'I need to get ahead of him.' Thomas was talking more to himself than to Keane. But why Toulouse? 'Because it's safe,' he said aloud.

'Safe?'

'Toulouse,' Thomas said, 'we can't follow him into Toulouse. It belongs to the Count of Armagnac, and his men patrol the road north, but that means it's a safe route for de Verrec.' De Verrec needed to keep Genevieve unharmed till she was exchanged. Then the answer was tumbling in his head. 'He's not going to Toulouse, he's taking the road through Gignac.'

Keane looked blank. 'Gignac?'

'There's a road through Gignac, it joins the main road north from Toulouse. He'll be safer on that route.'

'You're sure the man is going north?'

'He's going to Labrouillade!' That was the obvious destination. Genevieve could be held there until Bertille was surrendered.

'How far's Labrouillade?'

'Five or six days on horseback,' Thomas said. 'And we can go through the hills, it's quicker.' Or it would be quicker if he was sure that no *coredor* ambushed him on the way. He needed his men-at-arms. He needed his archers with their long war bows and goose-fledged arrows. He needed a miracle.

There were villages ahead. They had to be skirted. The countryside was coming alive as more men went to the fields or vineyards. Those labourers were all far away, but Thomas had grown up in the countryside and knew that such men missed nothing. Most of them would never travel more than a few miles from home in all their lives, but they knew every tree, bush and beast within that small area, and something as small as the flight of a bird could alert them to an intruder, and once they thought that the reward of gold equal to the weight of a man's hand was within their reach they would be implacable. Thomas felt despair. 'If I were you,' he said to Keane, 'I'd go back to the city now.'

'Why, for God's sake?'

'Because I'm wasting my time,' Thomas said bitterly.

'You've reached this far,' Keane said, 'so why give up now?'

'And why the hell are you with me? You should just go and fetch that reward.'

'Oh Jesus, if I have to sit through another year of Doctor Lucius's lectures and listen to that miserable worm Roger de Beaufort I'll go mad, I will. They say you make men rich!'

'Is that what you want?'

'I want to be on a horse,' Keane said, 'riding the world like a free man. A woman would be nice, or two. Three even!' He grinned and looked at Thomas. 'I want to be outside the rules.'

'How old are you?'

'I'm never sure because I was never good at counting, but it's probably eighteen by now. That or nineteen.'

'The rules keep you alive,' Thomas said. His damp clothes were chafing and his boots had broken a seam.

'The rules keep you in your place,' Keane said, 'and other people make the rules and thump you if you break them, which is why you broke them, yes?'

'I was sent to Oxford,' Thomas said. 'Like you I was meant to be a priest.'

'So that's how you know the Latin?'

'My father taught me from the first. Latin, Greek, French.'

'And now you're Sir Thomas Hookton, leader of the Hellequin! You didn't keep to the rules now, did you?'

'I'm an archer,' Thomas said. And an archer without a bow, he thought. 'And you'll find I make the rules for the Hellequin.'

'What are they?'

'We share the plunder, we don't abandon each other, and we don't rape.'

'Ah, they said you were remarkable. Did you hear that?'

'What?'

'A hound? Two perhaps? Giving tongue?'

Thomas stopped. They had left the river and were walking faster because they had entered a chestnut wood that hid them from prying eyes.

He heard the small wind in the leaves, a wood-pecker far off, then the baying. 'Damn,' he said.

'Could just be hunting.'

'Hunting what?' Thomas asked, then moved to the wood's edge. There was a dry ditch, and beyond it neatly bound stacks of chestnut stakes that were used to support vines. The terraces of the vineyard curved away and down to the river valley and the sound of the dogs, there was more than one, came from that low ground. He ran a few paces into the vineyard, keeping low, and saw three horsemen and two hounds. They could have been hunting anything, he thought, but he suspected their quarry was an archer's hand. Two were holding spears. The hounds had their noses to the ground and were leading the horsemen towards the chestnuts. 'I forgot about dogs.' Thomas said when he was back among the trees.

'They'll be just fine,' Keane said with a blithe confidence.

'They're not after your right hand,' Thomas said, 'and they'll have our scent by now. If you want to leave me this would be a good time.'

'Christ no!' Keane said. 'I'm one of your men, remember? We don't abandon each other.'

'Then stay here. Try not to get savaged by a hound.'

'Dogs love me,' the Irishman said.

'I'm relying on the idea that they'll call the hounds off before they bite you.'

'They'll not bite me, just you see.'

'Just stand there,' Thomas said, 'and be quiet. I want them to think you're alone.' He leaped for the low branch of a tree and, using the huge muscles made by the war bow, hauled himself up till he was hidden among the leaves. He crouched on a branch. Everything depended on where the horsemen stopped, and surely they would. He could hear them now, hear the heavy fall of the hooves and the faster sound of the dogs who were racing ahead. Keane, to Thomas's astonishment, had fallen to his knees and was holding his clasped hands high in prayer. Much good that would do him, Thomas reckoned, and then the hounds were in sight. A pair of grey-coated wolfhounds with slavering jaws who raced towards the Irishman, and Keane simply opened his eyes, spread his arms and clicked his fingers.

'Good doggies,' the Irishman said. The wolf-hounds were whining now. One had laid itself at Keane's knees, the other was licking an outspread hand. 'Down, boy,' Keane said in French, then scratched both dogs between the ears. 'And what a fine morning it is to be chasing an Englishman, yes?'

The horsemen were close now. They had slowed their horses to a trot as they ducked beneath the low branches. 'Goddamned dogs,' one of them said in astonishment at the sight of the wolfhounds succumbing to Keane's blandishments. 'Who are you?' the man called.

'A man at prayer,' Keane answered, 'and good morrow to you all, gentlemen.'

'Prayer?'

'God has called me to His priesthood,' Keane said in a sanctimonious tone, 'and I feel closest to Him when I pray beneath the trees in the dawn of His good day. God bless you, and what are you gentlemen doing abroad this early in the day?' His black homespun gown gave him a convincingly clerical appearance.

'We're hunting,' one of the men said in an amused tone.

'You're not French,' another said.

'I am from Ireland, the land of Saint Patrick, and I prayed to Saint Patrick to quell the anger of your dogs. Aren't they just the sweetest beasts?'

'Eloise! Abelard!' the horseman called his hounds, but neither moved. They stayed with Keane.

'And what are you hunting?' Keane asked.

'An Englishman.'

'You'll not find him here,' Keane said, 'and if it's the fellow I'm thinking you're after then surely he'll still be inside the city?'

'Maybe,' one said. He and his companions were to Thomas's left, Keane was to his right, and Thomas needed the horsemen to be closer. He could just see them through the leaves. Three young men, richly dressed in fine cloth with feathers in their caps and long boots in their stirrups. Two were holding wide-bladed boar-spears with cross-pieces just behind the heads, and all three had swords. 'And maybe not,' the man said. He kicked his horse forward. 'You come here to pray?'

'Isn't that what I said?'

'Ireland is close by England, isn't it?'

'She's cursed by that, right enough.'

'And in town,' the rider said, 'a beggar saw two men by the Widow. One in a student's gown and the other climbing aboard a shit-cart.'

'And there was me thinking I was the only student who got up early from bed!'

'Eloise! Abelard!' the owner of the dogs snapped their names, but the hounds just whined and settled even closer to Keane.

'So the beggar went to find the consuls,' the first man said.

'And found us instead,' another man said, amused. 'No reward for him now.'

'We helped him to a better world,' the first man took up the tale, 'and perhaps we can help your memory too.'

'I could always do with help,' Keane said, 'which is why I pray.'

'The hounds picked up a scent,' the man said.

'Clever doggies,' Keane said, patting the two grey heads.

'They followed it here.'

'Ah, they smelled me! No wonder they were running so eagerly.'

'And two sets of footprints by the river,' another man added.

'I think you have questions to answer.' The first man smiled.

'Like why he wants to be a crow,' the dog's owner said. 'You don't like women, perhaps?' The other two horsemen laughed. Thomas could see them more clearly now. Very rich young men, their saddlery and harness were expensive, their boots polished. Merchants' sons, perhaps? He reckoned they were the kind of wealthy young sons who could break the city's curfew with impunity because of their fathers' status, young bucks who roamed the city looking for trouble and confident that they could avoid the consequences. Men who had apparently killed a beggar so they would not need to share the reward with him. 'Why does a man want to be a priest?' the horseman asked scornfully. 'Perhaps because he isn't a man, eh? We should find out. Take your clothes off.' His companions, eager to join the sport, kicked their mounts forward and so passed under Thomas's branch. He dropped.

He fell onto the rearmost horseman, hooked his right arm around the man's neck and seized the boar-spear with his left. The man fell. The horse reared and whinnied. Thomas slammed onto the ground, the unseated rider on top of him. The man's left foot was trapped in the stirrup and the horse skittered away, dragging the man with him, and Thomas was already rising, the spear in both hands now. The other spearman was turning his horse and Thomas swung the weapon fiercely, and the flat of the blade cracked hard against the rider's skull. The man swayed in the saddle as Thomas ran at the leading horseman, who was trying to draw his sword, but Keane was holding the man's forearm while the horse circled frantically. The dogs were leaping at Keane and the horse, thinking it a game. Thomas swung the spear, and the wide blade sliced under the horseman's ribs. The man yelled in pain, and Keane dragged him from the saddle and brought his right knee up to meet the man's head and the rider dropped, stunned. The first man had managed to disentangle his foot from the stirrup, but he was dizzy. He attempted to stand, and Thomas kicked him in the throat and he too went down. The dazed rider was still in the saddle but he was just staring at nothing, his mouth opening and closing. 'Get the horses,' Thomas ordered Keane, then ran out of the trees, crossed the ditch and used his knife to cut the twine that held the bundles of chestnut stakes. 'We'll tie the bastards up,' he told Keane, 'and if you need a change of clothes, help yourself.' He hauled the third man from his saddle and dazed him even more with a slam of his hand that drew blood from the man's ear.

'Is that velvet?' Keane asked, fingering one of the young men's jackets. 'I always saw myself in velvet.'

Thomas dragged the boots off all three men and found a pair that fitted him. One of the horses had saddlebags with a flask of wine, some bread, and a hunk of cheese, and he split them with Keane. 'You can ride a horse?'

'Jesus, I'm from Ireland! I was born on horseback.'

'Tie them up. Strip them naked first.' Thomas helped Keane truss the three men, then stripped off his damp clothes and found a pair of hose that fitted him, a shirt, and a fine leather jacket that was too tight around his archer's muscles, but dry. He strapped a sword belt around his waist. 'So you killed the beggar?' he asked one of the three. The man said nothing so Thomas hit him hard around the face. 'You're lucky I'm not cutting your balls off,' he said, 'but the next time you ignore my question I'll take one of them. Did you kill the beggar?'

'He was dying,' the young man said sullenly.

'So it was an act of Christian charity,' Thomas said. He stooped and held his knife between the man's legs. He saw the terror on the sullen face. 'Who are you?'

'My name's Pitou, my father's a consul, he'll pay for me!' He was gabbling desperately.

'Pitou's a big man in town,' Keane said, 'a vintner who lives like a lord. Eats off gold plates, they say.'

'I'm his only son,' Pitou pleaded, 'he'll pay for me!'

'Oh, he will,' Thomas said, then cut the twine from Pitou's ankles and wrists. 'Get dressed,' he said, kicking his own damp clothes towards the frightened youth. He tied Pitou's wrists again when the boy was dressed, and he was little more than a boy, perhaps seventeen years old. 'You're coming with us,' he said, 'and if you hope to see Montpellier again you'd better pray that my servant and two men-at-arms are alive.'

'They are!' Pitou said eagerly.

Thomas looked at the other two. 'Tell Pitou's father his son will be returned when my men reach Castillon d'Arbizon. And if they don't have their own weapons, mail, horses and clothes then his son will be sent home without his eyes.' Pitou stared at Thomas when he heard those words, then suddenly bent forward and vomited. Thomas smiled. 'He's also to send a grown man's right glove filled with genoins, and I mean filled. Do you understand?'

One of them nodded, and Thomas lengthened the stirrups of the largest horse, a grey stallion, and swung into the saddle. He had a sword, a spear, a horse, and hope.

'The hounds will come with us,' Keane announced as he climbed onto a brown gelding. He took the reins of the third horse on which Pitou was mounted.

'They will?'

'They like me, so they do. Where do we go now?'

'I have men waiting close by, we go north.'

They rode north.

Roland de Verrec was unhappy. He should have been ecstatic, for the successful completion of his quest was in sight. He had captured Thomas of Hookton's wife and child, and, though he had no doubt that they would be exchanged for the adulterous Countess Bertille de Labrouillade, Roland had still hesitated before making the capture. It went against the grain of his romantic ideals to use a woman and child, but the men-at-arms who supported him, all six of them loaned by the Count of Labrouillade, had persuaded him. 'We're not going to hurt them,' Jacques Sollière, the leader of the count's six men, had persuaded Roland, 'just make use of them.'

The capture had been simple. The consuls of Montpellier had lent him even more men, and Genevieve and her son had been taken as they tried to leave the city with two men-at-arms and a servant as their only protection. Those three attendants were now in Montpellier's citadel, but they were none of Roland's business. His duty was to reach Labrouillade and exchange his captives for the count's wayward wife, and then his quest would be done.

Yet somehow it did not feel chivalric. Roland insisted that Genevieve and her child be treated with courtesy, yet she returned that favour with defiant scorn, and her words hurt him. If Roland had been a more perceptive man he would have seen the terror beneath the scorn, but he felt only the lash and he tried to deflect it by telling tales to young Hugh. He told the boy the story of the golden fleece, then how the great hero Ipomadon had disguised himself to win a tournament, and then how Lancelot had done the same, and Hugh listened in fascination while his mother appeared to despise the tales. 'So why did they fight?' she asked.

'To win, my lady,' Roland said.

'No, they fought for their lovers,' Genevieve said. 'Ipomadon fought for Queen Proud, and Lancelot for Guinevere who, like the Countess of Labrouillade, was married to another man.'

Roland coloured at that. 'I would not call them lovers,' he said stiffly.

'What else?' she asked with reeking scorn. 'And Guinevere was a prisoner, as I am.'

'Madame!'

'If I'm not a prisoner,' she demanded, 'let me go.'

'You are a hostage, madame, and under my protection.'

Genevieve laughed at that. 'Your protection?'

'Until you are exchanged, madame,' Roland said stiffly, 'I swear no harm will come to you if it is in my power to prevent it.'

'Oh stop your witless blathering and tell my son another tale of adultery,' she spat.

So Roland told what he thought was a much safer story, the glorious tale of his namesake, the great Roland de Roncesvalles. 'He marched against the Moors in Spain,' he told Hugh. 'Do you know who the Moors are?'

'Pagans,' Hugh said.

'That's right! They are heathens and pagans,

followers of a false god, and when the French army came back across the Pyrenees they were treacherously ambushed by the pagans! Roland commanded the rearguard and he was outnumbered twenty to one, some say fifty to one! Yet he possessed a great sword, Durandal, that had once belonged to Hector of Troy, and that great blade slew his enemies. They died in their scores, but not even Durandal could hold back that pagan horde and the poor Christians were in danger of being overwhelmed. But Roland also possessed a magic horn, Olifant, and he blew the horn, he blew it so hard that the effort killed him, but the sound of Olifant brought King Charlemagne and his magnificent knights to slaughter the impudent enemy!'

'They may have been impudent,' Genevieve said, 'but they were never Moors. They were Christians.'

'My lady!' Roland protested.

'Don't be absurd,' she said. 'Have you ever been to Roncesvalles?'

'No, madame.'

'I have! My father was a juggler and fire-eater. We went from town to town collecting pennies and we listened to the stories, always the stories, and in Roncesvalles they know it was the Basques, Christians to a man, who ambushed Roland. They killed him too. You just pretend it was the Moors because you can't abide thinking that your hero was killed by peasant rebels. And how glorious a death is it? To blow a horn and fall down?'

228

'Roland is a hero as great as Arthur!'

'Who had more sense than to kill himself by blowing a horn. And speaking of horns, why do you serve the Count of Labrouillade?'

'To do right, lady.'

'Right! By returning that poor girl to her pig of a husband?'

'To her lawful husband.'

'Who rapes his tenants' wives and daughters,' she said, 'so why aren't you punishing him for adultery?' Roland had no answer except to frown at Hugh, distressed that such a subject should be aired in front of a small boy. Genevieve laughed. 'Oh, Hugh can listen,' she said. 'I want him to be a decent man like his father, so I'm educating him. I don't want him to be a fool like you.'

'Madame!' Roland protested again.

Genevieve spat. 'Seven years ago, when Bertille was twelve years old, she was carried to Labrouillade and married to him. He was thirty-two then and he wanted her dowry. What choice did she have? She was twelve!'

'She is lawfully married, before God.'

'To a disgusting creature whom God would spit on.'

'She is his wife,' Roland insisted, yet he felt exquisitely uncomfortable. He wished he had never taken this quest, but he had, and honour demanded it must be seen through to its end and so they rode northwards. They stayed at a tavern in the marketplace of Gignac, and Roland insisted on sleeping just outside the chamber where Genevieve slept. His squire shared the vigil. Roland's squire was a clever fourteen-year-old, Michel, whom Roland was training in the ways of chivalry. 'I don't trust the Count of Labrouillade's men,' Roland told the boy, 'especially not Jacques, so we sleep here with our swords.' The count's man had been eyeing the fair-haired Genevieve all day, and Roland had heard the laughter behind him and suspected the men-at-arms were discussing his captive, but they made no attempt to get past Roland during the night, and next morning they rode northwards and joined the high road heading towards Limoges while Genevieve tormented Roland by suggesting that her husband would have escaped Montpellier.

'He's difficult to capture,' she said, 'and terrible in revenge.'

'I do not fear fighting him,' Roland said.

'Then you're a fool. You think your sword will protect you? Do you call it Durandal?' She laughed when he reddened, for he obviously did. 'But Thomas has a span of dark-painted yew,' she said, 'and a cord of hemp with arrows of peeled white ash. Have you ever faced an English archer?'

'He will fight courteously.'

'Don't be such a fool! He'll cheat you and trick you and deceive you, and at the end of the fight you'll be as stuck full of arrows as a brush has bristles. He might already be ahead of you! Maybe the archers are waiting on the road? You won't see them. The first you'll know is the strike of the arrows, then the screams of horses and the death of your men.'

'She's right,' Jacques Sollière put in.

Roland smiled bravely. 'They will not shoot, lady, for fear of hitting you.'

'You know nothing! At two hundred paces they can pick the snot out of your nose with an arrow. They'll shoot.' She wondered where Thomas was. She feared that the church would seize her again. She feared for her son.

The next night was spent in a monastery's guest house, and again Roland guarded her threshold. There was no other way from the room, no escape. On the road, before they reached the monastery, they had passed a group of merchants with armed guards, and Genevieve had called out to them, saying she had been captured against her will. The men had looked worried until Roland, with his calm courtesy, had said she was his sister and moon-touched. He said the same thing whenever Genevieve appealed to passers-by. 'I take her to a place where she might be treated by holy nuns,' he said, and the merchants had believed him and passed on.

'So you're not above telling lies,' she had mocked him.

'A lie in God's service is no lie.'

'And this is God's service?'

'Marriage is a sacrament. My life is dedicated to God's service.'

'Is that why you're a virgin?'

He blushed at that, then frowned, but still answered the question seriously. 'It was revealed to me that my strength in battle rests on purity.' He paused to glance at her. 'It was the Virgin Mary who spoke to me.'

Genevieve had been mocking him, but something in his tone checked her scorn. 'What did she say?'

'She was beautiful,' Roland said wistfully.

'And she spoke to you?'

'She came down from the chapel ceiling,' he said, 'and told me I must live a chaste life until I marry. That God would bless me. That I was chosen. I was only a boy then, but I was chosen.'

'You had a dream.' Genevieve sounded dismissive.

'A vision,' he corrected her.

'A boy dreams of a beautiful woman,' Genevieve said, the scorn back in her voice, 'that's no vision.'

'And she touched me and told me I must stay pure.'

'Tell that to the arrow that kills you,' she had said, and Roland had fallen silent.

Now, on the third day of travel, he constantly searched the road ahead for any sign of the Hellequin. There were plenty enough travellers, merchants, pilgrims, drovers, or folk going to market, but none reported seeing armed men. Roland was becoming ever more cautious and had sent two of the count's men-at-arms a quarter-mile ahead to scout the road, but as the day passed they reported nothing threatening. He worried that their progress was so slow, suspecting that Genevieve was deliberately causing delay, yet he could not prove it and his courtesy demanded that he respect every request she made for privacy. Were women's bladders really that small? Yet in two days more, Roland thought, he would reach Labrouillade and could send a message to the Hellequin demanding Bertille's return in exchange for the safety of Thomas's wife and child, and so he tried to reassure himself that the quest was almost finished. 'We must find a place to spend the night,' he said to Genevieve as the sun sank on their third day of travel.

Then he saw his scouts hurrying from the north. One of them was gesturing wildly.

'He's seen something,' Roland said, more to himself than to any of his companions.

'Jesus,' one of the men-at-arms said, because now they could see what had alarmed the scouts. The evening was drawing in and the sun cast long shadows across the countryside, but on the northern skyline, suddenly bright in that fading sunlight, were men. Men and steel, men and iron, and men and horses. The light glinted off armour and off weapons, from helmets and from the finial of a banner, though the flag was too far off to be seen clearly. Roland tried to count them, but the distant horsemen were moving around. Twelve? Fifteen?

'Maybe you won't live to see the night,' Genevieve said.

'They can't have got in front of us,' Jacques said, though without much conviction.

Panic made Roland hesitate. He rarely felt panic. In a tournament, even in a wild melee, he was calm amidst the chaos. He felt, in those moments, as if an angel guarded him, warned him of danger, and showed opportunity. He was fast, so that even in the most disastrous turmoil, it seemed to him as if other men moved slowly. Yet now he felt real fear. There were no rules here, no marshals to stop the fighting, just danger.

'The first you'll know,' Genevieve said, 'is the flight of an arrow.'

'There's some kind of village over there!' One of the scouts, his horse white with sweat, galloped up to the hesitant Roland and pointed to the east. 'There's a tower there.'

'A church?'

'God knows. A tower. It's not far, maybe a league?'

'How many men did you see?' Roland asked.

'Two dozen? There could be more.'

'Let's go!' Jacques snarled.

A rough track led through a wooded valley towards the hidden tower. Roland took it, leading Genevieve's mare by its reins. He hurried. He glanced back to see that the distant men had vanished from the skyline, then he was among trees and ducking to avoid low branches. He fancied he heard hooves behind, but saw nothing. His heart was pounding in a way it never did in the tournament lists. 'Go ahead,' he told his squire, Michel, 'find who owns the tower and demand shelter. Go! Go!'

Roland told himself it could not be Thomas pursuing him. If Thomas had escaped Montpellier then he would be south of Roland surely, not north? Maybe no one pursued him? Perhaps the armed men were on some innocent journey, yet why would they be armoured? Why wear helmets? His horse pounded through the leaf mould. They splashed through a shallow stream and cantered beside a puny vineyard. 'Thomas's men call their arrows the devil's steel hail,' Genevieve said.

'Be quiet!' Roland snapped, forgetting his courtesy. Two of the count's men were riding close to her, making sure she did not try to fall off her horse and so slow them down. He rode up a slight slope, looked behind and saw no pursuer, then they breasted the shallow crest and there was a small village and, just beyond, the tower of a half-ruined church. The sun had almost gone and the tower was in shadow. It showed no lights.

The horses crashed through the village, scattering fowl, dogs and goats. Most of the houses were derelict, their thatch blackened or fallen in, and Roland realised this must be a village denuded by the plague. He made the sign of the cross. A woman snatched her child from the path of the big horses. A man called out a question, but Roland ignored it. He was imagining the devil's steel hail. Imagining the arrows slicing from the twilight to slaughter men and horses, and then he was in a small graveyard and one of his men was in the broken nave of the church and had found the steps that climbed into the old bell tower. 'It's empty,' he called.

'Inside,' Roland ordered.

And so, in the dusk, Roland to the dark tower came.

CHAPTER 7

Thomas, Keane, and their prisoner reached the mill to find Karyl and nine remaining men-at-arms ready, though what they were ready for none of them knew. They were all in mail, their horses were saddled, and they were nervous. 'We know about Genevieve,' Karyl greeted Thomas.

'How?'

Karyl jerked his scarred face towards a man dressed only in hose, shirt, boots, and coat. The man had been shrinking from Thomas's sight, but Thomas spurred towards him. 'Keep an eye on that bastard,' he told Karyl, indicating Pitou, 'if he annoys you, hit him.' He curbed his horse by the reluctant man and looked down into a very anxious face. 'What happened to your monk's habit?' he asked.

'I still have it,' Brother Michael said.

'Then why aren't you wearing it?'

'Because I don't want to be a monk!' Brother Michael protested.

'He brought us news.' Karyl had followed Thomas. 'He said Genevieve was taken, and you are hunted.'

'They have taken Genevieve,' Thomas confirmed.

'De Verrec?'

'I assume he's taking her to Labrouillade.'

'I sent the rest of the men to Castillon,' Karyl said, 'and told Sir Henri to send at least forty men towards us. It was his idea.' He nodded down at Brother Michael.

Thomas looked at the monk. 'Your idea?'

Brother Michael looked about the hilltop anxiously, as if seeking somewhere to hide. 'It seemed a sensible idea,' he said finally.

Thomas was not so certain it was sensible. He had ten men, twelve if you counted the reluctant student and even more reluctant monk, and they would be pursuing Roland de Verrec while the men from Castillon d'Arbizon would be roaming an unfriendly country looking for Thomas. That could lead to disaster if either small group was confronted by a much larger enemy. Yet if they did link up? He nodded approval. 'It was probably a good idea,' he said grudgingly. 'So now you'll go back to Montpellier?'

'Me? Why?' Brother Michael asked indignantly.

'To learn how to sniff piss.'

'No!'

'So what do you want?'

'To stay with you.'

'Or with Bertille?'

Brother Michael coloured. 'To stay with you, sire.'

Thomas nodded towards Keane. 'He doesn't want

to be a priest and you don't want to be a monk. Now you're both Hellequin.'

Brother Michael looked disbelieving. 'I am?' he asked excitedly.

'You are,' Thomas said.

'So all we need now is a pair of ripe young girls who don't want to be nuns,' Keane said cheerfully.

Karyl had not seen Roland de Verrec pass northwards with Genevieve. 'You told us to stay hidden,' he said reproachfully, 'away from the road. So we did.'

'He didn't come this way,' Thomas said, 'he's on the Gignac road, at least I think he is, and the bastard has a day's lead on us.'

'We follow?'

'We'll use the roads through the hills,' Thomas said. He did not know those roads, but they had to exist because, looking north, he could see villages in the higher ground. He could see a mill on the skyline and smoke rising from a shadowed valley, and where there were people there were roads. They would be slower than the high roads, but with luck, with no thrown horseshoes and no *coredors*, he might catch up with de Verrec before the virgin knight reached Labrouillade. He dismounted and walked to the southern edge of the small plateau on which the ruined mill stood. He could see Montpellier clearly and also see small bands of horsemen scouring the scorched ground where the houses outside the city walls had been burned to deny an English attack any shelter or cover. There were at least six bands of men, no group larger than seven or eight, all of them exploring the bushes at the edges of the cleared ground. 'They're hunting me,' he told Karyl, who had come to stand beside him.

Karyl shaded his eyes. 'Men-at-arms,' he grunted. Even at this distance it was possible to see that at least two of the bands were in grey mail. The sun glinted off helmets.

'City guards, probably,' Thomas said.

'Why don't they make one group?' Karyl asked.

'And share the reward?'

'There is a reward?'

'A big one.'

Karyl grinned. 'How big?'

'Probably enough to buy you a decent farm in, where is it, Bohemia?'

Karyl nodded. 'Have you ever been to Bohemia?'

'No.'

'Cold winters,' he said, 'I think I'll stay here.'

'They'll be searching the city,' Thomas said, 'but when they find nothing, then a whole lot more of them will come outside.'

'We'll be gone.'

'And they'll guess that.'

'And pursue us?'

'I hope so,' Thomas said. The horses from the city would likely be well fed and rested, while the horses at the mill had fed sparsely, and if he was to travel fast through the hills he would need good horses. He also needed mail and weapons for Keane and Brother Michael.

He said as much to Karyl, who turned to look at the monk. 'A weapon would be wasted on him,' he said scornfully, 'but the Irishman looks useful.'

'They both need to look like men-at-arms,' Thomas said, 'even if they're not. And we need spare horses too. We'll be riding hard.'

'Ambush,' Karyl said with relish.

'Ambush,' Thomas agreed, 'and we need to make it quick, brutal and effective.' Now that he was with his men he was feeling vengeful. Genevieve's plight tortured him, even though he assumed she was merely a bargaining piece for Bertille, and Bertille was safe in Castillon d'Arbizon and he doubted that Sir Henri would release her without Thomas's permission. All the same he wanted to avenge Genevieve, and the anger overflowed when, just before midday, they sprang the ambush.

It was simplicity itself. Keane and Brother Michael, the two men without mail or helmets, simply showed themselves in an olive grove that was visible to one of the bands searching the countryside. Those men whooped and hollered, put spurs to horses, drew swords and galloped. Keane and Brother Michael ran, vanishing from their pursuers into a small valley where Thomas's men waited.

And the anger was spewed into sword-strokes. Six men were in the hunt and they were racing one another to catch the fugitives. The first two were mounted on small fast horses, and they outstripped their companions to gallop over the crest and down into the valley. Their horses were splashing through a tiny stream before they realised that they were in trouble. Thomas's men closed from both sides as the remaining four hunters thundered over the skyline, saw the melee below, and desperately tried to curb and turn their horses.

Thomas kicked his horse up the slope. A man wearing the livery of Montpellier was trying to turn away, then changed his mind and swung his sword back at Thomas, who leaned left in the saddle, let the blade slide past his face, then brought his own sword in a savage blow that struck the back of the man's neck just beneath the helmet rim. He did not bother to see what happened, he knew the man was out of the fight, just drove his horse higher up the slope and rammed the blade at a second man, as Arnaldus, one of the Gascons in the Hellequin, backswung a battleaxe into the man's face. Karyl had hauled a man out of the saddle, now turned and stabbed down with his sword, and Thomas saw blood spurt higher than Karyl's battered helmet. Keane was holding one of the first horsemen under the water, drowning him as the two hounds savaged a flailing arm.

Six men down in fewer seconds and not one of the Hellequin was injured. 'Keane! Get the horses!' Thomas shouted.

A second band of men had seen the first group

spur northwards and they were now following, but the sight of mail-clad horsemen waiting at the top of the olive grove dissuaded them. They turned away.

'You,' Thomas pointed at Brother Michael, 'find a coat of mail that fits you. Find a helmet, find a sword. Get a horse.'

They rode north.

Roland de Verrec ordered the horses tied in the ruined nave, then climbed the steep, narrow steps of the bell tower. There was no bell any more, just an open space. Each of the four walls was pierced by a wide arch, the roof was rotted rafters from which most of the tiles had fallen, while the floor creaked dangerously under the weight of his men. 'The arrows will fly through the arches,' Genevieve told him.

'Be silent,' he said and then, because he always tried to be courteous, added 'please'. He was nervous. The horses stamped in the nave, someone called from the village, but otherwise the world seemed silent. Darkness was falling fast and throwing lumpy shadows across the graveyard next to the church. The graves had no markers. This village must have been struck hard by the terrible plague that had carried away so many souls, and the bodies lay in their shallow pits. Roland remembered seeing the wild dogs dig up plague victims. He had been a boy, and he had wept for the pity of seeing the dogs tear the rotting flesh of his mother's tenants. His father had died, as had his only brother. His mother had said that the sickness was sent as a punishment for sin. 'The English and the plague,' she had said, 'both are works of the devil.'

'They say the English have the plague too,' Roland had pointed out.

'God is good,' the widow had said.

'But why did Father die?' Roland had asked.

'He was a sinner,' his mother had said, though she had still turned her house into a shrine for her husband and for her eldest son, a shrine with candles and crucifixes, black hangings and a chantry priest who was paid to say masses for the father and heir who had died vomiting and bleeding. Then the English had come, and the widow was turned out of her land and had fled to the Count of Armagnac who was a distant cousin, and the count had raised Roland to be a warrior, but a warrior who knew that the world was a battlefield between God and the devil, between light and darkness, between good and evil. Now he watched the darkness darken as the shadows crept across the plague-humped land. The devil was out there, he thought, sliding through the dusk-blackened trees, a serpent coiling about the ruined church.

'Perhaps they didn't follow us,' he said almost in a whisper.

'Perhaps the first bows are being drawn now,' Genevieve said, 'or perhaps they'll light a fire beneath us.'

'Be quiet,' he said, and his tone now was pleading, not commanding.

The first bats were flying. A dog barked in the village and was hushed. The dry branches of pine trees rattled in a small wind, and Roland closed his eyes and prayed to Saint Basil and Saint Denis, his two patron saints. He gripped his scabbarded sword, Durandal, and touched his forehead to the big pommel. 'Let not evil come to me in this darkness,' he prayed. 'Make me good,' he prayed as his mother had taught him.

A hoof sounded in the trees. He heard the creak of saddle leather and the chink of a bridle. A horse whinnied and there were more footsteps. 'Jacques!' a voice called from the dark. 'Jacques! Are you there?'

Roland lifted his head. The first stars were glinting above the hilltops. Saint Basil's mother had been a widow. 'Let not my mother lose her only son,' he prayed.

'Jacques, you bastard!' the voice shouted again. The men-at-arms sheltering in the tower looked at Roland, but he was still praying.

'I'm here!' Jacques Sollière called into the dark. 'Is that you, Philippe?'

'I'm the Holy Ghost, you idiot,' the man called Philippe shouted back.

'Philippe!' The men-at-arms in the tower were on their feet now, shouting a welcome.

'They're friends,' Jacques told Roland, 'the count's men.'

'Oh God,' Roland breathed. He could not believe the relief that flooded through him, so much relief that he felt weak. He was no coward. No man who had faced Walter of Siegenthaler in the lists could be called a coward. The German had killed and maimed men in a score of tournaments, always claiming the carnage was an accident, but Roland had fought the man four times and humiliated him in every bout. He was no coward, but he had been terrified in this creeping dusk. War, he was realising, had no rules, and all the skill in the world might not be enough to help him survive.

Philippe appeared as a shadow beneath the tower. 'The count sent us,' he called up.

'Labrouillade?' Roland asked, though the question was unnecessary. The count's men-at-arms had greeted their comrades familiarly.

'The English are marching,' Philippe explained. 'Are you the Sire de Verrec?'

'Yes. Where are the English?'

'Somewhere north,' Philippe said vaguely, 'but that's why we're here. The count wants all his men-at-arms.' More soldiers were coming from the dark, leading their horses into the ruined nave. 'Can we light a fire?'

'Of course.' Roland hurried down the steps. 'The count sent you because the English are marching?'

'He's been summoned to Bourges, and he wants to take at least sixty men to war. He needs the men who went with you.' Philippe watched as a servant struck steel and flint to light a twist of straw. 'Did you find *le Bâtard*?'

'He's in Montpellier, a prisoner, I hope.' Roland was still feeling weak, astonished by the fear that had driven him to his knees. 'He's in Montpellier,' he said again, 'but I have his wife.'

'The boys will enjoy that,' Philippe said.

'She is under my protection,' Roland said stiffly. 'I propose exchanging her for the countess.'

'The boys will enjoy that even more,' Philippe said.

'Because justice will have been served.'

'Damn justice, they'll enjoy watching the bitch being punished. Oh, and some fellows have come to Labrouillade. They want you.'

'Who?'

'A churchman,' Philippe said vaguely.

'How did you know where to find me?' Roland asked, still surprised at the relief he was feeling.

'We weren't looking for you,' Philippe said curtly. 'It's Jacques and his men we want, but we knew you'd gone to Montpellier. We have a man in Castillon d'Arbizon. He owns a tavern, listens to the talk, and sends us messages. He told us *le Bâtard* had gone to Montpellier, which means you'd have followed him. Your churchman wants him as well.'

'My churchman?'

'The one who's looking for you. Bastard might even be following us. Very eager he is.' Philippe stopped abruptly, watching Genevieve as she came down the steps into the light of the small fire, which was now blazing with straw and rotted wood. 'Oh, that's nice,' he said.

'I told you,' Roland said, 'she is under my protection.'

'Won't count for much if her husband doesn't give us the countess, will it? And he's in Montpellier, you say. Anyway, the count wants his men-at-arms back. The English bastards are burning, plundering, raping, killing. We've got a proper war to fight.'

'There'll be a battle?' Roland asked, suddenly aware of taking part in a fight where there were no rules.

'God knows,' Philippe said. 'Some say the king's bringing an army south, some say he's not, and the truth is no one knows. We're all ordered to Bourges, and they want us there as fast as possible.'

'I won a tournament at Bourges,' Roland said.

'You'll find war a bit different,' Philippe said. 'No marshals to stop the killing, for a start. Though God knows if it will come to a fight. For now our job is just to keep an eye on the bastards.'

'And mine is to return the countess to her husband,' Roland said firmly.

'He'll be glad of that,' Philippe said, then grinned, 'as will the rest of us.' He clapped his hands to draw the men's attention. 'We're leaving at dawn! Get some rest! Horses stay here; if you want to kick some bastards out of bed in the village, do it. Jean, other Jean, François, you're on guard duty.'

'My prisoner will sleep in the tower,' Roland said, 'and I shall guard her.'

'Good, good,' Philippe said absently.

Roland hardly slept that night. He sat on the church tower's stone stairs and thought how the world was crumbling. To Roland's mind there was a proper order of things. A king ruled, advised by his nobles and by the wise men of the church, and together they made justice and prosperity. The people should be grateful for that governance and show their gratitude in deference. There were enemies, of course, but a wise king dealt with those enemies with courtesy, and God would decide the outcome of any disagreement by the workings of destiny. That was the proper order, but instead the world was infested with men like Jacques and Philippe, hard men, men who showed no respect, men who robbed and cheated and were proud of it. If the English were marching then that was regrettable and plainly against the will of God, but the King of France, with his bishops and lords, would bring the banner of Saint Denis to destroy them. That was a holy duty, a lamentable duty, but to Roland's disgust, Philippe positively relished the thought of warfare. 'It's a chance to make money,' he had told Roland over the sparse evening meal. 'Take a rich prisoner? That's the best thing.'

'Or get into the enemy's baggage train,' Jacques had said wolfishly.

'There's usually nothing but wounded men and

servants with the baggage,' Philippe had explained to Roland, 'so you just cut the bastards down and help yourself.'

'And the women,' Jacques had said.

'Oh Jesus, the women. Remember that fight at . . . where was it?' Philippe had frowned, trying to remember. 'Place with the broken bridge?'

'I never knew the name. South of Reims, wasn't it?'

Philippe had laughed at the memory. 'The English were one side of the river and their women on the other. I had four of them tied to my horse's tail, all of them naked. Jesus, that was a good month.'

'He was hiring them out,' Jacques had told Roland.

'Except to the count, of course,' Philippe had said, 'he got it for nothing on account of being the count.'

'Lords have privileges,' Jacques had said.

'The privilege not to fight too,' Philippe had added, sounding resentful.

'He's too fat,' Jacques had defended the Count of Labrouillade, 'but when he does fight he's a devil! I've seen him crush a man's head, skull, helmet and everything, with one swipe of that morningstar. There was brains everywhere!'

'The fight was already over,' Philippe had said scornfully. 'He only joined in when it was safe.' He had shaken his head at the memory, then looked at Roland. 'So you'll be joining us, sire?'

'Joining you?'

'To fight the damned English!'

'When I have completed my . . .' Roland had hesitated. He had been about to say 'quest', but suspected these two older and more hardened men would mock him for that. '. . . my duty,' he had said instead.

So Roland, uncomfortable on the stone stairs, had slept hardly at all. He was galled by the memory of the two men-at-arms' mocking laughter. He could have defeated either in the lists, but suspected fate would prove very different on the battlefield. He had a sudden vision of the siege tower collapsing at Breteuil, of the men screaming as they burned. He reassured himself that he had not panicked then, he had kept calm and rescued a man, but it had still been a defeat, and none of his skill could have averted that shame. He feared war.

Next morning, at dawn, they rode on north-wards. Roland felt a great deal safer now that he was escorted by almost a score of armed and armoured men, while Genevieve was quiet. She kept looking eastwards hoping that mounted archers would appear, but nothing moved in the low summer hills. The sun was relentless, baking the fields, slowing the horses and making the men sweat in their heavy mail. Philippe was leading now, using tracks away from the high road. They passed another village ruined by plague. Sunflowers grew in abandoned gardens. There must have been folk working in the fields and vineyards, but they hid whenever they saw horsemen in mail. 'How much further?' Roland asked as they watered the horses at a ford that crossed a shrunken field.

'Not far,' Philippe said. He had taken off his helmet and was wiping his face with a scrap of cloth. 'Maybe two hours' riding?'

Roland gestured for his squire to take his horse. 'Don't let him drink too much,' he ordered, then looked at Philippe again. 'And once you're at Labrouillade,' he asked, 'you'll have to leave for the north?'

'Within a day or two.'

'And you follow the English?'

Philippe shrugged. 'I assume so,' he said. 'If the king reaches us we join him, but otherwise we harass their foragers, cut off their laggards and keep them worried.' He hitched up his mail coat to piss against a tree. 'And with any luck we take some rich prisoners.'

And the first arrow struck.

Thomas led his men and tired horses into a small town. He had no idea what it was called, only that there was no easy way around it and so they must ride through the narrow streets and hope no one delayed them. He took the precaution of tying the prisoner's hands and stopping his mouth with a gag made of rags.

'We should buy food,' Karyl suggested.

'But do it quickly,' Thomas said.

The horsemen clattered into a small square at the town's centre, though to call it a town was to flatter a place that had neither walls nor fortress. Market stalls lined the western side of the square while a tavern lay hard under a steep hill to the north, and Thomas gave Karyl some coins. 'Dried fish, bread, cheese,' he suggested.

'No one's selling,' Karyl grumbled.

The stallholders and their customers had all gathered by the church. They looked with curiosity at the horsemen, but none asked their business, though a couple, seeing that the horsemen were interested in the food offered for sale on the stalls, hurried to help. Thomas walked his horse across the cobbles to where the crowd was thickest and saw that a broad-shouldered man was reading aloud from the top of the church steps. The man had lost his right hand and instead wore a wooden spike on which a parchment was impaled. He had a close-fitting helmet, a short grey beard, and wore a faded jupon that displayed golden fleurs-de-lys against a blue field. He lowered the parchment as he saw Thomas draw close. 'Who are you?' he called.

'We serve the Count of Berat,' Thomas lied.

'You'd do well to return there,' the man said.

'Why?'

The man flourished the parchment. 'This is the *arrière-ban*,' he said. 'Berat and every other lord is summoned to make war for the king. The English are out.' The crowd made a low growling noise and some even looked nervously northwards as if expecting to see the old enemy appearing from the hills.

'Are they coming this way?' Thomas asked.

'God be praised, no. Those goddams are well north of here, but who knows? The devil could bring them south any day.'

Thomas's horse stamped a hoof on the cobbles. Thomas leaned forward and stroked its neck. 'And the king?' he asked.

'God will bring him victory,' the grey-bearded man said piously, meaning that he had no news of the French king's movements, 'but until God does, my lord summons every man-at-arms to assemble at Bourges.'

'Your lord?'

'The Duke de Berry,' the man said proudly. That explained the royal fleurs-de-lys on his jupon because the Duke de Berry was a son of King Jean and the holder of a slew of dukedoms, counties, and fiefs.

'The duke plans to fight them on his own?' Thomas asked.

The messenger shrugged. 'The king has ordered it. All forces from the south of France are to gather at Bourges.'

'Where's Bourges?'

'North,' the messenger said, 'but to be honest I don't know precisely, except you go to Nevers and there's a fine road from there.'

'Wherever the hell Nevers is,' Thomas grumbled. 'Has your lord summoned Labrouillade too?' he asked.

'Of course. The *arrière-ban* summons every lord

and every vassal. With God's grace we're going to trap the bastards and destroy them.'

'And these good people?' Thomas gestured at the crowd that numbered perhaps sixty or seventy people, and which contained no men-at-arms as far as he could tell.

'He wants our taxes!' a man in a butcher's bloodied apron shouted.

'Taxes must be paid,' the messenger said firmly. 'If the English are to be beaten, the army must be paid.'

'The taxes are paid!' the butcher shouted, and the rest called out their support.

The messenger, fearing the anger of the crowd, pointed at young Pitou. 'A prisoner?' he asked Thomas. 'What has he done?'

'Stolen from the count,' Thomas lied.

'You want to hang him here?' the man asked hopefully, plainly wanting a distraction from the crowd's hostility.

'He must go back to Berat,' Thomas said. 'The count likes to hang thieves himself.'

'Pity.' The man pulled the document off the wooden spike and pushed his way through the crowd until he reached Thomas's stirrup. 'A word, monsieur?' he asked.

Now that he was close, Thomas could see that the messenger had a shrewd and weathered face which suggested that this man had experienced too much, and that nothing that happened in the future could surprise him. 'You were a man-at-arms?' Thomas asked.

'I was, till some whoreson Gascon chopped off my hand.' He used the wooden spike to wave away the men who had followed in hope of over-hearing his conversation, and gestured Thomas towards the square's centre. 'My name is Jean Baillaud,' he introduced himself, 'Sergeant to Berry.'

'A good master?'

'He's a goddamned child,' Baillaud said.

'Child?'

'Fifteen years old. Thinks he knows everything. But if you help me, I'm sure I can persuade him to be grateful.' He paused, smiling. 'And a prince's gratitude is worth having.'

'Then how can I help?' Thomas asked.

Baillaud looked back at the small crowd and lowered his voice. 'The poor bastards have paid their taxes,' he said, 'or at least most of them have.'

'But you want more?'

'Of course. There are never enough taxes. Be stupid enough to pay once and you can be sure we'll be back to squeeze you again.'

'And the count sent you on your own to do the squeezing?'

'He's not that foolish. I have seven men-at-arms here, but the town knows just why we came.'

Thomas looked at the tavern. 'And the town has been generous with wine?' he guessed.

'With wine and with whores,' Baillaud said.

'So,' Thomas said, and let the word hang in the hot midday air.

'So squeeze the bastards for me and you can take ten per cent back to Berat.'

'The count would like that,' Thomas said.

'That butcher is the town treasurer,' Baillaud said. 'He has the tax list but claims to have lost it. You might start by helping him find it?'

Thomas nodded. 'Let me talk to my men,' he said, and kicked his horse towards the tavern. Once out of Baillaud's earshot he beckoned for Keane. 'There are eight horses in the tavern stables,' he said, 'and we're taking all of them. You and Brother Michael, get around the back and make sure they're bridled. Karyl!'

The German had finished buying supplies and was pushing food into saddlebags. 'You want more?' he called.

Thomas beckoned him close. 'There are seven men whoring in the tavern. We'll take their mail and weapons.'

'Kill them?'

'Only if they cause trouble.'

Karyl strode towards the tavern as Baillaud caught up with Thomas. 'They'll do it?'

'Willingly,' Thomas said.

'I didn't hear your name,' Baillaud said.

'Thomas,' Thomas said, and reached down to shake Baillaud's hand, then realised there was nothing to shake.

'You sound Norman,' Baillaud said.

'That's what folk tell me. Is that where the English are going? You said they were going north.'

'Christ knows,' Baillaud said. 'They marched out of Gascony and the last I heard they were at Périgueux.'

'They could be coming this way,' Thomas said.

'More plunder northwards,' Baillaud said. 'The English princeling stripped everything to the south last year.' He scowled. 'It's a goddamned scandal,' he said angrily.

'Scandal?'

'Edward of Wales! He's a nothing! A spoiled, privileged puppy! Women and gambling are all he cares about, and he's running riot around France because King Jean is scared of arrows. We should catch the bastard, take his hose down and spank him like a seven-year-old.' Baillaud suddenly turned and stared at the inn. He could hear shouting. 'What?' he began, then stopped abruptly as a naked man was hurled backwards through an upstairs window. The man landed heavily on his back and lay there, stirring slightly. 'That's . . .' Baillaud said.

'One of your men,' Thomas said. 'They must have very tough whores in this town.'

'God's blood,' Baillaud protested, and started towards the prostrate man, then stopped because a second naked man had come out of the tavern door. He was backing away frantically, pursued by two of Thomas's men.

'I surrender!' the man shouted. 'Enough! Enough!'

'Let him be!' Thomas said.

'Bastard threw a full piss-pot at me,' Arnaldus snarled.

'It'll dry,' Thomas said.

'It wasn't filled with piss,' the Gascon said, and kicked the naked man hard between the legs. 'Now I'll let him be.'

'What are you . . .' Baillaud began

Thomas smiled down from the saddle. 'Men call me *le Bâtard*,' he said, 'and we're the Hellequin.' He touched the hilt of the sword just to remind Baillaud that it existed. 'We're taking your horses and weapons,' he went on, then turned his horse and kicked it towards the townsfolk who were still gathered around the church steps. 'Pay your taxes!' he shouted. 'Make your lords rich, so that when we capture them they can afford to pay us a large ransom. You'll be poor, but we shall be rich! You have our gratitude.' They just gaped at him.

Thomas now had more spare horses, more weapons, more mail. If there was any pursuit from Montpellier it was left far behind, but no such pursuit worried him. Genevieve worried him.

So they rode on northwards.

The arrow struck Philippe full in the chest. The crunching sound reminded Roland of a butcher's axe driving into a carcass. Philippe was thrown back by the force of the blow. The arrow had pierced his mail coat, broken a rib, and punctured a lung. He tried to speak, but instead bubbled blood at his lips, then fell backwards. More arrows flew. Two more men were down. Blood was swirling in the stream. An arrow slashed by Roland's head, missing his ear by a hand's breadth. The wind of it was like a slap. A horse was screaming, an arrow in its belly. The arrows were much longer than Roland expected. He was amazed he even noticed that, but even as the missiles whipped in from the west he was astonished by the length of the shafts, so much longer than the short arrows he used for hunting. Another struck a tree and shivered there.

Philippe was dying. Men were scrambling to hide behind trees, or else beneath the shallow stream bank, but it was Jacques who saved them. He ran to Genevieve's side and snatched her son from her protective arms. He gripped the boy's belt and held him high with one strong hand and slid a long knife from its sheath with the other hand. He held the blade at the boy's throat. Genevieve screamed, but the arrows stopped. 'Tell them your son dies if there's one more arrow,' Jacques said.

'You . . .' Genevieve began.

'Tell them, bitch!' Jacques snarled.

Genevieve cupped her hands. 'No more arrows!' she called in English.

Silence, except for the gurgling in Philippe's throat. Every gasp brought more blood to spill from his mouth. The horse began whinnying, white-eyed.

'Tell them we're going,' Jacques said, 'and the boy dies if they try to stop us.'

'You must leave us alone!' Genevieve shouted.

Then the archers appeared from a copse a hundred yards to the east. There were sixteen of them, all holding the long war bows. 'Genny!' one of them called.

'They'll kill Hugh if you try to stop them,' she called back.

'Any news of Thomas?'

'No, Sam! Now let them go!'

Sam waved, as if to suggest they could leave, and Roland began to breathe again. Two men were lifting the dying Philippe onto a horse, and two corpses were draped over other saddles. The men mounted, but Jacques took care to keep hold of the boy. 'Break the arrows,' he ordered a man.

'Break them?'

'So they can't use them again, you half-brained idiot.'

The man snapped as many fallen arrows as he could find, then Jacques led them northwards. Roland was silent. He was thinking of the arrows searing in. By God's grace none had struck him, but the terror of those shafts was still making him tremble, and that had been a mere handful of archers. What could a thousand such men do? 'How did they find us?' he asked.

'They're archers,' Genevieve said, 'they'll find you.'

'Quiet, bitch,' Jacques shouted. He had Hugh across his saddle bow and still held the knife.

'Be courteous!' Roland said more angrily than he had intended.

Jacques muttered something under his breath, but spurred ahead to get out of Roland's company.

Roland looked back down the road and saw that the archers were mounted now and following, but keeping a good distance. He wondered how far an English war bow could shoot, then forgot the question as the men-at-arms crested a small rise, and there was Labrouillade. The castle lay at the centre of a wide, shallow valley, the moat fed by a meandering stream that looped through calm pastureland. No trees grew close to the castle, nor was any building allowed within a quarter-mile, so that no besieger could find shelter for a bowman or a siege engine. The stones of the curtain wall looked almost white in the strong sun. The moat glittered. The count's green banner hung listless from the topmost tower, then Jacques spurred on and the other horsemen followed, and Roland saw the great drawbridge creak down. The hooves echoed loud on the bridge's planks; he plunged through the sudden darkness of the entrance arch and there, waiting in the castle's courtyard, was a tall churchman with green eyes and a hawk on his wrist.

The huge capstan in the gatehouse creaked as two men turned its handle to close the heavy drawbridge. The pawl that held it closed clattered on the metal teeth, then the planks met the arch with a crash and two men ran to bolt the massive bridge upright.

And Roland felt safe.

CHAPTER 8

Thomas arrived at last light. His horses were worn out, stumbling into the grove of chestnut and oak where an archer, seeing horsemen dark against the furnace of the sunset, shouted a challenge. 'Who are you?'

'It's no good shouting in English, Simon,' Thomas called back.

'God's belly,' Simon lowered his bow. 'We thought you was dead.'

'I feel dead,' Thomas said. He and his companions had ridden hard all day, then cast around the Count of Labrouillade's castle in search of the men who had ridden from Castillon d'Arbizon, not knowing if they would be there, but finding them on this tree-covered hill that offered a view of the castle's sole entrance. Thomas slid from the saddle, his spirits as low as the swollen sun, which threw long shadows down the wide valley where Labrouillade had his fortress.

'We tried to stop them,' Sam told him.

'You did well,' Thomas said when he had heard the whole story. Sam and his archers had reached the stream only minutes before Roland and his

263

escort came into sight and they had indeed done well to set up an ambush.

'We'd have taken down every last man if it hadn't been for Hugh,' Sam went on. 'Bastard had a knife at his throat. We killed a couple though.'

'But Genevieve's inside?'

Sam nodded. 'She and Hugh.'

Thomas stared at the castle from the edge of the trees. No chance, he thought. The sun reddened the curtain wall, glimmered the moat scarlet, and reflected a wink of lurid light from the helmet of a sentinel. With a cannon, he thought, he could shatter the drawbridge in a day, but how would he cross the moat?

'I brought your bow,' Sam said.

'You were expecting me?' Thomas asked. 'Or planning to use it yourself?'

Sam looked confused for a moment, then changed the subject. 'And we fetched the countess as well,' he said.

'Fetched her?'

Sam jerked his head southwards. 'She's in a farm back there. Pitt's making sure the silly bitch doesn't run off.'

'Why the hell did you bring her?'

'In case you want to exchange her,' Sam said. 'It was Father Levonne's idea. He's here too.'

'Father Levonne? Why?'

'He wanted to come. He's not sure you should exchange her, but . . .' Sam's voice died away.

'It would be a simple solution,' Thomas said. He

was thinking that he should not be wasting time here. There was *la Malice* to discover and, more importantly, the news that the Prince of Wales was marching an army somewhere through France. Archers and men-at-arms were ravaging a swathe of countryside, wrecking estates, burning towns and spreading panic, all in hope of luring a French army into range of the long war bows and their goose-feathered arrows. Thomas knew his place was with that army, but instead he was trapped here because Genevieve and Hugh were prisoners, and the simple solution was indeed to offer Bertille, Countess of Labrouillade, back to her vengeful husband, but if he did that Thomas would face Genevieve's wrath. Well, he thought, let her be angry. Better to be enraged and free than imprisoned and helpless.

'You have sentinels?' he asked Sam.

'All along the wood's edge. Couple more on the road east, dozen around the farm.'

'You did well,' Thomas said again. The moon was rising as the last daylight drained from the west. Thomas gestured for Keane to join him as he walked towards the farm where Bertille was held. 'I want you to ride within hailing distance of the castle,' he told the Irishman. 'No weapons. Hold your hands out wide to show you're unarmed.'

'And will I be unarmed?'

'You will.'

'Jesus,' the Irishman said. 'So how far can a crossbow shoot?'

'Much farther than you can shout.'

'You want me dead, then?'

'If I went,' Thomas said, 'I think they might shoot, but they don't know you, and you have a brisk tongue.'

'You noticed that, did you?'

'They won't shoot,' Thomas said reassuringly, hoping it was true, 'because they'll want to hear what you have to say.'

Keane snapped his fingers and the two wolfhounds came to his heels. 'And what do I have to say?'

'Tell them I'll exchange the countess for Genevieve and my son. There are to be no more than three men as escorts on either side, and the exchange will happen halfway between the wood and the castle.'

'Is that what all this fuss is about?' Keane asked. 'The countess?'

'Labrouillade wants her back.'

'Ah, that's touching. The man must love her.'

Thomas preferred not to think why the count wanted Bertille back because he knew that by exchanging her he was condemning her to misery and possibly death, but Genevieve and Hugh were infinitely more important to him. It was a pity, he thought. It was unavoidable.

'And just when do I deliver this message?' Keane asked.

'Now,' Thomas said. 'There's enough moonlight for them to see you're not armed.'

'Enough to aim a crossbow too.'

'That too,' Thomas agreed.

He found the countess in the farm's enormous kitchen, a room crossed by heavy beams from which hung drying herbs. Father Levonne, the priest from Castillon d'Arbizon, was there, and Pitt was guarding her. Pitt, he owned to no other name, was a tall, lean and taciturn man with a gaunt face, lank hair tied with a frayed bowstring, and deep-set eyes. He was English, from Cheshire, but he had joined the Hellequin in Gascony, riding out of a forest as though he belonged to them and then just falling into line and saying nothing. He was black-humoured, morose, and Thomas suspected he had deserted from some other company, but he was also a superb archer and knew how to lead men in battle. 'Glad you're back,' he growled when he saw Thomas.

'Thomas,' Father Levonne said in relief, and stood up from the chair beside Bertille.

Thomas waved the priest down. Bertille sat at the big table where two candles burned smokily. A maid, provided by Genevieve from among the girls at Castillon d'Arbizon, knelt beside her. The countess's eyes were red from crying. She looked up at Thomas. 'You're going to give me back, aren't you?'

'Yes, my lady.'

'Thomas . . .' Father Levonne started.

'Yes,' Thomas said harshly, cutting off whatever protest the priest was about to make.

Bertille lowered her head and began crying again. 'Do you know what he'll do to me?'

'He has my wife and son,' Thomas said.

She sobbed quietly.

'Jesus,' Keane hissed beside Thomas.

Thomas ignored the Irishman. 'I'm sorry, my lady,' he said.

'When?' she asked.

'Tonight, I hope.'

'I'd rather be dead,' she said.

'Thomas,' Father Levonne said, 'let me go and talk to the count.'

'What the hell good do you think that will do?' Thomas asked more curtly than he had intended.

'Just let me talk to him.'

Thomas shook his head. 'The Count of Labrouillade,' he said, 'is an evil bastard, a fat malevolent angry bastard, and by this time of night he'll probably be half drunk, and if I let you go into his castle you probably won't come out.'

'Then I stay there. I'm a priest. I go where I'm needed.' Father Levonne paused. 'Let me talk to him.'

Thomas thought for a moment. 'From outside the castle, maybe.'

Levonne hesitated, then nodded. 'That will do.'

Thomas plucked Keane's elbow and took him into the farm's yard. 'Don't let Father Levonne go into the castle. They'll likely make him another hostage.'

The Irishman, for once, seemed lost for words, but finally found his tongue. 'God's blood,' he said wistfully, 'but she's a beautiful creature.'

'She belongs to Labrouillade,' Thomas said harshly.

'She could dim the stars,' Keane said, 'and turn a man's mind to smoke.'

'She's married.'

'A creature so lovely,' Keane said wonderingly, 'it just makes you believe that God must really love us.'

'Now find a fresh horse,' Thomas said, 'and you and Father Levonne take that message to Labrouillade.' He turned to the priest who had followed them into the moonlight. 'You can say your words, father, but unless you can persuade the count to let Genevieve go, then I'm exchanging the countess.'

'Yes,' Father Levonne said unenthusiastically.

'I want this finished,' Thomas said harshly, 'because tomorrow we're riding north.'

Riding north. To join a prince, or to find *la Malice*.

Roland de Verrec felt his soul soar like a bird in a clear sky, a bird that could pierce the clouds of doubt and rise to the heights of glory, a bird with wings of faith, a white bird, white as the swans that swam in the moat of the Count of Labrouillade's castle, where now he knelt in the candle-lit chapel. He was conscious of his heart beating, not just beating, but drumming hollowly in his chest as if it kept time with the beating wings of his rising soul. Roland de Verrec was in ecstasy.

That evening he had learned about the Order

of the Fisherman. He had listened to Father Marchant tell him of the Order's purpose and of the quest to retrieve *la Malice*. 'But I know about *la Malice*,' Roland had said.

Father Marchant had been taken aback, but recovered. 'You know?' he had asked. 'So what do you know, my son?'

'It is the sword Saint Peter carried in Gethsemane,' Roland had said, 'a sword that was drawn to protect our Saviour.'

'A holy weapon,' Father Marchant had said gently.

'But cursed, father. They say it is cursed.'

'I have heard that too,' Father Marchant had said.

'Cursed because Saint Peter drew it and Christ reproved him.'

'"*Dixit ergo Iesus Petro mitte gladium in vaginam . . .*"' Father Marchant had begun the quote from the gospel, then checked because Roland had looked so distressed. 'What is it, my son?'

'If evil men hold the sword, father, they will have such power!'

'That is why the Order exists,' the priest had explained patiently, 'to ensure that *la Malice* belongs only to the church.'

'But the curse can be lifted!' Roland had said.

'It can?' Father Marchant had seemed surprised.

'It is said,' Roland had told him, 'that if the blade is taken to Jerusalem and blessed within the walls of the Church of the Holy Sepulchre then the curse will be lifted and the sword will become a weapon of God's glory.' No other sword, not Roland's Durandal, not Charlemagne's Joyeuse, not even Arthur's Excalibur could compare to *la Malice*. She would be the holiest weapon on God's earth if her curse could be lifted.

Father Marchant had heard the awe in Roland's voice, but instead of saying that a journey to Jerusalem was about as likely as Saint Peter reappearing he had nodded solemnly. 'Then we must add that duty to the Order's tasks, my son.'

Now, in the candle-bright chapel, Roland was inducted into the Order. He had made his confession, he had received absolution, and now he knelt at the altar step. The other knights were behind him, standing in the small, white-painted nave. Roland had been pleased to find Robbie in the Order, but the second Scotsman, the bone-hung Sculley, had shocked him. Even a few moments in Sculley's presence was to be struck by the man's coarseness: the perpetual sardonic grin, the curses, the malevolence of the man, the mockery and the appetite for cruelty. 'He is indeed a crude instrument,' Father Marchant had told Roland, 'but God makes use of the humblest clay.'

Now Sculley was shuffling his feet and mumbling about wasting time. The other knights were silent, watching as Father Marchant prayed in Latin. He blessed Roland's sword, laid his hands on Roland's head, and placed a sash with the fisherman's embroidered keys around Roland's neck. And as he prayed, the candles in the chapel were being extinguished one by one. It was like the service of Good Friday, when to mark the Redeemer's death the churches of Christendom were plunged into darkness. And when the last candle guttered, there was only the pale light of the moon beyond the chapel's sole high window and the small red flame of the eternal presence, which cast shadows the colour of dark blood on the silver crucified Christ at which Roland gazed with adoration in his eyes. He had found his cause, he had found a quest worthy of his purity, and he would find *la Malice*.

Then Genevieve screamed.

And screamed again.

Keane and Father Levonne had ridden close to the drawbridge where the Irishman shouted up at the sentinel, who just glanced at the two horsemen in the moonlight and then walked a few paces along the gatehouse parapet. 'Are you listening?' Keane shouted. 'Tell your lord we've got his woman! He wants her back, doesn't he?' He waited. His horse stamped its foot. 'Jesus, man, are you hearing me?' he called. 'We've got his lady here!' The sentinel leaned between two of the merlons to look at Keane again, but he offered no answer, and after a moment he pulled back behind the stones. 'Are you deaf?' Keane asked.

'My son,' Father Levonne shouted, 'I am a priest! Let me talk to your lord!'

There was no answer. The moon illuminated the castle and shivered white on the wind-rippled moat.

There had only been the one man visible on the gatehouse wall, but he had now vanished to leave Keane and Levonne seemingly alone. The Irishman knew Thomas and a dozen other men were looking on from the trees, but he wondered who else watched from the dark slits in the curtain wall and in the moon-shadowed towers, and whether those watchers had tensioned crossbows loaded with short heavy bolts tipped with steel. The two wolf-hounds who had followed Keane whined. 'Is anyone hearing us?' Keane called.

A gust lifted the flag on the castle's keep. The banner stirred, then dropped as the small wind died. An owl called across the valley, and the two hounds lifted their heads and smelt the air. Eloise growled softly. 'Gentle now,' Keane told her, 'quiet yourself, girl, and tomorrow we'll run some hares. Maybe a deer if you're lucky, eh?'

'Englishman!' a voice bellowed from the castle.

'If you must insult a man,' Keane called back, 'can you not be clever about it?'

'Come back in the morning! Come at first light!'

'Let me talk to your lord!' Father Levonne shouted.

'You're a priest?'

'I am!'

'Here's your answer, father,' the man shouted, and a cord thrummed in one of the towers and a crossbow bolt slammed through the moonlight to strike the track twenty yards short of the two horsemen. The bolt tumbled on the turf, skidding to a halt between the startled dogs.

'It seems we have to wait till morning, father,' Keane said. He turned his horse, kicked back his heels, and rode out of range of the crossbows.

Till the morning.

The Count of Labrouillade had been at supper. There was a venison pastry, a roasted goose, a ham coated in thick lavender-flavoured honey, and a platter of millet-fattened ortolans, which was the count's favourite dish. He had a cook who knew how to drown the tiny birds in red wine, then roast them fast on a fierce fire. The count sniffed one. Just perfect! The aroma was so delicious it almost made his head swim, and then he sucked on the tiny bird and the yellow fat dribbled down his chins as he scrunched the fragile bones. The cook had roasted three woodcock too, drenching the needle-beaked birds with a mixture of honey and wine.

The count liked to eat. He was mildly annoyed that his guests, the severe Father Marchant, Sir Robbie Douglas, and the risible virgin knight, were fooling around in the chapel, but he would not wait for them. The ortolans were piping hot, and the woodcocks' dark breasts too delicious to delay, and so he left word that his guests could join him at their leisure. 'Sire Roland has done well, eh?' he remarked to his steward.

'Indeed, my lord.'

'Fellow got hold of *le Bâtard*'s wife! Roland might be a virgin,' the count chuckled at that, 'but he can't be a total idiot. Let's have a look at her.'

'Now, my lord?'

'Better entertainment than that fool,' the count said, gesturing towards a minstrel who played a small harp and sang of the count's excellence in battle. The song was largely invented, but the count's household pretended to believe it. 'Is everything ready for the morning?' the count asked before the steward could leave on his errand.

'Everything, my lord?' the steward asked, confused.

'Packhorses, armour, weapons, provisions. Christ's belly, man, do I have to do it all?'

'Everything is ready, my lord.'

The count grunted. He had been summoned to Bourges by the Duke of Berry. The duke, of course, was just some snot-nosed child, and the count had been tempted to pretend the summons had never arrived, but the snot-nosed child was a son of the French king and the *arrière-ban* had been delivered with a letter which delicately pointed out that the count had ignored two previous summonses, and that a failure to obey an *arrière-ban* justified the confiscation of land. 'We are sure,' the letter said, 'that you wish to retain your estates and so we anticipate your arrival at Bourges with joy, knowing you will come with many arbalists and men-at-arms.'

'Arbalists,' the count grumbled. 'Why can't he call them crossbowmen? Or archers?'

'My lord?'

'The duke, you fool. He's a damned child. Fifteen? Sixteen? Still wet. Arbalist, by Christ.' Still, the count would take forty-seven arbalists and sixty-seven men-at-arms to Bourges, a considerable force, greater even than the small army he had led against Villon to retrieve Bertille. He had thought to let one of his captains lead the force while he stayed at home where he would be guarded by the twenty crossbowmen and sixteen men-at-arms who would garrison the castle, but the threat of losing his land had persuaded him to travel himself. 'So fetch the woman!' he snapped at his steward, who had hesitated, thinking his lordship might have further questions.

The count crammed a woodcock against his mouth and gnawed at the honey-flavoured flesh. Not as delicate as the ortolan, he thought, and so he let the woodcock fall and thrust a tenth ortolan into his mouth.

He was still sucking on the little carcass as Genevieve and her son were brought into the small hall where he had chosen to eat. The great hall was filled with his men-at-arms, who were drinking his wine and eating his food, though he had made sure they were not served venison, ortolans or woodcock. The count crunched the bones of the songbird, swallowed, and pointed to a space close enough to the table for the big candles to illuminate Genevieve. 'Put her there,' he said, 'and why did you bring the boy?'

'She insisted, my lord,' one of the men-at-arms said.

'Insisted? It's not her place to insist. Skinny bitch, isn't she? Turn around, woman.' Genevieve stayed still. 'I said turn around, all the way around, slowly,' the count said. 'If she doesn't obey, Luc, you can hit her.'

Luc, the man-at-arms who had held Genevieve's arm to bring her into the hall, drew back his hand, but had no need to strike. Genevieve turned around, then looked defiantly into the count's eyes. He dabbed at his mouth and chins with a napkin, then drank wine. 'Strip her,' he said.

'No,' Genevieve protested.

'I said strip her,' the count said, looking at Luc.

Before Luc could obey, the door of the chamber opened and Jacques, now the count's senior captain, stood there. 'They've sent two messengers, my lord,' he said, 'offering to exchange the woman for the countess.'

'So?'

'They have the countess here, my lord,' Jacques said.

'Here?'

'So he says.'

The count stood and limped around the table. The arrow wound in his leg throbbed, though it was healing well enough. It still hurt to put his considerable weight on that leg, and he flinched as he stepped off the dais to confront Genevieve. 'Your husband, madame,' he growled, 'defied me.' He waited for her to respond, but she stayed silent. 'Tell their messengers to come back in the morning,' the count ordered, not taking his eyes off Genevieve, 'we'll exchange her at dawn.'

'Yes, my lord.'

'But I have another use for the bitch first,' he said, and with those words a terrible anger overwhelmed the count. He had been humiliated, first by his wife and then by *le Bâtard*. He suspected his own men mocked him behind his back, which is why he preferred to eat in a separate hall. Indeed, he knew that all France laughed at him. He had been insulted, he had been crowned with the cuckold's horns, and he was a proud man, and the wound to his honour went deep so that the rage was suddenly red in him, and he roared in what sounded like pain as he reached out, took hold of Genevieve's linen dress and ripped it open.

Genevieve screamed.

The scream only enraged the count further. All the hurt of the last weeks was seething in him, and all he could think of was to wreak revenge on the men who had belittled him, and how better than to take the horns from his own head and put them on *le Bâtard*? He tore the dress down as Genevieve screamed a second time and staggered backwards. Her son was crying and the count cuffed him hard around the head, then tugged at Genevieve's dress again. She clutched the torn linen to her throat. 'You foul bitch!' the count shouted. 'Show me your tits, you skinny bitch!' He struck her a stinging blow, and just then half a dozen men came through the chamber door.

'Stop!' It was Roland de Verrec who shouted. 'Stop!' he called again. 'She is my hostage.'

Still more men came through the door. Robbie Douglas was there, gaping at Genevieve, who was now crouching on the flagstones and trying to pull the ripped fragments of her dress up to her neck. Sculley was grinning. The count's men-at-arms were looking from the furious Labrouillade to the calm Roland, while Father Marchant took stock and stepped between them. 'The girl,' he told the count, 'is the captive of the Order, my lord.'

That statement puzzled Roland who thought she was his hostage, but he took the words as a statement of support and so made no protest.

The count was breathing heavily. He was a cornered boar. For a heartbeat it seemed that prudence might govern his rage, but then, like a wave breaking inside him, the rage overwhelmed him again. 'Get out,' he snarled at the newcomers.

'My lord . . .' Father Marchant started emol-liently.

'Get out!' the count roared. 'This is my castle!' No one moved.

'You!' the count pointed at Luc. 'Get rid of them!'

Luc did try to shepherd Roland, Father Marchant and the other knights of the Order of the Fisherman from the hall, but Roland stayed firm. 'She is my hostage,' he said again.

'Let's fight for the bint,' Sculley said cheerfully.

'Quiet,' Robbie hissed. Robbie was aware of all the old turmoil that he thought had been calmed by the Order of the Fisherman. He knew Genevieve, he had been in love with her since the day he had first seen her in the cells at Castillon d'Arbizon. That unrequited love had broken his friendship with Thomas, it had led to the breaking of oaths, to his arguments with the Lord of Douglas, and had only ended, Robbie had thought, with the sacred duty of the Order of the Fisherman. Now he saw Roland put a hand on the hilt of his sword, and he dreaded the choice that must follow. Genevieve was staring up at him, surprise and appeal in her hurt eyes.

The count saw Roland's hand go to Durandal's sword hilt and, foolishly, he reached for his own blade. Father Marchant held up both hands. 'In the name of God!' he shouted, and snatched at Roland's arm. 'In the name of God!' he said again, and held a cautionary hand towards the count. 'My lord,' he said in a reasonable voice, 'you are right. This is your castle. What happens in these walls is by your command, by your privilege, and we cannot prevent it. But, my lord,' and here Father Marchant bowed low to the count, 'this woman must talk to us. His Holiness the Pope demands it, the King of France demands it, and, my lord, His Holiness and His Majesty will be grateful to you if you will allow me, your most humble servant,' and here he bowed again to Labrouillade, 'to question this wretched woman.'

Father Marchant had invented the interest of the Pope and the king, but it was an inspired invention, sufficient to cool Labrouillade's fury. 'I am right?' the count demanded.

'Entirely, and if any of us has impeded you, my lord, if any of us has challenged your undoubted authority, then you have our humblest apology.'

'But the Pope and the king have an interest here?'

'Astonishing though that may seem, my lord, yes. It is why I am here, sent by Cardinal Bessières. My lord, if you would earn a reputation as a man who has fought valiantly for the kingdom of heaven here upon earth then I would beg you to allow me some time with this creature.'

'And when you're done with her?'

'As I said, my lord, this is your castle.'

'And your men would do well to remember that,' the count snarled.

'Indeed, my lord.'

'Then take her,' the count said magnanimously.

'The church will be for ever in your debt, my lord,' Father Marchant said, and beckoned to Sculley and Robbie to take Genevieve out. He pointed at Hugh. 'Take him too.'

And Robbie breathed a sigh of relief.

Thomas knelt at the wood's edge. 'What did he say?' he asked for the tenth time.

'To go back at first light.' Keane said.

And between now, the night's heart, and first light, what would happen to Genevieve? This was the question that tortured Thomas, and to which imagination provided a foul answer, and for which intelligence offered no solution. He could not rescue her. He could not cross a moat, climb a wall, and fight his way inside. For that he would need an army and time. 'You should get some sleep,' he said to his men, and that was true, but the archers had chosen to keep their vigil with Thomas. None wanted to sleep. 'How many men inside?' Thomas wondered aloud.

'The bastard had about a hundred men when we fought at Villon,' Sam offered.

'They can't all be inside,' Thomas said, though that was hope speaking.

'It's a big enough place,' Keane said.

'And we have thirty-four archers here,' Thomas said.

'And we have men-at-arms,' Karyl added.

'He had about forty crossbows,' Sam said, 'maybe more?'

'He didn't say he'd exchange her?' Thomas asked, for the tenth time.

'He just said to come back,' Keane said. 'I'd have asked the fellow a few questions if I could, but they dropped a hint with a crossbow that Father Levonne and I weren't exactly welcome.'

If Genevieve was hurt, Thomas thought, he would forget *la Malice*, he would forget the Prince of Wales, he would forget everything until he had tied the Count of Labrouillade down onto a table and cut him as the count had cut Villon. And that was a futile hope in this moonlit night. There were times when all a man could do was wait and fortify himself with dreams against despair.

'At dawn,' Thomas said, 'I want every archer,

every man-at-arms. We'll show ourselves. We'll be ready to fight, but stay just out of crossbow range.' It was a gesture, he knew, nothing more, but right now he was reduced to gestures.

'We're ready now,' Sam said. Like all the archers he had his bow, though in the expectation of dew he had taken the cord from the stave and stored it in his hat. 'And it'll be an early dawn.'

'You should sleep,' Thomas said, 'all of you who aren't sentries, you should sleep.'

'Aye, we should,' Sam said.

And no one moved.

Father Marchant laid a gentle hand on Roland's arm. 'You did right, my son. She is your prisoner and you had to defend her, but you must use caution.'

'Caution?'

'This is the count's demesne. He rules here.' He smiled. 'But that is past. Now you must give the prisoner to us.'

'Prisoner?' Roland asked. 'She is a hostage, father.'

Father Marchant hesitated. 'What do you know of her?' he asked.

Roland frowned. 'She is base-born and married to *le Bâtard*, but beyond that nothing of consequence.'

'You like her?'

Roland hesitated, then remembered his duty to the truth. 'I didn't like her at first, father, but I've come to admire her. She has spirit. She has a quick mind. Yes, I like her.'

'She has bewitched you,' Father Marchant said sternly, 'and for that you are not to blame. But you should know she is excommunicated, condemned by Holy Mother Church. She was to be burned for heresy, but *le Bâtard* rescued her, and then, to compound her evil, she killed a pious Dominican who had discovered her heresy. In all conscience, my son, I cannot let her go now, I cannot permit her to spread her loathsome doctrines. She is condemned.'

'I swore to protect her,' Roland said uneasily.

'I release you from that oath.'

'But she seems such a good woman!'

'The devil masks his work, my son,' Father Marchant said, 'he cloaks the vile in raiments of light and sweetens their foulness with honeyed words. She looks fair, but she is the devil's creature, as is her husband. They are both excommunicated, both heretics.' He turned as his servant approached down the shadowed corridor. 'Thank you,' he said, taking the hawk from the man. He had pulled on a leather glove and now wrapped the bird's jesses around his wrist before stroking the hood that covered the bird's eyes. 'Do you know,' he enquired of Roland, 'why the heretics went to Montpellier?'

'She told me they went to escort an English monk who would enrol at the university, father.'

Father Marchant smiled sadly. 'She lied about that, my son.'

'She did?'

'Her husband seeks *la Malice*.'

'No!' Roland said, not in protest, but in astonishment.

'It's my surmise that he heard the weapon might be there.'

Roland shook his head. 'I wouldn't think so,' he said confidently.

It was Father Marchant's turn to be astonished. 'You wouldn't . . .' he said weakly, then stopped.

'Well, of course I don't know,' Roland said, 'and perhaps you have news of *la Malice* that I haven't heard?'

'We heard it was at a place called Mouthoumet, but it was gone when we arrived.'

'It's possible it was taken to Montpellier,' Roland said dubiously, 'but a man who cares for *la Malice* would surely return it to its proper place.'

'There is a proper place?' the priest asked cautiously. He was stroking the bird's hooded head, his finger gentle against the soft leather.

Roland smiled modestly. 'My mother, God bless her, is descended from the ancient Counts of Cambrai. They were great warriors, but one of them defied his father and gave up the profession of arms to become a monk. Junien, he was called, and family tradition says that the blessed Saint Peter appeared to him in a dream and gave him the sword. Saint Peter told Junien that only a man who was both a saint and a warrior was fit to protect the blade.'

'Saint Junien?'

'He's not well known,' Roland admitted sadly, 'indeed, if he's famous at all it's for sleeping through a snowstorm that should have killed him, but he was protected by the grace of God . . .' He paused because Father Marchant had gripped his arm so tightly that it hurt. 'Father?' he asked.

'Does this Junien have a shrine?'

'The Benedictines at Nouaillé keep his earthly remains, father.'

'At Nouaillé?'

'It's in Poitou, father.'

'God bless you, my son,' Father Marchant said.

Roland heard the relief in the priest's voice. 'I don't know that *la Malice* is there, father,' he warned cautiously.

'But she may be, she may be,' Father Marchant said, then paused as a servant carried a chamber pot down the passageway that was lit by what small glow leaked from the candle-lit hall. 'I don't know,' he finally admitted when the servant had passed. 'I don't know,' he repeated, sounding weary. 'It could be anywhere! I don't know where else to look, but perhaps *le Bâtard* knows?' He stroked the hawk that was stirring restlessly on his wrist. 'So we must discover just what he knows and why he went to Montpellier.' He lifted his arm on which the hawk was perched. 'Soon, my dear one,' he spoke to the hawk, 'we shall unhood you very soon.'

'Unhood her?' Roland asked. It seemed a strange thing to do in the night-time.

'She is a *calade*,' Father Marchant said.

'A *calade*?' Roland asked.

'Most *calades* discover sickness in a person,' Father Marchant explained, 'but this bird also has the God-given talent of discovering the truth.' He stepped away from Roland. 'You look tired, my son. Might I suggest you sleep?'

Roland smiled ruefully. 'I've slept little these past nights.'

'Then rest now, my son, with God's good blessing on you, rest.' He watched Roland walk away, then turned to where his other knights were waiting at the passage's end. 'Sir Robbie! Will you bring the girl and her boy?' He pushed open a random door and found himself in a small room where wine barrels were stacked around a table on which stood jugs, funnels, and goblets. He swept them off, clearing the table's top. 'This will do,' he called, 'and bring candles!'

He stroked the hawk. 'Are you hungry?' he asked the bird. 'Is my darling hungry? We shall feed you very soon.' He stood to one side of the small chamber as Robbie brought Genevieve through the door. She was clutching her torn dress to her breasts. 'It seems you have met the heretic before?' Father Marchant suggested to Robbie.

'I have, father,' Robbie said.

'He's a traitor,' Genevieve said, and spat into Robbie's face.

'He is sworn to God's purpose,' Father Marchant said, 'and you are cursed by God.'

Sculley dragged Hugh through the door and pushed him down beside the table.

'Candles,' Father Marchant demanded of Sculley. 'Fetch some from the hall.'

'Like to see what you're doing, eh?' Sculley said with a grin.

'Go,' Father Marchant ordered harshly, then turned back to Robbie. 'I want her on the table. If she resists, you may strike her.'

Genevieve did not resist. She knew she could not fight Robbie, let alone Robbie and the ghastly man with the bones in his hair who now brought two huge candles that were placed on wine barrels. 'Lie flat,' Father Marchant ordered her, 'as if you were dead.' He saw her shivering. She had placed her hands on her breasts to keep the torn dress in place, and the priest now unwound the jesses from his glove and put the hawk on her topmost wrist. The claws dug into her thin flesh and she made a small whimpering sound. '*In nomine Patris*,' Father Marchant said softly, '*et Filii, et Spiritus Sancti*, amen. Sir Robert?'

'Father?'

'We have no notary to record this sinner's confession, so you will pay attention and be a witness to what is said. You have a holy duty to remember the truth.'

'Yes, father.'

The priest looked at Genevieve who lay with closed eyes and clasped hands. 'Sinner,' he said gently, 'tell me why you went to Montpellier.'

'We took an English monk there,' Genevieve said.

'And why?'

'He was to study medicine at the university.'

'You wish me to believe that *le Bâtard* went all the way to Montpellier just to escort a monk?' Father Marchant asked.

'It was a favour to his liege lord,' Genevieve said.

'Open your eyes,' the priest ordered. He still spoke softly. He waited till she obeyed. 'Now tell me,' he said, 'have you heard of Saint Junien?'

'No,' Genevieve said. The hooded hawk did not move.

'You are excommunicated, are you not?'

She hesitated, then gave a small nod.

'And you went to Montpellier as a favour to a monk?'

'Yes,' she said in a small voice.

'It would be in your interest,' Father Marchant said, 'to tell the truth.' He leaned forward and unlaced the hood, slipping it off the hawk's head. 'This is a *calade*,' he told her, 'a bird that can tell whether you speak true or false.' Genevieve looked up into the hawk's eyes and shuddered. Father Marchant stepped back. 'Now tell me, sinner,' he said, 'why you went to Montpellier?'

'I told you, to escort a monk.'

Her scream echoed through all the castle.

CHAPTER 9

Roland was startled awake by the scream. The count had not thought to provide beds. The castle was crammed with men waiting to march to Bourges, and they slept where they could. Many were still drinking in the great hall, while some had bedded down in the courtyard where the horses that had no room in the stables were sleeping, but Roland's squire, Michel, had cleverly found a chest filled with banners that he spread on a stone bench in the antechamber to the chapel. Roland had just fallen asleep on that makeshift bed when the scream echoed down the passageways. He woke confused, thinking he was back home with his mother. 'What was that?' he asked.

Michel was staring down the long passage. The boy said nothing. Then a bellow of anger echoed down the corridor, and that brought Roland to full wakefulness. He rolled off the bench and snatched up his sword. 'Your boots, sire?' Michel said, offering them, but Roland was running. A man at the passage's far end was looking alarmed, but no one else seemed to have been disturbed

290

by the scream and the shout. Roland pushed open the door of the wine store and gaped.

The room was almost totally dark because the candles had been knocked over, but in the dim light Roland saw Genevieve sitting on the table with one hand clasped to an eye. Her torn dress had fallen around her waist. Father Marchant was sprawling on his back with bloody lips, a beheaded hawk was twitching on the floor, while Sculley was grinning. Robbie Douglas was standing with a drawn sword over the priest, and, as Roland took in the scene, the Scotsman used the sword's hilt to hit Marchant again. 'You bastard!'

Hugh was crying, but on seeing Roland he ran to him. Roland had told him stories, Hugh liked him, and he clung to Roland, who flinched as Robbie hit the priest a third time, knocking Marchant's head back hard against a wine barrel. 'You'd blind her, you bastard?' Robbie shouted.

'What . . .' Roland began.

'We must go!' Genevieve shouted.

Sculley seemed to be amused by what he had seen. 'Nice titties,' he said to no one in particular, and that seemed to startle Robbie into a realisation of what he had done.

'Go where?' Robbie asked.

'Find a hole and bury yourself,' Sculley advised, then looked back to Genevieve. 'Bit small, but nice.'

'What happened?' Roland at last managed to ask.

'The bastard wanted to blind her,' Robbie said.

'I like titties,' Sculley said.

'Quiet,' Robbie snarled at him. He had thought he had found purpose and spiritual reassurance in the Order of the Fisherman, but the sight of the hawk slashing its beak at Genevieve's eye had opened his own eyes. He realised he had run from his old oaths, that he had betrayed his promises, and now he would make good. He had ripped his sword out of its scabbard and taken the hawk's head off in one sweep, then turned on Father Marchant and punched him with the sword's hilt, breaking the priest's lips and teeth. Now he had no idea what he should do.

'We have to leave now,' Genevieve said.

'Where?' Robbie asked again.

'A very deep hole,' Sculley said, amused, then frowned at Robbie. 'Are we fighting anyone?'

'No,' Robbie said.

'Get my cloak,' Roland ordered Michel, and when the squire brought the garment the virgin knight draped it around Genevieve's bare shoulders. 'I am sorry,' he said.

'Sorry?'

'You were under my protection,' he said, 'and I failed.'

Robbie looked at Roland. 'We must go,' he said, sounding frightened.

Roland nodded. Like Robbie he was finding his world turned inside out. He was desperately trying to think what he should do, what was the right thing to do. The girl was a heretic and, only this same evening, he had sworn an oath before God to join the Order of the Fisherman, yet here was the Order's chaplain, moaning and bleeding, and the heretic was looking at him with one eye, the other still covered by her hand, and Roland knew he had to save her. He had promised her protection. 'We must go,' he echoed Robbie.

Both were aware that they were deep inside a castle that was suddenly a hostile place, but when Roland looked out into the passage there was no one there, and the noise from the great hall where men still drank had surely been loud enough to smother the sound of Genevieve's scream. Roland strapped on his sword belt. 'We just go,' he said, sounding astonished.

'Your boots, sire,' Michel said.

'There's no time,' Roland said. He was feeling panicky. How were they to leave?

Father Marchant tried to get up and Robbie turned and kicked his head. 'Kick him hard, Sculley, if he moves again.'

'Am I fighting for him or for you?' Sculley asked.

'Who do you serve?' Robbie demanded.

'The Lord of Douglas, of course!'

'And what am I?'

'A Douglas.'

'Then don't ask stupid questions.'

Sculley accepted that. 'So you want me to kill the bastard?' he asked, looking at the priest.

'No!' Robbie said. To kill a priest was to invite

excommunication, and he was in trouble enough already.

'I don't mind,' Sculley offered. 'I haven't killed anyone in a week. No, it's been even longer. It must be at least a month! Jesus! Are you sure we're not fighting anyone?'

Roland looked at Robbie. 'We just walk out?'

'We don't have a great deal of choice,' Robbie said, sounding nervous again.

'Then let's go!' Genevieve wailed. She had found a cleaning rag that she was clutching to her eye with one hand, while the other held the cloak at her neck.

'Take the boy,' Roland ordered Michel, then he stepped out into the passageway. 'Sheathe your sword,' he said to Robbie.

'Sheathe it?' Robbie seemed confused.

Roland glanced at the sword, which had a smear of bloody feathers. 'We're guests here.'

'For the moment.'

'What in Christ's name are we doing?' Sculley demanded.

'Fighting for the honour of Douglas,' Robbie said curtly.

'So we are fighting?'

'For Douglas!' Robbie snarled.

'No need to shout,' Sculley said, and, as Robbie sheathed his sword, he drew his own long blade. 'Just tell me who you want slaughtering, eh?'

'No one for now,' Roland said.

'And keep quiet,' Robbie added. Roland glanced

at Robbie as if seeking reassurance, but the young Scotsman was just as nervous as the Frenchman. 'We must keep moving,' Robbie suggested.

'Are we leaving the castle?'

'Think we have to, yes,' he paused, looking around, 'if we can.'

Roland led the way into the courtyard. A few fading fires on which men had baked oatcakes smoked in the wide space, but the moonlight was bright, the shadows dark. No one took any particular notice of them. Genevieve was swathed in the cloak, and Hugh was clutching at its folds as they threaded their way through the sleeping horses and men. Other men passed wineskins and talked in low voices. Someone sang. There was the low chuckle of laughter. Lantern light glimmered in the gatehouse.

'Look for my horse,' Roland said to Michel.

'You think they'll just let us ride out?' Robbie whispered.

'Don't look for my horse,' Roland said, wondering how they were to escape on foot.

'Your boots, sire?' Michel offered them.

'No time,' Roland said. His world had fragmented; he no longer knew where his salvation lay, unless it was his honour, which meant he must save a heretic even if it meant breaking a church-sworn oath. 'I'll tell them to lower the drawbridge,' he told Robbie, and strode towards the gatehouse.

'Stop them!' The shout came from the door behind them. Father Marchant, holding onto the doorpost, was pointing at them. 'Stop them! In the name of God!'

The men in the courtyard were slow to respond. Some were sleeping, others were trying to sleep, and many were lulled by wine, but now they stirred as more men took up the shouts. Sculley swore, then nudged Robbie. 'Are we fighting yet?'

'Yes!' Robbie shouted.

'Who?'

'Everyone!'

'About bloody time!' Sculley said, then slammed his sword in a backhanded blow against a man struggling to free himself of a cloak. The man collapsed, blood dark on his forehead, and Sculley sawed the sword through a skein of ropes tethering three horses to a ring set in the wall. He pricked one of the horses with his sword's point, and the animal bolted, causing chaos among the waking men. He slapped the other two, and all through the yard horses were whinnying and rearing.

'Drawbridge!' Roland shouted. Two men were facing him, both with swords, but he was suddenly calm. This was his trade. So far he had only fought in tournaments, but his victories in the lists were the result of hours of practice, hour upon hour of obsessive sword practice, and he flicked one enemy's blade wide, feinted back, stepped forward and his sword slid between the ribs of the left-hand man, and he stepped into the other man, inside his wild swing, and brought his sword arm back so his elbow smashed into the man's belly.

'I have him,' Robbie called, just as if they were in a tournament's melee.

Roland stepped to his left and gave a short downswing, and the first man was out of the fight and he had hardly drawn breath. Now two sentinels had come from the gatehouse, and he went for them fast. One carried a spear, which he jabbed, but Roland could see the nervousness on the man's face and he hardly even had to think to parry the thrust and then flick the sword up so that its tip raked a horrid wound across the man's face. He cut lips, nose and an eyebrow, and the man, one eye filling with blood, reeled back into the second guard, who panicked, backing into the guardhouse. 'Bring Lady Genevieve,' Roland called to Michel, 'into the arch!'

Roland vanished into the guardroom, while Robbie and Sculley barred the entrance to the deep arched tunnel that was blocked at its further end by the closed drawbridge. 'It's got bloody bolts,' Sculley said.

Michel spoke no English, but he had seen the bolts and dragged the right-hand one free of its stone socket. Genevieve reached up and tried to free the other, but it would not budge and the cloak fell off her shoulders. Men in the courtyard saw her naked back and shouted to see more. Michel came to help her and the vast iron bolt squealed back.

'Hold them, Sculley!' Robbie shouted.

'Douglas!' Sculley bellowed his war shout at the men in the courtyard.

297

One guard was left inside the guardroom, but he shrank away from Roland who ignored him. Instead, Roland climbed the winding stairs that led to the big chamber above the gate-arch. There was no one there, but it was dark, the only light was the moon's dim glow leaking through the arrow slits, but Roland could see the vast windlass on which the drawbridge's chains were spooled. The windlass's drum was as wide as the arch and stood four feet high. There were huge handles at either end, but Roland could not budge the nearer one. He heard shouts below and the clash of blades. He heard a scream. A horse whinnied. For a few seconds he stood helpless, wondering how to release the mechanism, then as his eyes became accustomed to the gloom he saw a vast wooden lever by the far handle. He ran to it, took hold and pulled. For an instant it resisted his strength, then it suddenly gave way and there was an appallingly loud click and the vast drum spun fast and the chains whipped off the spools, jerking and shaking, and one snapped and the broken links whipped back to slash the side of Roland's face just as an almighty crash announced that the drawbridge was down.

He staggered, half stunned by the whiplashing chain, then recovered to pick up his sword that he had dropped to pull the lever, and started down the stairs.

The gate was open.

★   ★   ★

'Sir?' Sam touched Thomas's shoulder.

'Jesus.' Thomas breathed the name. He had been half asleep, or rather his mind was drifting vaguely like the tenuous mist that was sifting off the moon-touched moat of Labrouillade's castle. He had been thinking of the Grail, of the common clay bowl he had hurled into the sea, and been wondering, as he often did, whether it truly was the Holy Grail. Sometimes he doubted it, and sometimes he shivered for the audacity of concealing it beneath the eternal roll and thunder of the waves. And before that, he thought, he had sought the lance of Saint George, and that too was gone, and he had been thinking that if he did find *la Malice* then perhaps that also should be hidden for ever, and while his mind was wandering he had seen the sudden dull glimmer of firelight appear in the castle's arch and then came the great crash confirming that the drawbridge had fallen.

'Are they coming out?' Sam wondered aloud.

'Bows!' Thomas called. He stood and bent his great black yew stave, looping the cord over the horn nock. He touched the inside of his left wrist, confirming that the leather bracer was there to protect him from the string's lash. He pulled an arrow from his bag.

'No horsemen,' a man said. The archers had moved out of the trees to where they could shoot unimpeded.

'Someone's coming out,' Sam said.

Why would they lower the drawbridge, Thomas

thought, unless it was to make a sortie? But if they planned a surprise night attack on his encampment then why were the horses not already galloping across the open meadow that stretched down to the moon-whitened castle? He could see a few people crossing the bridge, but no horsemen. Then he saw more men following, and there was the glint of moonlight on blades. 'Forward!' he called. 'Get in range!'

Thomas cursed his limp. It was not crippling, but he could not run as fast as he had once run, and his men easily outstripped him. Then Karyl and two other men cantered past on horseback, their swords drawn. 'That's Hugh!' someone shouted.

'And Genny!' Another English voice. Thomas had a glimpse of shapes against the lit gateway, thought he saw Genevieve and Hugh, but then saw another shape, a man with a crossbow. He halted, raised the great war bow and drew the cord.

The muscles of his back took the enormous tension. Two fingers drew the cord, two more steadied the arrow on the stave as he tilted the bow towards the stars. This was as long a range as any longbow could shoot, maybe too long. He gazed at the gateway, saw the crossbowman kneel and raise the weapon to his shoulder, and Thomas drew the cord back past his right ear.

And loosed.

★ ★ ★

Roland expected to die. He was frightened. It seemed that the screeching, hammering, clangorous noise of the unreeling windlass drum was still ringing in his ears like the scream of some unearthly devil who was filling him with terror. He just wanted to hide, to curl into a ball in some dark corner and hope the world passed him by, yet he moved instead. He leaped down the stairs, still without his boots, and he expected that Labrouillade's men would have retaken the guardhouse and that he would be cut down by vengeful blades, yet to his astonishment there was only the one man still in the guardhouse chamber, and he was even more frightened than Roland. Robbie was shouting at Roland to hurry.

'Jesus,' Roland said, and it was a prayer.

Sculley was bellowing at the men in the courtyard to come and be killed. Three men lay at his feet and the firelight reflected from the glossy black of their blood that filled the spaces between the cobbles. 'Genevieve's gone,' Robbie shouted at Roland, 'now come on! Sculley!'

'I'm no finished,' Sculley snarled.

'You are finished,' Robbie said, and tugged at Sculley's shoulder. 'Run!'

'I hate running away.'

'Run! Now! For Douglas!'

They ran. They had survived thus far because the men in the courtyard were half asleep and confused, but they were awake now. Men pursued the fugitives, then Roland heard a sound he feared, the ratchet of a crossbow being tensioned. He pounded in his bare feet across the drawbridge, heard the snap of the crossbow being released, but the bolt went wide. He did not see the bolt, but he knew there must be others. He snatched at Hugh's hand and dragged him onwards and just then something white flashed by the corner of his sight. Another white flash! In his panic and fear he thought they must be doves. At night? A third slashed past and a shout sounded behind and he realised they were arrows in the night. Goose-feathered arrows, arrows of England, arrows whipping through the darkness to strike the men coming from the castle. One skidded on the path, skittering past Roland, and then the arrows paused as four horsemen thundered across the grassland, swords drawn, and the horses went past the fugitives, turned and the long blades slashed down at the pursuers. The horsemen did not stop, but kept going, curling around behind Roland, and the arrows flew again, pouring relentlessly into the gateway's open arch where the crossbowmen were crammed.

Then suddenly the fugitives were surrounded by men with longbow staves, and the horsemen were a shield behind and they kept going out of range of the castle till they reached the trees, and there Roland fell to his knees. 'Dear God,' he said aloud, 'thank you.' He was panting, shaking, and still held Hugh's hand.

'Sir?' Hugh asked nervously.

'You're safe,' Roland told him, and then someone came and scooped the boy up, carrying him away to leave Roland alone.

'Sam!' a harsh voice shouted. 'Keep a dozen men on the tree line. Bows strung! The rest of you! Back to the farm. Brother Michael! Where are you? Come here!'

Roland saw men crowding around Genevieve. He was still on his knees. The night was filled with excited English voices, and Roland had rarely felt so solitary. He glanced around to see that the long moonlit meadow between the wood and the castle was empty. If the Count of Labrouillade or Father Marchant were planning a pursuit it had not yet started. Roland thought how he had only been trying to be honourable, and yet it had turned his life upside down. Then Michel tapped his shoulder. 'I lost your boots, sire.' Roland did not answer, and Michel crouched. 'Sire?'

'It doesn't matter,' Roland said.

'I lost the boots and the horses, sire.'

'It doesn't matter!' Roland said more sharply than he had intended. What was he to do now? He had thought he was employed on two quests, one of them of high sanctity, yet they had led to this lonely despair. He closed his eyes in prayer, begging for guidance, then became aware that someone was breathing in his face. He shuddered, then felt a wet lick and opened his startled eyes to see a pair of wolfhounds standing over him.

'They like you!' a cheerful voice said, but as the

man spoke in English Roland had no idea what was said. 'Now come away, you two,' the man went on, 'not everyone wants to be christened by a pair of bloody hounds.'

The dogs romped away and Thomas of Hookton took their place. 'My lord?' he said, though there was no respect in the voice. 'Should I kill you or thank you?'

Roland stared up at *le Bâtard*. The virgin knight was still shaking and did not know what to say, so he turned and stared at the castle again. 'Will they attack?' he asked.

'Of course not,' Thomas said.

'Of course not?'

'They were half asleep or half drunk. Maybe they'll be ready for a sortie by dawn? Though I doubt it. That's why my men have two rules, my lord.'

'Rules?'

'They can get drunk as much as they like, but only when I tell them. And no rape.'

'No . . .' Roland began.

'Unless they want to be hanged off the nearest tree. I hear Labrouillade wanted to rape my wife?' Thomas asked and Roland just nodded. 'Then I owe you thanks, my lord,' Thomas said, 'because what you did was brave. So thank you.'

'But your wife . . .'

'She'll live,' Thomas said, 'maybe with only one eye. Brother Michael will do what he can, though I doubt that he can do much. Only I'm not sure

I should call him "brother" any more. I'm not certain what he is now. Come, my lord.'

Roland allowed himself to be raised up and led through the trees towards the farm. 'I didn't know,' he said, then faltered.

'Didn't know what a bastard Labrouillade is? I told you he was, but so what? We're all bastards. I'm *le Bâtard*, remember?'

'But you don't let your men rape?'

'For God's sake,' Thomas said, turning on him. 'You think life is easy? It might be easy in a tournament, my lord. A tournament is artificial. You're on one side or the other and no one thinks God takes sides in a tournament, and there are marshals to make sure you don't get carried off dead, but there are no marshals here. It's just war, war without end, and the best you can do is try not to be on the wrong side. But who in God's name knows which side is right? It depends where you were born. I was born in England, but if I'd been born in France I'd be fighting for King Jean and reckoning God was on my side. In the meantime I try not to do evil. It might not be much of a rule, but it works, and when I do evil I say prayers and give alms to the church and pretend my conscience is clear.'

'You do evil?'

'It's war,' Thomas said. 'Our job is to kill. The scriptures say *non occides*, but we do. A clever doctor at Oxford told me that the commandment means we shouldn't commit murder, and that isn't

305

the same as thou shalt not kill, but when I lift some poor bastard's visor and slide a sword into his eye socket that isn't a great comfort to me.'

'Then why do you do it?'

Thomas gave him an almost hostile look. 'Because I like it,' he said, 'because I'm good at it. Because in the dark of night I can sometimes persuade myself I'm fighting for all those poor folk who can't fight for themselves.'

'And are you?'

Thomas did not answer, but instead called to a man standing beside the farm's door. 'Father Levonne!'

'Thomas?'

'This is the bastard who caused all the trouble. The Sire Roland de Verrec.'

'My lord,' the priest said, bowing to Roland.

'I need to talk to Robbie, father,' Thomas said, 'and look after Genevieve. So maybe you can find Sire Roland some boots?'

'Boots?' the priest asked, astonished. 'Here? How?'

'You're a priest. Pray, pray, pray.'

Thomas unslung his bow, chiding himself for not having done it earlier. A bow that was left tensioned by the cord too long could become permanently bent; it would have followed the string, as the archers said, and such a bow had less power. He coiled the cord and pushed it into a pouch and went into the farmhouse, which was lit with feeble rush wicks. Robbie was sitting in the cattle's byre, which was otherwise occupied by only a brindled cow with one horn. 'He had this bird,' Robbie said as soon as Thomas came through the heavy door, 'a hawk. He called it a *calade*.'

'I've heard the word,' Thomas said.

'I thought *calades* discovered sickness in a person! But he tried to blind her! I killed it. I should have killed him!'

Thomas half smiled. 'I remember,' he said, 'when Genevieve killed the priest who had tortured her. You disapproved of that. Now you'd kill a priest yourself?'

Robbie lowered his head and stared at the rotted straw on the byre's floor. He was silent for a while, then shrugged. 'My uncle's here, in France I mean. He's not much older than me, but still my uncle. He killed my other uncle, the one I liked.'

'And you don't like this uncle?'

Robbie shook his head. 'He frightens me. The Lord of Douglas. I suppose he's my clan chief now.'

'And demands what of you?'

'That I fight against the English.'

'Which you vowed not to do,' Thomas said.

Robbie nodded, then shrugged. 'And Cardinal Bessières released me from that vow.'

'Cardinal Bessières is a slimy turd,' Thomas said.

'Aye, I know.'

'Why is your uncle here?'

'To fight the English, of course.'

'And expects you to fight alongside him?'

'He wants that, but I said I couldn't break the

oath. So he sent me to Bessières instead.' He looked up at Thomas. 'The Order of the Fisherman.'

'What in God's name is that?'

'Eleven knights, well, there were eleven before tonight, sworn to discover . . .' He stopped suddenly.

'*La Malice*,' Thomas said.

'You know,' Robbie said flatly, 'the cardinal said you knew. He hates you.'

'I dislike him too,' Thomas said mildly.

'It's a sword,' Robbie said, 'supposedly a magic sword.'

'I don't believe in magic.'

'But other folk do,' Robbie said, 'and if he gets the sword he'll have power, won't he?'

'Power to become Pope,' Thomas said.

'I suppose that's not really a good thing?' Robbie suggested.

'You'd make a better Pope. Hell, I would. That cow would.'

Robbie half smiled, but said nothing.

'So what do you do now?' Thomas asked, and again Robbie said nothing. 'You saved Genevieve,' Thomas said, 'so I release you from your oath. You're free, Robbie.'

'Free?' Robbie grimaced and looked up at Thomas. 'Free?'

'I release you. All your oaths to me, they're gone. You're free to fight the English, do what you will. *Te absolvo*.'

Robbie smiled at the priestly Latin. 'You absolve me,' he said tiredly, 'to be free and poor.'

'You're still gambling?'

Robbie nodded. 'And losing.'

'Well, you're free. And thank you.'

'Thank you?'

'For what you did tonight. Now I need to see Genny.'

Robbie watched Thomas walk to the door. 'So what do I do?' he blurted out.

'It's your choice, Robbie. You're free. No oaths any more.' Thomas paused at the door, saw that Robbie was not going to answer and so walked out. The cow lifted her tail and filled the byre with stench.

Sculley pushed the door wide. 'They're bloody English,' he protested.

'Yes.'

'Still, that was a good fight,' Sculley said, then laughed. 'I had a son of a whore try to axe my feet away and I jumped over the bastard's swing and put my sword in his mouth and he just stared at me and I gave him a moment to think about it, then pushed. Bloody Christ, the noise he made! I think he was calling for his mama, but that's no bloody use when you've a Douglas sword down your gullet.' He laughed again. 'Aye, a rare good fight, but for the English?'

'We were fighting for Genevieve,' Robbie said, 'and she's French.'

'The thin bitch? Pretty enough, but I like them with more meat. So what do we do? What happened to the bloody fisherman?'

Robbie smiled wanly. 'I don't think Father Marchant will want us back.'

'It was a waste of time anyway. Pissing about for a daft priest with a magic bird.' Sculley stooped and picked up a handful of straw and scrubbed at his sword blade. The bones woven into his hair rattled as he bent over the weapon. 'So we leave?' he asked.

'Leave?'

'Jesus! To join the lord, of course!'

He meant the Lord of Douglas, Robbie's uncle. 'Is that what you want?' Robbie asked, his voice dull.

'What else? We came here to do a bloody job, not piss about with bloody fishermen.'

'I'll talk to Thomas,' Robbie said, 'and I'm sure he'll give you a horse. Money too.'

'The lord will want you back.'

'I took an oath,' Robbie said, then remembered that Thomas had just freed him of all his commitments. He could choose his own fate now. 'I'm staying, Sculley,' he said.

'Staying?'

'You can go to my uncle, but I'm staying here.'

Sculley frowned. 'If you stay with this fellow,' he gestured towards the other part of the house where he assumed Thomas had gone, 'then the next time I see you I'll have to kill you.'

'Yes, you will.'

Sculley gobbed towards the cow. 'I'll make it

quick. No hard feelings. You'll talk to the man about a horse?'

'I will, and I'll ask him to give you coins for the journey.'

Sculley nodded. 'That sounds fair,' he said, 'you stay, I go, and then I'll kill you.'

'Yes,' Robbie said.

He was free.

Father Levonne, to his own astonishment, discovered a pair of boots in a chest that stood in a small upstairs room of the farm. 'The farmer fled,' he said, watching as Roland tried the boots on, 'but we shall leave him money. Do they fit?'

'They do,' Roland said, 'but we can't steal them.'

'We'll leave more money than they're worth,' Father Levonne said. 'Trust me, he's a French farmer, he'd rather have gold than shoes.'

'I have no money,' Roland said, 'or rather the money I have is in the castle.'

'Thomas will pay,' Father Levonne said.

'He will?'

'Of course. He always pays.'

'Always?' Roland sounded surprised.

'*Le Bâtard*,' Father Levonne explained patiently, 'lives on the edge of English Gascony. To eat he needs grain and cheese and meat and fish, he needs wine and hay, and if he steals those things then the country folk won't like him. They'll betray him to Berat or Labrouillade, or to any of the other lords

311

who'd like to hang Thomas's skull in their hall, so Thomas makes sure they appreciate him. He pays. Most lords don't pay, so who do you think is more popular?'

'But . . .' Roland began, then faltered.

'But?'

'*Le Bâtard*,' Roland said in puzzlement, 'the Hellequin?'

'Ah, you think they're the devil's creatures?' Father Levonne laughed. 'Thomas is a Christian, and even, I dare say, a good one. He's not sure of that, but he does try.'

'But he was excommunicated,' Roland pointed out.

'For doing what you did, saving Genevieve's life. Maybe you'll be excommunicated next?' Father Levonne saw the horror on Roland's face and tried to alleviate it. 'There are two churches, sire,' he said, 'and I doubt God takes any notice of an excommunication from one of them.'

'Two? There's only one church,' Roland said. He gazed at the priest as though Father Levonne was a heretic himself. '*Credo unam, sanctam, catholicam et apostolicam Ecclesiam*,' he said sternly.

'Another soldier who speaks Latin! You and Thomas! And I too believe in one holy, catholic and apostolic church, my son, but that church is Janus-faced. One church, two faces. You were serving Father Marchant?'

'Yes,' Roland said in some embarrassment.

'And whom does he serve? Cardinal Bessières.

Cardinal Louis Bessières, Archbishop of Livorno and Papal Legate to the court of France. What do you know of Bessières?'

'He's a cardinal,' Roland said, but plainly knew no more.

'His father was a tallow merchant in the Limousin,' Father Levonne said, 'and young Louis was a clever boy and his father had enough cash to see that he was educated, but what chance does a tallow merchant's son have in this world? He can't become a lord, he wasn't born, as you were, to privilege and rank, but there is always the church. A man can rise far in the holy, catholic and apostolic church. It matters not if he was born in a gutter, so long as he has a good brain, and a tallow merchant's son can become a prince of the church, and so the church draws in all those clever boys, and some of them, like Louis Bessières, are also ambitious, cruel, greedy and ruthless. So one face of the church, sire, is our present Pope. A good man, a little dull, a little too attached to canon law, but a man who tries to do Christ's will in this wicked world. And the second face is Louis Bessières, an evil man, who wants, above everything, to be Pope.'

'Which is why he seeks *la Malice*,' Roland said quietly.

'Of course.'

'And I told Father Marchant where to find it!' Roland went on.

'You did?'

313

'Or perhaps where he can find it. I don't know. It might not be there.'

'I think you must talk to Thomas,' Father Levonne said gently.

'You can tell him,' Roland said.

'Me? Why me?'

Roland shrugged. 'I must ride on, father.'

'To where?'

'An *arrière-ban* has been pronounced. I must obey.'

Father Levonne frowned. 'You'll join the army of the King of France?'

'Of course.'

'And how many enemies will you have there? Labrouillade? Marchant? The cardinal?'

'I can explain to Father Marchant,' Roland said hesitantly.

'You think he's amenable to reason?'

'I took an oath,' Roland said.

'Then take it back!'

Roland shook his head. 'I can't do that.' He saw the priest was about to interrupt so hurried on, 'I know things are not black and white, father, and perhaps Bessières is evil, and I know Labrouillade is a vile creature, but is his wife any better? She is an adulteress! A fornicator!'

'Half Christendom is guilty of that sin, and most of the other half wish they were too.'

'If I stay here,' Roland said, 'then I condone her sin.'

'Good God,' Father Levonne said in astonishment.

'Is it so bad to wish for purity?' Roland asked, almost pleadingly.

'No, my son, but you're not making sense. You accept that you made oaths to evil men, but now you won't break them. How pure is that?'

'Then maybe I break the oaths,' Roland allowed, 'if my conscience tells me to, but why break an oath to support a man who fights against my country and who shelters an adulteress?'

'I thought you were a Gascon. The English rule Gascony, and no one disputes their right.'

'Some Gascons do,' Roland said, 'and if I fight I will fight for what I think is right.'

Father Levonne shrugged. 'You can do no more than that,' he agreed, 'but at the very least you can say farewell to Thomas.' He glanced out of the casement and saw that dawn was greying the world's edge. 'Come, he'll want to thank you.'

He led Roland downstairs into the big kitchen. Genevieve was there, a bandage across her left eye, and Hugh was sleeping in the corner while Thomas sat beside his wife with an arm about her shoulder. 'Father,' he greeted Levonne.

'The Sire Roland wishes to leave,' Father Levonne said. 'I tried to persuade him to stay, but he insists he will go to King Jean.' He turned and gestured for Roland to say whatever he wished, but Roland said nothing. He was staring, entranced, at the third person sitting at the table. He seemed incapable of speech or, indeed, of motion. He just stared, and through his head were running all the lines of poetry that the troubadours had sung in his mother's castle, lines about lips that looked like crushed rose petals, about cheeks as white as doves' wings, about eyes that could light the darkest sky, and about hair that was the colour of ravens' wings. He tried to speak again, but nothing came, and she was gazing back at him with eyes just as wide.

'You haven't met the Countess of Labrouillade,' Thomas said. 'My lady, this is the Sire Roland de Verrec . . .' He paused, then added pointedly, 'who swore an oath to return you to your husband.'

But it seemed Bertille did not hear Thomas's words any more than Roland heard them, because she was just gazing at Roland. They each stared at the other and for both the world had ceased to exist. Time had stopped, heaven was holding its breath, and the virgin knight was in love.

PART III

POITIERS

CHAPTER 10

The two dice rolled across the table.
It was a very fine table, made from dark walnut and inlaid with a pattern of unicorns made from silver and ivory, but it was now covered with a cloth of darkest blue velvet fringed with golden tassels. The velvet muffled the sound of the dice, which were being watched by five men.

'God's bowels,' the youngest one said when the dice stopped.

'Have emptied upon you, sire,' another man said as he stooped over the table, 'thrice!' He needed to stoop because the dice, though made of the finest and whitest ivory, were marked with gold, which made them hard to read, and the difficulty was compounded by the strange light inside the vast tent, which was sewn from canvas dyed in red and yellow stripes. Not that there was much light to be coloured by the canvas for, although it was mid-morning, the sky was thick with dense cloud. The man looked quizzically at the prince, seeking permission to scoop up the dice. The prince nodded. 'A two and a one,' the man said, grinning,

319

'which I believe, sire, make three, and increases your debt to me by three hundred.'

'Your enjoyment is unseemly,' the prince said, though without any anger.

'It is indeed, sire, but it is enjoyment all the same.'

'Oh God, no.' The prince looked up because the tent was suddenly loud with the sound of a hard rain falling. It had been pattering on the canvas all morning, but now drummed, then cascaded so fast that the men needed to raise their voices to be heard. 'God doesn't love me today!'

'He adores you, sire, but loves my purse more.'

The prince was twenty-six years old, a fine-looking man with thick fair hair darkened by the tent's peculiar light. His face was bony with deep-set eyes as dark as the jet buttons that decorated the high collar of his tunic, which was fashionably short, tight-waisted, and dyed royal blue. The skirt was stiffened with bone and tailored into points that were edged with pearls, lined with yellow silk and finished with tassels woven from cloth of gold. His sword belt was made from the same cloth, though embroidered with his badge of three feathers made from ivory-coloured silk. The scab-barded sword itself was leaning against a chair that stood at the tent's entrance, and the prince crossed to it so he could peer up at the rain-drenched sky. 'Good God, will it never stop?'

'Build an ark, sire.'

'And fill it with what? Women? Two by two? Now that is a beguiling notion! Two girls with golden hair, two with black, and a pair of redheads for variety?'

'They'll prove better company than animals, sire.'

'You know that from experience?'

The men laughed. Men always laugh at the jests of princes, but this laughter was genuine enough because Edward of Woodstock, Prince of Wales, Duke of Cornwall, Earl of Chester and lord of Lord knew how many other territories, was a genial, easygoing and generous young man. He was tall and would have attracted the eyes of women even if he had not been heir to the throne of England and, according to the lawyers and lords who served his father, heir to the throne of France too. King Jean II disputed that, naturally enough, but the pursuit of that claim was why the English army was in France. The prince's coat-of-arms was the royal coat, showing the three golden lions of England quartered with the fleur-de-lys of France, above which was a silver bar with three pendant labels indicating that he was the eldest son of the king, though the prince himself preferred to carry a shield painted black on which his three feathers glowed alabaster white.

The prince looked moodily at the sky. 'Goddamned rain,' he said.

'It must stop soon, sire.'

The prince made no answer to that comment, but stared between the twin oak trees that stood like sentinels at the tent's entrance. The city of Tours was barely visible because of the heavy rain.

The place did not look formidable. True, the Cité was well enough protected with towers and heavy stone walls, but the *bourg*, which was surely where much of the city's wealth lay, was low-lying and ringed only by a shallow ditch and by a wooden wall that was broken in many places. The prince's troops, hardened by war, could cross that barrier in their sleep, except that the River Loire had overflowed its banks, and Tours was now protected by flooded fields, by farmland turned to marsh, and by thick mud. 'Goddamned rain,' the prince said again, and God answered with a peal of thunder so sudden and loud that every man in the tent flinched. A jagged sky-splitting lance of lightning slid down to the low hill on which the tent stood, making everything stark white and black for an instant, then a second crash of thunder echoed across the sky and, though it had seemed that it could not rain any harder, the intensity of the downpour was doubled. Rain bounced off the muddy ground, poured off the tent and made streams on the hill. 'Jesus,' the prince said, 'Jesus, Jesus, Jesus!'

'Saint Martin has his ear, sire,' one of his companions remarked.

'Saint Martin?'

'Patron saint of Tours, sire.'

'Did he drown to death?'

'I believe he died in his bed, sire, but I'm not sure.'

'The bloody man bloody deserved to bloody drown if he sent this bloody rain.'

A horseman appeared at the foot of the hill. His horse was draped in a cloth showing a badge, but the cloth was so wet that the device could not be distinguished. The horse's mane lay flat on its neck, dripping water. Its hooves slopped through the mud while the rider, who was wearing a mail hood beneath a bascinet, slumped in the saddle. He kicked the reluctant beast up the shallow slope and squinted towards the tent. 'Is His Majesty there?'

'That's me!' Edward called. 'No, no, don't dismount!' The man had been about to get out of the saddle to kneel to the prince, but instead he just bowed. Rain bounced off his helmet.

'I was sent to tell Your Majesty that we're going to try again,' the messenger shouted. He was only five paces away, but the rain was too loud for a normal voice.

'You're going to swim to the damned place?' the prince called and waved to show he wanted no answer. 'Tell him I'll come!' he shouted, then turned back into the tent and snapped his fingers towards a servant who waited in the shadows. 'A cloak! A hat! Horse!'

Another crash of thunder deafened the world. Lightning stabbed onto the ruined church of Saint Lidoire, the remnants of which had been pulled apart to provide stone to repair the Cité's walls. 'Sire,' one of the men at the gaming table called, 'you needn't go!'

'If they're attacking then they need to see me!'

'You've no armour, sire!'

The prince ignored that, lifting his arms so a servant could attach the sword scabbard to the silver chains hanging from the belt. Another servant swathed Edward in a thick black cloak. 'Not that one,' the prince said, pushing the cloak away, 'the red one! The one with gold fringes!'

'The dye will run, sire.'

'Damn the dye, they must see me. The red one! They need to recognise my pretty face. Give me that hat, the small one. Is a horse ready?'

'Always, sire,' a servant said.

'Which horse is it?'

'Foudre, sire.'

The prince laughed. 'That's bloody apt, eh? Foudre!' *Foudre* was the French for lightning, and the prince, like his entourage, preferred to speak in French. It was only when he needed to speak with the common soldiers that he used English. He ran into the rain, cursing as he slipped on the wet grass. He steadied himself by grabbing the groom holding Foudre. 'Help me up!' He was already soaked through. 'I'll want dry clothes when I get back!' he called to a servant inside the tent, then tugged on the reins.

'Wait!' someone shouted, but the prince was already spurring away, squinting because the rain was lashing into his eyes. The wind had risen, thrashing wet branches, and Foudre shied away from a low, heavy-leaved oak bough that shook in the gale. Lightning ripped across the sky, revealing the limestone bluffs beyond the river with a sudden brilliant white light and was followed a few seconds later by a crash of thunder that sounded as if the towers of heaven were collapsing.

'You're an idiot, sire!' Another horseman had caught up with the prince, who was laughing.

'I'm a wet idiot!'

'We can't attack in this!'

'Maybe that's what the bloody enemy thinks?'

The prince's horse pounded across a waterlogged meadow towards a stand of willows where a mass of mailed men looked dark in the day's gloom. The river was just beyond them, its wide surface made turbulent by the incessant rain. To the prince's left, closest to the feeble defences of the *bourg*, but separated from them by a wide stretch of half-flooded marsh, were archers. They were wading north towards the town, but the prince noted none of them was drawing bows and loosing arrows. 'Sir Bartholomew!' he called as he ducked under a willow branch.

'Bloody strings are wet,' Sir Bartholomew Burghersh said without looking at him. He was a stocky, dark-faced man a little older than the prince, and a man noted for his violent hatred of all things French, except possibly for their wine, gold, and women. 'Bloody strings are sopping wet. Might as well spit at the bastards rather than loose arrows. Let's go!'

The mass of mailed men-at-arms trudged north behind the archers, who, because their bowstrings were soaked, could not shoot at anything near to their usual range. 'Why are the bowmen out there?' the prince called.

'A fellow slipped into our lines and said the bastards had pulled back into the Cité,' Burghersh said. His men-at-arms, all on foot and carrying shields, swords and axes, were struggling through the soggy ground and into the face of the rain-drenched gale. The wind was so strong that it was making waves on the flood water; there were even whitecaps. The prince spurred behind the men-at-arms, staring into the tempest and wondering if it could be true that the enemy had abandoned the *bourg*. He hoped so. His army was bivouacked on what higher ground they could find. A few lucky men had cottages or hovels for shelter, a handful possessed tents, but most had to put together a shelter from branches, leaves, and turf. The *bourg* could shelter all his men till this wretched weather relented.

Sir Bartholomew, mounted on a fine destrier, rode alongside the prince. 'Some of the bows will shoot, sire,' he said, somewhat nervously.

'Are you sure of your fellow? The one who said the bastards had fled?'

'He seemed very certain, sire. He claimed the Count of Poitou ordered every defender into the Cité.'

'So the puppy Charles is here, is he?' the prince said. Charles was the eighteen-year-old dauphin, heir to King Jean of France. 'The boy made a quick march from Bourges, didn't he? And he's just going to let us take the town?' The prince peered through the rain. 'His banners are still on the wall,' he added dubiously. The feeble defences of the *bourg* were hung with banners, though it was hard to distinguish what they displayed because the rain had smeared the dyes in the cloth, but there were saints and fleurs-de-lys, and the presence of the flags suggested the defenders were still behind their palisade.

'They want us to think they're still in the *bourg*, sire,' Burghersh said.

'And I want this town,' the prince said.

He had led six thousand men out of Gascony, and they had burned towns, captured castles, razed farms, and slaughtered livestock. They had captured noble prisoners whose ransoms would defray half the cost of the war, indeed they had taken so much plunder that the men could not carry all they had stolen. From the treasury at Saint-Benoît-du-Sault alone they had taken no less than fourteen thousand golden écus, each worth three English silver shillings. Over two thousand pounds in good French gold! They had met almost no resistance. The great castle at Romorantin had held out for a couple of days, but when the fire arrows of the prince's archers had succeeded in setting fire to the roof of the great keep, the garrison had stumbled out, escaping the falling rafters that were collapsing in spectacular gouts of flame. A priest in the prince's household reckoned the army had covered two hundred and fifty miles so far, and it had been two hundred and fifty miles of plunder and destruction and pillage and killing, two hundred and fifty miles of impoverishing the French and showing that England could march with impunity throughout the enemy's land.

Yet the prince knew his army was small. He had led six thousand men for two hundred and fifty miles, and now he was in the very centre of France, and France could assemble thousands of men to oppose him. Rumour said the King of France was gathering an army, but where, and how large, the prince did not know. But of one thing he could be certain: the army of King Jean would be larger than his army, and the reason he wanted Tours so badly was that this was the route by which he could join the smaller force of the Earl of Lancaster. Lancaster had marched out of Brittany to lay waste a swathe of land in northern France, and was now said to be coming south, hoping to join the prince, while the prince was working his way northwards, but to join Lancaster he needed to cross the Loire, and to cross the Loire he needed the bridge, and to take the bridge he needed to capture Tours. If the prince could join Lancaster he would command enough men to keep going north towards Paris, to ravage the enemy's heartland and take on the French royal army, but if he could not cross the river then he would have no choice but to retreat.

The archers edged their way through the swamp. The rain seethed and the wind drove the water in quick wavelets. One man drew his bow and loosed an arrow at the *bourg*'s wooden palisade, but the bow's string had been weakened by the rain and the arrow fell well short. 'Don't waste your bloody sticks!' a ventenar, a man who led a score of archers, called angrily. 'Wait till you can kill a bloody Frenchman.'

'If there are any to kill,' Burghersh said. No enemy showed on the *bourg*'s feeble defences. 'Maybe the bastards really have gone?' he added hopefully.

'But why would he abandon the *bourg*?' the prince asked.

'Because he's an idiot, sire?' Burghersh suggested.

'I've heard the dauphin's ugly,' the Prince said, 'but no fool.'

'Whereas you, sire?' his other companion suggested, and Burghersh looked astonished at such insolence, but the prince laughed, enjoying the jest.

Some of the archers were using their bows as staffs, probing for firmer ground or else just balancing themselves. And still no enemy showed. One group of archers, closest to the river, found a strip of higher land that gave firm footing and they ran towards the pathetic wall beyond which were the rich houses and fat churches of Tours's *bourg*. Other archers moved towards the same drier ground, and the men-at-arms, struggling through the floods and mud, followed them till there was a crowd of men on the slightly higher and drier land.

And the crossbows shot.

Dozens of crossbows, kept dry because their

archers were in the upper floors of houses close to the wall. The bolts slashed through the rain, and the first archers were being thrown backwards by the force of the missiles. A couple of men tried to reply with their long war bows, but the damp strings had stretched and the arrows fell feebly short of the wooden wall that suddenly bristled with men holding axes, swords, and spears.

'Jesus,' the prince cursed.

'Another fifty paces,' Burghersh said, meaning that in another fifty yards his archers would be able to shoot into the *bourg*, but the crossbows were spitting quarrels too fast. The prince saw a man struck in the face, saw the blood misting sudden and almost immediately washed out of the air by the rain as the man fell back and splashed into the flood with a short black bolt protruding from an eye.

'Call them back,' the prince commanded.

'But . . .'

'Call them back!'

Burghersh shouted an order at his trumpeter who sounded the retreat. The wind and rain were loud, but not loud enough to drown the jeers of the defenders.

'Sire! You're too close!' the prince's companion insisted. He was Jean de Grailly, the Captal de Buch, a Gascon who had followed the prince from his lavish tent. 'You're too close, sire!'

'There are four hundred men closer than I am,' Edward said.

'You're wearing a red cloak, sire. It's called a target.' The captal spurred his own horse next to the prince's. 'Bastards,' he spat. He was as young as the prince, a black-browed young man with intense dark eyes and, despite his youth, he had a formidable reputation as a leader of men. He had brought his own followers out of Gascony, all of them wearing his badge of five silver scallop shells on a black cross displayed against a field of gold. His horse wore the badge, and his cloak was striped black and yellow, making him as prominent a target as the prince. 'If a bolt hits you, sire,' he said, but did not finish the sentence because a bolt hissed close to his face, forcing him into an involuntary flinch.

Prince Edward was watching the archers and men-at-arms struggle back through the watery mud. 'Sir Bartholomew!' he called to Burghersh, who had ridden a few paces closer to the wading men.

'Sire?'

'The bastard who told you they'd retreated. Where is he?'

'At my quarters, sire.'

'Hang him. Hang him slowly. Make it very slow.'

A crossbow bolt struck the marshland just in front of Foudre and tumbled in a spray of water past the horse's hooves. Two more missiles came close, but still the prince would not move. 'They can't see me running away,' he told the captal.

'Better to run away than die, sire.'

'Not always,' the prince said. 'Reputation, my lord, reputation.'

'Being dead before your time isn't the way to great reputation,' the captal said.

'My time isn't now,' the prince said. 'I had my fortune told in Argenton.'

'You did?'

'A filthy crone, she was, but folk said she sees the future. She smelled like a cesspit.'

'And what did she say?'

'She said I was destined for marvellous things,' the prince said.

'Did she know you were the Prince of Wales, sire?'

'Oh yes.'

'Then she'd hardly say you were going to die in a mucky rainstorm a week later, would she? The better the fortune they give the better you pay them. And I'll wager you were generous?'

'I think I was, yes.'

'And most likely one of your courtiers told the crone what to say. Did she say you'd be lucky in love?'

'Oh yes.'

'That's an easy prophecy to give a prince. A prince can look like a toad and they'll still spread their legs.'

'God is indeed good,' the prince said happily. Scarlet dye was leaking from his hat and making faint trickles on his face so that he looked as if he was bleeding.

'Come away, sire,' the captal pleaded.

'In a moment, my lord,' the prince said. He was determined to wait until the last Englishman or Welshman had retreated past his horse.

A crossbowman on the upper floor of a leather-worker's house that lay close to the southern gate had seen the two horsemen's rich cloaks. He wound the handles of his weapon, drawing the cord back inch by slow inch, tensioning the wood and metal bow that creaked as it took the enormous strain of the thick cord. He felt the cord click over the pawl that held it, then searched through his bolts to find one that looked sharp and clean. He laid it in the groove, then rested the weapon on the casement sill. He sighted it. He noted that the wind was gusting hard from left to right and so he edged the weapon slightly leftwards. He put the stock against his shoulder, took a breath and felt for the trigger with his right hand. He waited. The horsemen were not moving. The foot soldiers were fleeing, some were falling as the bolts struck through leather or mail to pierce bone and flesh, but the crossbowman ignored them. He sighted on the red cloak again, raised his aim very slightly to allow for the missile's fall, steadied himself, held his breath, and pulled the trigger. The crossbow thumped into his shoulder as the bolt sped away, a black streak in the torrential silver rain.

'Maybe the rain will stop tonight,' the prince said wistfully.

333

The crossbow bolt went between his right thigh and the saddle. It cut the fine cloth of his hose without scratching his skin, it pierced the saddle's thick leather, was slowed by the wooden frame and finally jarred against one of Foudre's ribs. The horse whinnied and shied away from the pain. The prince calmed the stallion. 'Christ,' he said, 'two inches higher and I'd be singing in the front row of the choir.'

'Sire,' the captal said, 'you can punish me for this, but I don't want to lose you.' He leaned over, took hold of Foudre's bridle, and dragged the prince back towards the willows. The prince called encouragement to the defeated foot soldiers as he allowed himself to be pulled out of danger.

'Tomorrow,' he called, 'tomorrow we'll have our revenge! Tomorrow we'll sack Tours!'

Yet the next dawn brought no reprieve. The wind still howled across the wet land and the rain fell and the thunder bellowed and lightning tore the sky. God, it seemed, wanted Tours to be safe. He wanted to trap the English and their Gascon allies south of the River Loire. And the next day after that, because to remain still was to invite the French to surround them, the prince's army turned back towards the south.

The retreat had begun.

The weapons were stored in the dungeons beneath the keep of Castillon d'Arbizon's castle. There were five cells there, and one of those was occupied by Pitou, who was waiting for his father to send Thomas's men back from Montpellier. Two other cells were empty. 'I put the drunks in those,' Thomas explained to Keane.

'Jesus, they must be full all the time.'

'Rarely,' Thomas said, leading the Irishman into the largest cell, which was his makeshift armoury. The two wolfhounds sniffed in the passageway, anxiously watching Keane as he ducked into the cell. 'They know they can get drunk as much as they like,' Thomas went on, 'but not when they're supposed to be sober.' He raised the lantern and hung it on a hook embedded in the ceiling, though the flickering candle gave small light. 'You stay alive by being good,' he said.

'By being sober?' Keane sounded amused.

'By being good,' Thomas said, 'by practice, by being fast, by being strong enough to pull a bow or carry a heavy sword. Weapons need skills and the man you end up fighting might have been practising those skills for twenty years so you have to be better. If not, you're dead. And out here? We're a small garrison surrounded by enemies, so we have to be the best.'

'And if a man's not good enough?'

'I discharge him. There's plenty want to serve here. They make money.'

Keane grinned. '*Coredors* with a castle, eh?'

He had meant it as a jest, but Thomas flinched anyway because there was truth in the jest. *Coredors* were bandits, men and women driven from their

335

land to live wild in the hills and prey on travellers or small communities, and the incessant wars in France meant that there were many *coredors*. The largest highways were patrolled by men-at-arms, but other roads were dangerous except to formidable bands of armed men. The *coredors* were hated, but what were the Hellequin if not *coredors*? Except that they served a lord, in this case William Bohun, Earl of Northampton, who was God knows how many miles away watching the border between Scotland and England, and it was the Earl of Northampton's wish that Thomas dominated this stretch of France. Did that make it right? Or was Saint Sardos's church in Castillon d'Arbizon rich in silver and bright with wall paintings because Thomas suspected otherwise? 'I first met Genevieve in this cell,' he told Keane.

'Here?'

'They were going to burn her as a heretic,' Thomas said. 'They'd already built the fire. They had piles of straw for kindling and they'd stacked the faggots upright because they burn more slowly. That way the pain lasts longer.'

'Jesus,' Keane said.

'Not pain,' Thomas corrected himself, 'but agony. Can you imagine Jesus burning someone alive?' he asked. 'Can you imagine him making a fire to burn slowly, then watching someone scream and writhe?'

Keane was surprised by the pure anger in Thomas's voice. 'No,' he said cautiously.

'I'm a devil's whelp,' Thomas said bitterly, 'a priest's son. I know the church, but if Christ came back tomorrow he wouldn't know what the hell the church was.'

'We're all evil bastards,' Keane said uncomfortably.

'And you're not fast enough with a sword,' Thomas said. 'Another five years' practice and you might be swift enough. Here, try this.'

The weapons in the cell were all captured from enemies. There were swords, axes, crossbows, and spears. Many were useless, their blades just waiting to be melted down and recast, but there was plenty of good weaponry, and Thomas had chosen a poleaxe. 'Christ, that's wicked,' Keane said, hefting the heavy axe.

'The head's weighted with lead,' Thomas explained. 'It doesn't take a lot of skill, but it needs strength. Mind you, skill helps.'

'To hack?'

'Think of it as a quarterstaff with a blade. You can trip with it, thrust with it or hack with it.' The poleaxe was short, just five feet long, with a thick wooden haft. The head, forged from steel, had an axe blade and opposite it a hooked spike, while both ends of the haft had short spikes. 'A sword isn't much good against an armoured man,' Thomas said. 'Mail will stop a cut, and even boiled leather will stop most sword slashes. A sword thrust might work against mail, but that,' he touched the spike at the tip of the poleaxe, 'works against all armour.'

'Then why do men carry swords?'

'In battle? Most don't. You have to batter a man down if he's in armour. A mace, a morningstar, a flail, an axe will all do better.' He turned the head to show the hooked spike. 'You can pull a man off balance with the fluke. Hook or trip him onto the ground and beat the bastard to death with the axe head. If you like it, take it, but tie some rags under the head.'

'Rags?'

'You don't want blood trickling down the haft and making it slippery. And ask Sam to weave you some bow cord to improve the grip. You know the blacksmith in town?'

'The one they call Squinting Jacques?'

'He'll put an edge on it for you. But go into the courtyard first and practise with it. Hack one of the stakes to bits. You've got two days to become an expert.'

The courtyard was already filled with men practising. Thomas sat on top of the keep's steps and smiled a greeting to Sir Henri Courtois, who sat beside him, then flexed an ankle and flinched. 'It still hurts?' Thomas asked.

'Everything hurts. I'm old.' Sir Henri frowned. 'Give me ten?'

'Six.'

'Sweet Jesus, only six? How about arrows?'

Thomas grimaced. 'We're short of arrows.'

'Six archers and not many arrows,' Sir Henri said unhappily. 'We could just leave the castle gates wide open?'

'It would be much less trouble,' Thomas agreed, provoking a smile from Sir Henri. 'I'll leave you a thousand arrows,' he suggested.

'Why can't we make arrows?' Sir Henri asked unhappily.

'I can make a bow in two days,' Thomas said, 'but one arrow takes a week.'

'But you can get arrows from the Prince of Wales?'

'I'm hoping so,' Thomas said. 'He'll have brought hundreds of thousands. Wagonloads of arrows.'

'And each takes a week?'

'It takes a lot of people,' Thomas said, 'thousands of folk in England. Some cut the shafts, some forge the heads, some collect the feathers, some glue and bind them, some nock them, and we shoot them.'

'Ten men-at-arms?' Sir Henri suggested.

'Seven.'

'Eight,' Sir Henri said, 'otherwise you're leaving me unlucky thirteen.'

'Fourteen with you,' Thomas said, 'and you should have sixteen soon.'

'Sixteen?'

'That prisoner downstairs. He's to be exchanged for Galdric and our two men-at-arms. They should arrive any day now. So sixteen. Jesus! I could hold this castle till Judgement Day with sixteen men!'

They were discussing how the castle was to be protected. Thomas planned to ride north and wanted to take as many of the Hellequin as he could, but he dared not leave the castle too lightly garrisoned. There were chests in the great hall that contained the gold and silver that Thomas wanted to take back to England. A third of it belonged to his lord, the Earl of Northampton, but the rest would buy him a fair estate. 'In Dorset,' he said, thinking aloud, 'back home.'

'I thought this was home?'

'I'd rather live in a place where I don't need sentinels every night.'

Sir Henri smiled. 'That sounds good.'

'Then come to Dorset with us.'

'And listen to your barbaric language every day?' Sir Henri asked. He was over fifty now, a man who had spent his long life in mail and plate. He had been the commander of the old Count of Berat's men-at-arms, and thus had been an enemy of Thomas, but the new count had reckoned Sir Henri was too old and too cautious. He had scornfully promised Sir Henri command of the small garrison at Castillon d'Arbizon when it was recaptured, but instead the count's siege had been defeated. Sir Henri, abandoned by the count, had been taken prisoner by Thomas, who, recognising the older man's vast experience and common sense, had kept the count's promise by making Sir Henri his own castellan. He had never regretted it. Sir Henri was reliable, honest, stoic, and determined to make his former lord regret his scorn. 'I hear Joscelyn has gone north,' Sir Henri said.

Joscelyn was the new Count of Berat, a headstrong

man who had still not given up his dream of re-claiming Castillon d'Arbizon. 'To Bourges?' Thomas asked.

'Probably.'

'Where is Bourges?'

'North,' Sir Henri said, though he was plainly uncertain. 'If it was me I'd ride to Limoges and ask the way from there.'

'And the Prince of Wales?'

'He was near Limoges,' Sir Henri said cautiously, 'or so they say.'

'They?'

'A friar was here last week. He said the English had ridden somewhere north of Limoges.'

'And where's Limoges?' Thomas wondered. 'Is Bourges to the east or the west of Limoges?'

'I know it's north of it,' Sir Henri said, 'but I have a mind it's eastwards of it too? You could ask Father Levonne. He's travelled a lot.'

Thomas was trying to make a picture of unknown territory and to fit within that vague idea an esti-mation of what the armies did. He knew the French were gathering forces, and that the men from southern France were assembling at Bourges while the northerners, under the king, would surely gather somewhere near Paris. But what of the Prince of Wales? He was making another *chevauchée*, a destructive march through the heart of France that left farms burned, mills destroyed, towns ruined, and livestock slaughtered. A *chevau-chée* was brutal and cruel, but it left the enemy impoverished. Eventually, if the French wanted to stop the English, they had to come out from their castles and fortresses to fight, and that was when the arrows would fly. Hundreds upon thousands of goose-fledged arrows.

'If I was you,' Sir Henri said, 'I'd go westwards. Limoges first, then up to Poitiers and keep going north from there towards Tours. You're bound to come across the prince somewhere.'

'Is Poitiers in Poitou?'

'Of course.'

'The man who tried to blind Genevieve might be there,' Thomas said, and did not add that *la Malice* might be there too, but he was not sure he even believed in *la Malice*.

'And what about Genny?' Sir Henri asked. 'Will she stay here?'

Thomas shook his head. 'Saint Paul said wives should be submissive to their husbands, but no one bothered to tell Genny that.'

'How is her eye?'

Thomas grimaced. Genevieve had made herself a leather eye-patch which she hated wearing, but she preferred it to the milky white of her ruined eyeball. 'Brother Michael thinks she'll keep it, but it's blinded.' He shrugged. 'She thinks she's ugly now.'

'Genny couldn't be ugly if she tried,' Sir Henri said gallantly. 'And what about Brother Michael? Will you take him?'

Thomas grinned. 'He's all yours. Give him a

crossbow; he should manage to shoot one of those without killing himself.'

'You don't want him?'

'And watch him despair over Bertille?'

Sir Henri chuckled. 'God, he's fast!' He was watching the Sire Roland de Verrec, who was fighting two men at once, fending them off with his swift sword. He seemed to do it effortlessly, though the two men attacking him were plainly straining every muscle to get past his parries. 'He'll go north with you,' Sir Henri said.

'He wants to, yes.'

'You know why? He doesn't want to be the virgin knight any more.'

Thomas laughed. 'That's easily remedied. I'm amazed it isn't already.'

Sir Henri watched Roland fight. 'He's extraordinary! How did he parry that thrust?'

'Skill,' Thomas said, 'and practice.'

'And purity,' Sir Henri said. 'He believes his skill lies in his purity.'

'God, I must be such a weakling. Really?'

'Which means he must make Bertille a widow before he can marry her, and he won't lose his virginity until he is married.'

'Dear God,' Thomas said. 'Truly?'

'He says they're betrothed. Can you be betrothed to a married woman? Anyway, he's talked to Father Levonne, and reckons he can keep his purity by marrying, but to marry the countess she has to be a widow, so first he has to kill the husband.'

'I hope Father Levonne explained that Labrouillade probably won't die in battle.'

'He won't?' Sir Henri asked.

'Of course not. He's too rich. He's worth a fortune as a prisoner. If things go badly for him he'll surrender, and no one will forgo a vast ransom to help Roland de Verrec lose his virginity.'

'I don't think our virgin knight has quite reckoned with that,' Sir Henri said. 'And what about Sir Robbie?'

'He goes with me,' Thomas said, his voice sounding grim.

Sir Henri nodded. 'You don't trust him?'

'Let's say I want him where I can see him.'

Sir Henri massaged his ankle. 'His man went back north?'

Thomas nodded. Sculley had wanted to go back to the Lord of Douglas and so Thomas had thanked him, given him a purse and let him ride north. 'The last thing he said to me was that he looked forward to killing me,' Thomas said.

'God, he was a horrible thing.'

'Horrible,' Thomas agreed.

'You think he'll make it to the French army?'

'I think Sculley could ride through hell untouched,' Thomas said.

'Is that a Scottish name? Sculley?'

'He told me his mother was English,' Thomas said, 'and he took her name because she didn't know who his father was. She was captured from

Northumberland by a Scottish raiding party and they evidently took turns on her.'

'So he's really an Englishman?'

'Not according to him. I just hope I don't have to fight the bastard.'

Then there were two days of preparation, days of rubbing bows with lanolin, of trimming the fledging on hundreds of arrows, of mending harness, of sharpening swords and axes, of looking at the future and wondering what it held. Thomas could not get the fight at Crécy out of his mind. Not that he remembered much outside the chaos of battle, the screams of horses and the screams of men, the whimpering of the dying and the stink of shit across a field of slaughtered soldiers. He did remember the noise of a thousand arrows leaping off their strings, and the Frenchman in a pig-snouted helmet that had been decorated with long red ribbons, and how those ribbons had swirled around so prettily as the man fell from his horse and died. He remembered the heavy thunder of the French drums driving their horsemen onto murderous blades, and the destriers breaking their legs in the pits dug to trap them; he remembered the proud banners in the mud, the weeping women, the dogs feasting on eviscerated soldiers, and the peasants creeping in the dark to plunder the corpses. He remembered all the glory of battle: the red ribbons of a dying man, the blood-laced corpses, and the lost child weeping inconsolably for his dead father.

And he knew the French were gathering an army.

And he was ordered to join the prince.

And so, as the first leaves turned yellow, he led the Hellequin north.

Jean de Grailly, Captal de Buch, sat his horse in the shadow of oak trees. Every time the courser moved its hooves there was the crunch of acorns. It was autumn already, but at least the driving rain that had defeated the army's attempt to capture Tours had ended, and the ground had been dried by days of warm weather.

The captal was not wearing his bold colours this morning. The striped yellow and black made him conspicuous and so, like the thirty-two men he led today, he was wearing a plain brown cloak. The courser was brown too. In battle the captal would ride a great destrier, trained to fight, but for this kind of combat the courser was better. It was faster and had more stamina.

'I see sixteen,' a man said softly.

'There are more of them in the trees,' another said.

The captal said nothing. He was watching the French horsemen who had appeared at a tree line beyond a stretch of pasture. Beneath the brown cloak, the captal wore a sleeveless haubergeon of leather covered with mail. He wore a bascinet with no visor, and other than that he had no protection except the plain shield on his left arm. A sword hung at his left hip, while in his right hand was a lance. It had been shortened. A heavy lance, such as a man would carry in a tournament, was too clumsy for this work. The lance's tip, which rested in the leaf mould, had a small triangular pennant showing the captal's silver scallop shell on a field of black and yellow stripes. It was his one concession to the vanity of nobility.

The prince's army was a mile or more behind him, travelling south on roads leading through apparently endless forests, and all around the army were small bands of horsemen like this one that the captal led. They were the army's scouts, and beyond the scouts were the enemy's scouts. There was an enemy army somewhere too, but the prince's scouts just saw bands of horsemen.

Those horsemen had tracked the army from the day it had left the safety of Gascony, but now there were far more. At least a dozen groups of French horsemen were keeping track of the English. They rode as close as they dared and sheered away if they were opposed by a larger force, and the captal knew they were sending their messages back to the French king. But where was he?

The prince, having been turned away from the river at Tours and thwarted of his ambition to join the Earl of Lancaster, was going back southwards. He was riding for the safety of Gascony and taking his plunder with him. The whole army was mounted, even the archers had horses, and the baggage carts were mostly light and horse-drawn so that the army could move fast, but it was evident the French were travelling just as fast, and any fool could understand that King Jean was doing his utmost to get ahead of the prince. Get in front, choose a battlefield, and kill the impudent English and Gascons.

So where were the French?

There was a faint smudge of grey in the eastern sky, which the captal suspected was smoke from the remnants of the fires that the French had lit in their encampment the previous night. And that smudge was close, too close and too far to the south. If that smudge was a marker of the French night-time position then they were already abreast of the prince, and a prisoner, taken two days before, had confirmed that King Jean had dismissed the foot soldiers from his army. He travelled like the English, every man on horseback. Foot soldiers would slow his march and he did not want to be slowed. It was a race.

'Twenty-one now,' a man said.

The captal stared at the horsemen. Were they a lure? Were a hundred other cavalry waiting in the trees to pounce if any Englishman or Gascon rode to attack the twenty-one? Then he would set his own lure. 'Hunald!' he called to his squire. 'The bag. Eude? Your horse and two men to go with you.'

The squire took a leather bag that hung from his saddle, dismounted and rooted around the forest floor to find stones. There were not many that were heavy enough, and so it took time to fill the bag. The Frenchmen, meanwhile, were gazing westwards. They were being cautious, and that, the captal decided, was good. They would be more confident if they were supported by a larger band of hidden cavalry.

The filled bag was tied by its laces to the right forefoot of Eude's horse. 'Ready, sire,' Eude said. He had dismounted.

'Then go.'

The three men, two in their saddles and with Eude leading his horse, left the cover of the trees and went southwards. The horse, cumbered by the bag of stones, walked awkwardly. It shied every few steps, and when it did walk docilely it dragged its right forefoot, and to a distant observer it looked as though the beast was painfully lame and that its owner was trying to lead it back to safety. The three men appeared to be easy prey, and the French, doubtless hoping that one of them was rich enough to yield a ransom, took the bait.

'It works every time,' the captal said in wonderment.

He was watching and counting the French horsemen who were coming from the trees. Thirty-three. The years of our Lord, he thought, and saw the enemy turning towards their prey and spreading apart. Lances dropped to the rest, swords were drawn, and then the Frenchmen spurred their horses across the pasture that separated the two stretches of woodland. They went from the trot to the canter. They were racing themselves now, eager to take the prisoners, and the captal waited a few heartbeats longer, then jerked up his own lance and touched the courser with his spurs. The horse leaped forward.

Twenty-nine horsemen burst from the trees. Lances were levelled. The French had not shortened their lances, and so had an advantage, but they had been taken by surprise and to meet the charge they needed to turn. They were slow, and the long lances were ponderous, and the captal struck them hard before they had a chance to realign themselves.

His own lance caught a man beneath his shield. The captal felt the shock of the blow as he tightened his arm on the lance's stock. The high cantle of his saddle held him in place as the lance bored deep. It went through mail and leather, through skin and muscle into soft tissue and there was blood on the enemy's saddle and the captal had already let go of the lance and was drawing his sword. He backslashed the blade, hitting the dying man's helmet, and used his knees to turn the courser hard to the right and so towards another Frenchman whose lance was tangled in a companion's horse. The man panicked, let go of the long ash lance and tried to draw his sword, and he was still drawing it as the captal's blade gouged his unprotected throat. A massive blow crashed against the captal's shield, but then one of his horsemen drew off that assailant. A horse was screaming. A dismounted man was staggering with blood spilling from a gash in his bascinet. 'I want a prisoner!' the captal shouted. 'At least one prisoner!'

'And their horses!' another man shouted.

Most of the Frenchmen were fleeing and the captal was content to let them go. He and his men had killed five of the enemy, wounded another seven, and they had their prisoners as well as the valuable horses.

He took them all back to the woodland where the ambush had been sprung and there he questioned the captives whose horses all bore the brand of the Count of Eu. That brand, a stylised lion burned into the horses' flanks, told the captal that these men were Normans. They were talkative Normans too. They told how the Count of Poitou's men, drawn from the southern counties of France, had joined the French king's army. So now the enemy was reinforced. They said, too, that they had ridden less than five miles from their overnight encampment to the meadow where the captal's men had torn into their flank.

So the French were nearby. They had been reinforced, they were marching hard, they were trying their best to cut the prince off from safety. They wanted a battle.

The captal went to find the prince to tell him the hunters had become the hunted.

And the retreat went on.

CHAPTER 11

It was a strange journey.

Thomas could feel the nervousness in the land. Towns kept their gates closed. Villagers hid when they saw horsemen coming; they either fled to nearby woods or, if taken by surprise, sheltered in their churches. Harvesters dropped their sickles and ran. Twice the Hellequin found cows lowing in pain because they needed to be milked after their owners had fled. Thomas's archers, nearly all of them countrymen, milked the animals instead.

The weather was uncertain. It did not rain, yet it always seemed about to rain. The clouds were low and the incessant north wind unseasonably cold. Thomas led thirty-four men-at-arms, which, except for those left to guard Castillon d'Arbizon, was every man fit enough to travel, and each of those men had two horses, and some had three or four. They had squires and servants and women who, like Thomas's sixty-four archers, were all mounted, and horses inevitably cast shoes or went lame, and each incident took time to remedy.

There was little news, and what there was could

not be trusted. On the third day of the journey they heard church bells clanging. It was too noisy and discordant to be the tolling for a funeral and so Thomas left his men hidden safe in a wood and rode with Robbie to discover what caused the commotion. They found a village large enough to boast two churches, and both were ringing their bells, while in the market square a Franciscan friar in a stained robe was standing on the steps of a stone cross proclaiming a great French victory. 'Our king,' the friar shouted, 'is rightly called Jean le Bon! He is indeed Jean the Good! John the Triumphant! He has scattered his enemies, taken noble prisoners, and filled the graves with Englishmen!' He saw Robbie and Thomas and, assuming them to be French, pointed at them. 'Here are the heroes! The men who have given us victory!'

The crowd, which seemed more curious than jubilant, turned to look at the two horsemen.

'I wasn't at the battle,' Thomas called, 'do you know where it was fought?'

'To the north!' the friar declared vaguely. 'And it was a great victory! The King of England is slain!'

'The King of England!'

'Glory be to God,' the friar said. 'I saw it myself! I saw the pride of England slaughtered by Frenchmen!'

'The last I heard,' Thomas said to Robbie, 'the king was still in England.'

'Or fighting Scotland,' Robbie said bitterly.

'There's a truce, Robbie, a truce.'

'The Lord of Douglas doesn't recognise a truce,' Robbie said bleakly. 'That's why I'm here, because I told him I couldn't fight against the English.'

'You can now. You're bound by no oaths.'

'By gratitude, then?' Robbie asked. Thomas gave a brief smile, but said nothing. He was watching a small boy, probably no older than Hugh, who was annoying an equally small girl by trying to lift her skirts with a nuthook. The boy saw Thomas's gaze and pretended to be interested in what the friar was saying. 'You think he's right?' Robbie asked. 'There's been a battle?'

'No, it's rumour.'

The friar was now haranguing the crowd to donate coins to two younger men, both in friar's robes, who were carrying small barrels about the crowd. 'Our brave men have suffered wounds!' the friar shouted. 'They have suffered for France! For the love of our Lord Jesus Christ help them in their distress! Be generous and receive Christ's blessing! Every coin will help our wounded heroes!'

'He's a fraud,' Thomas said dismissively. 'Just a rogue making some money.'

They moved on northwards. The Hellequin had to avoid towns because any place that had a wall inevitably had a score of men capable of shooting a crossbow, and Thomas wanted to finish his journey without losing a man to some squalid skirmish. He had tended to the eastward because he was more likely to find Englishmen in that direction, and he found a score of them in a village dominated by a high-towered church. That church was the only stone building; the rest were all made of timber, plaster, and thatch. There was a smithy with a furnace built in the back yard beneath a scorched oak tree, and a tavern surrounded by a huddle of small cottages, and when Thomas first glimpsed the village amidst the vineyards he had also seen a crowd of horses being watered in the small stream that flowed beside the impressive church. There were more than fifty horses, which suggested at least twenty men, and he had presumed the horses must belong to Frenchmen, but then he had seen the flag of Saint George, its red cross bold against the white field, leaning against the tavern wall. He had led his men down the hill and into the small square where men-at-arms leaped up in alarm. 'We're English!' Thomas called.

'Jesus,' a tall man said in relief as he ducked under the tavern's lintel. He wore a jupon showing a golden lion rampant against a background of fleurs-de-lys on a blue field. 'Who are you?' he asked.

'Sir Thomas Hookton,' Thomas said. He rarely used the honorific 'sir', but he had been knighted by the Earl of Northampton and it was useful sometimes.

'Benjamin Rymer,' the tall man said. 'We serve the Earl of Warwick.'

'You're with the army?' Thomas asked in hope.

'We're looking for the bloody army,' Rymer said, then explained that he and his conroi of men had been aboard a ship that had sailed from Southampton, but had become separated from the fleet that had been carrying the rest of the earl's reinforcements to Gascony. 'The wind blew up and the bloody shipmaster panicked and we ended up in Spain,' he said, 'and it took the bastard two months to make repairs and get us to Bordeaux.' He looked at Thomas's men. 'It's a relief to be with some archers again. Ours were on another ship. Do you know where the prince's army is?'

'No idea at all,' Thomas said.

'The blind leading the blind,' Rymer said. 'And there's no ale here, so no end to bad news.'

'Is there wine?'

'They say so. Tastes like cat piss to me. Did you come from Bordeaux?'

Thomas shook his head. 'We're from a garrison east of Gascony,' he said.

'So you know the damn country?'

'Some of it. It's big.'

'So where do we go?'

'North,' Thomas said. 'The last rumour I heard said the army was at Tours.'

'Wherever the hell Tours is.'

'It's to the north,' Thomas said, and slid out of the saddle. 'Rest the horses,' he called to his men. 'Walk them! Let them drink! We're moving again in an hour.'

Rymer and his troop travelled with Thomas's

men, and Thomas wondered how the man had survived so far because he expressed surprise when Thomas sent scouts ahead. 'Is it that dangerous?' he asked.

'It's always dangerous,' Thomas said. 'This is France.'

Yet no enemy disturbed them. Once in a while Thomas saw a castle and led his column on a wide detour to avoid trouble, but the garrisons made no attempt to challenge or even identify the mounted soldiers. 'They've probably sent most of their men north,' Thomas told Rymer, 'and just left a handful to hold the battlements.'

'Pray God we're not too late for any battle!'

'Pray to Saint George there isn't a battle,' Thomas said.

'We have to beat them!' Rymer said cheerfully, and Thomas thought of Crécy, of blood in the grass and of the weeping in the night after battle. He said nothing, and his thoughts wandered to Saint Junien. He sensed they must be nearing the abbey where the saint was entombed, though that was merely a suspicion that could have been inspired by hope rather than by reality. Yet the country was changing, the hills were smaller and more rounded, the rivers wider and slower, the leaves were turning faster. Whenever he found a village or a traveller, he asked for directions, but usually folk only knew how to reach the next village or perhaps a town that Thomas had never heard of, and so he just kept going north.

'You're trying to reach Poitiers?' the Sire Roland asked him on the sixth day.

'I'm told the prince might be there,' Thomas said, but as it had been Sir Henri who suggested that, and as Sir Henri knew no more than Thomas, it was at best a vague destination.

'Or are you going there because it's near Nouaillé?' Roland asked.

'Nouaillé?'

'That's where the blessed Junien rests.'

'You've been there?'

Roland shook his head. 'I've only heard of it. Are you going there?'

'If it's on the way,' Thomas said.

'Because you want *la Malice*?' Roland asked, and it was almost an accusation.

'Does it exist?'

'I've heard so, yes.'

'Cardinal Bessières believes it,' Thomas said, 'and the Black Friars must too, and my lord has ordered me to find it.'

'So he can use it to fight against France?' Roland asked indignantly. He might have joined the Hellequin and be willing to fight against King Jean's army, but that was for Bertille. His deep loyalty was still with France, which meant he would do this thing for Bertille, only for Bertille, because she had asked him to do it and what she asked, he gave. He twisted in his saddle to look at her. She rode with Genevieve. Thomas had not wanted either woman to come north, but Bertille had insisted, and it had been impossible to deny her when so many of the archers and men-at-arms had their women mounted on rounceys.

A grumble of thunder sounded somewhere to the north. 'You're worried,' Thomas said, 'that I'll find *la Malice*?'

'I wouldn't want the blade in the hands of France's enemies,' Roland said.

'You want the church to have it?'

'That's to whom it should belong,' Roland said, but his memories of Father Marchant made his tone uncertain.

'Let me tell you a story,' Thomas said. 'Have you heard of the Seven Dark Lords?'

'They were the men charged with guarding the treasures of the Cathar heretics,' Roland said disapprovingly.

Thomas reckoned it wise not to say that he was descended from one of those same Dark Lords. 'It's said that they possessed the Holy Grail,' he said instead, 'and I've heard they rescued it from Montségur and then hid it, and that not so long ago other men set out to find it.'

'I've heard the same thing.'

'But what you have not heard,' Thomas said, 'is that one of those men found it.'

The Sire Roland crossed himself. 'Rumour,' he said dismissively.

'I swear to you on the blood of Christ,' Thomas said, 'that the Grail was found, though the man who discovered it sometimes doubted what he had found.'

Roland stared at Thomas for a few seconds, then saw the sincerity in Thomas's face. 'But if it was found,' he said urgently, 'why isn't it shrined in gold, mounted on an altar, and worshipped by pilgrims?'

'Because,' Thomas said gravely, 'the man who found the Grail hid it again. He took it to a place where it cannot be found. He hid it at the bottom of the ocean. He gave it back to God because man cannot be trusted with it.'

'Truly?'

'I promise you,' Thomas said, and he remembered the moment when he had hurled the clay bowl into the grey sea and had seen the small splash, and it had seemed to him that the world went silent after the Grail vanished, and it had been moments before he heard the sound of the waves and the noise of shingle being dragged to the ocean and the forlorn cry of gulls. Heaven itself, he thought, had held its breath. 'I promise you,' he said again.

'And if you find *la Malice*,' Roland began, then faltered.

'I shall give it back to God,' Thomas said, 'because man cannot be trusted with it.' He paused, then looked at Roland. 'So yes,' he said, 'I want *la Malice*, even if it's only to stop Cardinal Bessières from finding it.'

The thunder murmured far off to the north.

There was no rain, just the dark clouds, and the Hellequin rode towards them.

The rain had moved southwards leaving a cloudless sky and a hot sun. It was mid September and felt like June.

The prince's army was following the clouds, going south, labouring on a high wooded ridge. The baggage train, heavy with the plunder of the *chevauchée*, was to the west, using roads in the valley, but the main part of the army, the mounted archers and men-at-arms, were following tracks through the high trees.

It had become a race, though to what conclusion no one yet knew. The prince's advisers, those wise and experienced warriors sent by his father to keep Edward out of trouble, believed that if they could get ahead of the French king and find a suitable place to make a stand, then they could fight a battle and win it. If they could force the French to climb a steep hill into the face of the lethal English archers, then there was the chance of a great victory, but those same advisers feared what would happen if King Jean turned the tables and managed to put his army across the path of the retreating English. 'I'd rather not attack,' the Earl of Suffolk told the prince.

'God, it's hot,' the prince said.

'It is always better to defend,' the earl, who was riding on the prince's right, said.

'Where in God's name are we?' the prince asked.

'Poitiers is over there,' the Earl of Oxford, on Edward's left, pointed vaguely eastwards.

'Your grandfather, forgive me, made that mistake at Bannockburn,' Suffolk said.

'Mistake?'

'He attacked, sire. There was no need, and he lost.'

'He was an idiot,' the prince said cheerfully. 'I'm not an idiot, am I?'

'Indeed not, sire,' Suffolk said, 'and you will remember your father's great victory at Crécy. Yours too, sire. We defended.'

'We did! My father's no idiot!'

'God forbid, sire.'

'But grandfather was. No need to apologise! Had the brains of a squirrel, that's what my father says.' The prince ducked under the low branch of an elm. 'But what if we see the bastards on the road? We should attack then, yes?'

'If the circumstances are propitious,' the Earl of Oxford said cautiously.

'And what if we don't find that convenient hill?' the prince asked.

'We keep going south, sire, till we do find one,' Suffolk said, 'or till we reach one of our fortresses.'

The prince grimaced. 'I don't like running away.'

'You'll find it preferable to imprisonment in Paris, sire,' Oxford said drily.

'I hear they have very pretty girls in Paris?'

'There are pretty girls everywhere, sire,' Suffolk said, 'as you know better than most men.'

'God is good,' the prince said.

'Amen,' Oxford added.

'And pray God he's slowing the French,' Suffolk said grimly. The last reliable information he had heard said that the French king was only some ten or twelve miles away, and his army, which, like the prince's, was all mounted, was travelling faster. King Jean, having dallied all summer, was now suddenly full of energy and, Suffolk assumed, confidence. He was looking for a battle, though he was not so foolish as to risk fighting on disadvantageous ground. The French wanted to trap the prince, force him to fight in a place they chose, and Suffolk was apprehensive. A prisoner taken by the Captal de Buch had confirmed that King Jean had sent all his foot soldiers away because they would slow his army, yet even without that infantry he still outnumbered the prince, though by how many no one knew, and he was not being forced to travel over this damned wooded ridge. He was using good roads. He was racing south. He was looking to close the trap.

Yet the damned wooded ridge was the prince's best hope. It was a short cut. It might gain a day's march, and a day's march was worth gold. And perhaps, at the end of the ridge, there would be a place to ambush the French. Or perhaps not. And Suffolk worried about the baggage. So long as it was separated from the army it was vulnerable, and even if the day's march was gained they would need to wait half a day for the baggage to catch up. And he worried about the horses. There was no water in this high land, the animals were thirsty, and the men riding them were hungry. The army's food supplies were desperately low. They needed to reach low, fertile land where the granaries were full, they needed water, they needed rest, they needed respite.

Four miles ahead of where the prince and the two earls rode through the trees, the Captal de Buch sat in his saddle at the ridge's end. Ahead of him a long slope dropped to a road and the glint of a river, while to his right, beyond some low wooded hills, was a smudge of smoke dirtying the sky that he knew must mark the cooking fires of Poitiers. The far slope of the valley was covered in vineyards, row after row of thick vines.

It was a beautiful day. Warm and sunny, with just a few high white clouds. The trees were heavy with leaves that had started to show a tinge of autumn colour. The grapes were plump, almost ripe for picking. It was a day, the captal thought, to take a girl to the river and swim naked there, and afterwards make love in the grass and drink wine before making love again.

Instead he was watching the enemy.

An army had passed through the gentle valley. The ground on either side of the road had been churned by hooves, thousands upon thousands of hooves, to leave a dark scar of broken turf. One of the captal's scouts, mounted on a small fast horse, had watched the army pass. 'Eighty-seven banners, sire,' he said.

The captal grunted. Only the greatest lords flew their banners on the march so that their followers would know their place in the column, but how many men did that mean? No great lord would take fewer than a hundred men to battle, so ten thousand? Twelve? A lot, the captal thought grimly. The English and their Gascon allies would not be flying more than forty such banners, but his scout had counted eighty-seven! Yet now, as the sun shone on the scarred valley and the gentle river, the captal could only see two banners flying above a crowd of men and horses who rested beside the river. 'This is the rearguard?' he asked.

'Yes, sire.'

'You're sure?'

'There's no one behind them.' The scout gestured eastwards. 'I rode a league that way. Nothing.'

And the French rearguard was resting. They were in no hurry, and why should they hurry? They had overtaken the English and the Gascons. The prince had not gained a day's march, the French had won the race, and the captal summoned one of his men and told him to take that bad news back to Edward. 'Go,' he said, 'hurry,' and then, like the French, the captal waited.

'How many do you reckon?' he asked a man-at-arms, nodding at the men beside the river.

'Six hundred, sire? Seven?'

So six or seven hundred Frenchmen were motionless in the valley. Most wore no helmets because of the day's heat, though many were wearing wide-brimmed hats with extravagant white feathers, clear evidence that they expected no trouble. There was a handful of light carts, which carried lances and shields. These Frenchmen had no idea that an enemy was this close to them. Some had dismounted and a few were even lying in the grass as if catching up on sleep. Servants were walking riderless horses in the pasture where others grazed. Men stood in small groups, handing around wine-skins. The captal could not distinguish the two banners because they hung listless in the windless heat, but their presence meant that there were lords among those men-at-arms, and lords meant ransoms.

'They outnumber us,' the captal said, then paused as his horse thumped the leaf mould with a forefoot. 'We're outnumbered two to one,' he continued, 'but we're Gascons.'

He had just over three hundred men-at-arms, all helmeted, all with shields, all ready to fight.

'Why are they waiting?' a man-at-arms asked.

'Water?' the captal suggested. The day was hot, both armies had marched fast, the horses were thirsty and there was no water on the high ground, and he guessed that this rearguard was letting their stallions drink from the small river. He turned in his saddle and gestured to Hunald, his squire. 'Helmet, shield, lance, have the axe ready.' He looked at his standard bearer, who caught his eye and grinned. 'Close up!' he called to his men. He took the helmet, pushed up the visor and crammed it over his mail hood. He pushed his left arm through the loop of the black and yellow shield, then gripped the handle. His squire helped him couch the lance. All along the edge of the trees men were doing the same thing. Some men just drew swords, while Guillaume, a huge man mounted on an equally huge horse, carried a spiked morning-star. 'No trumpet,' the captal called. If he signalled the charge with a trumpet then the enemy would gain a few seconds of warning. Better just to burst from the woods and be halfway down the slope before the French realised that death had come visiting on a warm afternoon. His horse whinnied and thumped its hoof again. 'In the name of God, Gascony and King Edward,' the captal said.

And kicked his heels back.

And by God, he thought, there was nothing like this feeling. A good horse, a tight high saddle, a lance, and an enemy taken by surprise. The thunder of hooves filled the afternoon, clods of earth hurled high by heavy feet as three hundred and seventeen horsemen erupted from the trees and hurled themselves down the slope. The captal's banner, its silver scallop shells bright on the black cross against the yellow field, flapped as the standard bearer raised it high. Men were shouting now, 'Saint Quiteira and Gascony!'

The captal laughed. Saint Quiteira? She had

been a Christian virgin who, refusing to marry a pagan lord, had been beheaded, but her headless trunk had picked up its own severed, bloody head and carried it uphill to a place where, to this day, miracles were said to happen. She was Gascony's saint. A damned virgin! But maybe she would bring the miracle they needed. Eighty-seven enemy banners might need a miracle? 'Saint Quiteira and Saint George!' he shouted, and he saw a Frenchman turn a horse to meet the charge, and the man had neither lance nor shield, just a drawn sword, and the captal pressed his left knee against his destrier's flank and the horse turned obediently. It seemed to sense where the captal wanted to go, and the destrier was at the full gallop as it crossed the road, and the captal let the lance slide into the enemy's belly, just a slight jar as it went through mail and struck a lower rib and he let go of the lance and held out his right hand so that his squire could give him the axe. He preferred an axe to a sword. An axe would smash through mail, even plate, and he touched the horse with his knee again and pursued a fleeing man, swung the axe and felt the blade crunch through the skull. He wrenched the blade free, raised his shield to parry a feeble sword stroke from his left, and glimpsed that man vanish in a welter of misting blood as Guillaume's morningstar obliterated a white-feathered hat, skull and brain together.

The Gascon horsemen drove into the enemy. It was not a fair fight. The French rearguard had been relaxing, confident that if anyone in their army saw the enemy it would be their vanguard, but instead that enemy was among them and killing them. The captal killed and spurred forward, not letting the Frenchmen form in any kind of order. They were thickest about the ford where there was a crowd of men and horses beneath some willows, and the captal swerved towards them. 'Follow me!' he shouted. 'Follow me! Saint Quiteira!'

His men turned their destriers to follow, men in mail carrying bright steel on heavy horses. The destriers were white-eyed, teeth bared and hung with blood-spattered trappers. The captal plunged into the disorganised mass of Frenchmen and swung the axe, hearing the screams, panicking the enemy horses, driving into the crowd, and shouting all the while. The French were already running. Men were scrambling into saddles and spurring away. Other men were shouting that they yielded, and all across the water meadow the Gascons were galloping, killing, wheeling, and spurring back to kill again. The captal had thought he would need to fight through the crowd of men, but instead the crowd was falling apart, it was fleeing, and he was in pursuit and there was no easier way to kill than when a man was in pursuit. His destrier would line itself on a fugitive's horse, speed up, wait for the pressure of a knee to say the axe had done its work, and then look for another victim, and to the captal's left and right other Gascons were doing the same. They left a trail of bleeding, wounded, twitching men, of riderless horses, of dead men, and still they spurred on, pursuing and killing, all the frustrations of days of retreat being salved by this orgy of death. A Frenchman panicked and turned his horse hard to the left and the beast lost its footing. The bloodied bodies of two plundered geese were tied to the saddle's cantle, and feathers flew as the horse collapsed. The man screamed as his leg was trapped and broken by the falling horse, then tried to twist away as the captal's axe swung. The screaming stopped. A woman was calling for help, but her man had fled and she was left surrounded by Gascons in a bloodied field.

The captal shouted for his trumpeter. 'Sound the disengage,' he ordered.

His men had killed, they had triumphed, they had taken at least three great lords captive, they had left scores of dead with hardly a scratch to themselves, but the pursuit was galloping towards the main body of the French, and it would be only a matter of minutes before that army reacted and sent heavily armed and armoured men to counterattack. And so the captal swerved up the small slope and vanished back into the trees. The valley, which had looked so peaceful, was flecked blood red, and littered with bodies.

The armies had met.

'Saint Junien's abbey?' the peasant had said. 'For sure, my lord, along the valley,' he pointed north with a grubby finger, 'not far, lord. You can drive an ox there and back in a morning.' The man had been threshing grain when the Hellequin came to his village, and he had been oblivious of the horsemen until their shadows darkened the door of his barn. He had stared in dumb astonishment at the mounted men, then gone to his knees and scrabbled a hand at his forelock. Thomas had told him he was safe, that they meant him no harm and then, as he had a hundred times on this journey, asked the man whether he knew of the abbey of Saint Junien, and now, for the first time, someone did. 'There are monks there, my lord,' the man said nervously, trying to be helpful. His eyes flickered to the left, doubtless to where his family lived. His flail, two wooden clubs joined by a length of leather, lay discarded in case these grim men on horseback mistook it for a weapon.

'Who is your lord?' Thomas asked.

'The abbot, my lord,' the man said.

'What sort of monks?' Thomas asked.

The question puzzled the man. 'Black monks, lord?' he suggested.

'Benedictines?'

'Ah yes! Benedictines. I think.' He smiled, but it was obvious he did not know what a Benedictine was.

'Have other soldiers been here?'

He was more sure of this answer. 'Not in a long while, lord, but some came on Saint Perpetua's day, I remember that. They came; they didn't stay.'

'None since?'

'No, lord.'

Saint Perpetua's day was half a year past. Thomas tossed the man a silver coin and turned his horse away. 'We go north,' he told his men curtly, and spurred that way.

It was dusk, which meant it was time to seek shelter for the night. A river twisted in the valley bottom where a pair of hovels lay dark under oak trees, but at the valley's northern end, hidden by a spur of wooded land, was a village or small town, betrayed by the thickness of smoke from its kitchen fires. The abbey had to be there. Two crows flew across the river, black against the darkening sky. A bell rang, calling men and women to their evening prayers.

'Is there a town here?' Rymer, the Earl of Warwick's man, had spurred alongside Thomas.

'I don't know, but usually a village grows beside a monastery.'

'A monastery!' Rymer seemed surprised.

'I'm going there.'

'To pray?' Rymer suggested lightly.

'Yes,' Thomas replied.

Rymer was embarrassed by that answer and went silent. Thomas rounded a bend in the valley and he could see a willow-edged river, and, just beyond it, a large village and the towers of a monastery. The monastery was surprisingly big, surrounded by a high wall and dominated by its large abbey church. 'We can stay in the village,' Rymer said.

'There'll be a tavern there,' Thomas said.

'That's what I was hoping.'

'My men will stay there too.' Thomas stared at the monastery, its high walls dark in the gathering dusk. Those walls looked as formidable as any castle's ramparts. 'Is that the place?' he asked the Sire Roland, who had spurred his horse to catch up with Thomas.

'I wouldn't know,' Roland replied.

'It looks more like a fortress than a monastery,' Thomas said.

The virgin knight frowned at the distant walls. 'Saint Junien was told to keep Saint Peter's sword safe, so maybe it is a fortress?'

'If it even is Saint Junien's.' As Thomas rode closer he could see that the monastery's huge gates were open. He supposed they would not be closed till the sun finally vanished in the west. 'He's buried there, yes?'

'His earthly remains are there, yes.'

'So perhaps *la Malice* is there too.'

'And maybe we should leave it there,' Sire Roland said.

'I would, if I didn't believe Bessières is looking for it, and if he finds it he'll use it, not for God's glory, but for his own.'

'And will you use it?'

'I told you,' Thomas said curtly, 'I shall lose it.' He turned in the saddle. 'Luc! Gastar! Arnaldus! With me. The rest of you stay in the village! And pay for your victuals!' He had chosen Gascons to stay with him so that the monks would not suspect their allegiance to England.

Robbie, Keane and the Sire Roland also stayed with Thomas, then Genevieve and Bertille insisted on accompanying him too, though Hugh was taken under the care of Sam and the other archers. 'Why not take the archers?' Genevieve asked.

'All I'm doing,' Thomas said, 'is asking the abbot some questions. I don't want to frighten the man. We go, we ask and we leave.'

'That's what you said at Montpellier,' Genevieve said tartly.

'These are monks,' Thomas said, 'just monks. We question them and we leave again.'

'With *la Malice*?' Genevieve asked.

'I don't know,' Thomas said. 'I don't even know if *la Malice* exists.' He kicked his heels to reach the gate before the sun vanished behind the western skyline. He cantered across a pasture where a herd of goats was being guarded by a small boy and a big dog who both watched the riders pass in silence. A fine stone bridge spanned the river beyond the pasture and, on the bridge's far side, the road forked. The left-hand road led into the village, and the right to the monastery. Thomas could see that the monastery was half surrounded by a channel of the river that had been diverted to make a kind of wide moat, maybe so the monks could keep fish. He could also see two robed figures walking towards the open gate, and he spurred again. The two monks saw him coming and waited. 'You're here for the pilgrims?' one of them called in greeting.

Thomas opened his mouth to ask the man what he meant, then had the sense to nod instead. 'We are,' he said.

'They arrived an hour ago. They'll be glad of protection, they think the English are close.'

'We didn't see any English,' Thomas said.

'They'll still be glad to see you,' the monk said. 'It's a dangerous time to be on pilgrimage.'

'All times are dangerous,' Thomas said, and led his followers beneath the high arch. The sound of their hooves echoed from the stone walls as the bell's tolling stopped. 'Where are they?' Thomas called back.

'In the abbey!' the monk shouted.

'Someone's waiting for us?' Genevieve asked.

'They're not waiting for us,' Thomas said.

'Who?' she asked urgently.

'Just pilgrims.'

'Send for the archers.'

Thomas glanced at his three Gascons, at Robbie and the Sire Roland. 'I think we're safe from a band of pilgrims,' he said drily.

The horses filled the small space between the walls and the abbey church. Thomas swung down from the saddle and instinctively checked that his sword was running free in its scabbard. He heard the monastery gates crash shut, then the thump as the locking bar was dropped into place. It was almost dark now and the monastery's buildings were black against a faintly luminous sky in which the first stars shone. A becketed torch burned between two stone houses that might have been dormitories, while two more blazed bright at the abbey steps. A cobbled street ran in front of the abbey and at its far end, where another gate through the monastery's high wall was still open, Thomas could see a mass of saddled horses and four sumpter ponies being held by servants. He dismounted, turning towards the abbey steps where the torches' sparks flickered and died by the open door through which Thomas could hear monks chanting, the sound slow and beautiful, deep and rhythmic, ebbing and flowing like the tides of the sea. He climbed the steps slowly, and gradually the interior of the building revealed itself, a glory of bright candles and painted stone and carved pillars and shining altars. So many candles! And the long nave was filled with black-cowled monks, chanting and genuflecting, and it struck Thomas that the sound was threatening now, as if the swelling tide was breaking into deep waves of menace. He could distinguish the words as he stepped into the light of the candles and he recognised them as coming from a psalm. '*Quoniam propter te mortificamur tota die*,' the male voices chanted, drawing out the long syllables, '*aestimati sumus sicut oves occisionis*.'

'What is it?' Genevieve whispered.

'For your sake we look on death all day,' Thomas translated softly, 'and we are judged as sheep to be slaughtered.'

'I don't like it,' she said nervously.

'I just need to speak with the abbot,' Thomas reassured her. 'We'll wait for the service to end.'

He gazed into the lofty choir where he could just see a great wall painting of Christ in judgement. Sinners were tumbling to a fiery hell on one side, their ranks surprisingly filled with gowned priests and mantled monks. Closer, in the nave, was a painting of Jonah and the whale, which struck Thomas as a strange subject for a monastery so far inland, but reminded him of his father telling him that old tale and how as a small boy he had gone down to the shingle beach at Hookton and stared in hope of seeing a great whale that might swallow a man. Opposite Jonah, and half shadowed by pillars, was another painting that Thomas realised was Saint Junien. It showed the monk kneeling in a patch of land cleared of snow and gazing upwards in rapture towards an arm that reached down from heaven to offer him a sword. 'That's it!' he said in wonderment.

The monks standing at the back of the nave heard him and most of them turned to see Genevieve and Bertille. 'Women!' one of them hissed in alarm.

A second monk hurried towards Thomas. 'Pilgrims can only come to the church between Matins and None,' he said indignantly, 'not now! All of you, leave!'

Robbie, Keane, Sire Roland and the three Gascons

377

had followed Thomas into the church, and the indignant monk spread his arms as if to drive them all away. 'You're wearing swords!' the man protested. 'You must leave!' More monks turned, and the chanting was interrupted by a growl, and Thomas remembered his father saying that a pack of monks was more frightening than any band of brigands. 'Folk think they're nothing but gelded milksops,' Father Ralph had said, 'but they're not, by God they're not! They can fight like savages!' These monks were spoiling for a fight, and there had to be at least two hundred of them. They must have reckoned that no man-at-arms would dare draw a sword inside the abbey, and the monk closest to Thomas had to believe that because he thrust a meaty hand hard against Thomas's chest just as a bell rang from the high altar. It rang frantically, and was reinforced by the sound of a staff being beaten on the stone floor. 'Let them stay!' a great voice bellowed. 'I order them to remain!' The remnants of the chant drained away raggedly, finally fading to nothing. The monk still had his hand on Thomas's chest.

'Take it away,' Thomas said softly. The man looked at him with hostile eyes, and Thomas reached up and took hold of the hand. He bent it backwards, using the strength that comes from hauling back a war bow's cord. The monk resisted, then his eyes widened in fear as he felt the archer's strength. He tried to pull his hand away and

Thomas bent it harder until he felt the wrist bones fracture. 'I told you to take it away,' he said.

'Thomas!' Genevieve gasped.

Thomas looked at the high altar and saw a figure rising there, a massive man swathed in red, gross and tall and commanding. The pilgrims were led by Cardinal Bessières. And he was not alone. There were crossbowmen at the edges of the nave and Thomas heard the clicks as their cords were caught by the trigger mechanisms. There were at least a dozen archers, all wearing the livery of a green horse on a white field, and with them were men-at-arms, and there, beside the cardinal at the top of the altar steps, was the Count of Labrouillade. 'You were right,' Thomas said softly, 'I should have brought the archers.'

'Bring them here!' Bessières ordered. The cardinal was smiling, and no wonder; his enemies had come straight to him and he had them at his mercy, and Cardinal Bessières, Archbishop of Livorno and Papal Legate to the throne of France, had no mercy. Father Marchant, tall and grim, stood just behind the cardinal, and Thomas, as he was forced up the nave between the monks who parted to let them through, could see more men-at-arms in the shadows at the abbey's edges. 'Welcome,' the cardinal said, 'Guillaume d'Evecque.'

'Thomas of Hookton,' Thomas said defiantly.

'*Le Bâtard*,' Father Marchant said.

'And his heretic whore of a wife!' the cardinal said.

'My wife too,' Labrouillade muttered.

'Two whores!' the cardinal said, sounding amused. 'Keep them there!' He snarled that order to the crossbowmen who were guarding Thomas. 'Thomas of Hookton,' he said, '*le Bâtard*. So why are you here in this place of prayer?'

'I was given a task,' Thomas said.

'A task! And what was that?' The cardinal spoke in mock kindness, as though he indulged a small child.

'To prevent a sacred relic from falling into evil hands.'

The cardinal's mouth twitched in a half-smile. 'What relic, my son?'

'*La Malice.*'

'Ah! And what hands?'

'Yours,' Thomas said.

'You see what infamy *le Bâtard* is capable of!' The cardinal was addressing the whole abbey now. 'He has taken it upon himself to deny Holy Mother Church one of her most sacred relics! He is an excommunicate already! He has been declared outside of salvation, and yet he dares come here, bringing his whores into this most holy place to steal what God has given to his faithful servants.' He raised a hand and pointed at Thomas. 'Do you deny that you are an excommunicate?'

'I plead guilty to only one thing,' Thomas said.

The cardinal frowned. 'And that is?'

'You had a brother,' Thomas said. The cardinal's face darkened and the outstretched finger quivered,

380

then dropped. 'You had a brother,' Thomas said, 'and he is dead.'

'What do you know of that?' the cardinal asked in a dangerous tone.

'I know he was killed with an arrow shot by a devil's whelp,' Thomas said. He could have begged for his life, but he knew that would achieve nothing. He was trapped, surrounded by crossbows under tension and by men-at-arms, and all that was left was defiance. 'I know he was killed by an arrow cut from an ash tree at sundown,' he went on, 'killed by an arrow peeled of its bark with a woman's knife, tipped by steel that was forged in a starless night and fledged with feathers taken from a goose killed by a white wolf. And I know that the arrow was shot from a bow that had lain for a week in church.'

'Witchcraft,' the cardinal whispered.

'They must all die, Your Eminence,' Father Marchant spoke for the first time, 'and not just the whores and excommunicates, but those men too!' He pointed at Robbie and the Sire Roland. 'They have broken their oaths!'

'An oath to a man who tortures women?' Thomas sneered. He could hear horses' hooves in the cobbled yards outside the abbey. There were voices there and they were angry.

The cardinal had also heard the voices and he glanced towards the abbey's door, but saw nothing menacing there. 'They will die,' he said, looking back to Thomas. 'They will die by *la Malice*.' He snapped his fingers.

There had been a dozen monks standing beside the high altar, but they now moved aside, and Thomas saw a friar there. He was an older man, and he had been beaten so that his white robe was spattered with blood that had dripped from his broken lip and nose. And beyond him, in the shadows behind the altar, there was a tomb. It was a stone casket, carved and painted, resting on two stone pedestals that stood in a niche of the apse. The lid of the casket had been slid aside and now a familiar figure came from the shadows. It was the Scotsman, Sculley, the bones tangled in his long hair clicking as he walked to the tomb and reached inside. He had more bones attached to his beard that knocked against the breastplate he wore over his mail coat. 'You lied to me,' he called to Robbie, 'you made me fight for the goddamned English, and your uncle says you must die, that you're a weak fart of a man. You're not worthy of the name Douglas. You're a piece of dog shite is what you are.'

And from the tomb he drew a sword. It was nothing like the swords in the wall paintings. This sword looked like a falchion, one of those cheap blades that could serve as a hay knife as well as a weapon. It had a thick curved blade, widening towards its tip, a weapon for crude hacking rather than piercing. The blade itself looked old and uncared for, it was pitted, darkened, and crude, yet still Thomas had an urge to fall to his knees. Christ himself had looked on that sword, he had maybe touched it, and on the night before his agony he had refused to let that weapon save him. It was the sword of the fisherman.

'Kill them,' the cardinal said.

'Blood should not be shed,' a tall grey-bearded monk protested. He had to be the abbot.

'Kill them,' the cardinal repeated, and the cross-bowmen raised their weapons. 'Not with arrows!' Bessières called. 'Let *la Malice* do her duty and serve the church as she is intended to serve. Let her do her glorious work!'

And the archer loosed, and the arrow flew.

CHAPTER 12

The arrow struck Sculley plumb on his breastplate. The missile was tipped with a bodkin, an arrowhead made to pierce armour. Bodkins were forged from steel. They were long, slim and pointed arrowheads without tangs, and this arrow's leading inches of ashwood had been replaced with a short length of heavier oak. If any arrow could slide through steel it was a heavy bodkin that concentrated the arrow's weight and impetus onto one small point, but this arrowhead crumpled like cheap iron. Few blacksmiths knew how to make good steel, and some smiths cheated, sending iron bodkins instead of steel, but though the bodkin had failed to pierce Sculley's breastplate, the force of the arrow's strike was sufficient to throw him three staggering paces backwards so that he tripped on the altar steps and sat down heavily. He picked up the arrow that had struck him, looked at the bent head and grinned.

'If anyone does any killing in this damned church,' a voice shouted from the back of the abbey, 'it will be me. Now what the damned hell is happening here?'

Thomas turned. The back of the abbey was filling with men-at-arms and archers, all of them wearing the same badge: a golden lion rampant against a background of golden fleurs-de-lys on a blue field. It was the same badge Benjamin Rymer wore, the livery of the Earl of Warwick, and the snarl of the voice and the confidence of the newcomer suggested it had to be the earl himself who now strode up the nave. He was wearing a suit of fine mud-spattered armour that clinked as he walked, and his steel-shod boots crashed brutally loud on the nave's stones. He wore no jupon, so displayed no badge, though his status was proclaimed by a short, thick chain of gold that hung over a blue silk scarf. He was a few years older than Thomas, thin-faced, unshaven, and with unruly brown hair that had been compressed by the helmet that was now held by a squire. He scowled. His quick eyes darted around the abbey and seemed to scorn everything he saw. A second man, older and with grizzled grey hair, a short beard and wearing much-battered armour, followed him, and there was something familiar to Thomas about the man's blunt, sun-darkened face.

The cardinal slammed his staff on the altar steps. 'Who are you?' he demanded.

The earl, if it was the earl, ignored him. 'Who the devil is killing who here?' he asked.

'This is a church matter,' the cardinal said loftily, 'and you will leave.'

'I will leave when I'm goddamned ready to leave,'

the newcomer said, then turned fast as a scuffle sounded at the back of the abbey. 'If there is any damned trouble in here I shall have my men clear the goddamned lot of you out of the monastery altogether. You want to spend the night in the goddamned fields? Who are you?'

This last question was directed at Thomas, who, assuming it was the earl, went to one knee. 'Sir Thomas Hookton, sire, pledged to the Earl of Northampton.'

'Sir Thomas was at Crécy, my lord,' the man with grizzled grey hair said quietly, 'one of Will Skeat's men.'

'You're a bowman?' the earl demanded.

'Yes, my lord.'

'And knighted?' He sounded both surprised and disapproving.

'Indeed, my lord.'

'Deservedly knighted, my lord,' the second man said firmly, and Thomas remembered him then. He was Sir Reginald Cobham, a man renowned as a soldier.

'We were at the ford together, Sir Reginald,' Thomas said.

'Blanchetaque!' Cobham said, remembering the ford's name. 'Oh my sweet God, but that was a rare fight!' He grinned. 'You had a priest fighting with you, yes? Bastard was splitting French heads with an axe.'

'Father Hobbe,' Thomas said.

'You two have finished?' the earl snarled.

'Nowhere near, my lord,' Cobham said happily, 'we could reminisce for another few hours.'

'Damn your bloody guts,' the earl said, though without rancour. He might be an earl of England, but he knew well that he had better listen to the advice of men like Sir Reginald Cobham. Such men were attached to all the great lords, appointed by the king as advisers. A man could be born to wealth, rank, title, and privilege, but that did not make him a soldier, and so the king made sure his nobles were advised by lesser men who knew more. The earl might command, but if he was wise then he only commanded after Sir Reginald had decided. The Earl of Warwick was experienced, he had fought at Crécy, yet he was also wise enough to listen to advice. At this moment, though, he seemed too angry to be prudent, and his anger grew when he saw the red heart on Sculley's grubby jupon. 'Is that the crest of Douglas?' he asked in a dangerous voice.

'It is the most sacred heart of Christ,' the cardinal answered before Sculley had a chance to speak. Not that Sculley had understood the question, which had been asked in French. The Scotsman had got to his feet and was now glowering at Warwick so fiercely that the cardinal, thinking the bone-hung Sculley might start a fight, pushed him back into the small crowd of monks who stood by the altar. 'These men,' Bessières gestured at the crossbowmen and men-at-arms wearing the livery of Labrouillade, 'are serving the church. We are on a mission for His Holiness the Pope, and you,' he raised a threatening finger to point at the earl, 'are hindering our duties.'

'I'm hindering goddamned nothing!'

'Then leave this precinct and allow our devotions to continue,' the cardinal demanded grandly.

'Devotions?' the earl asked, looking at Thomas.

'Murder, my lord.'

'Righteous execution!' the cardinal thundered. His finger quivered as he pointed at Thomas. 'This man is an excommunicate. He is hated by God, loathed by man and an enemy to Mother Church!'

The earl looked at Thomas. 'Are you?' he asked, sounding thoroughly disgruntled.

'He says so, my lord.'

'A heretic!' The cardinal, seeing an advantage, pressed it hard. 'He is condemned! As is that whore, his wife, and that whore, an adulteress!' He pointed at Bertille.

The earl looked at Bertille, a sight that seemed to lift his evil mood. 'You were going to kill these women too?'

'The judgement of God is just, it is sure, it is merciful,' the cardinal said.

'Not while I'm standing here, it isn't,' the earl said belligerently. 'Are the women under your protection?' he asked Thomas.

'Yes, my lord.'

'Stand up, man,' the earl said. Thomas was still kneeling. 'And you're English?'

'Indeed, my lord.'

'He is a sinner,' the cardinal said, 'and condemned by the church. He is outside man's law, subject only to God's.'

'He's English,' the earl said forcefully, 'and so am I. And the church does not kill! It hands men over to the civil power, and right now I am that power! I am the Earl of Warwick and I won't kill an Englishman for the church's benefit unless the Archbishop of Canterbury tells me to.'

'But he is excommunicated!'

The earl mocked that claim with laughter. 'Two years ago,' he said, 'your goddamned priests excommunicated two cows, a caterpillar, and a toad, all in Warwick! You use excommunication like a mother uses a birch rod to correct her children. You can't have him, he's mine, he's English.'

'And right now,' Sir Reginald Cobham added softly, and speaking in English, 'we need every English archer we can find.'

'So why are you here?' the earl asked the cardinal and, after a deliberately insulting pause, added, 'Your Eminence.'

The cardinal grimaced with anger at being denied the revenge he sought, but controlled it. 'His Holiness the Pope,' he said, 'sent us to beseech both your prince and the King of France to make peace. We travel under the protection of God, recognised as mediators by your king, by your prince and by your church.'

'Peace?' The earl spat the word. 'Tell the usurper Jean to yield the throne of France to its rightful owner, Edward of England, then you'll have your peace.'

'The Holy Father believes there has been too much killing,' the cardinal said piously.

'And you were about to add to it,' the earl rejoindered. 'You'll not make peace by killing women in an abbey church, so go! You'll find the prince that way.' He pointed north. 'Who's the abbot here?'

'I am, sire.' A tall, bald-headed man with a long grey beard stepped out of the apse's shadows.

'I need grain, I need beans, I need bread, I need wine, I need dried fish, I need anything men or horses can eat or drink.'

'We have very little,' the abbot said nervously.

'Then we'll take what little you've got,' the earl said, then looked at the cardinal. 'You're still here, Your Eminence, and I told you to go. So go. This monastery is now in English hands.'

'You cannot give me orders,' Bessières said.

'I just did. And I have more archers, more swords, and more men than you. So go before I lose my temper and have you carried out.'

The cardinal hesitated, then decided prudence was better than defiance. 'We shall leave,' he announced. He gestured to his followers and stalked down the nave. Thomas moved to intercept Sculley, then saw that the Scotsman had vanished.

'Sculley,' he said, 'where is he?'

The abbot gestured towards a shadowed archway beside the apse. Thomas ran to it, pushed the door open, but there was nothing outside except a strip of flame-lit cobbles and the monastery's outer wall. The sword of the fisherman had gone.

There was a fitful moon sliding between high clouds, which, with the torches, gave enough light to see that the cobbled yard behind the church was empty. The hairs at the back of Thomas's neck prickled and, fearing that the Scotsman was in deep shadow waiting to ambush him, he drew his sword. The long blade rasped on the scabbard's throat.

'Who was he?' a voice asked, and Thomas turned fast, heart racing, to see it was the bloodied Black Friar who had spoken.

'A Scotsman,' Thomas said. He stared back into the shadows. 'A dangerous Scotsman.'

'He has *la Malice*,' the friar said flatly.

A noise in the bushes made Thomas turn, but it was just a cat that stalked from the low-hanging branches and crossed towards some far buildings. 'Who are you?' he asked the friar.

'My name is Fra Ferdinand,' the friar said.

Thomas looked at him, seeing an older man, his weathered face bloody. 'How did your nose and lip get broken?'

'I refused to say where *la Malice* was,' the friar said.

'So they hit you?'

'The Scotsman did, on the cardinal's orders. Then the abbot told him where she was hidden.'

'In the tomb?'

'In the tomb,' Fra Ferdinand confirmed.

'You were at Mouthoumet,' Thomas said accusingly.

'The Lord of Mouthoumet was a friend,' the friar said, 'and good to me.'

'And the Lord of Mouthoumet was a Planchard,' Thomas said, 'and the Planchard family were heretics.'

'He was no heretic,' Fra Ferdinand said fiercely. 'He might have been a sinner, but which of us is not? He was no heretic.'

'The last of the Dark Lords?' Thomas asked.

'They say one still lives,' the friar said, and crossed himself.

'He does,' Thomas said, 'and his name is Vexille.'

'They were the worst of the seven,' Fra Ferdinand said. 'The Vexilles knew no pity, showed no mercy, and carry the curse of Christ.'

'My father was called Vexille,' Thomas said. 'He didn't use the name, and nor do I, but I am a Vexille. Lord of God knows what and Count of somewhere or other.'

Fra Ferdinand frowned, looking at Thomas as though he were some dangerous beast. 'So the cardinal is right? You are a heretic?'

'I'm no heretic,' Thomas said savagely, 'just a man who crossed Cardinal Bessières.' He thrust the sword back into its sheath. He had just heard a gate being slammed and barred and he reckoned

Sculley and the cardinal were gone. 'So tell me about *la Malice*,' he demanded.

'*La Malice* is Saint Peter's sword,' the friar said, 'the one he used in the Garden of Gethsemane to protect our Lord. It was given to Saint Junien, but the Dark Lords found it and, when their heresy was burned from the land, they hid it so their enemies could not find it.'

'They hid it here?'

Fra Ferdinand shook his head. 'It was buried in a Planchard tomb in Carcassonne. The Sire of Mouthoumet asked me to find it so the English wouldn't discover it.'

'And you brought it here?'

'The sire was dead when I returned from Carcassonne,' the friar said, 'and I didn't know where else to take it. I thought it would be safer hidden here.' He shrugged. 'This is where it belongs.'

'It will never have peace here,' Thomas said.

'Because it isn't hidden any more?'

Thomas nodded.

'And is that what you want?' Fra Ferdinand asked suspiciously. 'That it should have peace?'

Thomas took one last look around the monastery grounds, then walked back towards the abbey. 'I'm no Dark Lord,' he said. 'My ancestors might have been Cathars, but I'm not. But I'll do their bidding anyway. I'll make sure their enemies can't use it.'

'How?'

'By taking it from that bastard Sculley, of course,'

Thomas said. He went back into the abbey church. The monks were leaving and the candles were being snuffed out, but there was enough light left to see into the half-opened stone casket that stood in its place of honour behind the altar. Saint Junien lay there, his hands crossed and the yellow-brown skin of his face stretched tightly across his skull. The eye sockets were empty and the shrunken lips pulled back to show five yellow teeth. He wore a Benedictine habit, and in his hands was a simple wooden cross.

'Rest in peace,' Fra Ferdinand said to the corpse, and reached in to touch the saint's hands. 'And how will you make sure your enemies can't use *la Malice*?' he asked Thomas.

'By doing what you wanted to do,' Thomas said. 'I'll hide it.'

'Where?'

'Where no one can find it, of course.'

'Sir Thomas,' Sir Reginald Cobham called from the far end of the nave, 'you're coming with us!'

Fra Ferdinand put a hand on Thomas's arm to stop him leaving. 'Do you promise me?'

'Promise you what?'

'You'll hide it?'

'I swear on Saint Junien,' Thomas said. He turned and put his right hand on the dead saint's forehead. The skin felt like smoothed vellum beneath his fingers. 'I swear I will lose *la Malice* for ever,' he said, 'I swear it by Saint Junien, and may he intercede with God to send me to everlasting hell if I break this solemn promise.'

The friar nodded, satisfied. 'Then I'll help you.'

'By praying?'

The Black Friar smiled. 'By praying,' he said. 'And if you keep your oath my work is done. I'll return to Mouthoumet. It's as good a place to die as any.' He touched Thomas's shoulder. 'You have my blessing,' he said.

'Sir Thomas!'

'Coming, Sir Reginald!'

Sir Reginald led Thomas briskly down the abbey steps to the cobbled street where two wagons were being loaded with beans, grain, cheese, and dried fish from the monastery stores. 'We're the rearguard,' Sir Reginald explained, 'which means goddamned nothing because we're ahead of the prince's army right now. But he's up on the hill.' He pointed north to where Thomas could see the tree-fringed loom of a high hill dark in the wan moonlight. 'The French are somewhere beyond, God knows where, but not far.'

'We'll be fighting them?'

'Christ only knows. I think the prince would like to get closer to Gascony? We're short of food. If we stay here more than a couple of days we'll strip the country bare, but if we keep going south the bloody French might get ahead of us. They march fast.' He said all this as he paced beside the wagons, which were being loaded by archers. 'But it'll be the devil's own job to get away from here. They're close, and we'll need to get the wagons and pack-horses across the river without the bastards attacking us. We'll see what the morning brings. Is that wine?' He called the question to an archer heaving a barrel onto a cart.

'Yes, Sir Reginald!'

'How much is there?'

'Six barrels like this.'

'Keep your thieving hands off it!'

'Yes, Sir Reginald!'

'They won't, of course,' Sir Reginald said to Thomas, 'but we need it for the horses.'

'For the horses?' Thomas asked.

'There's no water on the hill; poor beasts are thirsty. So we give them wine instead. They'll be wobbly in the morning, but we fight on foot so it doesn't matter.' He stopped suddenly. 'God, that's a pretty woman.' Thomas thought he was talking of Bertille who was standing with Genevieve, but then Sir Reginald frowned. 'What happened to her eye?'

'One of the cardinal's priests tried to gouge it.'

'Jesus God! There are some evil bastards in the church. And he's been sent to make peace?'

'I think the Pope would rather see the prince surrender,' Thomas said.

'Ha! I hope we fight.' He said those four words grimly. 'And I think we will, I think we'll have to, I think they'll make us fight, and I think we'll win. I want to see our archers cut the bastards down.'

And Thomas remembered the bodkin striking

Sculley's breastplate. The arrows were made in their hundreds of thousands in England, but were they well made? He had seen too many crumple. And Sir Reginald thought there would be a battle.

And the steel of the arrowheads was weak.

The king could not sleep.

He had dined with his eldest son, the dauphin, and with his youngest boy, Philippe, and they had listened as minstrels sang of ancient battles full of glory, and the king had become ever gloomier as he considered what was expected of him. Now, wanting to be alone and have time to think, he walked in the walled orchard of a fine stone house that had been commandeered for his quarters. All around him, spread through a village whose name he did not know, the fires of his army glowed in the darkness. He could hear men laughing or shouting in delight when their dice or cards were lucky. He had heard that Edward, Prince of Wales, was a gambler, but how would that prince gamble now? And was he lucky?

The king walked to the northern wall of the orchard where, by standing on a bench, he could see the red glow of the English fires. They seemed to spread across the night sky, but the brightest glow outlined a long, high hill. How many men were there? And were they there at all? Perhaps they had lit the fires to persuade him they were staying and then marched away south, carrying their plunder with them. And if they had stayed should he fight them? It was his decision and he did not know how to make it. Some of his lords advised him to avoid battle, saying that the English archers were too deadly and their men-at-arms too feral, while others were confident that this gambling prince could be defeated easily. He growled to himself. He wished he were back in Paris where musicians would be entertaining him and dancers surrounding him; instead he was God knows where in his own country and he did not know what he should do.

He sat on the bench. 'Wine, Your Majesty?' A servant spoke from the shadows.

'Thank you, Luc, no.'

'The Lord of Douglas is here, sire. He wishes to speak with you.'

The king nodded tiredly. 'Bring a lantern, Luc.'

'You'll speak with him, sire?'

'I'll speak with him,' the king said, and wondered if the Scotsman would have anything new to say. He supposed not. Douglas would urge an attack. Fight now. Kill the bastards. Attack. Slaughter them. The Scotsman had been saying the same thing for weeks. He just wanted a battle. He wanted to kill Englishmen, and the king was sympathetic to that wish, but he was also haunted by the fear of failure. And now Douglas would harangue him again and King Jean sighed. He was frightened of Douglas and, though the man was never anything but respectful, the king suspected that the Scotsman despised him. But Douglas did not have the responsibility. He was a confident brute, a fighter, a man born for blood and steel and battle, but King Jean had a whole country to tend and he dared not lose a fight to the English. It had taken a huge effort to raise this army, the treasury was empty, and if the king suffered a defeat then God only knew what chaos would descend on poor France. And poor France was already raped. English armies roamed the country burning, plundering, destroying, killing. And this army, the prince's army, was trapped. Or nearly trapped. And there was a chance to destroy it, to cut down the pride of the enemy, to give France a great victory, and King Jean allowed himself to imagine riding into Paris with the Prince of Wales as his captive. He imagined the cheers, the flowers being thrown in front of his horse, the fountains running with wine, and the *Te Deum* being sung in Notre-Dame. That was a beguiling dream, a wonderful dream, but its nightmare brother was the possibility of defeat.

'Your Highness.' Douglas appeared under the pear trees carrying the lantern. He went onto one knee and bowed his head. 'You're awake late, sire.'

'As are you, my lord,' the king said, 'and please, my lord, stand.' King Jean was wearing a blue velvet gown, fringed with gold, embroidered with golden fleurs-de-lys and draped with a thick collar of silver fur. He wished he was wearing something more martial because Douglas was impressive in mail and leather, all of it scarred and battered. He had a short jupon showing the faded red heart of his family, and a thick sword belt from which hung a monstrously heavy blade. He was also carrying an arrow. 'Some wine, my lord?' the king offered.

'I'd prefer ale, your highness.'

'Luc! Do we have ale?'

'We do, Your Majesty!' Luc called from the house.

'Bring some for the Lord of Douglas,' the king said, then made a great effort and smiled at the Scotsman. 'I suspect, my lord, you have come to encourage me to attack?'

'I trust you will, sire,' Douglas said. 'If the bastards stay on that hill we'll have a rare chance to crush them.'

'It seems, though,' the king said mildly, 'that the bastards are on the top of the hill and we are not. Does that not seem pertinent?'

'The slopes to the north and west are easy,' Douglas said dismissively, 'long, gentle, easy slopes, sire. In Scotland we wouldn't even call that a hill. Nothing but a stroll. A crippled cow could walk up there without losing a breath.'

'That is reassuring,' the king said. He paused as the servant brought a great leather pot of ale, which the Scotsman gulped down. The gulping sound was horrible, as was the sight of ale trickling from the edges of Douglas's mouth and soaking into his beard. A brute, King Jean thought, a brute from the edge of the world. 'You were thirsty, my lord,' he said.

'As are the English, sire,' Douglas said, then casually tossed the leather pot back towards Luc. The king sighed inwardly. Did the man have no manners? 'I talked with a farmer,' Douglas went on, 'and he tells me there's no damned water on that hill.'

'A river flows past it, I think?'

'And how do you carry enough water for thousands of men and horses uphill? They'll carry a little, sire, but not enough.'

'Then perhaps we should allow them to expire of thirst?' the king suggested.

'They'll break away south first, sire.'

'So you want me to attack,' Jean said wearily.

'I want you to see this, sire,' Douglas said, and handed the king the arrow.

'An English arrow,' Jean said.

'I have a man,' Douglas said, 'who has been helping the Cardinal Bessières these last few weeks. I'm not sure he is a man, sire, because he's more of an animal and he fights like a demented fiend. Christ's bowels, he frightens me, so God knows what he does to the enemy. And earlier this evening, sire, an English archer shot that arrow at my animal. It hit him plumb on the breastplate. The bastard shot the thing from no more than thirty or forty paces away, and my creature is still alive. He's more than alive, the lucky animal is making babies with some girl in the village right now. And if a man is shot by an English arrow at forty paces and survives to make the two-backed beast a couple of hours later, then there's a message for us all.'

The king fingered the arrowhead. It had once been four inches long, smooth and sharp, but was now bent and squashed. So the arrow had not penetrated a breastplate. 'We have a saying, my lord,' the king said, 'that one swallow does not make a summer.'

'We have the same saying, sire. But look at it!'

The Scotsman's peremptory tone irritated the king who was notoriously short-tempered, but he managed to control his anger. He ran his finger over the crumpled arrowhead. 'You're telling me it's badly made?' he asked. 'One arrow? Your beast was simply lucky.'

'They make arrows by the thousands, sire,' Douglas said. He was talking in a low voice now, earnest rather than hectoring. 'Every shire in England has a duty to make so many thousands of arrows. Some men cut the wood, some men trim the shafts, others collect goose feathers, some men boil the glue, and smiths make the arrowheads. Hundreds of blacksmiths, all across the land, forging heads by the thousand, and all those things, the shafts, the feathers and the heads are collected, assembled, and sent to London. Now one thing I know, sire, is that when you make things in the hundreds of thousands then they're not as well made as a single object fashioned by a craftsman.

You eat from gold plates, sire, and so you should, but your subjects eat off cheap clay. Their platters are made by the thousand, and they break easily. And arrows are harder to make than bowls and plates! The blacksmith has to judge how much bone to add to the furnace, and who is going to make certain he even did that in the first place?'

'Bones?' the king asked. He was fascinated by what Douglas was saying. Was that really how the English made their arrows? Yet how else? They shot hundreds of thousands in a single battle and so they had to be made in vast numbers, and clearly that demanded organisation. He tried to imagine arranging such a thing in France, and sighed at the impossibility of the thought. 'Bones?' he asked again, then made the sign of the cross. 'It sounds like witchcraft.'

'If you smelt iron ore in a furnace, sire, you get iron, but if you add bones to the fire you get steel.'

'I didn't know.'

'They say the bones of a virgin make the best steel.'

'That would make sense, I suppose.'

'And virgins are in short supply,' Douglas said, 'but your armourers, sire, take care over their steel. They make good breastplates, good helmets, good greaves. So good that they'll stop a cheap English arrow.'

The king nodded. He had to admit that the Scotsman was making sense. 'You think we're too frightened of English archers?'

'I think, sire, that if you charge the English on horseback then they'll rip you to shreds. Even cheap arrows will kill a horse. But fight on foot, lord, and the arrows will bounce off well-made steel. They might pierce a shield, but they won't pierce armour. They might as well throw rocks at us.'

The king stared at the arrow. At Crécy, he knew, the French had charged on horseback and the horses had been killed in their hundreds, and in the chaos that followed the men-at-arms had died in their hundreds too. And the English had fought on foot. They always fought on foot. They were famous for it. They had been beaten in Scotland, cut down in their hundreds by Scottish pikemen, and that was the last time they had charged on horseback, and the king reflected that his enemies had learned their lesson. So must he, then. French knights believed there was only one way to fight, on horseback. That was the noble way to fight: the magnificent, frightening way, men and metal and horse together; but common sense said that Douglas was right. The horses would be slaughtered by the arrow storm. He fingered the bent arrowhead. So fight on foot? Do what the English did? And then the arrows would fail? 'I shall think on what you've said, my lord,' he told Douglas, offering the arrow back to the Scotsman, 'and I thank you for your counsel.'

'Keep the arrow, sire,' Douglas said, 'and win this great victory tomorrow.'

The king abruptly shook his head. 'Not tomorrow, no! Tomorrow is Sunday. The Truce of God. The cardinals have promised to talk to the prince and persuade him to yield to our demands.' He glanced north. 'If the English are still there, of course.'

The Lord of Douglas restrained himself from ridiculing the idea of keeping a holy truce on a Sunday. So far as he was concerned one day was as good as any other for killing Englishmen, but he sensed he had persuaded the king that the enemy was vulnerable so there was no point in antagonising the man. 'But when you do win this great victory, sire,' he said, 'and take your prisoners back to Paris, then take that arrow too and keep it as a reminder of how the English put their faith in a weapon that doesn't work.' He paused, then bowed. 'I bid you good night, sire.'

The king said nothing. He was turning the bent arrow over and over in his hands.

And dreaming of Paris echoing with cheers.

At dawn there was a mist in the trees. Everything was grey. Smoke from a thousand fires thickened the mist through which men in mail coats walked like ghosts. A horse broke from its tether and stamped through the oaks, then down the slope towards the distant river. The hoofbeats faded in the mist. Archers kept their strings dry by coiling them inside their helmets or in pouches. Men drew stones along the edges of grey blades. No one spoke much. Two servants kicked acorns out of reach of picketed horses. 'It's strange,' Keane said, 'you can feed acorns to ponies, but not to horses.'

'I hate acorns,' Thomas said.

'They poison the horses, but not ponies. I've never understood that.'

'They taste too bitter.'

'You should soak them in running water,' Keane said, 'and when the water runs clear they'll not be bitter any more.'

The acorns were thick beneath their feet. Mistletoe hung in the oak branches, though as Thomas and Keane walked to the western edge of the woods the large oaks gave way to chestnut, wild pear, and juniper. 'They used to say,' Thomas said, 'that an arrow made of mistletoe couldn't miss.'

'How in God's name would you make an arrow of mistletoe? It's nothing but a bundle of twigs.'

'It would be a short arrow.'

The two hounds ranged ahead, noses to the ground. 'They'll not go hungry,' Keane said.

'You feed them?'

'They feed themselves. They're hunting dogs.'

They left the trees, crossing a rough strip of grassland to where the hill dropped steeply to the river valley. The river itself was hidden by mist. The army's wagons were down there somewhere, parked on a track that led to a ford. Treetops showed above the mist. To the west was another valley, much shallower. In Dorset, Thomas thought, they would call it a combe. The nearer slope was terraced for vines, the farther slope was arable land that rose to a wide, flat-topped plateau. Nothing moved there. 'Is that where the French are?' Keane asked, seeing where Thomas was staring.

'No one seems to know. They're close, though.'

'They are?'

'Listen.'

They fell silent, and after a pause Thomas heard the distant sound of a trumpet. He had heard it a moment before and wondered if he had imagined it. The two hounds pricked their ears and stared northwards, and Thomas, out of curiosity, walked towards the sound.

The English and their Gascon allies were camped among the high trees on a long, wide and high hill that ran north from the River Miosson. If they were to escape the French they must cross that river. It was not large, but it was deep, and to cross it the army could use the bridge by the abbey and a ford that lay farther to the west, and such a crossing would take time and give the French an opportunity to attack while the army was only partway across the river. So perhaps the army would stay here. No one knew.

Though it was certain the army would stay for at least a while, because banners were being planted on the grassland that edged the high woods at the crest of the long hill. The banners ran from the south to the north and they marked where the men-at-arms must assemble. The distant trumpet was sounding more insistently now, and its call was bringing the English and Gascons from the trees. They wondered if the sound presaged an attack. The Earl of Warwick's lion banner was at the southernmost point of the crest and, though that was Thomas's place, he kept walking northwards. The combe was to his left. The combe's slope was precipitately steep where the hill met the River Miosson, but as he and Keane walked northwards the slope became ever more gentle as the valley floor rose, and by the time Thomas reached the great banner blazoned with the Prince of Wales's feathers the slope to his left was long and shallow, a mere dip between this crest and the flat-topped hill to the west, though it would hardly be an easy approach if the French chose to attack from that far hill. The long slope was crossed by vineyards, the grapes tied with willow slips to hemp lines stretched between chestnut posts. To make things more difficult there was the thickest hedge Thomas had ever seen stretching across the slope, a hedge as wide as ten or twelve feet to make a long and impassable thicket of brambles and saplings. There were two wide gaps in the hedge where carts had left great ruts in the soil, and archers were now gathering at either side of those gaps. The English banners were some forty or fifty paces behind the rutted openings.

Keane watched the English army assembling.

Lines of men in mail and steel. Lines of men with axes and hammers, with flails, clubs, swords, and lances. 'They're expecting an attack?' he asked, sounding anxious.

'I don't think anyone knows,' Thomas said, 'but nothing's happening yet.'

Then a trumpet sounded again, but much closer. The archers, who had been sitting, stood up and some strung their bows. They planted arrows in the turf, ready to be plucked up and shot.

'That came from the hill there,' Keane said, staring at the wide, flat hill to the west.

Nothing showed on that far hill. Two horsemen wearing the Prince of Wales's livery galloped from the trees and stood in one of the hedge's great gaps from where they gazed westwards. Men-at-arms were thick beneath the English banners now, and Thomas knew he should go back to the southern end of the line where the hill loomed over the Miosson valley, but just as he turned to go the trumpet called again. Three brazen notes, each held for a long time, and when the third note faded a horseman appeared on the flat-topped hill. He was a half-mile away, perhaps more, but Thomas could see he wore a gaudy tunic, then watched as the man raised and waved a thick white stick over his head. 'A herald,' he said.

There was a pause. The French herald just sat watching the English-held hill, though he could see little of the prince's army because it was obscured by the thick hawthorn hedge. 'Is he just going to stay there?' Keane asked.

'He's waiting for an English herald,' Thomas guessed, but before any of the prince's heralds had a chance to meet his French colleague, a group of horsemen showed on the far skyline. They were dressed in red or black and they spurred their horses down the long slope to where the vines began. 'Three cardinals!' Thomas exclaimed. There were six men-at-arms in plate armour, but the riders were mostly churchmen: priests and monks in black, brown or white being led by three men in cardinal's bright red robes. One of them was Bessières. Thomas recognised the bulk of the man and pitied the horse that had to carry him.

The horsemen, all but one, stopped in the dip of the land, while one cardinal came up the slope alone. He threaded the vines on a narrow track, watched by scores of Englishmen and Gascons who were crowding into the hedge's wide gaps.

'Make way! Make way!' voices shouted behind Thomas. Men-at-arms wearing royal livery were ploughing through the crowd, dividing it to make a space for the Prince of Wales. Men went on their knees.

The prince, mounted on a grey stallion and wearing a jupon with his coat of arms above a mail coat, and with a helmet surrounded by a gold coronet, frowned in puzzlement as the cardinal came closer. 'It's Sunday, isn't it?' he asked loudly.

'Yes, sire.'

'Perhaps he's come to give us a blessing, boys!'

Men laughed. The prince, not wanting the approaching cardinal to see too much of what lay behind the hedge, walked his horse a few paces forward. He waited, his right hand resting on the gilded hilt of his sword. 'Anyone recognise him?' he called.

'That's Talleyrand,' one of the prince's older companions grunted.

'Talleyrand of Périgord?' The prince sounded surprised.

'The same, sire.'

'We are honoured,' the prince said sarcastically. 'Stand up!' he called to the men behind him. 'We don't want the cardinal to think we're worshipping him.'

'He'd like us to worship him,' the Earl of Warwick growled.

The cardinal reined in his mare. The horse was bridled in red leather that was trimmed with silver. The saddlecloth was scarlet with gold fringes, the saddle's pommel and cantle were edged with gold. Even the stirrups were gold. Talleyrand of Périgord was the richest churchman in all France. He had been born into the nobility and had never taken to heart his church's preaching on humility, though he respectfully bowed low in his saddle when he reached the waiting prince. 'Your Majesty,' he said.

'Your Eminence,' the prince replied.

Talleyrand glanced at the archers and men-at-arms, and they gazed back, seeing a tall, thin-faced man with haughty dark eyes. He leaned forward and patted his horse's neck with a red-gloved hand on which a thick gold ring, set with a ruby, glowed bright. 'Your Majesty,' he said again. 'I come with a plea.'

The prince shrugged, but said nothing.

Cardinal Talleyrand looked up at the sky as if seeking inspiration, and when he looked back to the prince there were tears in his eyes. He stretched out his arms. 'I pray you will listen to me, sire. I beseech you to hear my words!'

He had looked to where the sun was burning through a layer of thin cloud, Thomas thought, to make his eyes water.

'This is no time for a sermon!' the prince said brusquely. 'Say what you have to say and say it quickly.'

The cardinal flinched at the prince's tone, but then recovered his sorrowful look and, gazing into the prince's eyes, declared that a battle would be a sinful waste of human life. 'Hundreds must die, sire, hundreds will die, and they will die far from their homes to be buried in unconsecrated ground. Have you marched this far just to gain a shallow grave in France? For you are in peril, Your Majesty, you are in dreadful peril! The might of France is close, and they outnumber you! They will crush you, and I beg you, I beg you, sire, to allow me to seek another answer. Why fight a battle? Why die for pride? I promise you, sire, by the crucified Christ and by the Blessed Virgin that I will do all that I can to satisfy your wishes! I speak for the church, for the Holy Father, for Christ himself, who does not wish to see men die here. Let us parley, sire. Let us sit down and reason together. This is Sunday, a day unfit for slaughter, a day for men of goodwill to talk. In the name of the living Christ I beg this of you, sire.'

The prince was silent. There was a murmur in the English ranks as men translated the cardinal's words. The prince raised a hand for quiet, then just gazed at the cardinal without speaking for what seemed a long while. Then he shrugged. 'Do you speak for France, Your Eminence?'

'No, sire. I speak for the church and for the Holy Father. The Holy Father desires peace, in the name of Christ, I swear it. He has beseeched me to prevent bloodshed, to end this senseless warfare and to make peace.'

'And will our enemy keep a truce this day?'

'King Jean has promised as much,' Talleyrand said. 'He has sworn to give this day to the church in the prayerful hope that we can forge an everlasting peace.'

The prince nodded, then again sat silent for a while. The high clouds drifted to unveil the sun, which blazed in the pale sky, promising a warm day. 'I shall keep the truce this day,' the prince finally spoke, 'and send emissaries to treat with you. They can talk there.' He pointed to where the remaining churchmen waited at the foot of the slope. 'But the truce is for this day only,' the prince added.

'Then I declare this day to be the Truce of God,' Talleyrand said grandly. There was an awkward pause as if he felt he should say something more, but then he just nodded to the prince, turned his horse, and spurred back down the long sunlit slope.

And the prince let out a long sigh of relief.

CHAPTER 13

'Truce of God.' Sir Reginald Cobham said the words sourly.

'They'll keep it, won't they?' Thomas asked.

'Oh, they'll keep it. They'd like the whole of next week to be a Truce of God,' Sir Reginald said, 'the bastards would love that.' He kicked his horse down the slope towards the River Miosson. The mist had burned away under the September sun so that Thomas could see the river winding in the valley. It was a small river, scarcely more than thirty feet across at its widest, but as he followed Sir Reginald down the steep slope he could see that the valley bottom was marshy, which suggested the river flooded often. 'They'd like us to stay here,' Sir Reginald said, 'and exhaust our supplies. Then we'd be hungry, thirsty, and vulnerable. Which we are already. Nothing to eat, no water on the hill, and we're outnumbered.'

'We were outnumbered at Crécy,' Thomas said.

'Which doesn't make it a good thing,' Sir Reginald said. He had summoned Thomas with a curt, 'You'll do. Get on your horse and bring a half-dozen archers,' then led him to the southern-most end of the English line where the Earl of Warwick's banner stirred in the light breeze. Sir Reginald kept going, leading Thomas and his archers down the steep hill into the marshy valley of the Miosson. The English baggage train, a mass of carts and wagons, was parked under the trees. 'They could cross the river by the bridge,' Sir Reginald explained, gesturing east towards the monastery that was hidden by the big trees growing in the lush land about the river, 'but the village streets are narrow and you can wager your last penny that some bloody idiot will break a wagon wheel on a house corner. It will be quicker if they can get across the ford here. So that's what we're doing. Seeing if the ford is passable.'

'Because we're retreating?'

'The prince would like that. He'd like to get over the river and head south as fast as we can. He'd like us to sprout wings and fly to Bordeaux.' Sir Reginald stopped close to the river where he turned and looked at Thomas's six archers. 'All right, boys, just stay here. If any bastard Frenchman comes near just sing out. Don't shoot. Just sing out, but make sure your bows are strung.'

A raised track curved through the marsh. The causeway was firm and rutted, showing that carts used the track, which dipped into the ford where both horses stopped to drink. Sir Reginald let his horse slake its thirst, then spurred into the river's centre. 'Splash about,' he told Thomas. He was letting the horses feel the river bottom, looking for a treacherous dip or a marshy place that could trap a wagon, but the horses found firm footing all the way across.

'Sir!' Sam shouted, and Sir Reginald twisted in the saddle.

A dozen horsemen were watching from the trees halfway down the western hill. They were in mail and helmets. Three wore jupons, though they were too far away for Thomas to see what badge they bore. One carried a small banner, red against the green and yellow of the trees.

'Le Champ d'Alexandre,' Sir Reginald said and, when Thomas looked at him quizzically, he pointed to the flat-topped western hill. 'That's what the local folk call it, Alexander's Field, and my guess is that those bastards are exploring the whole damned hill.' The Frenchmen, they had to be French if they were on that western slope, were well out of bowshot. Thomas wondered if they had even seen the archers, who were in the shadow of the willows growing close to the ford. 'I didn't want to bring a score of men,' Sir Reginald said, 'because I don't want the bastards to think we're interested in the ford. And I certainly don't want the goddam bastards to see our wagons.' Those wagons were parked on the Miosson's northern bank, hidden from le Champ d'Alexandre by trees and by the high shoulder of the hill on which the forest of Nouaillé grew and where the prince had formed his line of battle. Sir Reginald frowned as he watched the Frenchmen who, in turn, gazed back at the two horsemen in the river. 'It might be a truce,' Sir Reginald went on, 'but they still could be tempted by us.'

The Frenchmen were indeed tempted. Their job was to probe the English position and, as far as they could see, the two horsemen were a long way from the rest of the prince's troops and so they spurred forward, not charging, just coming slowly and deliberately towards the river. 'They want to have a chat with us,' Sir Reginald said sourly. 'How good are your archers?'

'As good as any.'

'Boys! Have some target practice! Kill some trees, all right? Don't aim at the men or horses, just frighten the bastards away.'

The French had divided into two files, which were now coming faster down the hill, picking their way through the thick trees as the riders ducked under branches. Sam shot the first arrow. The fledging flickered white against the leaves, then buried itself in the trunk of an oak. Five more arrows followed. One struck a branch and tumbled, the others slammed hard into bark, and the closest was no more than two paces from a French horseman.

Who abruptly curbed his horse.

'Another shot each!' Sir Reginald called. 'Just a few paces short of them, boys. Let them know you're here and you're hungry!'

The bows shot again, the arrows flew to thud

into trees with appalling force and the Frenchmen turned away. One waved genially towards Sir Reginald, who waved back. 'Thank God for archers,' he said. He watched the Frenchmen push back up the hill until they were out of sight.

'Sam,' Thomas called, 'fetch the arrows back.' He had resupplied his men with arrows from the prince's baggage train, but there were never enough.

'I want you to stay here,' Sir Reginald said. 'All night. I'll send the rest of your men down to join you. Do you have a trumpeter?'

'No.'

'I'll send one. Stay here, and sound the alarm if the French come back in force. But keep them away if they do come. If they see the wagons close to the ford they'll guess what we're doing.'

'Retreating?' Thomas asked.

Sir Reginald shrugged. 'I don't know.' He frowned and gazed blankly northwards as if trying to gauge what the enemy might do. 'The prince thinks we should keep marching. He's given orders that tomorrow morning, first thing, we cross the river and march south as if the devil himself was at our heels. A French attack would stop that, of course, but my guess is they won't attack at first light. They'll need at least two hours to draw their army up, and I want the wagons gone before they even know we were here, and then the rest of the army can slip over the river and steal a day's march.' He kicked his horse out of the ford, back onto the track that crossed the marsh. 'But who knows what those goddamned churchmen are proposing? If we could have joined Lancaster . . .' He let that thought trail away.

'Lancaster?'

'The idea was to join the Earl of Lancaster and make havoc in northern France, but we couldn't cross the Loire. And nothing's gone right since then, and now we're trying to get back to Gascony without the bloody French killing us. So stay here till dawn!'

To help an army escape.

The Captal de Buch took twenty men-at-arms northwards. They rode past the Earl of Salisbury's men who guarded the northern end of the ridge. Most of the earl's men were arrayed beyond the northern end of the protective hedge and so his archers were busy digging and disguising pits to break the legs of charging horses. A bowman guided the captal and his men past the pits, and once past the traps the captal could look back and see the cardinals and churchmen who were attempting to forge a peace. They and the French negotiators had met the English emissaries in the open fields, just beneath the vineyard. Someone had brought benches to the place and the men were sitting and talking, while heralds and men-at-arms waited a few paces away. There was no tent or awning. A single banner was planted behind the churchmen. It showed the crossed keys of Saint Peter, a sign that a Papal Legate was present.

'What are they talking about?' one of the captal's men asked.

'They're trying to delay us,' the captal said, 'they want to keep us here. They want us to starve.'

'I hear the Pope sent them. Maybe they want peace?'

'The Pope shits French turds,' the captal said curtly, 'and the only peace he wants is to see us in his chamber pot.' He turned away and led his Gascons down the long slope that dropped gently to the north. They were heading into a tangled landscape of woods, vineyards, hedges, and hills, and somewhere in that tangle was a French army, but no one was quite certain where it was or how big it was. It was certainly close. The captal could tell it was close because the smoke of French cooking fires was thick on the northern skyline, but the prince had asked him to try to discover just where the enemy was camped and how many they were, and so he spurred down the slope, keeping now in the shelter of the trees. Neither he nor his men were mounted on their great destriers, the trained war horses that went into battle, but on coursers, fast light horses that could speed them out of trouble. The men wore mail, but not plate, and had helmets and swords, but no shields. They were Gascons and that meant they were accustomed to perpetual war, to countering French raids or making raids themselves.

They rode in silence. There was a cart track to their left, but they stayed away from it, keeping hidden. They slowed when they reached the foot of the slope, for now they were well beyond English bowshot and if the French had posted sentinels then they could be anywhere among these trees.

The captal gestured to spread his men out, then gestured again to signal them forward. They went very slowly, searching the woods ahead for a movement that might betray a hidden crossbowman. They saw nothing. They were climbing through thick woods, and still there was no sign of the enemy. The captal stopped. Was he being lured into a trap? He waved a hand indicating that his men should wait where they were, and he swung out of the saddle and went alone on foot. The slope was not steep and he could see the crest not far ahead. Surely that was a place to put sentinels? He was moving quietly, furtively, watching for the flight of a bird, but for all his caution he sensed he was alone. He watched the skyline for a moment, then moved on up to the crest and suddenly he could see far to the north and west.

He crouched.

The main French encampment was only half a mile away, the tents clustered about a village and a manor, but what interested him was the sight of men going west. They would be invisible to the English on their hill, but the captal could see that the French forces were being led around to the west and south, curling closer to the river. They were not in battle order, indeed they were in no order that he could see, but they were undeniably moving westwards. It looked to him as if they were going to the flat-topped hill, to le Champ d'Alexandre. He could not count them, they were too many and there was too much dead ground. Eighty-seven banners, he remembered.

He backed away, stood, and went to his horse. He mounted, turned and waved his men southwards again. They rode fast now, sure that no enemy was within sight or earshot, and the captal wondered if the French would keep the truce.

But of two things he was sure. The enemy were readying to attack, and the attack would come from the west.

The Earls of Warwick and Suffolk came back to the prince's tent in the late afternoon. They sat wearily when the prince offered them chairs, then drank the wine that his servant brought. All the prince's advisers were there, all waiting for the results of the long negotiations to be announced.

'The terms are these, sire,' the Earl of Warwick spoke flatly. 'We must return all the land, fortresses and towns captured in the last three years. We must yield all the plunder in our baggage train. We must release all prisoners held here or in England without further payment of ransom. And we are to pay France an indemnity of sixty-six thousand pounds to compensate for the destruction we have wrought over the years.'

'Dear God,' the prince said faintly.

'In return, sire,' the Earl of Oxford took up the tale, 'your army will be permitted to march to Gascony, the King of France will betroth one of his daughters to you, and she will bring you the County of Angoulême as her dowry.'

'Are his daughters pretty?' the prince asked.

'Prettier than a hill covered in English corpses, sire,' the Earl of Warwick said sharply. 'There is more. You and all England must swear not to take up arms against France for a period of seven years.'

The prince looked from one earl to the other, then to the captal, who sat to one side of the tent. 'Advise me,' he said.

The Earl of Warwick flinched as he stretched his legs out. 'We're outnumbered, sire. Sir Reginald believes we can slip away in the dawn, cross the river and be on our way before the enemy notices, but I confess I'm sceptical. The bastards aren't fools. They'll be watching us.'

'And they're moving south and west, sire,' the captal put in. 'They must be thinking we'll try to cross the Miosson and they're trying to close that escape.'

'And they're confident, sire,' the Earl of Oxford said.

'Because of numbers?'

'Because our men are tired, outnumbered, hungry and thirsty. And the fat cardinal said something strange. He warned us that God has sent France a sign that He is on their side. I asked him what he meant, but the fat bastard just looked smug.'

'I thought the cardinals spoke for the Pope?'

'The Pope,' Warwick said dourly, 'is in France's grip.'

'And if we fight tomorrow?' the prince asked.

There was silence. Then the Earl of Warwick shrugged and used his hands to imitate a weighing scale. Up and down. The thing could end either way, his hands were suggesting, but his face showed nothing but pessimism.

'We hold a strong position,' the Earl of Salisbury, who commanded the troops at the northern end of the English hill, said, 'but if the line breaks? We've made pits and trenches that will stop them, but we can't entrench the whole damned hill. And it's my belief they have at least twice our numbers.'

'And they're eating well today,' the captal said, 'while our men make acorn stew.'

'The terms are harsh,' the prince said. A horsefly landed on his leg and he slapped at it angrily.

'And they demand noble hostages, sire, as a surety that the terms are honoured,' the Earl of Oxford said.

'Noble hostages,' the prince said flatly.

'Noble and knightly, sire,' the earl said, 'which includes everyone in this tent, I fear.' He took a piece of parchment from a pouch on his sword belt and held it towards the prince. 'That's a partial list, sire, but they will undoubtedly add other names.'

The prince nodded and a servant took the list and went on one knee to give it to his master. The prince grimaced as he read the names. 'All our best knights?'

'Including Your Royal Majesty,' Oxford said.

'So I see,' the prince said. He frowned as he read the names. 'Sire Roland de Verrec? Surely he's not in our army?'

'It seems he is, sire.'

'And a Douglas? Are they mad?'

'Sir Robert Douglas is also here, sire.'

'He is? Christ's bowels, what's a Douglas doing with us? And who in God's name is Thomas Hookton?'

'Sir Thomas, sire,' Sir Reginald spoke for the first time. 'He was one of Will Skeat's men at Crécy.'

'An archer?'

'Now a vassal of Northampton, sire. A useful man.'

'Why in Christ's name is Billy knighting archers?' the prince asked petulantly. 'And why in hell's name do the French know he's here and I don't?'

No one answered. The prince let the parchment drop onto the carpet that covered the turf. What would his father think? What would his father do? But Edward the Third, the most feared warrior-king in Europe, was in faraway England. So this was the prince's decision. True, he had advisers and he was wise enough to listen to them, but in the end the decision was his alone. He stood and walked to the tent door and stared past the

426

banners, through the trees to where the light was fading in the west. 'The terms are harsh,' he said again, 'but defeat will be harsher.' He turned and looked at the Earl of Warwick. 'Beat them down, my lord. Offer half of what they demand.'

'It's hardly a demand, sire, but a suggestion from the cardinals. The French must accept the terms too.'

'Of course they'll accept them,' the prince said, 'they dictated them! Even half of what they want means victory for them! Christ! They win everything!'

'And if the French won't accept lesser terms, sire? What then?'

The prince sighed. 'It's better to be a hostage in Paris than a corpse in Poitiers,' he suggested, then flinched as he thought again of the French demands. 'It's a surrender, really, isn't it?'

'No, sire,' the Earl of Warwick said firmly. 'It's a truce and an arrangement.' He frowned, trying to find some good news amid the bad. 'The army will be allowed to march on to Gascony, sire. No prisoners will be demanded.'

'And hostages are not prisoners?' the Earl of Salisbury asked.

'Hostages pay no ransom. We'll be treated honourably.'

'You can drape it in velvet,' the prince said unhappily, 'and drench it in perfume, but it's still a surrender.' But he and his army were trapped. Call it a truce, an arrangement, or a treaty, he knew it was really a surrender. Yet he had no other choice. So far as he could see it was surrender or be slaughtered.

Because the English were beaten.

The Hellequin guarded the ford. The Sire Roland de Verrec and Robbie Douglas had stayed on the hill with the rest of the Earl of Warwick's men-at-arms, but the remainder of Thomas's men were camped just south of the river. A cordon of archers was on the northern bank, and Keane was there with his wolfhounds. 'They'll howl if they smell men or horses,' he said.

'No fires,' Thomas had ordered. They could see the glow of the English and Gascon campfires on the hill, and a greater glow stretching around the northern and western horizon that marked where the French army was spending the night, but Thomas would have no fires. Sir Reginald did not want to draw the enemy's attention to the crossing over the Miosson, and so the men-at-arms and archers shivered in the cold autumn darkness. Clouds smothered the moon, though there were gaps through which bright stars showed. An owl called and Thomas made the sign of the cross.

Some time in the night and somewhere in that darkness hooves sounded. The wolfhounds stood and growled, but then a voice called softly, 'Sir Thomas! Sir Thomas!'

'I'm here.'

'Sweet Jesus, it's dark.' It was Sir Reginald who

appeared out of the blackness and eased himself out of his saddle. 'Good man, no fires. Any visitors?'

'None.'

'But we reckon they've moved men onto that hill.' He gestured towards the dark loom of le Champ d'Alexandre. 'Damn it, they must know the ford's here; they must have realised we'll try to escape. Except we might not.'

'Might not?'

'The churchmen have come up with terms. We pay the bastard French a fortune, give them hostages, return all the land we've conquered, and promise to behave ourselves for the next seven years. The prince has agreed.'

'Jesus,' Thomas said quietly.

'I doubt he has anything to do with it. And if the French agree to the church's proposal? Then tomorrow we give them hostages and slink away.' He sounded disgusted. 'And you're one of the hostages.'

'Me!'

'Your name's on the list.'

'Jesus,' Thomas said again.

'So why would the French want you?'

'Cardinal Bessières wants me,' Thomas said. 'I killed his brother.' This was not the time to talk of *la Malice*, and the killing of the cardinal's brother was explanation enough.

'His brother?'

'An arrow. Bastard deserved it too.'

'He was a churchman?'

429

'God no, a rogue.'

Sir Reginald chuckled. 'Then my advice, Sir Thomas, is to ride away from here if the truce is declared.'

'And how will I know?' Thomas asked.

'Seven trumpet calls. Long blasts, seven of them. That means there'll be no battle, just humiliation.'

Thomas thought about the last word. 'Why?' he finally asked.

He sensed that Sir Reginald shrugged. 'If we fight,' the older man said, 'we'd probably lose. We think they might have ten thousand men, so we're badly outnumbered, we're exhausted, there's no food and the damned French have plenty of everything. So if we fight we condemn a lot of good Englishmen and loyal Gascons to death, and the prince doesn't want that on his conscience. He's a good man. Too easily distracted by ladies, perhaps, but who'd blame a man for that?'

Thomas smiled. 'I knew one of his ladies.'

'You did?' Sir Reginald sounded surprised. 'Which one? God knows there are enough.'

'She was called Jeanette. The Countess of Armorica.'

'You knew her?' The surprise was still there.

'I often wonder what happened to her.'

'She died, God rest her soul,' Sir Reginald said bleakly, 'she and her son both. The pestilence.'

'Dear God,' Thomas said, and made the sign of the cross.

'How did you know her?'

'I helped her,' Thomas said vaguely.

'I remember now! There was talk that she escaped Brittany with an English archer. That was you?'

'Long time ago now,' Thomas said evasively.

'She was a beauty,' Sir Reginald said wistfully. He was silent for a moment and when he spoke again his voice was brusque. 'One of two things will happen tomorrow, Sir Thomas. One, you hear seven blasts on the trumpet and if you've any sense you mount up and ride like hell to escape the cardinal. And two? The French decide they win more by fighting us, which means they'll attack. And if that happens I want the baggage over the river. The damned French usually take hours to ready for a battle so we've a chance to slip away before they know it. And to escape we need this ford. You'll have help if there's going to be fighting, but you know as well as I do that nothing goes to plan in a battle.'

'We'll hold the ford,' Thomas said.

'And I'll ask Father Richard to come here before dawn,' Sir Reginald said, going back to his horse.

'Father Richard?'

There was the creak of leather as Sir Reginald climbed back into the saddle. 'He's one of the Earl of Warwick's chaplains. You'll want to hear mass, won't you?'

'If there's a fight, yes,' Thomas said, then helped

Sir Reginald find his stirrups. 'What do you think will happen in the morning?'

Sir Reginald's horse stamped on the track. The rider was a dark shadow against a dark sky. 'I think we'll surrender,' Sir Reginald said bleakly. 'God help me, but that's what I think.' He turned the horse and rode towards the hill.

'You can see your way, Sir Reginald?' Thomas called.

'The horse can. One of us must have some sense.' He clicked his tongue and the horse's pace quickened.

It seemed the night would never end. Darkness was complete, and with it came the sense of doom that darkness brings. The river ran loud over the shallow ford. 'You should try to sleep,' Genevieve said, surprising Thomas. She had waded the ford to join him on the northern bank.

'You too.'

'I brought you this,' she said.

Thomas held out his hand and felt the familiar heft of his bow. A yew bow, tall as a man, the stave thick in the centre and straight as an arrow. It felt smooth. 'You waxed it?' he asked.

'Sam gave me the last of his wool fat.'

Thomas ran his hand up the stave. At its thick centre, where the arrow rested before the cord sent it on death's mission, he could feel the little silver plate. It was incised with a yale holding a cup, the badge of the disgraced Vexille family, his family. Would God punish him for casting

432

the Grail into the cold sea? 'You must be frozen,' he said.

'I pulled up my skirts,' she said, 'and the ford isn't deep.' She sat beside him and rested her head on his shoulder. For a time neither spoke, but just stared into the night. 'So what happens tomorrow?' she asked.

'It's today,' Thomas said bleakly. 'And it depends on the French. Either they accept the church's terms or they decide they can do better by beating us. And if they do accept, we ride south.' He did not tell her that his name was on a list of men who must be surrendered as hostages. 'I want you to make certain the horses are saddled. Keane will help you. They have to be ready before dawn. And if you hear seven trumpet calls then we go. We go fast.'

He felt her head nod. 'And if the trumpet doesn't call?' she asked.

'Then the French will come to kill us.'

'How many are there?'

Thomas shrugged. 'Sir Reginald thinks they have about ten thousand men? No one really knows. Maybe more, maybe fewer. A lot.'

'And we have?'

'Two thousand archers and four thousand men-at-arms.'

Genevieve was silent and he supposed she was thinking about the disparity in numbers. 'Bertille is praying,' she said.

'I suppose lots of people are praying.'

'She's kneeling by the cross,' Genevieve said.

433

'Cross?'

'Beyond the cottage, at the crossroads, there's a crucifix. She says she'll stay all night and pray for her husband's death. Do you think God listens to prayers like that?'

'What do you think?'

'I think God is weary of us.'

'Labrouillade won't fight in the front rank,' Thomas said. 'He'll make sure other men are in front of him. And if things go badly he'll just surrender. He's too rich to kill.' He stroked her face, feeling the leather patch she wore across her injured eye. She was blind in that eye, and it had gone milky white. He told her it did not disfigure her and he believed that, but she did not. He hugged her close.

'I wish you were too rich to kill,' she said.

'I am,' Thomas said with a smile. 'They could ransom me for a fortune, but they won't.'

'The cardinal?'

'He doesn't forgive or forget. He wants to burn me alive.'

Genevieve wanted to tell him to be careful, but that was as much a waste of words as Bertille's prayers at the roadside cross. 'What do you think will happen?' she asked instead.

'I think we'll hear the trumpet sound seven times,' Thomas said.

And then he would ride south as if all the fiends of hell were at his heels.

★   ★   ★

434

King Jean and his two sons knelt to receive the wafer that was Christ's body. *'In nomine Patris, et Filii, et Spiritus Sancti,'* the Bishop of Châlons intoned. 'And may Saint Denis guard you and keep you and bring you to the victory that God wills.'

'Amen,' the king grunted.

Prince Charles, the dauphin, stood and went to a window. He pulled open a shutter. 'It's still dark,' he said.

'Not for long,' the Earl of Douglas said, 'I hear the first birds.'

'Let me go back to the prince.' Cardinal Talleyrand spoke from the room's edge.

'To what purpose?' King Jean asked, annoyed that the cardinal had not called him 'sire' or 'Your Majesty'.

'To offer them a truce while the terms are clarified.'

'The terms are clear,' the king said, 'and I am not inclined to accept them.'

'You proposed the terms, sire,' Talleyrand said respectfully.

'And they accepted them too easily. That suggests they're frightened. That they have cause to be frightened.'

'With respect, sire,' Marshal Arnoul d'Audrehem intervened. He was fifty, wise in war, and wary of the archers in the enemy army. 'Every day they linger on that hilltop, sire, weakens them. Every day increases their fear.'

'They're frightened and weak now,' Jean de Clermont, the second marshal of the French army, said. 'They're sheep to be slaughtered.' He sneered at his fellow marshal. 'You're just afraid of them.'

'If we fight,' d'Audrehem said, 'you'll be staring at my horse's arse.'

'Enough!' King Jean snapped. Men feared his notorious temper and fell silent. The king frowned at a servant who carried a pile of jupons over his arm. 'How many?'

'Seventeen, sire.'

'Give them to men in the Order of the Star.' He turned and looked at the window where the faintest light showed in the east. The king already wore a jupon of blue cloth decorated with golden fleurs-de-lys, and the seventeen coats the servant carried were identical. If there was to be a battle then let the enemy be confused as to who was the king, and the men in the Order of the Star were among the greatest fighters of France. It was King Jean's own order of chivalry, an answer to England's Order of the Garter, and today the Knights of the Star would protect their monarch. 'If the English are stupid enough to accept a few days more on the hilltop, so be it,' he told Talleyrand.

'So I may extend the truce?' the cardinal asked.

'See what they say,' the king said and waved Talleyrand away. 'If they beg for time,' he told the men remaining in the room, 'it means they're scared.'

'Scared men are easily beaten,' Marshal Clermont observed.

'Oh, we'll beat them,' King Jean said, and felt a flutter of nervousness about the decision he had made.

'So we fight, sire?' the Lord of Douglas asked. He was confused as to whether the king really meant to fight or extend the truce. All the men in the room had been awake half the night as armourers clad them in leather, mail and steel, and now the king was again flirting with the idea of a truce?

The king frowned at the question. He paused. He shifted his weight and scratched at his nose, then reluctantly nodded. 'We fight,' he said.

'Thank God,' Clermont muttered.

The Lord of Douglas went to one knee. 'Then with your permission, sire, I would ride with Marshal d'Audrehem.'

'You?' The king sounded surprised. 'You're the one who told me to fight on foot!'

'I shall indeed fight on foot, sire, and take pleasure in beating your enemies into bloody pulp, but I would ride with the marshal first.'

'So be it,' the king allowed. The French feared the enemy archers and so they had assembled five hundred knights whose horses were elaborately armoured, heavy with mail, plate, and leather. Those great destriers, protected from arrows, would charge the archers on the English flanks, and when the horsemen had scattered the bowmen and beaten them down with axes, swords and lances, the rest of the army would advance on foot. 'When the archers are dead you will join Prince Charles,' the king commanded Douglas.

'I am honoured, sire, and I thank you.'

The dauphin Charles, just eighteen years old, would command the first battle of French men-at-arms. Their job was to advance up the long slope and crash into the English and Gascon knights and slaughter them. The king's brother, the Duke of Orléans, commanded the second line, while the king himself, along with his youngest son, would lead the rearmost troops. Three great battles, led by princes and a king, would assault the English, and they would attack on foot because horses, unless they were armoured like men, were too vulnerable to arrows.

'Order all lances to be shortened,' the king commanded. Men on foot could not wield long lances, so they must be cut down to manageable lengths. 'And to your battles, gentlemen.'

The French were ready. The banners were flying. The king was armoured in the best steel Milan could make. It had taken four hours to clad the king in plate steel, each piece first blessed by the Bishop of Châlons before the armourers buckled, strapped or tied the item comfortably. His legs were protected by cuisses, by greaves, and by roundels over his knees, while his boots had scales of overlapping steel. He wore strips of steel fixed to a leather skirt, above which were his breast- and backplates, which were buckled tightly over a mail coat. Espaliers covered his shoulders, vambraces and rerebraces his arms, while his hands were in gauntlets that, like the boots, had scales of steel. His helmet had a snouted visor and was circled by a crown of gold, and over his body was a surcoat blazoned with the golden fleur-de-lys of France. The oriflamme was ready; the French were ready. This was a day to go into history, the day that France cut down its enemies.

The Lord of Douglas knelt for the bishop's blessing. The Scotsman was still nervous that the king might change his mind, but he dared not ask questions in case those very queries made Jean cautious. Yet what Douglas did not know was that the king had received a sign from heaven. During the night, as the armourers had fussed and measured and tightened, the Cardinal Bessières had come to the king. He had dropped to his knees, grunting with the effort, and then looked up at the king. 'Your Majesty,' he had said, and offered with both hands a rusty, feeble-looking blade.

'You're giving me a peasant weapon, Your Eminence?' the king had said, irritated that the fat cardinal had interrupted his preparations. 'Or do you want me to reap some barley?' he asked because the crude sword, its blade broader at its tip than at the base, looked like a grotesquely lengthened hay knife.

'It is the sword of Saint Peter, Your Majesty,' the cardinal had said, 'given into our hands by the providence of God to ensure your great victory.'

The king had looked startled, then disbelieving, but the earnestness with which Bessières had spoken was reassuring. He had reached out and touched *la Malice* nervously, then held his finger on the pitted blade. 'How can you be sure?'

'I am sure, Majesty. The monks of Saint Junien were given guard of it, and they delivered it to us as a sign from God.'

'It has been missing these many years,' the Bishop of Châlons had said reverently, then knelt to the relic and kissed the pitted blade.

'So it is real?' the king had asked, amazed.

'It is real,' Bessières had replied, 'and God has sent it to you. This is the sword that protected our Saviour and the man who possesses this sword cannot know defeat.'

'Then God and Saint Denis be praised,' the king had said, and he had taken the sword from the cardinal and touched it to his lips. The cardinal had watched, hiding his pleasure. The sword would bring victory, and victory would raise King Jean to be the mightiest monarch of Christendom, and when the Pope died the King of France would add his persuasion to the men who would advocate Bessières's candidacy for the throne of Saint Peter. The king closed his eyes momentarily and kissed the blade a second time before returning it to the cardinal's gloved hands.

'With Your Highness's permission,' the cardinal

had said, 'I shall give this holy blade to a deserving champion so he can cut down your enemies.'

'You have my permission,' the king had said. 'Give it to a man who will use it well!' His voice was firm because the sight of the blade had given him a new confidence. He had been wanting a sign, some hint that God would grant France a victory, and now he had that sign. Victory was his. God had decreed it.

Yet now, as dawn edged the world, the king felt his old doubts return. Was it wise to fight? The English prince had accepted humiliating terms, so perhaps France should impose those terms? Yet victory would yield much greater riches. Victory would bring glory as well as treasure. The king made the sign of the cross and told himself that God would prosper France this day. He had confessed his sins, he had been forgiven, and he had been sent a sign from heaven. Today, he thought, Crécy will be avenged.

'What if the cardinal arranges a truce, sire?' d'Audrehem interrupted his thoughts.

'The cardinal can fart for all I care,' King Jean said.

Because he had made his choice. The English were trapped, and he would slaughter them.

He led the way from the house into a world made grey by the day's first wolfish light. He put an arm around the shoulder of his youngest son, the fourteen-year-old Philippe. 'Today, my son, you will fight at my side,' he said. The boy had been

441

equipped like his father, head to toe in steel. 'And today, my son, you will see God and Saint Denis shower glory upon France.' The king lifted his arms so an armourer could strap a great sword's belt about his waist. A squire held a war axe with a haft decorated with golden hoops, while a groom led a handsome grey stallion that the king now mounted. He would fight on foot like his men, but at this moment, as the dawn promised a bright new day, it was important that men should see their king. He pushed up his helmet's visor, then drew his polished sword and held it high above his blue-plumed helmet. 'Advance the banners,' he ordered, 'and unfurl the oriflamme.'

Because France was going to fight.

The Prince of Wales, like the King of France, had spent most of the night being armoured. His men had spent it in their lines, beneath their banners. They had been drawn up in battle order for twenty-four hours, and now, in the dawn, they grumbled because they were thirsty, hungry, and uncomfortable. They knew a battle had been unlikely the previous day; it had been a Sunday and the churchmen had proclaimed a Truce of God, though still they had waited in line in case the treacherous enemy broke the truce, but now it was Monday. Rumours flickered through the army. The French numbered twelve thousand, fifteen thousand, twenty thousand. The prince had surrendered them to the French, or the prince had arranged a truce, but despite the rumours there were no orders to relax their vigilance. They waited in line, all but those who went back to the woods to empty their bowels. They watched the skyline to the north and west, looking for an enemy, but it was dark and unmoving there.

Priests moved among the waiting men. They said mass, they gave men crumbs of bread and absolution. Some men ate scraps of earth. From earth they came, to earth they would go, and eating the soil was an old superstition before battle. Men touched their talismans, they prayed to their patron saints, they made the jokes that men always made before battle. 'Keep your visor lifted, John. Goddamned French see your face they'll run like hares.' They watched the wan light grow and the colour come back to a dead world. They talked of old battles. They tried to hide their nervousness. They pissed often. Their bowels felt watery. They wished they had wine or ale. Their mouths were dry. The French numbered twenty-four thousand, thirty thousand, forty thousand! They watched their commanders meet on horseback at the line's centre. 'It's all right for them,' they grumbled. 'Who'll kill a goddamned prince or earl? They just pay the bloody ransom and go back to their whores. We're the goddamned bastards who have to die.' Men thought of their wives, children, whores, mothers. Small boys carried sheaves of arrows to the archers who were concentrated at the ends of the line.

The prince watched the western hill and saw no one there. Were the French sleeping? 'Are we ready?' he asked Sir Reginald Cobham.

'Say the word, sire, and we go.'

What the prince wanted to do was one of the most difficult things any commander could attempt. He wanted to escape while the enemy was close. He had heard nothing from the cardinals and he had to assume the French would attack, so his troops would need to hold them off while the baggage and the vanguard crossed the Miosson and marched away. If he could do it, if he could get his baggage across the river and then retreat, step by step, always fending off the enemy attacks, then he could steal a whole day's march, maybe two, but the danger, the awful danger, was that the French would trap half his army on one bank and destroy it, then pursue the other half and slaughter that too. The prince must fight and retreat, fight and retreat, holding the enemy at bay with a dwindling number of men. It was a risk that made him make the sign of the cross, then he nodded to Sir Reginald Cobham. 'Go,' he said, 'get the baggage moving!' The decision was made; the dice were rolled. 'And you, my lord,' he turned to the Earl of Warwick, 'your men will guard the crossing place?'

'We will, sire.'

'Then God be with you.'

The earl and Sir Reginald galloped their horses south, and the prince, glorious in his royal colours

444

and mounted on a tall black horse, followed more slowly. His handsome face was framed in steel. His helmet was ringed with gold and crested with three ostrich feathers. He paused every few yards and spoke to the waiting men. 'We will probably fight today! And we shall do in this place what we did together at Crécy! God is on our side; Saint George watches over us! And you will stay in line! You hear that? No man will break the line! You see a naked whore in the enemy ranks you leave her there! If you break ranks the enemy will break us! Stay in line! Saint George is with us!' Again and again he repeated the words. Stay in line. Don't break the line. Obey your commanders! Stay together, shield to shield. Let the enemy come to us. Do not break the line!

'Sire!' A messenger galloped from the line's centre where there was a great gap in the thick hedge. 'The cardinal is coming!'

'Meet him, find what he wants!' the prince said, then turned back to his men. 'You stay in line! You stay with your neighbour! You do not leave the ranks! Shield next to shield!'

The Earl of Salisbury brought the news that the cardinal was offering a further five days of truce. 'In five days we starve,' the prince retorted, 'and he knows it.' The army had run out of food for men and horses and the presence of the enemy meant that no forage parties could search the nearby countryside. 'He's just doing the French king's bidding,' the prince said, 'so tell him to go say his prayers and leave us alone. We're in God's hands now.'

The church's mission had failed. Archers strung their bows. The sun was almost above the horizon and the sky was filled with a great pale light. 'Stay in line! You will not leave the ranks! Do you hear me? Stay in line!'

Beneath the hill, beside the river where the shadows of the night still lingered, the first wagons moved towards the ford.

Because the army would escape.

PART IV

BATTLE

CHAPTER 14

The axles squealed like pigs being slaughtered at winter's onset. The carts, wagons and wains, of which no two were alike, lurched on the rough track that led along the river's northern bank. Most were piled high, though with what it was impossible to tell because rough cloth was strapped over the loads. 'Plunder,' Sam said, sounding disapproving.

'I wonder how many monasteries, castles, and churches went to filling that big wain,' Thomas said as he watched the first wagon roll into the ford. It was hauled by four big horses and, to his relief, the cumbersome wagon crossed the river smoothly, the water scarce reaching the two axles.

'It's not just plunder from rich folk,' Sam said, 'they take anything! Spits, harrows, weed-hooks, cauldrons. I wouldn't mind if they just took from rich folk, but if it's metal it'll be taken.'

A horseman wearing the Earl of Warwick's golden lion badge spurred along the line of carts and wagons. 'Faster!' he shouted.

'Mother of God,' Sam said in disgust, 'the poor bastards can't go any quicker!' The drivers had to turn their vehicles onto the ford and it was an awkward place for the largest wagons. 'Slow and steady will do it.'

Scores of women and children walked beside the wagons. They were the camp followers every army attracted. One vast wain was driven by a woman. She was vast herself with a head of unruly brown curls on which a cap perched like a diminutive bird on a big nest. Two small boys were beside her, one holding a wooden sword and the other clinging to his mother's ample skirts. Her wagon was heaped with plunder and decorated with ribbons of every colour. She grinned at Thomas and Sam. 'He thinks the bloody Frenchies are coming for us!' she said, jerking her head towards the horseman. She flicked her whip at one of the lead horses and the wagon went into the ford. 'Hup, hup!' she called. 'Don't you boys get left behind!' she called merrily to Thomas's archers, then shook the reins so that her four horses put their weight into their collars and hauled the wagon up to the far bank.

Some of the women and children rode in empty wagons that had carried food and fodder, all of it eaten, while other carts just carried empty barrels in which the precious arrows had been held by leather discs so that their feathers were not crushed. There were plenty of those wagons, their barrels reminding Thomas of his escape from Montpellier. 'Keep going!' the horseman shouted. He looked nervously over his shoulder, staring north up the rising valley that led between the English-held hill and le Champ d'Alexandre.

Thomas looked that way and saw banners moving on the English hill. They were coming towards him, mere flickers of colour at the crest. It was the Earl of Warwick's men, marching to guard the river. So the retreat was happening. There had been no trumpet blasts, no seven long notes to herald a truce. Instead there would be a river to cross and, Thomas assumed, a long day keeping the French from interfering with the crossing.

'Don't goddamned dally, for Christ's sake!' the horseman shouted. He was annoyed because a heavily laden cart had paused at the place where the track turned, and so he spurred his horse alongside the two draught horses and slapped one of their rumps with the flat of his sword. The horse panicked, half reared, but was restrained by the harness. It twisted to the right and the other horse followed and both beasts bolted and the driver hauled on the reins, but the wagon bounced on the track, the horses tried to turn away from the river and the wagon slowly tipped over the causeway's edge. The horses screamed. There was a crash as the whole wagon fell sideways to block the ford. Plundered cauldrons clattered into the marsh. 'Jesus!' the panicking horseman who had caused the trouble shouted. Only two dozen wagons had crossed the Miosson, and at least three times that number was now baulked on the wrong bank.

'Jesus!' Sam echoed. Not because the wagon had

451

overturned, but because there were more banners in sight. Only these flags were not on the hill. They were in the wooded valley between the hills, a valley still shrouded in shadow because the sun had not yet reached it, and beneath the trees were flags and beneath the flags were horsemen. A mass of horsemen.

Coming to the river.

Marshal d'Audrehem and the Lord of Douglas led the heavily armoured horsemen whose task was to shatter the archers on the left wing of the English army. They had three hundred and twenty men, all of them experienced and renowned, all of them able to afford horse armour that could resist an English arrow. The destriers wore chamfrons, metal plates over their faces with holes for their eyes, while their chests were protected by leather, mail and even plate. The armour made the big horses slow, but almost invulnerable.

D'Audrehem and Douglas expected to attack across the valley and up the long slope towards the forest of Nouaillé, then skirt about the end of the hedge that protected and hid the enemy troops. They would walk their heavy horses across the valley, and walk up the slope, trusting to the armour to protect the great beasts. Once they had rounded the hedge they would spur the destriers into a lumbering gallop and so drive into the mass of English archers they expected to find. Maybe a thousand bowmen? And the big horses would carry them deep into that panicked mass where they would lay about with swords and axes. Destroy the archers, force them to run from the field, and then the horsemen would turn back to the French lines, dismount and take off their spurs, and then join the great attack that would fight on foot to hammer at the centre of the English army.

That was the plan of battle: to use the heavily armoured horse to destroy the English archers, then slaughter the men-at-arms, but as d'Audrehem and Douglas had led their men over the brow of the western hill they saw the tips of English banners beyond the hedge, and those banners were moving southwards.

'What are the bastards doing?' D'Audrehem asked the question of no one.

'Escaping,' Douglas answered anyway.

The eastern horizon was brightly lit by the rising sun and the forest was dark against that brightness, but the banners could be seen against the trees. There were a dozen flags, all of them moving southwards, and d'Audrehem looked that way and saw the glint of water in the depth of the valley. 'Bastards are crossing the river!' he said.

'They're running away,' Douglas said.

Marshal d'Audrehem hesitated. He was fifty years old and had spent almost all his adult years as a soldier. He had fought in Scotland, where he had learned to kill Englishmen, and then in Brittany, Normandy, and at Calais. He knew war.

He was not hesitating because he feared what was happening, but because he knew the plan of battle must change. If they charged the far hill, aiming for where they believed the English left wing lay, they would find men-at-arms, not archers, and his mounted knights had been ordered to destroy the hated enemy bowmen. So where were the archers?

'There's a ford down there,' a man said, pointing to the glint of water.

'You know that?'

'I grew up not three miles from here, sire.'

'We'll go to the ford,' d'Audrehem decided. He turned his horse, which was caparisoned in a great cloth that bore the broad blue and white diagonal stripes of his livery. He carried a shield with the same bright colours, and his visored helmet had one white plume and one blue. 'This way!' he called and led the horsemen southwards.

And this was easier than crossing the valley. Now, instead of pushing the heavy horses up the long slope of the English-held hill, they were riding downhill. They trotted. The horse armour clinked and jangled; the hooves thumped the dry turf. Some men carried lances, but most had swords. They were riding on open grassland, but ahead of them, where the valley dropped and widened into the larger valley of the Miosson, were trees, and beyond those trees d'Audrehem expected to find archers protecting the ford.

The Lord of Douglas was on the right where a dozen of his own Scotsmen joined him. 'Drop your visors when you see an arrow,' he reminded them, 'and enjoy the killing!' He would enjoy it. The sport of the Douglas clan was killing Englishmen, and Douglas felt a fierce joy at the prospect of battle. He had dreaded that the interfering churchmen would arrange an escape for this English army, but instead the negotiations had failed and he was released to cry havoc. 'And remember! If you see my cursed nephew then he's to live!' He doubted that he would find Robbie in the chaos of battle, but he still wanted the boy taken alive. Taken alive and then made to suffer. 'I want the little bastard alive and weeping! Remember that!'

'I'll make him weep,' Sculley answered, 'weep like a baby!'

Then the heavy horses were in the trees and the riders slowed as they ducked beneath heavy branches. Still no arrows. Still no enemy. Pray Christ d'Audrehem is right, Douglas thought. Were they riding into empty space? Were the English really retreating? Or were the horsemen pursuing a will-o'-the-wisp? The sound of his destrier's hooves had changed and he realised that they were riding into a marsh. There were willows and alders instead of oak, tussocks of earth and stretches of green liquid soil instead of leaf mould. The horses were sinking their heavy feet into the bog, but they were still moving, and then he saw the river ahead, a sliver of brightness in the green gloom, and he saw men there too, men and wagons, and there were archers!

Marshal d'Audrehem saw them too, and he saw that a wagon had overturned and that the English were in chaos, and an arrow flickered in the sky. He did not see where it went, but it told him he had made the right decision and he had found the archers. He slammed down his visor to turn his world dark, rowelled back his spurs, and charged.

The Earl of Warwick's archers were still streaming down from the hill. Thomas's men faced the horsemen and, because the archers were trained and experienced, they chose flesh arrows. These were the arrows made to kill horses because horses were vulnerable and every archer knew that to defeat a charge of mounted knights a man must aim at the horses. That was how Crécy had been won, and so they instinctively picked flesh arrows that had triangular heads, barbed heads, and the two edges of each head were razor sharp, edges to tear through flesh and cut blood vessels and rip apart muscles. They drew the bows back to their ears, picked their targets, and loosed.

The war bow was taller than a man. It was cut from the trunk of a yew grown in the sunny lands close to the Mediterranean, and it was cut where the golden sapwood met the dark-coloured heartwood, and the dark heart of the yew was stiff, it resisted bending, while the outer sapwood was springy so that it would snap back to its shape if it was bent, and the push of the compressed heartwood and the pull of the golden sapwood worked together to give the great war bow a terrible strength. Yet to release that strength the bow must be drawn to the ear, not the eye, so an archer must learn to aim by instinct, just as he had to train his muscles to pull the cord until it seemed that the stress in the yew must surely snap and break. It took ten years to make an archer, but give a trained man a war bow made of yew and he could kill at more than two hundred paces and be feared through all Christendom.

The bows sounded. The strings slapped on the bracers that protected the archers' wrists; the arrows leaped away. The archers aimed at the horses' chests, aiming to drive the flesh arrows deep into labouring lungs. Thomas knew what must happen. The horses would stumble and fall. Blood would froth at their nostrils and mouths. Men would scream as dying horses rolled on them. Other men would be tripped by the fallen beasts, and still the arrows would come, relentless, savage, searing white-tipped death driven by wood and hemp, except it did not happen.

The arrows struck. The horses kept coming.

Men were shouting. Wagon drivers were leaping from their seats and fleeing across the river. The horseman who had tried to hurry the retreat was gaping at the approaching French in disbelief. The first of the Earl of Warwick's archers were reaching the river and their ventenars were bellowing at them to start shooting.

And the French were still coming. They were coming slowly, relentlessly, apparently unaffected by the arrows. The closest horsemen were a hundred and fifty paces away now.

Thomas loosed a second shaft, watched the arrow fly, saw it arc low in the air to plunge dead centre into a bright trapper decorated with diagonal blue and white stripes and the horse did not miss a step, and Thomas saw other arrows were caught in the striped trapper. His arrow had gone just where he wanted, right into the horse's chest, and it had done nothing. 'They've got armour under the trappers!' he shouted at his men. 'Bodkins! Bodkins!' He plucked a bodkin from the ground where he had thrust a handful of arrows into the soft turf. He drew, looked for a target, saw the red heart of Douglas on a shield, loosed.

The horse kept coming.

Yet the horses were coming slowly. This was not a gallop, not even a canter. The big destriers were hung with mail and plate, restricted by thick skirts of boiled leather, carrying men in full armour, and ploughing through the marsh that bordered the river. That marsh slowed them, their weight slowed them, and Thomas saw an arrow slide by a horse's head, streak past the rider's knee and strike the destrier's rump and the horse sheered away from the pain. The armour was all in front!

'Hellequin! Follow me!' he shouted. 'Hellequin! Follow me!'

He snatched up his arrows and ran to his left.

He floundered in the mud and muck of the swamp-land, but he forced himself on. Get to the side, he told himself, get to the side. 'Follow me!' he repeated and snatched a look back to see his men obeying. 'Run!' he shouted, and hoped to God that no one thought they were running away.

He went forty, perhaps fifty paces, and thrust the arrows back into the marsh, plucked up a flesh arrow, laid it on the stave, pulled the bow up and drew the cord, aiming again at the horse with the red heart on its gaudy trapper. Now he was aiming at the horse's flank, just behind the front leg and in front of the saddle. He did not think. He looked where he wanted the arrow to go and his muscles obeyed his look and his two fingers released the string and the arrow slashed across the bog and vanished into the horse and the horse reared, and now more arrows were flying across the marsh and the arrows were biting at last and the horses were falling. The Earl of Warwick's archers had understood. The enemy's horses had all their armour in front and none on the flanks and backsides of the horses. A rider wearing a jupon quartered in red and yellow with a white star in one corner was shouting at the earl's archers to join Thomas's men. 'Go to the flank! Go, fellows, go, go, go!'

But the French were close. Their visors were down so their faces could not be seen, but Thomas could see where the trappers had been ripped and bloodied by their spurs. They were urging their horses on, and he loosed again and this time slapped a bodkin through the overlapping scales of a horse's neck armour. The beast stumbled to its fore knees, and its rider, trapped by the high pommel and cantle of his saddle, desperately tried to kick his feet from the stirrups before the horse rolled. The beast was still on its back legs, tilted forward, and the rider was falling onto its neck when two arrows struck his breastplate. One crumpled, the other pierced it and the man jerked back under the impact of the blows. He started falling forward again and was hit again. Archers jeered. Back and forward he went, tormented until a man-at-arms wearing the lion of Warwick stepped forward and swung an axe that cracked through the helmet to spray blood. A horseman tried to cut the Englishman down, but the arrows were flying thick from the flank now, striking the horses' unarmoured sides, and the rider's horse was hit in the belly by three arrows and the horse screamed, reared and bolted.

'Sweet Christ, kill them! Saint George!' The horseman with the white star on his jupon was just behind Thomas. 'Kill them!'

And the archers obeyed. They had been scared by the failure of their first arrows, but now they were vengeful. They could each loose fifteen arrows in a minute, and by now there were over two hundred archers on the French flank and those French were defeated. The leading riders were all down, their horses dying or dead, and some horses had turned and fled, screaming as they tried to escape the awful pain beside the river. The Earl of Warwick's men-at-arms were advancing into the chaos to hammer axes and maces on fallen riders. The horsemen at the rear were turning away. Two of Warwick's men-at-arms were leading a prisoner back to the ford, and Thomas saw that the man was wearing a jupon of bright blue and white stripes. Then he looked for the red heart of Douglas and saw the horse had fallen, trapping the man, and he sent a bodkin at the rider and saw it pierce the man's rerebrace. He shot again, driving an arrow into the man's side, just under the armpit, but before he could loose a third arrow three men, all dismounted, seized the fallen rider and dragged him out from under his horse. Arrows slapped at them, but two of them lived, and Thomas recognised Sculley. He was wearing a visored helmet, but his long hair with its yellowing bones hung beneath its rim. Thomas drew his bow, but two wounded horses galloped between him and Sculley, who had managed to heave the fallen rider onto an unwounded and riderless horse. Sculley slapped the horse's rump. The wounded horses galloped clear and Thomas shot, but his arrow bounced off Sculley's backplate. The horse with the rescued man struggled out of the marsh to the shelter of the trees, followed by Sculley and four other men wearing the red heart.

And then there was a sudden quiet, except for

the eternal sound of the river and the birdsong and the screams of horses and the beat of hooves striking the ground in the animals' death throes.

The archers unstrung their bows so that the yew staves straightened. Prisoners, some wounded, some staggering, were being led to the ford while Englishmen were stripping dead horses of precious armour and harness and saddlery. Some put horses out of their misery by unbuckling the chamfrons and then striking them hard between the eyes with a war axe. Other men unbuckled plate armour from dead knights and hauled mail coats off corpses. An archer strapped a French knight's sword around his waist. 'Sam,' Thomas shouted, 'fetch the arrows back!' Sam grinned and led a dozen men into the remnants of the carnage to collect arrows. It was also a chance for plunder. A wounded Frenchman tried to stand. He raised a hand to an English man-at-arms who knelt beside him. The two men spoke and then the Englishman lifted the Frenchman's visor and stabbed him through the eye with a dagger. 'Too poor to have a ransom, I suppose,' the rider behind Thomas said. He watched as the man-at-arms sheathed his dagger and began to strip the corpse. 'God, we're cruel, but we've captured Marshal d'Audrehem, and isn't that a good beginning to a bad day?'

Thomas turned. The man's visor was lifted to reveal a grey moustache and thoughtful blue eyes, and Thomas instinctively went to a knee. 'My lord.'

'Thomas of Hookton, isn't it?'

'Yes, sire.'

'I wondered who in Christ's name was wearing Northampton's colours,' the man said, speaking in French. Thomas had ordered his men to wear jupons with Northampton's badge, a badge that most men in the English army would recognise. A few had the red cross of Saint George strapped around an upper arm, but there were not enough armlets for all his men. The horseman who spoke to Thomas wore the white star on his red and yellow jupon, while the gold chain about his neck proclaimed his rank. He was the Earl of Oxford, brother-in-law to Thomas's lord. The earl had been at Crécy and afterwards Thomas had met him in England, and he was astonished that the earl remembered him, let alone remembered that he spoke French. He was even more astonished when the earl used his brother-in-law's nickname. 'It's a pity Billy isn't here,' the earl said grimly, 'we need all the good men we can get. And I think you should get your men back up the hill now.'

'Up the hill, sire?'

'Listen!'

Thomas listened.

And heard the war drums.

The French horsemen had attacked at the ford and at the right-hand end of the English line, but as those charges went home other horsemen rode in front of the dauphin's battle to challenge the English on their hill.

Six men chose to ride. Each was a tournament champion of fearsome reputation. They rode superbly trained destriers, and their winnings in the lists had bought them the finest armour that could be made in Milan. They rode close to the English hedge and called out their challenge, and the English archers ignored them. Six men did not make a battle, and there was no honour and not much usefulness in killing a solitary horseman when so many other men-at-arms were approaching on foot.

'Pass the word that they're to be ignored,' the Prince of Wales ordered.

The challengers were part of battle's dance. They went to taunt the English and in the hope of finding an opponent they could unhorse and kill, and so dispirit the English. They shouted their defiance. 'Are you women? Do you know how to fight?'

'Ignore them,' the commanders growled at their men.

But one man disobeyed. He owed no allegiance to any commander on the English side, and he knew the impudent challengers were meant to be ignored. Let them waste their breath, the real battle was not fought between champion and champion, yet still that one man mounted, took a lance from his squire, and rode out from the left of the English line.

He wore no jupon. His armour had been scrubbed so that it shone. His horse took small steps as he restrained it. His helmet was a tournament helmet, crowned with pale blue plumes, and his small black-painted shield bore the symbol of the white rose, the rose without thorns, the flower of the Virgin Mary. Around his neck he wore a blue scarf of finest silk, a woman's scarf, a gift from Bertille. He rode a track that twisted through the vineyard until he reached the open grassland in the valley's shallow base, and there he turned his horse and waited for one of the six to accept his challenge.

One man did. He was from Paris, a brutal man, quick as lightning and strong as a bull, and his armour was unpolished, his jupon a blue so dark it looked almost black. His device, embroidered on the jupon and painted on his shield, was a red crescent moon. He faced Roland de Verrec. 'Traitor!' he shouted.

Roland said nothing.

Both sides were watching. The other champions had withdrawn from the vineyard beneath the hedge and watched from behind their companion.

'Traitor!' the Parisian shouted again.

Still Roland said nothing.

'I won't kill you!' the Parisian called. His name was Jules Langier and his trade was fighting. He hefted his lance, sixteen feet of ash tipped with a steel head. 'I won't kill you! I'll take you in chains to the king and let him kill you instead. Would you rather run away now?'

Roland de Verrec's only answer was to prop his lance against his right knee and close his visor. He lifted the lance again.

'Jules!' one of the other champions called. 'Watch his lance. He likes to lift it at the last minute. Protect your head.'

Langier nodded. 'Hey, virgin,' he called, 'you can run away now! I won't chase you!'

Roland couched the lance. His horse took tiny skittering steps. A faint rough cart track crossed diagonally in front of him and he had noted it; he had seen where the wheels had made ruts in the soil. Not deep ruts, but enough to make a horse falter slightly. He would ride to the left of the ruts.

He felt little emotion. Or rather he felt as though he watched himself, as if he was disembodied. The next moments were all about skill, about cold-blooded skill. He had never faced Langier in the lists, but he had watched him and he knew the Parisian liked to bend low in the saddle as he struck home. That made him a small target. Langier would bend low and use his thick shield to throw off his opponent's lance, then turn snake-fast and use his short, heavy mace to attack from behind. It had worked many times. The mace was kept in a deep leather pocket attached to the right side of his saddle behind his knee. It could be snatched up in an eyeblink. Snatched and backswung, and all Roland would know was the sudden flare of white in his skull as the mace smashed into his helmet.

'Coward!' Langier called, trying to provoke Roland.

Roland still said nothing. Instead he held out

his left arm. He dropped his shield. He would fight without it.

The gesture seemed to infuriate Langier who, without another word, dug in his spurs so that his destrier leaped forward. Roland responded. The two horsemen closed. They were not far enough apart for either to reach a gallop, but the horses were straining as they closed. Both horses knew their business, both knew where their riders wanted them to go. Roland steered his mount with his knees, keeping it just to the left of the rut, and he raised his lance point so that it threatened Langier's eyes, and they were close now, their world the beat of hooves, and Langier swerved his horse slightly right and it faltered a tiny bit as a hoof hit uneven ground, and Langier was bending down, shield protecting his body as the lance was pointed plumb at the base of Roland's breastplate, and then the lance flew up and the horse was stumbling and Langier was desperately trying to pull it right with knee pressure, but the horse was down on its knees, sliding in grass that was slicked with frothy blood and Langier saw that his opponent's lance, instead of being aimed at his head, had pierced his horse's chest.

'This isn't a tournament.' Roland spoke for the first time. He had turned his horse, abandoned his lance and drawn the sword he called Durandal, and he rode back to where Langier was struggling to extricate himself from his fallen, dying horse.

Langier tried to find his mace, but the horse had fallen on the weapon, and then Durandal smacked across his helm. His head was jerked violently to one side, then to the other as the sword came back to smash the helmet again.

'Take your helmet off,' Roland said.

'Go and piss in your mother's arsehole, virgin.'

The sword swiped him again, half dazing Langier, then the point of the sword was thrust between the visor's upper edge and the helmet's rim. The blade bit into the bridge of Langier's nose, and stopped. 'If you want to live,' Roland said calmly, 'take the helmet off.' He pulled the sword free.

Langier fumbled at the buckles that held the helmet in place. The other champions watched, but made no effort to help. They were there to fight man against man, not two men against one because that would be unchivalrous, and so they just watched as Langier at last lifted the helmet clear of his lank black hair. A trickle of blood ran down his face from where Durandal had cut him.

'Go back to your army,' Roland said, 'and tell Labrouillade that the virgin is going to kill him.'

It was Langier's turn to say nothing.

Roland turned his horse away, sheathed Durandal, and kicked back his heels. He had delivered his message. He heard cheers from the Englishmen who had seen the fight through the hedge's gap, but it meant nothing to him.

It was all for Bertille.

★　　★　　★

468

The Lord of Douglas would kill no Englishmen this day. His leg had been broken when his horse fell, his arm was pierced to the bone by an arrow, and another had broken a rib and punctured a lung so that he was breathing bubbles of blood. He was in pain, horrible pain, and he was carried to the house where the king had spent the night, and there the barber-surgeons stripped him of his armour, cut the arrow flush with his skin, leaving the head embedded in his chest, and poured honey onto the wound. 'Find a cart and take him to Poitiers,' one of the surgeons ordered a retainer wearing the red heart. 'The monks of Saint Jean will care for him. Take him slowly. Imagine you're carrying milk and don't want it turning to butter. Go. If you want him to see Scotland again, go!'

'You can take him to the bloody monks,' Sculley said to his companions, 'I'm going to fight. I'm going to kill.'

More men were being carried to the house. They had charged with Marshal Clermont, attacking the archers at the right of the English line, but there the enemy had dug trenches and the horses floundered, others had broken their legs in pits, and all the while the arrows had struck, and the charge had failed as miserably as the attack in the marsh.

But now that the champions had flaunted their defiance and Langier had been unhorsed in full view of the French army, the main assault was closing on the English hill. The dauphin led the first French battle, though he was well protected

469

by chosen knights from his father's Order of the Star. The dauphin's battle was over three thousand strong and they came on foot, kicking down the chestnut stakes of the vineyard and trampling the vines as they climbed the gentle slope towards the English hill. Banners flew above them, while behind them, on the western hill, the oriflamme flew proudly from the ranks the king commanded. That flag, the long, twin-tailed banner of scarlet silk, was France's battle-flag and so long as it flew it meant that no prisoners were to be taken. Capturing rich men for ransom was the dream of every knight, but at a battle's beginning, when all that mattered was to break the enemy and shatter him and kill him and terrify him, there was no time for the niceties of surrender. When the flag was furled, that was when the French could look to their purses, but till then there would be no prisoners, only killing. So the oriflamme flew, waved from side to side like a ripple of red in the morning sky, and behind the dauphin's battle his uncle's second battle was advancing towards the valley's shallow bottom where the nakerers beat their vast drums in a marching rhythm to drive the dauphin's men uphill to a famous victory.

To the English and Gascons, at least to those who could see past the hedge, the far hill and the nearer valley were now filled with the panoply of war. With silk and steel, with plumes and blades. A mass of metal-clad men in bright surcoats of red and blue and white and green, marching beneath the proud banners of nobility. Drums hammered the morning air, trumpets seared the sky, and the advancing Frenchmen cheered, not because they had a victory yet, but to raise their spirits and frighten the enemy. 'Montjoie Saint Denis!' they shouted. 'Montjoie Saint Denis and King Jean!'

Crossbowmen were on the French flanks. Each archer had a companion who carried a great pavise, a shield large as a man behind which the crossbow could be rewound safe from the deadly English arrows. Those arrows were not flying yet. The leading men of the French advance could see the great hedge, and the wide gaps, and through those gaps were the English beneath their banners. The French visors were up and would stay up till the arrows came. The men in the foremost ranks were all in plate armour and most of those men did not carry shields; only the men who could not afford the expensive plate carried a willow shield. Some advanced with shortened lances, hoping to thrust an Englishman off balance and let another man kill the fallen enemy with axe or mace or morningstar. Few men carried swords. A sword would neither thrust nor cut through armour. An armoured man must be beaten down by lead-weighted weapons, beaten and crushed and pulped.

The dauphin did not shout. He insisted on being in the very front rank, though he was not a strong man like his father. Prince Charles was thin, weak-limbed, long-nosed, with skin so pale it looked like bleached parchment, and with legs so short and arms so long that some courtiers called him *le singe* behind his back, but the ape was a clever young ape, a judicious ape, and he knew that he must lead. He must be seen to lead. He wore a suit of armour made for him in Milan and burnished with sand and vinegar until it reflected the sun in dazzling shards of light. His breastplate was covered by a blue jupon on which fleurs-de-lys were embroidered in golden threads, while in his right hand was a sword. His father had insisted he learn to fight with a sword, but he had never mastered the weapon. Squires six years younger could beat him in mock combat, which was why the knights who flanked him were men seasoned in fighting and carrying heavy shields to protect the prince's life.

'We should have let them starve,' the dauphin said as they neared the hedge.

'Sire?' a man shouted, unable to hear the dauphin's voice over the sound of drums, trumpets and cheers.

'They have a strong position!'

'All the more glory when we beat them, sire.'

The dauphin thought that remark stupid, but he held his tongue, and just then a flicker of white caught his eye and the man who had made the stupid remark reached over and slammed down the prince's visor so hard that the dauphin was momentarily deafened and half stunned. 'Arrows, sire!' the man shouted.

The arrows were being shot from the ends of the hedge, slantwise across the advancing battle. More arrows came from small groups of archers who guarded the gaps in the hedge. The dauphin heard the missiles thumping into shields or clanging on armour. He could hardly see now. The visor had bars close together, his world was dark, sliced by bright sunlit slits, and he sensed, rather than saw, that the men about him had speeded up. They were closing ranks in front of him and he was too weak to force his way past them.

'Montjoie Saint Denis!' the men-at-arms shouted, and went on shouting so there was a great roar, an unending roar as the warriors of France hurried into the hedge's gap. The archers there had retreated. It occurred to the prince that the English were silent, and just then they shouted their war cry. 'Saint George!'

And there was the first harsh sound of steel on steel.

And screams.

And so the carnage began.

'Fetch your horses!' the Earl of Oxford called to Thomas. The earl, who was second in command to the Earl of Warwick, wanted most of the men who had protected the ford to return to the high ground. 'I'll leave Warwick's archers here,' he said to Thomas, 'but you take your men up the hill!'

It was a long way up the hill and it would be much quicker to ride. 'Horses!' Thomas shouted

473

across the river. Servants and grooms brought them over the ford, past the upturned wagon. Keane, riding a mare bareback, led them.

'Have the bastards gone?' the Irishman asked, looking past the dead and dying horses to where the French knights had vanished in the trees.

'Find out for me,' Thomas said. He did not want to abandon the ford only to discover that the French had renewed their attack on the baggage train.

Keane looked surprised, but whistled his two dogs and led them northwards towards the trees. The Earl of Oxford was sending Warwick's men-at-arms back up the steep hill and shouting at them to carry full waterskins. 'They're thirsty up there! Take water if you can! But hurry!'

Thomas, mounted on the horse he had captured outside Montpellier, found a wagon waiting to cross the river once the overturned cart was cleared away. The wagon bed was filled with barrels. 'What was in those?' he asked the driver.

'Wine, your honour.'

'Fill them with water, then get the damned wagon up the hill.'

The driver looked aghast. 'These horses will never make the hill, not with a load of full barrels!'

'Then get extra horses. More men. Do it! Or I'll come back and find you. And when you've done it once, come back for more.'

The man grumbled under his breath, Thomas ignored it and went back to the ford where his men were now mounted. 'Up the hill,' Thomas said, then saw Genevieve, Bertille, and Hugh were among the horsemen. 'You three! Stay here! Stay with the baggage!' He kicked back his heels and put the horse to the slope, going past Warwick's men who were climbing in their armour. 'Stirrup them!' Thomas called. He beckoned a man-at-arms who gratefully took hold of one stirrup leather and let the horse pull him up the hill.

Keane came back fast, looked for Thomas and saw him among the men streaming upwards. He kicked back his heels so the mare caught up. 'They've gone,' the Irishman said. 'But there are thousands up there!'

'Where?'

'Top of the valley. Thousands! Jesus!'

'Get to the top of the hill,' Thomas said, 'and find a priest.'

'A priest?'

The promised priest had never arrived at the ford. 'The men need shriving,' Thomas said. 'Find a priest and tell him we never heard mass.' There would be no time for a mass now, but at least the dying could receive the last rites.

Keane whistled to the hounds and kicked back his heels.

And Thomas heard the crash from the hilltop as men drove into men. Steel on steel, steel on iron, steel on flesh. He climbed.

The dauphin's battle aimed itself at the centre of the English line. The widest gap in the hedge was there and, as the French came closer, they saw the largest banners flying above the waiting men-at-arms beyond the gap, and those banners included the impudent flag that quartered the French royal arms with England's lions. That banner proclaimed that the Prince of Wales was there and, through the slits in their visors, the French could see the prince mounted on a horse, sitting close behind the line, and the battle anger was on them now. Not just anger, but terror, and for some men joy. Those men worked their way to the front rank. They were hungry for fighting, they were confident, and they were savagely good at their trade. Many other men were drunk, but the wine had given them bravado, and the arrows were slicing in from left and right, striking shields, crumpling on armour, sometimes finding a weak spot, but the attack flowed around the fallen men and, so very close now, the French broke into a run, screaming, and fell on the English.

That first rush was the most important. That was when the shortened lances could knock the enemy over, when the axes and hammers and maces would be given extra impetus by the charge, and so the dauphin's men screamed at the tops of their voices as they charged, as they swung, thrust, and chopped their weapons.

And the English line went back.

They were forced back by the fierceness of the charge and by the weight of men who crammed through the gap, but though they went back, they did not break. Blades crashed on shields. Axes and maces slashed down. Lead-weighted steel crumpled helmets, shattered skulls, forced blood and brains to spurt through split metal, and men fell and in falling made obstacles, and other men tripped on them. The impact of the charge was slowed, men tried to stand and were stunned by blows, but the French had forced their way through the gap and now were widening the fight, attacking left and right as more men came through the hedge.

The English and Gascons were still being driven back, but slowly now. The initial impact had left men dead, wounded, bleeding, and moaning, but the line was not broken. The commanders, their horses close behind the dismounted men-at-arms, were shouting at them to stay closed up. To keep the line. And the French were trying to break the line, to cut and hammer their way through the shields so they could shatter the English into small groups that could be surrounded and slaughtered. Men hacked with axes, screamed obscenities, thrust with lances, swung maces, and the shields splintered, but the line held. It went backwards under the pressure, and more Frenchmen came through the gap, but the Englishmen and Gascons were fighting with the desperation of trapped men and the confidence of troops who had spent months together, men who knew and trusted each other, and who understood what waited for them if the line broke.

'Welcome to the devil's slaughteryard, sire,' Sir Reginald Cobham said to the Prince of Wales. The two men were on horseback, watching from just behind the line, and Sir Reginald saw how the fight was slackening. He had expected the French to come on horseback and had been apprehensive when he understood they intended to fight on foot. 'They've learned their lesson,' he had remarked drily to the prince. He had watched as the lines crashed together and seen how the savage French charge had failed to rip the English and Gascons apart, but now it was hard to tell one side from the other, they were so close. The rear ranks of both sides thrust forward, crushing the front-rank men against their opponents and giving them small room to swing a weapon. The enemy was still forcing their way through the gaps in the hedge, widening their attack, but they were not breaking through the stubborn line. They were either crushed against their enemy, or else a group of men would assault, batter and cut, then step back to catch their breath and appraise their enemy. They were calling insults rather than fighting with fury, and Sir Reginald understood that. Attackers and defenders were each recovering from the initial shock, but more Frenchmen were still coming through the hedge's gap and the fight would get grimmer now, because the attacks would be more deliberate and the English, thirsty and hungry, would tire faster.

'We do well, Sir Reginald!' the prince said cheerfully.

'We must go on doing well, sire.'

'Is that the boy prince?' The Prince of Wales had seen the golden coronet surmounting a polished helmet in the French ranks and knew, from the largest banner, that the dauphin must be part of this attack.

'A prince, certainly,' Sir Reginald said, 'or maybe a substitute?'

'Real prince or not,' the real English prince said, 'it would be courteous to pay him my compliments.' He grinned, swung his leg over his saddle's high cantle, and dropped to the turf where he reached out to his squire. 'Shield,' he said, stretching out his left hand, 'and an axe, I think.'

'Sire!' Sir Reginald called, then fell silent. The prince was doing his duty and the devil was rolling the dice, and advising the prince to be cautious would achieve nothing.

'Sir Reginald?' the prince asked.

'Nothing, sire, nothing.'

The prince half smiled. 'What will be, Sir Reginald, will be.' He snapped down his visor and pushed through the English ranks to face the French. His chosen knights, there to protect the heir to England's throne, followed.

The enemy saw his bright jupon, recognised the insolent French arms quartered on his broad chest, and gave a roar of challenge and anger.

Then charged again.

CHAPTER 15

Thomas reached the hilltop just as the battle was widening. The French had forced their way through the gaps in the hedge and were spreading along its length, while others were hacking through the thick brambles to make new gaps. Somewhere to Thomas's right a man shouted, 'Archers! Archers! Here!'

Thomas slid from his saddle. His men were arriving in small groups and adding themselves to the left of the English line, which was not yet engaged, but he ran behind the line to where the call had sounded. Then he saw what had provoked the shout. Two crossbowmen had found a way to the hedge's centre with their pavisiers, and they were shooting into the Earl of Warwick's men. He paused to string his bow, placing one end on a protruding tree root and bending the other with his left hand so he could slip the loop of the cord onto the nocked horn at the bow's upper end. Most men could not even bend a bow sufficiently to string it, but he did it without thinking, then took a flesh arrow from his bag, shouldered his way through the rearmost ranks and drew the cord.

Both crossbowmen were about thirty paces away and both were being sheltered by their vast shields, which meant they were cranking the handles that rewound their cords. 'With you,' a voice said, and he saw Roger of Norfolk, known to everyone as Poxface, had joined him with his bow drawn. 'Yours is the one on the left,' Thomas said.

The shield of the man on the right suddenly swung to one side and the crossbowman was there, kneeling, his weapon aimed at the English men-at-arms. Thomas loosed, and the arrow took the French archer in the face. The man fell backwards, his finger reflexively tightening on the trigger so that his crossbow shot, and the bolt seared into the sky, then the man beside him spun away with Poxface's arrow in his chest. Thomas had already drawn again and sunk an arrow into the back of the fleeing pavisier. 'I love archers,' one of the men-at-arms said.

'You can marry me,' Poxface said, and there was a burst of laughter, then a shout because a mass of Frenchmen was coming along the hedge's inner face.

'Hold them back, fellows, hold them back!' a voice roared. The Earl of Oxford was behind the line now. His horse had a streak of blood on its rump where the stump of a crossbow bolt showed. Thomas pushed his way free of the tight ranks and ran back to the left where his men-at-arms were extending the line.

'Close up to the hedge!' Thomas called.

Keane was collecting abandoned horses, picketing them to a low oak branch. The archers were stringing their bows, though they had no targets because the men-at-arms concealed the enemy. 'Sam! Watch the end of the hedge!' Thomas called. 'Let me know if the bastards try to come around.' He doubted they would, the slope steepened there, which would make it a difficult place for the French to attack, but the archers could hold that flank against anything but the most determined assault.

The danger was inside the hedge where the French, sensing they were reaching the end of their enemy's line, were making rushes. A group of men would assault together, screaming their war shout. The drums were still beating. Trumpets were braying beyond the hedge, encouraging the French to break this enemy. Break them and split them and drive them back into the forest where they could be hunted down and slaughtered. That would be vengeance for all the damage the English had caused across France, for the burned cottages and slaughtered livestock, for the captured castles and weeping widows, for the countless rapes and stolen treasures. And so they came with renewed anger.

Thomas's men-at-arms were fighting now. If they broke there was nothing beyond them, but Karyl was standing like a rock, daring the French to come within range of his mace. They dared. There was a shout, a rush, and men were beating at each other with axes, maces and war hammers. A Frenchman latched his poleaxe over Ralph of Chester's espalier and pulled him hard, and the Englishman stumbled forward, dragged by the hook in his shoulder armour, and a mace slammed into the side of his helmet; he fell, and another Frenchman swung an axe to split his backplate. Thomas saw Ralph jerking; he could not hear his screams over the battle noise, but the mace slammed down again and Ralph went still. Karyl landed a glancing blow on the killer's arm, just enough to drive him back, but the French came again, sensing victory, and the clash of steel on wood and steel on iron was deafening.

Thomas laid his bow and his arrow bag at the tree line and forced his way into the line. There was an axe on the ground and he picked it up. 'Get back,' someone told him. Thomas wore nothing but mail and leather, and this was a place where men were sheathed in steel, but Thomas pushed into the second rank and used his archer's strength to swing the axe overhead, bringing its weighted blade down hard onto a French helmet and the weapon went through plume, steel and skull. The axe had been swung with such force that its blade had bitten deep into the enemy's chest cavity where it was trapped by a mangle of ribs, flesh, and steel. A mist of blood flared in the morning sun as Thomas tried to pull the weapon free, and a stout, broad-chested man wearing a snouted helmet saw his chance and rammed a shortened lance at Thomas's belly. Arnaldus, the Gascon, hit the man with an axe, knocking his head sideways, and Thomas abandoned his axe and seized the lance, pulling it to drag the man into his ranks where he could be killed, and the man pulled back. Karyl swung the mace and the snout-visor was knocked free, dangling from one hinge, and the Frenchman still would not abandon the lance. He was snarling, screaming insults, and Karyl slammed his mace into the moustached face, crushing the nose and breaking teeth, and now the man, his face a mask of blood, tried to ram the lance forward again, but Karyl punched the mace a second time and Arnaldus brought his axe down onto the man's shoulder, splitting his espalier, and the enemy went down onto his knees, spitting blood and teeth, and Arnaldus finished him with a mighty swing of the axe and kicked the kneeling body back towards the French.

The battle was now shrunken to the distance a man's weapon could reach. Enemy could smell enemy, smell the shit as bowels emptied in terror, smell the wine and ale on their breath, smell the blood that slicked the grass. There would be a brutal bout of fighting, then a pause as men pulled back and caught their breath. Thomas had picked up the shortened lance. He had no idea where his own weapons were, presumably on a packhorse that might have been brought up the hill. The lance must do for now. The French, of whom he could see perhaps a hundred close by, were watching through closed visors. Most wore a livery of pale blue with two red stars. He wondered which lord they served and whether the lord was among them. They watched, they judged, they were readying for another charge. Thomas's archers were holding poleaxes or maces. The Welsh archers were singing a battle song in their own language. Thomas assumed it celebrated a victory over the English, but if it helped them break the French then they could sing of English defeats till hell froze over.

'The line's holding!' the Earl of Oxford called from horseback. 'Don't let them break us!'

A big man carrying a morningstar pushed his way to the front of the enemy line. He wore plate armour, and had no jupon, while his helmet was a visored bascinet spattered with blood. He wore a heavy sword in a belted scabbard. Most men abandoned their scabbards in battle, fearing it might trip them, but this enemy needed the scabbard to hold his sword while he wielded the monstrous morningstar, which was fouled with blood.

The morningstar had a haft almost as long as a bow stave, while the head was an iron ball the size of a baby's skull. A long steel spike protruded from the tip of the ball, while a dozen shorter spikes surrounded it. The man hefted the weapon. The snout of his visor moved from side to side as he looked along the line of the Hellequin. Two companions, both carrying small battered tournament shields, joined him; one was armed with a poleaxe, the other with a *goupillon*, which had a short wooden handle connected by a thick chain to a spiked metal ball. It was a flail. 'They came here to die,' the tall man with the morningstar said loudly enough for Thomas to hear, 'so let's oblige the bastards.'

'Kill the poleaxe first,' Karyl said softly. The man carrying that weapon also had a shield, which meant he could not use the big hooked axe with full strength.

'You want to die?' the tall man shouted.

From somewhere to the north came the din of sudden frenzy: shouts, metal clashing, screams. The enemy must be making a frantic effort to pierce the line, Thomas thought, and he prayed the English and their Gascon allies held, then he could spare no thought for prayer because the huge man with the spiked morningstar was charging. He was charging straight at Thomas who, alone among the men-at-arms in the English line, wore no plate armour.

'Saint Denis!' the tall man bellowed.

And Saint Denis met Saint George.

Cardinal Bessières watched the battle from the French hill. He was mounted on a stout and patient horse, and wore his cardinal's robes though, incongruously, he had a bascinet perched on his head. He was a few yards from King Jean, who was also mounted, though the cardinal noted that the king had discarded his spurs, which suggested that if he fought he would fight on foot. The king's youngest son, Philippe, and the rest of the knights and men-at-arms were all dismounted. 'What is happening, Your Majesty?' the cardinal enquired.

The king was not entirely certain of the answer and he was irritated that the cardinal, with his ridiculous helmet, was staying so close. He did not like Bessières. The man was the son of a merchant, for God's sake, but he had risen in the church and was now a Papal Legate and, the king knew, had hopes of becoming Pope. And perhaps Bessières would be a good choice because, despite his humble birth, the cardinal was fiercely supportive of the French monarchy and it never hurt to have God's help, and so the king indulged him. 'Our first battle is breaking the enemy,' he explained.

'God be praised,' the cardinal said, then pointed to the Duke of Orléans's banner, which flew above the second battle that waited in the shallow valley between the two hills. The duke had well over two thousand men-at-arms. They were on foot, but their horses were close behind their ranks in case they were needed to pursue a broken enemy. 'Is there some reason,' the cardinal asked, 'why your brother is not advancing to do God's business?'

The king nearly lost his temper. He was nervous. He had hoped that the dauphin's battle would be sufficient to break the English, but it was evident that the fight was harder than anyone had expected. He had been assured that the enemy was weakened by hunger and thirst, but they were still fighting. Desperation, he supposed. 'My brother will advance when he is ordered to advance,' he said curtly.

'It is a question of space,' the Count of Ventadour intervened. He was a young man who was a favourite of the king, and he had sensed his monarch's irritation and moved to spare him from any further tedious explanations.

'Space?' the cardinal asked.

'The enemy, Your Eminence, has a strong position,' the count said, pointing. 'You see the hedge? It restricts us.'

'Ah,' the cardinal said as if he had only just noticed the hedge. 'But why not advance all our strength?'

'Because even a king or a cardinal cannot pour a quart into a pint pot, Your Eminence,' the count said.

'So break the pot,' the cardinal suggested.

'They are attempting to do just that, Your Eminence,' the count said patiently.

It was difficult to determine what happened beyond the hedge. There was plainly fighting, but who was winning? There were still Frenchmen on the hedge's western side, which suggested that they did not have space enough to fight on the farther side, or perhaps they were the fainthearts who did not want to risk their lives. A small trickle of wounded men retreated down the hill, and it seemed obvious to the cardinal that the French should send every man they had to put unbearable pressure on the enemy, but instead the king and his brother were waiting calmly, letting the dauphin's troops do the work. Geoffrey de Charny, the royal standard bearer, was still holding the oriflamme aloft, indicating that no prisoners should be taken, and the cardinal understood enough to know that the great flag would fly until the enemy was broken. Only when that bright red pennant vanished could the French be confident that they had time to secure rich ransoms, and Bessières was frustrated that it still flew. King Jean, he thought, was being tentative. He had sent a third of his army to fight, but why not all? Yet he knew he could utter no criticism. When the next Pope was elected he needed King Jean's influence.

'Your Eminence?' the Count of Ventadour broke into the cardinal's thoughts.

'My son?' the cardinal responded grandly.

'May I?' The count reached up towards the cheap-looking blade that the cardinal held.

'With reverence, my son,' the cardinal said.

The count touched *la Malice*, closed his eyes, and prayed. 'There will be victory,' he said when his prayer was finished.

'It is God's will,' the cardinal said.

Thirty paces away from the cardinal, the Count of Labrouillade stood in the ranks of the king's men. He was sweating. He wore linen underclothes and above those a close-fitting leather jerkin and a pair of trews. A mail coat covered the leather, and strapped over the mail was a full suit of plate armour. He needed to piss. The wine he had been drinking all night was swelling his bladder, but he feared that if he released that pressure then his bowels would release as well. His belly was sour. Christ, he thought, but let the dauphin win this quickly! And why was it taking so long? He shifted his weight from foot to foot. At least the Duke of Orléans would be the next into battle. The Count of Labrouillade had paid gold to Marshal Clermont to have himself and his men-at-arms posted to the king's battle, the last battle, and he fervently prayed that the king's three thousand men would not be needed. And why were they fighting on foot? Everyone knew that a nobleman fought on horse-back! Yet some damned Scotsman had persuaded the king to fight on foot as the English did. If the English and the Scots wanted to fight like peasants that was their business, but a noble of France should be in the saddle! How could a man run away if he was on foot? Labrouillade groaned.

'My lord?' His standard bearer thought the count had spoken.

'Be quiet,' Labrouillade said, then sighed with relief as he pissed. The urine soaked warm down his legs and dripped from under the steel-plated skirt that protected his groin. He clenched his bowels and, blessedly, stayed clean. He looked to his right to see that the oriflamme still flew, and he prayed for the moment when it would be furled and his men could be released to find Roland de Verrec, who had sent his insulting and threatening message with the man whose horse he had killed in full view of the French army. The count had vowed to do to Roland what he had done to the impudent Villon. He would geld him for his treachery. That prospect consoled the count. 'Messengers,' someone said, and he looked towards the distant fighting and saw that two horsemen were riding back across the valley. They brought news, he thought, and prayed that it was good and that he would not have to fight, but merely take prisoners.

Sculley, the frightening Scotsman, walked past Labrouillade, who thought he resembled a creature from nightmare. Blood had soaked his jupon so that the red heart of Douglas looked as though it had burst. There was blood on his gauntlets and on the vambraces that covered his forearms. His visor was up. He gave the count a feral look, then stalked on towards the cardinal.

'I want the magic sword,' Sculley said to the cardinal.

'What is the animal saying?' the cardinal asked Father Marchant, who was mounted on a mare that stood close behind Bessières's horse. Sculley had spoken in English and even if the cardinal had understood that language he would never have penetrated the Scotsman's accent.

'What is it?' Father Marchant asked Sculley.

'Tell your man to give me the magic sword!'

'*La Malice?*'

'Give it to me! The bastards have hurt my lord and I'm going to kill the bastards!' He spat the words out, glaring at the cardinal as though he wanted to begin his revenge by slicing open Bessières's huge stomach. 'That archer,' Sculley went on, 'he's a dead man. I watched the bastard! Shooting at my lord when he was on the ground! Just give me the magic sword!'

'Your Eminence,' Father Marchant spoke in French again, 'the creature wants *la Malice*. He expresses a desire to slaughter the enemy.'

'Thank God someone does,' the cardinal said. He had been wondering which man might best use the relic, but it seemed the man had chosen for him. He glanced at the Scotsman and shuddered at the crudity of his appearance, then he smiled, sketched a blessing, and gave the sword to Sculley.

And somewhere a trumpet called.

The Prince of Wales appeared in the English front line, his bright flag, the largest on the English side, behind and above him, and the French responded with a roar as they renewed their attack, but the English matched the war shout and surged forward themselves. Shield met shield with a crash, the weapons fell and thrust, and it was the English who forged ahead. The men trusted to guard the Prince of Wales were among the most experienced and savage in all the army.

They had fought a score of battles, from Crécy to minor skirmishes, and they fought with cold-blooded ruthlessness. The two Frenchmen closest to the prince were felled instantly. Neither was killed. One was half stunned by a mace blow, and he collapsed to his knees, and the other took an axe blow to his right elbow that shattered the bone and left him weaponless. He was dragged backwards by his companions, and that rearward movement spread to the neighbouring Frenchmen. The half-stunned man tried to stand, but the prince kicked him backwards onto the ground and trod on his armoured wrist. 'Finish him,' he said to the man behind him, who used a steel-shod foot to push up the fallen man's visor and rammed down with a sword point. Blood sprayed on the prince.

'Give me room!' the prince bellowed. He stepped forward and swung the axe, feeling the impact jar up his arms as the blade chopped into a man's waist. He wrenched the axe free and thrust it forward. The haft was topped with a steel spike that dented the wounded man's breastplate, but did not pierce it. That man staggered, and the prince took another step forward and sliced the heavy weapon at the enemy's neck where the sharp blade went through the mail aventail that he wore beneath his helmet to cover his neck and shoulders. The man staggered and the prince kicked him backwards and swung at another enemy. He was fighting without a visor and he could plainly see Charles, the dauphin, not ten paces away. 'Come and fight me!' he bellowed in French. 'You and me! Charles! Come and fight!'

The dauphin, so thin and awkward, did not bother to answer. He saw the Prince of Wales beat a man down with his axe, and saw a Frenchman plunge a shortened lance that ripped open the prince's jupon. Beneath the jupon the prince's cuirass was sculpted with his coat of arms. The lance thrust again and the prince slashed the axe down onto his assailant's shoulder. The dauphin saw the big blade bite through the armour and saw the blood spray sudden and bright. 'Back, Your Highness,' one of the dauphin's guards said. That guardian could see that the enemy prince was determined to fight his way through to the heir to the French throne. That could not happen. And the English were fighting like demons, so it might happen if he did not act. 'Back, Your Highness,' he said again, and this time pulled the dauphin away.

The dauphin was speechless. He had surprised himself by how little fear he had felt once the battle began. True, he was well guarded and the men charged with his safety were all brutally efficient fighters, but the dauphin had tried to do his best. He had thrust a sword hard at an enemy knight and thought he had hurt the man. Most of all he had been fascinated. He had observed the battle with an intelligent eye and, though he was appalled at the butchery, he found it intriguing.

It was a stupid way to decide great matters, he thought, for the decision was surely a lottery once the brawling began. There had to be a cleverer way to defeat the enemy?

'Back, sire!' a man bellowed at him, and the dauphin allowed himself to be drawn back through the gap in the hedge. How long had they been fighting? he wondered. It seemed like minutes, but now he saw that the sun was high above the trees and so it must have been at least an hour! 'Time flies,' he said.

'Did you speak, sire?' a man shouted.

'I said time flies!'

'Christ Jesus,' the man said. He watched the Prince of Wales, who was standing cocksure above the men he had beaten down with his bloodied axe.

The prince shook the axe at the retreating enemy. 'Come back!' he bellowed.

'He's a fool,' the dauphin said in puzzlement.

'Sire?'

'I said he's a fool!'

'A fighting fool,' the man said in grudging admiration.

'He's enjoying this,' the dauphin said.

'Why wouldn't he, sire?'

'Only a fool could enjoy it. To a fool this is paradise, and he's wallowing in idiocy.'

The man in charge of the dauphin's guards thought the eighteen-year-old prince was mad and he felt a surge of anger that he was trusted with the life of this pale-faced, hollow-chested weakling with his short legs and long arms, and now, it seemed, with a brain made of soft cheese. A prince should look like a prince, like the Prince of Wales. The Frenchman hated to admit it, but the enemy prince looked like a proper ruler in his broad-chested blood-spattered glory. He looked like a real warrior, not like this pale shred of an excuse for a man. But the pale shred was the dauphin, and so the man kept his voice respectful. 'We must send messengers to your father,' he said, 'to the king.'

'I know who my father is.'

'We must request him to send more men, sire.'

'Do so,' the dauphin said, 'but make sure he sends his most foolish fools.'

'Fools, sire?'

'Send the messengers! Do it now!'

So the French sent for help.

The huge man with the morningstar rushed at Thomas, while his companions, one with the flail and the other with an axe, charged with him. They bellowed their challenges as they came. Thomas was flanked by Karyl and by Arnaldus, hardened men both, one German, one Gascon, and Karyl faced the man with the poleaxe, while Arnaldus was challenged by the steel-faced man with the war-flail.

Thomas still carried the shortened lance. He dropped it.

The morningstar swung. Thomas, looking up, saw drops of blood being flicked from its spikes as it seared through the sky. He himself had no weapon now, so he just stepped forward, inside the swing, and put his archer's arms around the tall man and squeezed as he lifted.

Arnaldus had taken the flail's blow on his shield. Now, with his right hand, he chopped the axe down on his assailant's leg. Karyl had followed Thomas's example and stepped inside the pole-axe's long swing and rammed his mace into his enemy's groin. He rammed it again. Thomas heard a squeal. He was holding onto his enemy. The flail scraped down his back, tearing mail and leather. More Frenchmen were coming, but so were more Hellequin. The man with the poleaxe was bent double, and that was an invitation to Karyl, who took it gratefully. He held his mace close to its head, shortening the swing, and slammed it onto the nape of the Frenchman's neck. Once, twice, and the man went down in silence, and Karyl drew a dagger and prised up the lower rim of the breast-plate worn by the huge man clasped in Thomas's arms. Karyl slid the dagger up under the man's ribs.

'Jesus! Jesus!' the man screamed. Thomas tightened the embrace. The big man should have let go of the morningstar and tried to break Thomas's neck, but he stubbornly held the weapon as Karyl wriggled his long, thin blade, and the man screamed louder. Thomas smelt shit. He was squeezing as hard as he could and Karyl thrust the dagger again, ramming it up under the breastplate's edge so that his bloodied gauntlet vanished under the steel and into the mangled mail and wool.

'You can drop him now,' Karyl said.

The man fell heavily. He was jerking, gasping.

'Poor bastard,' Karyl said. 'Should have known better.' He picked up his mace, put a foot on the squirming man's chest and slammed the mace down hard onto his helmet. 'Good luck in hell,' Karyl said. 'Say hello to the devil for us.'

The French were pulling back. Step by step, watching their enemy, but going back along the hedge or else trying to force a way through the tangling brambles. The English and Gascons did not follow. Men on horseback behind the line were bellowing at them. 'Keep the line! No pursuit! Let them go!'

The temptation was to pursue the French and capture rich prisoners, but such a pursuit would break the line open, and if the French had failed to do that with steel then the English would not do it to themselves with greed. They stayed in line.

'You should try fighting with a weapon,' Karyl said to Thomas, amused.

Thomas was dry-mouthed. He could hardly speak, but as the French went, so the women from the English baggage came with wineskins filled with river-water. There was not enough for everyone to slake their thirst, but men drank what they could.

And trumpets sounded in the valley.

The enemy was coming again.

The first messenger to reach the king was dusty. Sweat had made channels through the dust on his face. His horse was white with sweat. He dismounted and knelt. 'My liege,' he said, 'the prince your son requests reinforcements.'

The king was gazing at the far hill. He could see the English banners through the widest gap in the hedge. 'What happened?' he asked.

'The enemy is weakened, sire. Very weakened.'

'But not broken.'

'No, sire.'

Two more messengers came and the king pieced together an account of what had happened so far that morning. The messengers heaped praise on his eldest son, saying the dauphin had fought magnificently, stories that the king disbelieved but pretended to accept. What did seem true was that the English had indeed been weakened, but had kept their discipline and held their line intact. 'They are stubborn, sire,' one of the messengers said.

'Ah yes, stubborn,' the king said vaguely. He watched his eldest son's troops come back down the far hill. They came slowly. They must have been weary because it had been a long fight. Most clashes of men-at-arms were over in minutes, but the two armies must have fought for at least an hour.

The king watched a wounded man limp up the hill, using a sword as a stave to support his weight. 'My son is unwounded?' he asked the messenger.

'Yes, sire, thank God, sire.'

'Thank God indeed,' the king said, then beckoned to the Count of Ventadour. 'Go to the dauphin,' he ordered him, 'and tell him he is to leave the field.'

'Leave the field?' The count was not certain he had heard correctly.

'He is the heir. He has fought enough. He has proved his courage, and now he must be kept safe. Tell him he is to ride to Poitiers with his entourage. I shall join him there this evening.'

'Yes, sire,' the count said, and called for his horse. He knew he was being sent with the message because the dauphin would distrust such a command unless it was brought by a man close to the king. And the count decided the king was right. The heir to the throne must be kept safe.

'And tell the Duke of Orléans to take up the fight,' the king commanded.

'He is to advance, sire?'

'He is to advance, he is to fight and he is to win!' the king said. He looked at his youngest son, just fourteen. 'You will not leave with Charles,' he said.

'I don't want to leave, father!'

'You will witness victory, Philippe.'

'Shall we fight, father?' the boy asked eagerly.

'Your uncle will fight next. We shall join him if we're needed.'

'I hope he needs us!' Philippe said.

King Jean smiled. He did not want to deprive his youngest son of any of the day's excitement, though he desperately wanted him kept safe. Perhaps, he thought, he would advance his three thousand men at the battle's end to join in the destruction of the English. His men were among the finest knights and men-at-arms that France possessed, which was why they served in the king's battle. 'You will see some fighting,' he promised his son, 'but you must swear not to leave my side!'

'I swear it, father.'

The Count of Ventadour had ridden his horse through the mass of men commanded by the king's brother. That was the shortest way to the dauphin. The king saw him deliver the message to the duke, then ride on to find the dauphin who was now halfway down the far slope. The English had not pursued him. They just waited behind the hedge, a sign, the king hoped, that they truly were weakened.

'When the duke attacks,' the king called to Marshal Clermont, 'we will advance our battle to his present position.'

'Yes, sire.'

The first hammer blow had weakened the English. Two more waited.

And then only one waited.

Because, as the king watched in disbelief, his brother decided to leave the field with the dauphin.

The Duke of Orléans had not fought, his sword was unstained by enemy blood, yet he called for his horses and led his troops northwards. 'What the devil?' the king asked the morning air.

'What in Christ's name is he doing?' Marshal Clermont asked.

'Sweet Jesus,' a man said.

'He's leaving!'

'You fool!' the king screamed at his brother, who was much too far away to hear. 'You spavined fool, you coward! You cretinous bastard! You gutless turd!' His face was red, spittle flying from his mouth. 'Advance the banners!' the king shouted. He dismounted and gave the reins of his horse to a groom. If his brother would not fight, then the king's battle, the finest in the army, would have to decide the day. 'Trumpets!' the king shouted, still angrily. 'Give me that damned axe! Sound the trumpets! Sound the advance! Forward!'

The trumpets sounded, the drums beat, and the oriflamme was carried towards the enemy.

'What are they doing?' The Prince of Wales had mounted his horse so that he could see the enemy better, and what he saw was worrying. The French second battle was going northwards. 'They plan to attack our right flank?' he suggested.

'And our centre at the same time, sire,' Sir Reginald Cobham, old in war, was watching the last French battle advance. This was the battle that flew the oriflamme and the royal standard. Sir

Reginald leaned forward and slapped at a horsefly that had settled on his destrier's neck. 'Maybe someone over there has some sense at last?'

'The Earl of Salisbury has archers?' the prince asked.

'Plenty, but does he have enough arrows?'

The prince grunted. A servant brought him a pitcher of wine diluted with water, but the prince shook his head. 'Make sure every other man drinks before I do,' he ordered in a voice loud enough to be heard thirty or forty paces away.

'A carter brought ten barrels of water up the hill, sire,' the Earl of Warwick said.

'He did? Good man!' The prince looked at a servant. 'Find him! Give him a mark!' The silver mark was a valuable coin. 'No, give him two! They're not very eager, are they?' He was looking at the Duke of Orléans's troops, whom he had presumed were about to attack the Earl of Salisbury's men on the English right, but to his bemusement those enemy troops were heading even farther north. Some had mounted their horses, some walked, and some lingered in the valley's bed as though uncertain what they should do. 'Jean!' the prince called. 'My lord!'

Jean de Grailly, Captal de Buch, who had stayed close to the prince for much of the battle, nudged his horse closer. 'Sire?'

'What are those devils doing?'

'A mounted attack?' the captal suggested, but he sounded very uncertain. If the French did plan a charge of mounted knights then they were taking their horses a long way from the English line. Some had already vanished over the distant skyline. 'Or perhaps they want to be first into the whore-houses of Poitiers?' the captal suggested.

'What sensible fellows they are,' the prince said. He frowned, watching the receding troops. About half of the Duke of Orléans's battle were going northwards, the other half had stayed where they were to be joined by the dauphin's men who had already fought. Then some of those began to follow the Duke of Orléans's banner northward. That banner, instead of being carried towards the right of the English line, was heading steadily north and westwards. 'By God,' the prince said in astonishment, 'I do believe you're right. They're racing to get the best whores! Giddy-up, fellows!' he shouted the encouragement towards the disappearing enemy, then patted his horse. 'Not you, old fellow. You have to stay here.' He looked back to the French king's troops who were now advancing towards him. 'He must be very confident,' he said, 'to send troops away?'

'Or very foolish,' the Earl of Warwick said.

There were a dozen horsemen about the prince. They were the wise men, the experienced men, their eyes creased from staring at distant enemies, their skin darkened by the sun, their armour scratched and dented, and their weapon hilts worn smooth from use. They had fought in Normandy, Brittany, Gascony, France, and Scotland, and they trusted each other, and, more importantly, the prince trusted them. 'And to think,' the prince said, 'that this morning I was expecting to be a hostage.'

'I'm sure Jean de Valois would accept the offer now, sire,' the Earl of Warwick said, refusing to call Jean the King of France, a title claimed by Edward of England.

'I don't believe what I think I'm watching,' the prince said. He was frowning at the retreating French troops, who really did seem to be leaving the battlefield, not just the dauphin's tired men, but the Duke of Orléans's fresh troops as well. Some had remained on the field, and those men were joining the king's battle. 'I suppose they think those fellows are sufficient.' He pointed at the approaching men-at-arms. The king's great standard, flamboyant in blue and gold, had reached the valley's bottom and now the great spread of armoured men began to climb. 'My lord,' the prince turned to the captal, 'you have horsemen?'

'I have sixty men mounted, sire. The rest are in the line.'

'Sixty,' the prince said thoughtfully. He glanced back at the approaching French. Sixty was not enough. His battered army might have around the same number of men as the King of France's approaching battle, but the enemy was fresh, the prince's men were tired, and he did not want to weaken his exhausted line by taking men-at-arms from the ranks. But then a happy thought occurred. 'Take a hundred archers with you. All mounted.'

'Sire?' the Earl of Warwick asked, wondering what the prince was thinking.

'They plan to strike us hard,' the prince said, 'so let's see how they like being struck themselves?' He turned back to the captal. 'Let them engage us first, my lord, then strike from the rear.'

The captal was smiling. It was not a pleasant smile. 'I need an English flag, sire.'

'So they know who's killing them?'

'So your archers don't use our horses for target practice, sire.'

'My God,' Warwick said, 'you're going to charge an army with a hundred and sixty men!'

'No, we're going to slaughter an army,' the prince said, 'with the help of God, Saint George, and Gascony!' The prince leaned from the saddle and clasped the captal's hand. 'Go with God, my lord, and fight like the devil.'

'Even the devil doesn't fight like a Gascon, sire.'

The prince laughed.

He smelt victory.

CHAPTER 16

Roland de Verrec had spent the battle on horseback. He would have felt uncomfortable fighting on foot, not because he had no skills at such combat, but because he had no close friends in the battle line. Men fought in pairs or in groups, united by kinship or friendship, and sworn to each other's defence. Roland de Verrec had no kin in this army, and his friendships were tenuous, and besides, he wanted to find his enemy. When the French had first burst through the gaps in the hedge to drive the English line backwards, Roland had searched the banners for the green horse of Labrouillade and had not seen it. So he had stood his destrier close to the Prince of Wales, though not so close that he would be noticed, and he had gazed through the hedge's widest gap trying to find the green horse among the two battles waiting to attack, and still he had not spied it. That was hardly surprising. The waiting battles were flamboyant with banners, flags, and pennants and there was little wind to spread them, so little wind that the man holding the oriflamme was waving it from side to side so it would be noticed.

That pennant was a ripple of bright red that was drawing ever closer to the English hill.

Robbie had joined him. The Scotsman, like Roland, was friendless in this army. It was true that he counted Thomas as a friend, but that friendship was marked by generosity on one side and ingratitude on the other, and Robbie felt shamed. In time the friendship could be mended, but for now Robbie did not think Thomas would trust him as a neighbour in battle and so, like Roland, he had watched the fight from behind the line. He had watched the English take the French charge, stop it, and repel it. He had heard the misery of battle, the screams of men being mangled by steel; he had watched the French try again and again to break the line and seen them lose heart. They had retreated. They left bodies behind, more bodies than the English, many more, but then it was always easier to defend. The English had to hold their line. Men who were reluctant to fight had small choice but to stay with their neighbours; they did not need to step forward and initiate battle, but the French had to advance. The more timid would hang back, leaving the bravest to fight, which meant the bravest were often isolated, set upon by half a dozen defenders, and it had been the French who had suffered most through their bravery. Now it would all start again.

'What happens now?' Roland asked suddenly.

Robbie gazed at the approaching French. 'They come, they fight, who knows?'

'I didn't mean that,' Roland said. He too watched the approaching French. 'They saved their best to last,' he added.

'Their best?'

Roland could see some of the banners now because the standard bearers were waving them to and fro. 'Ventadour,' he said, 'Dammartin, Brienne, Eu, Bourbon, Pommiers. And the royal standard too.'

'So what did you mean?'

'I mean what happens after the battle?'

'You marry Bertille.'

'With God's help, yes.' Roland said, touching the blue silk scarf at his neck. 'And you?'

Robbie shrugged. 'I stay with Thomas, I think.'

'You won't go home?'

'I doubt there'll be a welcome for me in Liddesdale, not any more. I'll have to make a new home.'

Roland nodded. He still watched the approaching battle. 'And I shall have to make my peace with France,' he said wistfully.

Robbie patted the neck of his horse, a piebald destrier that had been a gift from Thomas. 'I thought your lands were in Gascony?'

'They are.'

'Then do homage to the Prince of Wales. He'll restore your lands.'

Roland shook his head. 'I'm French,' he said, 'and I will ask France's forgiveness.' He sighed. 'I suppose it will cost money, but anything is possible with money.'

'Just make sure you kill him quickly,' Robbie said. 'I'll help you.'

Roland did not respond at once. He had seen a flash of green in the enemy ranks and was watching the place. Was it a green horse? 'Quickly?' he asked after a while, still staring. 'Did you think I would torment Labrouillade to death?' He sounded offended. 'He might deserve torment, but his death will be quick.'

'I mean kill him before he has a chance to surrender.'

Roland at last turned from the approaching French. His visor was lifted and he was frowning. 'Surrender?'

'Labrouillade's worth a fortune,' Robbie said. 'If the battle goes badly for him he'll surrender. He'd much rather pay a ransom than be buried. Wouldn't you?'

'My God,' Roland said. He had never thought of that possibility, but it was so obvious! He had dreamed of freeing Bertille with the sword, but Robbie was right. Labrouillade would never fight. He would yield.

'So kill him very quickly,' Robbie said. 'Don't give him a chance to say anything. Get in fast, ignore his pleas for mercy, and kill him.' He paused, watching Roland, who had looked back to the advancing enemy. 'If he's even there,' Robbie added.

'He's there,' Roland said bitterly. He had seen the green horse now. It was on the left of the

French line at the back of the king's battle. Somehow he would need to cut his way through that line if he was ever to free Bertille, and he knew that would be hopeless. He would have to kill too many men, and even if he succeeded he would give Labrouillade far too much time to see his death approaching. Robbie was right, he needed to do the killing fast and he did not see how that could be done.

And just then there was a crash of hooves. He turned and saw horsemen assembling beneath the trees and he guessed they were readying to make a charge. 'I need a lance,' he said.

'We need two lances!' Robbie said.

They turned their horses and went to find lances.

The Count of Labrouillade tripped on something. He still had his visor lifted, but it was difficult to look down because his helmet's lower rim, which covered his jaw, grated on his mail aventail and against the top of his thick breastplate, but he caught a glimpse of a discarded mace, smeared with blood and human hair. His bowels lurched. There was more blood on the ground, evidently left by a wounded man limping or crawling back from the first assault on the English line. He slowed his pace, making certain he was at the very back of the king's battle. The drums were close behind him, the drummers making a huge, ear-pummelling noise as their clubbed sticks thumped on the stretched goatskins. Armour clinked. The count was soaked in sweat; it was running down his face and stinging his eyes. He was tired from the long walk down from the flat hilltop and it was worse now because he was going gently uphill, every step an effort, his leg muscles nothing but ache, and his stomach was churning while his bowels had turned to water. He stumbled on a trampled vine, but managed to keep his footing. Trumpets called.

'No arrows!' someone shouted.

'The bastards have run out of arrows!'

'You can keep your visors up!' another man called, and just then an arrow flashed in from the left, slashing down into the ranks and glancing off a vambrace to bury its bodkin point in the earth. More arrows came, and all through the French ranks men fumbled to close their visors. The sound of arrows striking armour was like metal hail. A drummer was hit and he fell back, his vast drum on top of his bleeding stomach as he threw up a mixture of vomit and blood.

'Oh God,' the Count of Labrouillade moaned. The wine slopped in his belly. He felt sick. So many men had drunk their way to courage and now the wine was sour, and he stumbled as he struggled onwards. He could see almost nothing through the narrow slits of his visor. All he wanted was to keep his bowels closed and for this hell to be over. Pray God that the enthusiastic fools at the front of the attack surged through the English line and killed the enemy fools. With any luck he would take a prisoner worth a large ransom, but in truth he did not really care. He just wanted this to be finished.

The arrows dwindled. The archers on the right of the English line had only a handful left, and most of them discarded their bows and picked up poleaxes or maces, then watched the enemy close on the hedge.

The King of France was walking towards the widest gap in the hedge where he could see the great banner that proclaimed the presence of the Prince of Wales. His son Philippe was beside him and his bodyguard all around him. Seventeen other men were dressed in the king's colours, dressed to deceive the English. They were all renowned knights, members of the king's Order of the Star, and the hope was that the English would die in attacking them and so weaken themselves. 'You stay close beside me, Philippe,' the king said to his son.

'Yes, father.'

'Tonight we'll feast in Poitiers,' the king said. 'We'll have music!'

'And prisoners?'

'Dozens of prisoners,' King Jean said. 'Hundreds of prisoners! And we'll make you a nightshirt from the Prince of Wales's jupon.'

Philippe laughed. He carried a sword and a shield, though no one expected him to fight, and four Knights of the Star were detailed to protect him.

The front ranks of the French were converging on the gap in the hedge now. 'Montjoie Saint Denis!' they shouted, 'Montjoie Saint Denis!' The attacking line was ragged. The enthusiastic had forged ahead, the reluctant had deliberately slowed, and the French line was misshapen. The English were silent. The king had a glimpse of them through the ranks in front of him and saw a grey line of battered steel beneath tattered flags. 'Saint Denis,' he shouted, 'Montjoie Saint Denis!'

The Cardinal Bessières was a hundred paces behind the French attack. He was still mounted and escorted by Father Marchant and three men-at-arms. The cardinal was livid. The French army was supposedly led by men who knew their business, men experienced in warfare, yet the first attacks by horsemen had failed utterly, the second attack had been repulsed, and now at least half of the army had left the field, some without even trying to fight. What should have been an easy victory was being weighed in the balance, yet despite his anger he was still confident. The king's battle was the strongest of the three and filled with men of high reputation. They were fresh, the enemy was tired, and with God's help the king should prevail. The oriflamme still flew. The cardinal considered saying a prayer, but he had never been confident of God's help, preferring to rely on his own intelligence and cunning. 'When this debacle is over,' he said to Father Marchant, 'make sure you retrieve *la Malice* from that Scottish animal.'

'Of course, Your Eminence.'

And to the cardinal's surprise the recollection of Saint Peter's sword gave him a sudden surge of hope. He, above all men, knew the tawdry nature of most relics and the deceit that such things played on the credulous. Any scrap of old bone, whether from a goat, a bullock, or an executed thief, could be palmed off as the knuckle of a martyr, yet despite his scepticism he felt a certainty that *la Malice* was indeed the sword of the fisherman. It could not fail. The angels themselves would fight for France, and victory would propel Louis Bessières onto the throne of Saint Peter.

'Now go!' the cardinal called to the men in front, though they were too far away to hear him.

And the French charged. 'Montjoie Saint Denis!'

Thomas rode north along the English line. He could hear the French approaching, their big drums pounding the air, and he was curious to discover what was happening. So far his battle had been the short, vicious repulse of the horsemen by the ford, and then the equally short and savage battle inside the hedge. What had happened on the rest of the field was a mystery, and so he rode to find out and he saw, through the widest gap in the hedge, another French attack surging forward. What was strange was that there were no more Frenchmen on the distant skyline, except for a scatter of horsemen who appeared, like him, to be watching the battle.

He was about to turn back to tell his men what he had discovered and to warn them to be ready for another fight along the hedge when a voice shouted. 'Are you an archer?'

Thomas assumed the question was directed at someone else and ignored it, then it struck him as strange that the question should have been asked in French. He turned and saw a man in black livery on which a yellow shield was decorated with silver scallops. The man was staring straight at Thomas.

'I'm an archer,' Thomas called back.

'I need mounted archers!' The man was young, but had an unmistakable air of confidence and authority. 'Bring hand weapons!'

'I can give you at least sixty archers,' Thomas called back.

'Be quick!'

The French came through the gap, screaming their war cry and, just as before, they crashed into the English line and, just as before, steel met steel. 'Hold fast!' a man bellowed in English. 'Hold the line!' Trumpets raked the sky with noise, the drummers hammered their skins, the war cries were shouted, and Thomas rode, only stopping when he reached the southern end of the line, which was still unengaged. 'Karyl! It'll be the same fight as before! Just hold them! Sam! I want every archer on his horse. Bring axes, swords, maces, anything that kills, and hurry!'

Thomas wondered who the man in the black

jupon was or what in God's name he had just agreed to do. His men were running to the tree line where Keane had picketed the horses. 'Keane,' Thomas shouted, 'give me a poleaxe!'

The Irishman brought a poleaxe, then mounted his own horse. 'I'm coming. Where are we going?'

'I have no idea.'

'A mystery ride, is it? We used to do that at home. Just ride off and see where we ended. Usually an alehouse.'

'I doubt that's our destination,' Thomas said, then raised his voice. 'Come with me!' He kicked the horse back north. To his left the battle was loud. The English line was four men deep and it was holding. The men in the rear ranks were bracing the front rank, or thrusting with shortened lances between their comrades' bodies, while behind the line two horsemen were jabbing lances at any enemy whose visor was lifted. There was a mass of Frenchmen in the hedge's gap where banners waved, but most were still beyond the hedge, waiting for their leading men to hack out a space they could fill.

'Follow me!' the man in the black jupon shouted. He had sixty or so men wearing his black and yellow colours, and Thomas and his archers followed them into the trees. More archers joined, all following the man in black northwards. Thomas saw Robbie and Roland riding together and he kicked his horse to catch up with them.

'What are we doing?'

'Attacking from behind,' Robbie said. He grinned. 'Who's leading?'

'The Captal de Buch,' Roland said.

'Captal?'

'A Gascon title. He has reputation.'

My God, Thomas thought, but he needs to be good. As far as he could see the captal had fewer than two hundred men and he planned to assault the French army? And most of those men were mounted archers, not trained men-at-arms, but if the captal felt any trepidation he did not betray it. He led the men down the hill, staying in the woods and going far behind the Earl of Salisbury's battle that defended the right-hand end of the English line. The fighting was fierce there. Much of the earl's position was beyond the hedge, and the slope leading to the English line was gentle, and so the French assailed around the hedge's northern end to be met by men-at-arms and archers. Trenches trapped some Frenchmen. Archers fought with hand weapons, using their bow-given strength to batter armoured men. Thomas had a glimpse of that fight, then he was in the trees again. Acorns crunched under the hooves of his horse. Men ducked beneath the branches of oak and chestnuts. A handful of the men-at-arms carried long lances that had to be steered carefully between the thick trees, but they were not going fast. The strength of the horses needed to be conserved and so the captal led them at a trot, confident that he was hidden from the enemy. The sound of battle faded as they rode farther north.

They rode into a valley, crossed a trickle of a stream and climbed the further slope that was a field of stubble. Trees screened the northern and western skylines. Just before they reached the northern trees, the captal turned his horse to the left and rode into a thicket of oak that crowned a hill. When Thomas ducked into the trees he could see that the low hills to the north were covered with retreating men. Why? Had the French suffered a defeat that had escaped his notice? Yet there they were, hundreds and hundreds of men going northwards while the battle was still being fought on the English hill.

A small lizard skittered across Thomas's path. Was that a good omen or a bad? He wished he still had the dried dog paw he used to wear as a talisman about his neck, a paw he had boasted to be a relic of Saint Guinefort, a dog that had been declared a saint. How could a dog be a saint? He made the sign of the cross, remembering that he had not confessed before this battle and he had not received any absolution. If he was killed, he thought, he would go to hell. He thought of the paw again and curbed his horse. All the horses were standing now, pawing the ground and tossing their heads.

'Standard bearer!' the captal called.

'Sire?'

'The English flag.'

The standard bearer unfurled the white flag with the bold red cross of Saint George.

'Weapons, gentlemen,' the captal said in heavily accented English. He grinned and his teeth looked very white against his sun-darkened skin, which was shadowed by his helmet. 'Now let's destroy them!'

With those words he spurred his horse out of the trees. The men-at-arms and archers followed and as Thomas rode into the sunlight he suddenly saw the French army crowded at the hedge, and he saw that the captal had led them in a wide circle so that they were now riding at the French from the rear. The men-at-arms with lances held the weapons upright. All the long lances bore a black and yellow pennant: the captal's colours. There was a small hedge in front of them, but there were gaps, and the horsemen streamed through, re-forming on the far side as the captal spurred into a canter. Thomas's world was the thud of hooves, a devil's thud counterpointing the drums of the French, who seemed oblivious of the horsemen coming from behind.

They were riding on grassland now. Thomas kicked his horse into a canter. Not far. The French were just two bowshots away and the one hundred and sixty horsemen were spreading out. Down into the small combe, then up the slope where the horses trampled the broken grape vines. The flag of Saint George was high, the lances were lowered to the charge, the spurs went back, and a man screamed, 'Saint George!'

'Saint Quiteira!' a Gascon shouted.

'And kill them!' the captal bellowed, and the horsemen let their destriers and coursers run, and the French rear ranks, where the more timid men sheltered, turned to see the great beasts and armoured men crashing down on them and they broke even before the charge slammed home. Flags fell, men began to run, clumsy in their armour, and then the horses were among them and the lances slid into steel-clad bodies and axes swung to splinter backplates and shatter bone and to mist the autumn air with blood, and Thomas heard himself shouting like a fiend and feeling utter exhilaration. 'Saint George!' and he slammed the spike at the end of the poleaxe into a Frenchman's helmet and let the momentum of his horse drag the weapon free. A nakerer let his vast drum fall and ran, but a horseman turned and casually split the man's skull with a sword before turning back to attack a French knight. He swung again and his sword shattered the Frenchman's sword. A horse reared and beat a man down with its hooves. Sam was killing crossbowmen with an axe. 'I hate bloody crossbowmen!' he shouted and dropped the axe blade onto a man's head. 'Like cracking an egg!' he shouted at Thomas. 'Who's next?'

'Stay together,' the captal shouted. They were only one hundred and sixty strong, and the King of France's battle was three thousand men, but the one hundred and sixty had shattered the rear ranks of the French, who were now desperately running back towards the west. The front ranks, fighting beyond the hedge, heard the panic, and the whole battle moved backwards as the English line roared in triumph and moved forward. More horsemen appeared, this time from the southern end of the line, a more ragged charge of men coming to complete the panic. And the French had indeed panicked. They were fleeing, all of them, and the captal bellowed at his men to pull back.

A hundred and sixty men had broken an army, but they were still hugely outnumbered, and the French were realising it and forming lines to resist the horsemen. Three of them caught Pitt, the taciturn archer, and Thomas watched, horrified, as they cut his horse down with axes, dragged Pitt from the saddle and beat him to death with maces. Thomas rode at them, reaching them too late, but swinging the poleaxe wildly and slamming the blade into a man's neck. 'Bastards!' he shouted, then twisted his horse fast away from their axe blows. He followed the captal north, just out of range of the French weapons. The prince's men had come through the hedge and were falling on the French who again broke in panic. They fled, pursued by the dismounted men-at-arms coming in ever greater numbers through the hedge, and by the horsemen who had appeared to the south.

It was like shepherding a flock of sheep. The horsemen rode and threatened and the French made no effort to re-form, but kept going westwards. The oriflamme had vanished, but Thomas could see the blue and gold of the French royal standard still flying in the centre of the disorganised mass.

More and more of the English and Gascon men-at-arms had fetched their horses, and more and more came to join the pursuit. Down into the shallow valley they went, then up to the flat top of le Champ d'Alexandre from which the French had attacked that morning, and now it was the horsemen who attacked. Groups of men rode into the disorganised French, weapons swinging, horses snapping at men, and the French panic grew desperate as their ranks were split. Small groups stayed together and tried to defend themselves. The nobles were shouting that they were rich, that they surrendered. English archers, their bows discarded, were using their huge strength to wield axes, maces, and hammers. Men bellowed in bloodlust or in terror. All order had now vanished from the French, who were being broken into smaller and smaller groups assailed by battle-maddened men with sweaty faces and gritted teeth who only wanted to kill and kill. And so they did. A Frenchman fended off two archers, using his sword to foil their axes, then he stepped back and tripped on a fallen man and went down, and the archers jumped forward, axes swinging and the Frenchman screamed as a blade crashed into his shoulder; he tried to stand, fell back again and swung his sword in a great sweep that parried an axe. Thomas could see the man gritting his teeth, his whole face distorted with his desperate efforts. He parried another axe, then cried out as the second archer chopped into the meat of his thigh. He tried to lunge his sword at that man, spitting out teeth he had shattered because he had bitten down so hard, but his desperate lunge was parried, then an axe crunched down into his face and a poleaxe spike rammed into his belly and his whole body jerked in a great spasm as he died. For a moment his helmet's open face filled with blood, then it drained away as the two archers knelt to search his body.

Keane had dismounted and was standing over a corpse whose belly had been split open by the Irishman's poleaxe. The man's guts had been trampled into the stubble, while next to the corpse, and wearing the same livery of yellow circles on a blue field, was an older man with a pale, lined face, grey hair, and a neatly trimmed beard. He wore plate armour with a golden crucifix blazoned on his breastplate. He looked terrified. He had plainly surrendered to Keane, because the Irishman was holding the man's helmet that had a cross on its crest and a long blue plume trailing behind. 'He says he's the Archbishop of Sens!' Keane said to Thomas.

'Then you're rich. Hold onto him! Make sure no one steals him from you.'

'This fellow tried to protect him.' Keane looked down at the disembowelled man. 'Wasn't a clever decision, really.'

There was a wild melee in the centre of the field and Thomas, looking that way, saw the French royal standard still flying. Men were hacking at the standard's defenders, wild in their savagery as they tried to cut through to King Jean. Thomas ignored it, riding southwards to see men fleeing down the hill towards the Miosson, but the Earl of Warwick's archers were waiting there and the Frenchmen were fleeing towards death.

A man hailed Thomas and he turned to see Jake, one of his archers, leading a prisoner on a horse. The man wore a jupon showing a clenched red fist against a field of orange and white stripes, and Thomas could not help but laugh. It was Joscelyn of Berat, the man sworn to retake Castillon d'Arbizon. 'He says he'll only surrender to you,' Jake said, 'on account that I'm not a gentleman.'

'Nor am I,' Thomas said, then spoke in French: 'You are my prisoner,' he told Joscelyn.

'Fate,' Joscelyn said resignedly.

'Keane!' Thomas bellowed. 'Another one here to guard! Look after them both, they're rich!' Thomas looked back to Jake. 'Guard them well!' Men squabbled over the ownership of prisoners, but Thomas reckoned there were enough Hellequin to keep the archbishop and the Count of Berat from being poached by other men.

Thomas spurred northwards. More Frenchmen were fleeing that way, desperate to reach the safety of Poitiers. A few, very few, had managed to find their horses or else had taken a horse from an Englishman. Most ran, or rather stumbled, harried all the way by vengeful pursuers, but one man rode straight towards Thomas, who recognised the piebald destrier and then the red heart of Douglas, though the surcoat was so sodden with blood that for a moment Thomas thought it was coloured black. 'Robbie!' he called, glad to see his friend, then he saw that the rider was not Robbie, but Sculley.

'He's dead!' Sculley shouted. 'The traitor's dead! And it's your turn now.' He was carrying *la Malice*, the blade looking pathetically rusted and weak, but it was also discoloured by blood. 'It looks like shit,' Sculley said, 'but it's a canny weapon.' He had lost his helmet, and his long, lank hair rattled with bones. 'I took wee Robbie's head off,' Sculley said. 'One cut of the magic sword and wee Robbie went to hell. See?' He grinned and pointed to his saddle where Thomas saw Robbie's bloody head was hanging by its hair. 'I like a wee keepsake from a fight, and the sight of that will make his uncle happy.' He laughed at Thomas's expression. No one was attacking the Scotsman because any Englishman or Gascon assumed a horseman who was not fleeing northwards must be on their side even if, like Sculley, he did not wear a red cross of Saint George. Now Sculley curbed his stolen horse. 'Would you rather just surrender to me?' he asked, then suddenly rowelled his spurs so that the destrier charged straight at Thomas, who, taken by surprise, could only thrust his poleaxe at the

Scotsman, who easily avoided the clumsy blow and swept the ancient blade hard at Thomas's neck, trying to take his head as he had taken Robbie's.

Thomas jerked the axe back and upwards and somehow managed to parry the blow. The two weapons met with violent force and Thomas thought the old sword must break, but *la Malice* was still in one piece and Sculley backswung it with malevolent speed. Thomas ducked. *La Malice*'s blade hit his bascinet and scraped across the crown, and Thomas instinctively wrenched his horse to the left and saw the sword coming back, snake-fast, in a cut aimed at his face. He somehow leaned out of the way, aware of the broad tip of the sword flashing perilously close. He tried to lunge the poleaxe's spiked tip at the Scotsman, but Sculley just parried the heavy blade and struck again, this time slamming *la Malice* hard down, and the blade clashed onto Thomas's helmet so fiercely that he was half stunned, his ears ringing, but the bascinet's steel resisted the blade even though he was slumping in the saddle, grunting, trying to gather his wits and make room to swing his poleaxe.

'Christ's bowels, but you're feeble,' Sculley taunted. He grinned, prodded Thomas with the sword and laughed when Thomas swayed in the saddle. 'Time to say hello to the devil, Englishman,' Sculley said, and drew *la Malice* back for the killing blow, and Thomas dropped the axe, kicked his left foot free of the stirrup and lunged at the

Scotsman. He threw his arms around Sculley's chest and held on, gripping him, tearing Sculley out of the saddle so that they both thumped onto the ground, and Thomas was on top. He used his archer's strength to punch Sculley in the face, his iron-clad gauntlet shattering a cheekbone and nose. He hit him again, and Sculley tried to bite him and Thomas drove his gauntlet down again, but this time with out-thrust rigid fingers that drove into Sculley's left eyeball. The Scotsman gave a gurgling scream as the eye collapsed, then Thomas headbutted him with his helmet, and rolled off. He seized Sculley's right arm and wrenched the sword free. 'Bastard,' he said, and he held the sword in both hands, left hand on the hilt, right on the backblade, and he drove the fore-edge into Sculley's throat and sawed it hard so that he cut through gullet and blood vessels and sinew and muscle and Sculley still gurgled and blood jetted onto Thomas's face and he went on pushing as the blood pulsed warm and the pulses slowly slackened and still Thomas sawed and pushed until the old blade met bone.

And Sculley was dead.

'Jesus,' Thomas said, 'sweet Jesus.' He was on his knees, shaking. He stared at the sword. A miracle? He saw that someone had made a new wooden hilt for the ancient blade, and that hilt was slick with blood.

He stood. Robbie's horse was beside him and, in a spasm of anger, he cut the hair that held

Robbie's head. It thumped on the ground. He would have to find the rest of his old friend and dig a grave, but before he could think how he might do that he saw Roland de Verrec standing helpless in front of a fat man in armour. The fat man had a green and white jupon and, as Thomas watched, he drew his sword and held it towards Roland. It was the Count of Labrouillade. There was shit dribbling down the back of his armoured legs. 'I am your prisoner!' he announced loudly.

Thomas walked towards the two men. Sam and a half-dozen archers had seen Thomas and they now rode towards him, bringing Thomas's horse with them.

'He surrendered,' Roland called to Thomas.

Thomas said nothing. Kept walking.

'I have yielded,' the count said loudly, 'and will pay a ransom.'

'Kill the fat bastard!' Sam called.

'No!' Roland de Verrec held up his hand. 'You cannot kill him. That is dishonourable.' He stumbled over the English word.

'Dishonourable?' Sam asked, incredulous.

'Sir Thomas,' Roland looked desperately unhappy, 'a man who has surrendered is safe, is he not?'

Thomas ignored Roland, seemed not even to see him. He still said nothing. He walked up to the count, who was holding his sword out in surrender.

'Chivalry dictates that he must be kept alive,' Roland said. 'Is that not so, Sir Thomas?'

Thomas had not even looked at Roland. He just gazed at the count and then, almost as fast as Sculley, he backswung *la Malice* so that the blade chopped into the count's neck. The sword sliced beneath the helmet's rim, cutting through the aventail to bite deep into the fat neck, and Thomas sawed it back, thrust it forward with an archer's strength and was hit by even more blood as the Count of Labrouillade sank to his knees, and Thomas gouged the blade deeper and deeper until the life went from Labrouillade's eyes and he fell hard onto the grass.

'Sir Thomas!' Roland said in outrage.

Thomas turned wide-eyed on Roland. 'Did you say something?'

'He had surrendered!' Roland protested.

'I'm deaf,' Thomas said. 'I was hit on the head and I can't hear a thing. What are you telling me?'

'He had surrendered!'

'I can't hear what you're saying,' Thomas said. He turned away and winked at Sam.

Fifty yards away men were fighting around the King of France. His standard had fallen, the standard bearer was dead, and his son was trying to help his father. 'Look left, father! To the right! Watch out!' The king was fighting with an axe, though no one was trying to kill him, just to capture him. The decoys who had worn his colours were dead or had fled, but everyone knew this was the real king because his helmet was surmounted by a golden crown, and men wanted to take him alive because his ransom would be unimaginably huge. Men grabbed at the king, fought each other to get close to him, and the king shouted that he could make them all rich, but then two horsemen forced their great destriers into the crowd and bellowed at all the men to step back on pain of death.

The Earl of Warwick and Sir Reginald Cobham confronted King Jean and Prince Philippe. Both men dismounted and both men bowed low. 'Your Majesty,' the earl said.

'I am a prisoner,' the King of France said.

'Alas, Your Highness,' Sir Reginald said, 'it is the fate of battle.'

The king was taken.

One of the archers played pipes made from oat straw, the tune wistful and thin. A campfire burned, throwing twisting red light onto the branches of the oaks. A man sang; other men laughed.

The King of France was being feasted by the Prince of Wales, while on the flat hilltop where the battle had ended the birds and beasts gorged themselves on the dead. The dead went all the way to the gates of Poitiers because the English and Gascons had pursued the enemy that far, and the citizens of Poitiers, fearing an English invasion, had refused to open their gates and so the fugitives had been trapped under the walls and there the last of them had died. The old Roman road that ran to the city was littered with the dead, but now the living sat around fires and ate food they had plundered from the enemy's abandoned camp.

Thomas had joined the pursuit, riding with Sam and a dozen other archers. Those archers would all become rich on their plunder, but Thomas had not ridden to find jewels or plate armour or an expensive horse.

'You found him?' Genevieve asked. She sat beside him, her head on his shoulder, and Hugh leaned against her.

'I found them both.'

'Tell me again,' she said, like a child wanting to hear a familiar and comforting story.

So Thomas told her how he had caught up with Cardinal Bessières and how the cardinal's men-at-arms had tried to protect their master, and how Sam and the archers had beaten them down, and Thomas had confronted Father Marchant, who had loudly declared that he was a priest and not a combatant, and Thomas had used *la Malice* to disembowel him so that his guts slid out from his robe and spilt onto the saddle and then down to the ground, and Thomas had laughed at him. 'That's payment for my wife's eye, you bastard.' He had been tempted to let the priest die in agony, but then killed him with another swing of *la Malice*.

Cardinal Bessières had been begging for mercy.

'You are a combatant,' Thomas had said.

'No! I am a cardinal! I will pay you!'

'I see no red hat,' Thomas said, 'only a helmet,'

and the cardinal had tried to pull the bascinet off his head, then screamed as he saw *la Malice* coming, and the scream only stopped when Saint Peter's blade had ripped open his throat. Only then had Thomas turned back towards the battlefield where the dead now lay beneath the stars.

Roland was with his Bertille. 'I should have shouted at you,' he told Thomas, 'I didn't realise you had been deafened.'

'It was a terrible mistake,' Thomas lied gravely, 'and I apologise.'

'It was not dishonourable,' Roland said, 'because you were not to know he had surrendered. He was still holding a sword, and you were deafened.'

'It was God's will,' Bertille said. She looked radiant.

Roland nodded. 'It was God's will,' he agreed, then, after a pause. 'And *la Malice*?'

'She's gone,' Thomas said.

'Where?'

'Where she cannot be found,' Thomas said.

He had taken *la Malice* to the largest gap in the hedge where men were piling weapons discarded on the battlefield. The good weapons were put into one pile, the cheap and worthless weapons onto another. There were broken swords, shattered crossbows, an axe with a bent blade, and a score of rusted falchions. 'What happens to them?' Thomas had asked a man wearing the Prince of Wales's three-feathered badge.

'Melted down, like as not. That looks like a piece of shit.'

'It is,' Thomas had said, and he had tossed the Sword of the Fisherman onto the pile of worthless junk. It looked no different to all the other cheap falchions. A shattered spear had landed on top of it, then a broken sword had clattered onto the heap. When he had looked back Thomas could not even tell which sword was the relic and which was not. It would be put into the fire, melted, and then reforged. Perhaps a ploughshare?

'Now we go home,' he said. 'Castillon first, then back to England.'

'Home,' Genevieve said happily.

The Sword of Saint Peter had come. It had gone. It was over. It was time to go home.

HISTORICAL NOTE

Edward, Prince of Wales, eldest son of King Edward III, is best known as the Black Prince, though that name was not coined until long after his death. No one is quite sure why he was to be called the Black Prince, but even in France he was remembered as *le Prince Noir*, and I have come across references as late as the nineteenth century to French mothers threatening their disobedient children with a ghostly visit from this long-dead enemy. Some say the name arose from the colour of his armour, but there is little evidence to support that explanation, nor does it seem to be a reference to his character, which, so far as we can tell from the little information that remains, was anything but dark. He was generous, probably headstrong, probably romantic (he made an impractical marriage to the beautiful Joan, Maid of Kent), loyal to his father, but otherwise little is known of his personality. He is most famous as a soldier, though much of his life was spent in inefficient administration of his father's French possessions. He fought at Crécy, and shortly before his death won a victory at Najera in Spain, but

Poitiers is his most significant military achievement, and, despite his fame, the battle has receded from common memory while his father's great victory at Crécy, and Henry V's triumph at Agincourt remain celebrated.

Yet Poitiers deserves a place among England's most significant military achievements. It was an extraordinary battle. The prince was outnumbered, his army was thirsty, hungry, and travel-worn, yet it fought, by medieval standards, a very long battle and ended it as outright victors and with the King of France as their prisoner. King Jean II was taken back to London where he joined another royal prisoner, King David II of Scotland, who had been captured after the battle of Neville's Cross ten years before (described in Thomas of Hookton's adventure *Vagabond*).

The battle of Poitiers was the culmination of the prince's second great *chevauchée* through France. The first, in 1355, had struck south-east from Gascony and laid waste a great swathe of country, stopping just short of Montpellier, but ravaging, among many other towns and cities, the *bourg* of Carcassonne. A *chevauchée* was a destructive raid, designed to inflict severe economic damage on the enemy who, to end the losses, would need to fight a battle. If the enemy refused battle, as the French did in 1355, the *chevauchée* resulted in a shameful loss of face for the French and huge profit for the English. If they accepted battle, as King Jean chose in 1356, they risked defeat. Or perhaps they would achieve revenge and victory.

There are many riddles around the battle of Poitiers. One of the most puzzling is whether the prince really wanted to fight on that September morning. The previous day, a Sunday, had been spent in tortuous negotiations with the cardinals (Bessières is fictional, but Talleyrand was the principal negotiator). There is evidence that the prince was ready to accept the humiliating terms the church offered, but some historians believe he was merely playing for time. What does seem certain is that the battle began early on the Monday morning when the French perceived the English left wing retreating, and they feared that the prince planned to slip away across the Miosson and so escape them. That would have been an extraordinarily risky manoeuvre, to pass an army over a river while a dwindling rearguard defended against an enemy intent on stopping the retreat, but undoubtedly the Earl of Warwick's battle was intending to cross the Miosson. My own suspicion is that the prince hoped to evade the French and continue his retreat to Gascony, but was prepared to change that plan if the French attacked.

If the prince was in two minds, the same could be said of King Jean. He was no great warrior and he undoubtedly feared the power of the English archers. On the other hand he had the advantage of numbers and must have known his enemy was weakened by hunger. Some of his advisers suggested caution, others urged him to battle. He chose battle. It is possible that neither side was wholly committed to fighting that day, yet the hotheads on the French side prevailed and King Jean decided to attack. The prince, I am sure, would have preferred to retreat.

Yet one of the aims of a *chevauchée* was to bring the enemy to battle, so why not fight at Poitiers? Perhaps the prince hoped he would find a better place to fight further south, but he was given no choice. He did occupy a strong position, and here there are more puzzles. We know where the battle was fought, but the exact placement is frustratingly uncertain. The chroniclers mention the hedge, which was evidently a formidable obstacle, but the hedge has long vanished, and no one can tell precisely where it was. There are two fords across the Miosson (the novel only mentions one), and it is not certain which was the scene of the opening fight. Most historians agree that it was le Gué de l'Homme, the ford closest to the village and abbey at Nouaillé. We do know that the Captal de Buch led the cavalry attack of about one hundred and sixty men, of whom one hundred were mounted archers, which provoked the French panic and disintegration, but we cannot be sure of where that attack took place. It probably curved around the north of the French, though some people suggest it went around the south (I have preferred the northern route). We know roughly where the prince's army was drawn up. West of the village, now known as Nouaillé-Maupertuis, there is a bridge where once there was a ford, le Gué de l'Homme, and a minor road runs north from that bridge, passing the battlefield memorial as it climbs to the long ridge, and that road, once it gains the height, marks the prince's position. But from which direction did the French attack? There is disagreement. Some historians would have the attack coming from the north, while others prefer an attack from the west. Usually a visit to a battlefield will suggest answers, but I confess I found the topography confusing. I have preferred an attack from the west, simply because that approach looked easier to me, but there is no certainty. The French approach to the battlefield was from the north and, considering the difficulties of manoeuvring large bodies of men, an attack from the north makes sense, but the French were trying to stop the English crossing the Miosson, so they could well have marched parallel to the prince's position before turning to attack, a solution I have preferred. Any reader wanting a full discussion of the difficulties in placing the battle in the landscape should read Peter Hoskins's excellent book *In the Steps of the Black Prince* (The Boydell Press, 2011).

If the exact placement of the battle is problematic, at least we do know the course of the fight. It began with the cavalry attacks on the two wings of the English army, attacks that were repulsed by archery. The attack on the ford was made through marshland and, at the opening of that fight, the archers' arrows were making small impression on the heavily armoured French horses, but a quick move to the flank remedied that problem. William, Lord of Douglas, who had taken two hundred Scottish men-at-arms to aid the French, was badly wounded in that fight (though some believe he survived to be wounded in the dauphin's attack). Meanwhile, the dauphin, the clever but ungainly Charles, led the first attack on the main English line, an attack that had to deal with the frustrating hedge. The fight was long and hard, but Anglo-Gascon discipline prevailed, the line was not broken, and after some two hours the dauphin's men retreated. It should now have been the turn of the king's brother, the Duke of Orléans, to lead his battle against the battered English line, but the duke chose to leave the battlefield. Why? We do not know. It seems King Jean ordered his heir to leave. The dauphin Charles had done his duty and the king presumably did not want to put him at further risk, and it seems he instructed the dauphin to withdraw and the duke chose to withdraw with him. So now two-thirds of the French army had gone, and the king was left to attack with his own battle. That was when the captal led the impudent charge, the French ranks were shattered and the real slaughter began. It took place, we are told, on le Champ d'Alexandre, but where exactly is that?

Some claim it is a stretch of wetland beside the Miosson, but it seems improbable to me that the French would flee southwards, and my exploration of the battlefield convinced me that le Champ d'Alexandre was the plateau of the flat-topped hill west of the English position. But wherever it was, the Field of Alexander proved a death-trap to the French, and it was there that the king and his youngest son were captured. Men squabbled over who had taken Jean le Bon prisoner, but the Earl of Warwick and Sir Reginald Cobham took charge of the king and of his son, and escorted them back to Prince Edward, who treated the royal captives with elaborate courtesy.

The main battle was fought on foot. The Lord of Douglas advised this, knowing that archers were much less effective against foot soldiers than against horses, which makes it ironical that Douglas was probably wounded while on horseback. The archers at Poitiers were decisive in the defeat of the two French cavalry charges, but made little impression on the main battles, who attacked on foot. The English prevailed in this horrific fighting. There were two main reasons. First, the Anglo-Gascon command was efficient. The army had mostly been together for more than two years, their commanders were experienced, and though there was undoubtedly some rivalry, those commanders cooperated and, above all, trusted each other. The Earl of Warwick began the day expecting to lead his battle in retreat, but changed his tactics when events dictated a change, and did it quickly and effectively. The young Earl of Salisbury commanded the defence of the English right with admirable stubbornness and a personal display of bravery. The final cavalry charge, ordered by the prince, was timed to perfection and was devastating. In contrast, the French command was clumsy in the extreme. King Jean fed his troops piecemeal into a battle from which many fled without orders, and there was bitter rivalry between some of his senior commanders.

But the main reason for the Anglo-Gascon success was their discipline. They did not break the line. One man, Sir Humphrey Berkeley, did choose to leave the ranks and pursue the dauphin's retreating men, presumably in hope of securing a rich prisoner, and was captured himself. His ransom was £2,000, a fortune, but he was the only captive taken by the French, while the English had a glut of high-ranking prisoners: the king himself, his son, the Archbishop of Sens, Marshal Audrehem, the Counts of Vendôme, Dammartin, Tancarville, Joigny, Longueville, Eu, Ponthieu, Ventadour, and between two and three thousand French knights. Among the French dead were the Duke of Athènes, the Duke of Bourbon, Geoffrey de Charny (who carried the oriflamme), Constable Walter de Brienne, Marshal Clermont, the Bishop of Châlons, and some sixty or seventy other notables. Statistics for medieval battles are notoriously difficult, but it seems likely that the Anglo-Gascon army was about six thousand strong, of which one-third were archers, and that the French numbered about ten thousand. After the battle, heralds counted two and a half thousand French dead and a mere forty English or Gascons. The figure for the French appears credible, but are so few Anglo-Gascon casualties believable? There may have been some exaggeration by the winners, but the disparity also suggests that the greatest killing occurred after the French panicked. So long as men were in line, protected by their armour and supported by their neighbours, their chances of survival were high, but as soon as the line broke and men fled for their lives they became easy targets. There were certainly far too many bodies to be dealt with by the victors because, apart from those great nobles who could be identified, the rest were left on the field to rot, and stayed there till February when at last their remains were collected and buried.

Between two and a half and three thousand Frenchmen were captured. The less important prisoners and those who were badly wounded were paroled, meaning they were allowed to go home on a promise not to fight against the English until their ransom was settled, but any man worth a large fortune was taken back to England and kept there till the ransom was paid. Warwick Castle, in its present form, was largely constructed on the ransoms of Frenchmen. Jonathan Sumption, in his indispensable book, *Trial by Fire*, reckons the total ransoms collected from Poitiers amounted to around £300,000. It is almost impossible to offer an equivalent value in today's currencies, though one measure might be the price of ale, which today costs three thousand times what it did in the 1350s, so sufficient to say that many men became enormously wealthy. King Jean II's ransom was set at six million gold écus, much of which was paid before his death in London in 1364.

The name *la Malice* is an invention, and her connection with Saint Junien, whose body still lies behind the altar of the abbey church at Nouaillé-Maupertuis, is entirely fictional. All four gospels tell the story of Saint Peter drawing a sword in Gethsemane on the night of Christ's arrest, then using the blade to slice off the ear of the high priest's servant. The English have an old tradition that Joseph of Arimathea brought the sword to Britain and gave it to Saint George, but the Archdiocese of Poznań, in Poland, has a much better claim to the weapon, indeed the sword is one of their most precious possessions, and is on display in the Archdiocesan Museum. Is it the real thing? A sword in first-century Palestine was most likely to have been a *gladius*, a Roman short sword, while the weapon in Poznań is a falchion, a broad-tipped long sword. Still, there it is, and folk can believe it to be the genuine article if they wish.

I could not have written the novel without the help of several books, chief among them Jonathan Sumption's *Trial by Fire*, which is the second volume of his history of the Hundred Years War. Peter Hoskins gallantly walked the complete length of both the Black Prince's *chevauchée*s, and his story of those campaigns is told in his book *In the Steps of the Black Prince*. The best biography of Edward of Woodstock is Richard Barber's *The Black Prince*. By far the most authoritative account of the longbow and its effect is *The Great Warbow* by Matthew Strickland and Robert Hardy. Robert Hardy was generous in pointing me towards J. M. Tourneur-Aumont's massive *La Bataille de Poitiers, 1356*. The most intimate picture of everyday life in fourteenth-century France is provided in Ann Wroe's enchanting book *A Fool and His Money*. Other notable books are David Green's *The Battle of Poitiers, 1356*, *The Black Prince's Expedition* by H. J. Hewitt, *The Reign of Edward III* by W. Mark Ormrod, and *Edward III* by the same author. I owe thanks to all those historians.

The Prince of Wales owed thanks to his men and offered it in annuities and outright gifts of money. Many of the archers received grants of timber or rights of pasturage. In France there was shock and outrage at the battle's outcome, which was vented on the nobility. Poitiers was a disaster, propelling France into bankruptcy, chaos, and revolution. No wonder that Edward III, receiving the news of his son's triumph, proclaimed 'We rejoice in God's bounty'.

The war would continue, through Agincourt in 1415 and beyond, until eventually the French prevailed. But that is another story.